Beyond the Moonlit Sea

ALSO BY JULIANNE MACLEAN

WOMEN'S FICTION

These Tangled Vines

A Fire Sparkling

A Curve in the Road

The Color of Heaven Series

The Color of Heaven

The Color of Destiny

The Color of Hope

The Color of a Dream

The Color of a Memory

The Color of Love

The Color of the Season

The Color of Joy

The Color of Time

The Color of Forever

The Color of a Promise

The Color of a Christmas Miracle

The Color of a Silver Lining

CONTEMPORARY ROMANCE

Promise You'll Stay

HISTORICAL ROMANCE SERIES

The American Heiress Series

To Marry the Duke
Falling for the Marquess
In Love with the Viscount
Love According to Lily
To Annabelle, With Love
Where Love Begins

The Pembroke Palace Series

In My Wildest Fantasies
The Mistress Diaries
When a Stranger Loves Me
Married by Midnight
A Kiss Before the Wedding (a Pembroke Palace short story)
Seduced at Sunset

The Highlander Series

Captured by the Highlander
Claimed by the Highlander
Seduced by the Highlander
Return of the Highlander
Taken by the Highlander
The Rebel (a Highlander short story)

The Royal Trilogy

Be My Prince

Princess in Love

The Prince's Bride

Dodge City Brides Trilogy

Prairie Bride

Tempting the Marshal

A Time for Love

STAND-ALONE HISTORICAL ROMANCE

Adam's Promise

Beyond the Moonlit Sea

A NOVEL

JULIANNE MACLEAN

LAKE UNION PUBLISHING

This is a work of fiction. Names, characters, organizations, places, events, and incidents are either products of the author's imagination or are used fictitiously. Any resemblance to actual persons, living or dead, or actual events is purely coincidental.

Published by Lake Union Publishing, Seattle

www.apub.com

ISBN-13: 9781542036702
ISBN-10: 1542036704

Cover design by Caroline Teagle Johnson

Printed in the United States of America

Beyond the Moonlit Sea

CHAPTER 1
OLIVIA

Miami, 1990

I should have known better. I shouldn't have said the things I did.

That's what I told myself when I learned what happened to my husband on his return flight from the US Virgin Islands. But isn't that what we all say after something goes terribly wrong and we look back and wish we had behaved differently?

At least I was not directly to blame for what happened to Dean. I'm not sure whose fault it was, exactly. It's a mystery that will probably remain unsolved until the end of time. My own regret involves something of a more personal nature, a series of events that began on a Sunday morning when my mother called. Dean and I were still sleeping, and he groaned as he sat up to answer the telephone.

"Hello?" He ran a hand down his face to rouse himself. "Good morning, Liz. No, it's not too early. No, you didn't wake us. How are you?"

Dean gave me a look, and I responded by pulling the feather duvet up over my head.

"Yes, the weather's been great." He nudged me with his knee. "Olivia's right here. Hold on a sec . . ."

I poked my head out, crinkled my nose, and shook my head. He pushed the phone at me with a look that said, *Don't make* me *talk to her.*

I couldn't possibly torture him like that, because he and my mother weren't exactly close—which was a tactful way to say that they disliked each other immensely but remained civil for my sake.

None of that was Dean's fault, of course. It was entirely my mother's.

I sat up and took the phone from him. "Hi, Mom."

Dean kissed me on the cheek, slid out of bed, and padded toward the bathroom. Mom said something to me, but I was distracted by the image of my handsome husband as he stripped off his T-shirt before closing the door behind him.

"Olivia, are you listening?"

I sat up straighter against the thick pile of feather pillows. "Yes, Mom, I'm here."

"Did you hear what I said?"

"No. I'm still half-asleep. Say it again?"

"Can you come over for dinner tonight?" she repeated. "Sarah and Leon are in town until Wednesday, and Sarah was so sweet to call me yesterday. I haven't spoken to her in such a long time, probably not since your father's funeral, so I invited them."

I scratched the back of my head because I was surprised that Sarah had called my mother. Sarah was my half sister, almost twenty years older than me, and a product of my father's first marriage to a woman named Barbara who died before I was born.

"As I'm sure you know," my mother continued, "tomorrow is the second anniversary of your father's passing. Maybe that's why she called. I don't know. At any rate, you should be here too."

I was ashamed of myself for forgetting what day it was, but I'd had a lot on my mind lately. I'd been making a conscious effort to *not* look at a calendar.

Hearing the sound of the shower running in the bathroom, I slipped out of bed and pulled on my robe. "It'll be nice for us to get together. We'd be delighted to come. Assuming the invitation includes Dean as well?"

"Of course it includes Dean," she replied with a note of sassiness that confessed everything—that she didn't approve of him, we both knew it, but she didn't want to cause any more rifts.

"Just checking," I said, having decided long ago that it was pointless to try and convince her that she'd always been wrong about my husband—that he wasn't "beneath me," as she had once put it, simply because he didn't come from money.

Thank goodness Dean was a good sport about my mother's flagrant snobbery. Mostly we made fun of her, and he laughed it off. There was plenty of eye-rolling when she showed off a flashy new handbag that cost a thousand dollars or made a not-so-subtle dig about his financial situation growing up.

As I stood at the window watching a wispy cloud float lightly across the morning sky, I asked her if I could bring anything to the dinner.

"Just yourselves," she replied. Then we chatted for a minute or two before we hung up.

Dean was still in the shower, so I went to put some coffee on and grab the Sunday paper from outside the door. A short while later, I was seated at the kitchen table, reading the arts and entertainment pages. Dean appeared in shorts and a light-blue cotton T-shirt, his hair still wet.

"That's a nice clean shave," I said to him with a flirtatious grin, having commented about his rough stubble the night before when we were in bed.

He moved behind me and massaged my shoulders. "I'll try to be smoother next time." He kissed the top of my head and poured himself a cup of coffee. "What did your mother want?"

"She invited us to dinner tonight."

Dean faced me, his head drawing back slightly. "Both of us? Me included?"

"Yes, I know. I was surprised too," I said. "But Sarah is in town, and tomorrow is the second anniversary of Dad's passing, so Mom decided to do something, I guess. It's really last minute, nothing too elaborate. It'll just be us, a four-course meal, and a few bottles of Dad's favorite wine while Mom gets sentimental and tells romantic stories about him."

Dean was quiet while he sipped his coffee.

I sat in silence for a moment, knowing he wasn't going to enjoy any of that because he and my father had not been on speaking terms—not a word since Dad cut me off for marrying Dean. But nothing could have stopped me from walking down that aisle.

I rose from the chair and carried my empty cup to the dishwasher. "Do you still want to take Sarah's boat out today?" I asked. "Now that we have the dinner party to go to, we'll have to head back early."

Dean looked out the window and thought about it. "It's a gorgeous day. We should still go."

"Agreed. Life's too short. Let me grab a quick shower."

I was pleased we were on the same page because I wanted to talk to him about something important, and I wasn't sure how Dean would feel about it. I was banking on the gorgeous sailing conditions to help me present my case.

~

As I stood on the foredeck of *Daydreamer*—Sarah's thirty-nine-foot cruising yacht that she let us borrow from time to time—I felt revitalized and optimistic about the future. Dean was at the helm, breathing in the fragrance of the sea and enjoying the salty spray on his face, while I hung on to the shrouds, my ponytail whipping in the wind. The hiss of the waves beneath the leeward bow was music to my ears.

"Ready to come about!" Dean shouted, and I prepared to release the jib.

He turned the wheel hard over, hand over hand, and swung *Daydreamer* around. "Boom coming across!"

I ducked as it passed over my head, and within seconds, we were on a new tack, the sails snapping taut. The wind became still, and all was quiet as I hopped down to the cockpit.

"Want me to take over?" I asked.

"Sure." He stepped aside as I moved into position.

The return trip to the marina was a more relaxing affair with gentle but steady winds to take us home. I gripped the wheel while Dean reclined on the bench beside me, his face turned toward the sun.

"Can we talk about something?" I asked, gazing at him contentedly and feeling quite blessed.

He turned toward me, and I saw my reflection in his sunglasses. "Is everything okay?"

Dean had always been attuned to my moods and emotions. I was my truest self with him, and I felt accepted and loved. Perhaps even worshipped. I knew he would do anything for me. I was his whole world, and he was mine. I was a very lucky woman.

"Everything's wonderful," I replied, glancing up at the mainsail and adjusting the wheel slightly. "But I've been thinking . . ."

Dean sat forward on the bench and rested his elbows on his knees, attentively.

"You know how we decided that I would go off the pill and we'd see what might happen?"

He nodded.

"Well . . . it's been three months, and nothing's happened."

He nodded again and waited patiently for me to continue.

"We've been trying," I said, "sort of, but not officially. Not *actively* trying. We've just been doing what we usually do."

"And what is that exactly?" he asked with a sly, playful grin.

I laughed and shook my head at him. "Want me to describe it? Colorfully?"

"I'm game if you are."

I chuckled and looked up at the mainsail again to check the tension. Everything was perfect. We were cutting through the water on a fast and steady tack.

"I'm wondering if we should try a little harder," I continued. "I mean . . . I could keep track of my cycle on the calendar and take my temperature so that we know exactly when I'm ovulating."

"And start scheduling sex?" he asked without judgment. He merely seemed curious.

I made a face. "Yes, but I hate the sound of that. We've always been spontaneous, and I love that about us."

"We could still be spontaneous."

I was relieved he seemed open to what I was suggesting, but I was still wary of it, myself.

"I have to admit I'm hesitant," I explained, "because I read an article the other day about a couple who had trouble getting pregnant, and they put too much pressure on themselves. They started booking appointments for sex, and all the fun went out of it. And then they were devastated every month when she got her period. They grew impatient with each other and felt like failures. Then they started IVF, and that was a whole new can of emotional worms. Their marriage was never the same."

"Did they get pregnant?" Dean asked.

"No. They were still trying. And going to couples' therapy to fix their relationship."

"Couples' therapy . . ." After a pause, he rose from the bench and stood behind me, slid his arms around my waist, and buried his nose in the crook of my neck. "Don't worry about us. We're only just getting started. And if you want to get all clinical and start taking your temperature, I could get myself a lab coat. If you're really good to me, I might even wear it in the bedroom."

I laughed and turned around to kiss him, knowing he would instinctively take hold of the wheel. We kissed passionately until the mainsail began to flutter in the wind.

"I love you," I said, then faced forward again before we got stuck in the no-go zone.

"I love you too," he replied and hopped lightly onto the foredeck to adjust the lines while I steered us back on track. When that was done, he returned to the cockpit and sat down again. "Just out of curiosity, when will you be ovulating next? I want to make sure I'm free that night."

I smiled. "Tomorrow, as a matter of fact."

Impressed by my organizational skills, he checked his watch. "Well, if we want to get a jump on things, we could make an appointment for tonight. Midnight would count, correct?"

"I suppose, if you look at it that way."

"And we'd kill two birds with one stone."

"How so?"

"We'd have a legitimate excuse to make an early escape from your mother's dinner party."

I laughed again. "You're terrible."

"Guilty as charged." He sat back, put his feet up on the bench, and raised his face to the sun again. "Take us home, Captain."

A fresh breeze blew across the deck, and I looked up at the clear blue sky. It was a perfect day. Oh, how I loved my life.

~

When we arrived home, the red light on the answering machine was blinking. I pressed the button to listen to the messages and kicked off my shoes. "Are you hearing this?" I called out to Dean, who had gone into the washroom. "It's Richard. He wants you to call him."

Dean was a pilot who flew private jets in and out of Miami, and Richard was his boss. The clients were often business travelers, always wealthy, sometimes famous. Flying was Dean's passion, and he loved his work as much as I loved mine. Or at least my idea of it. I had graduated from film school with the intention of becoming a documentarian, but I hadn't produced anything yet. I just couldn't seem to find the right subject matter to inspire me, and funding was always an issue.

Dean returned to the kitchen. "Did he say what it was about?"

"No," I replied. "But he only left the message a few minutes ago. You should give him a call." I handed Dean the phone, then opened the fridge to grab a can of orange juice. I cracked it open and sat down at the kitchen table. I was thinking about what I should wear to my mother's house for dinner when I listened in on Dean's conversation with Richard.

"Tonight?" Dean said. "That's short notice, isn't it?" He looked at me, shook his head, and rolled his eyes. But then his expression changed. He perked up a little and turned away from me. "It's Mike Mitchell? Are you sure Kevin can't do it? How sick is he?"

My insides turned over with dread. Mike Mitchell was a singer and guitarist who had just broken into the Hollywood scene with a dramatic supporting role in an Oscar-nominated film, and his new album was currently number one on the *Billboard* charts. He was on the cover of every glossy magazine imaginable. It was not the first time Dean had flown him to his luxurious oceanside retreat in Saint Thomas.

Dean faced me with a sheepish look, a look that was asking my permission to take the job. Or perhaps *begging* was a more accurate description.

"Let me talk to Olivia about it, and I'll call you right back." He hung up the phone.

With a sigh of defeat, I drummed my fingers on the tabletop. "Don't tell me. You want to do it."

He winced a little, as if he were stepping on broken glass. "I doubt your mother will mind if I'm not there. She'd probably be overjoyed."

"But *I'd* mind," I argued. "I was looking forward to this. I haven't seen Sarah in ages, and—"

"You can still go," he said. "And you'll have more time to visit with her if I'm not there. You won't have to worry about leaving me alone with your mom."

I stared at him. "What about afterward? We were going to come home and . . . you know."

I couldn't deny that the postponement of our midnight rendezvous was the true root of my disappointment, because lately I'd developed a serious case of baby fever. I hadn't told Dean about it, but whenever I saw a young mother on the street pushing a baby carriage, an intense longing took hold of me. And when my period arrived last month, I'd cried on the bathroom floor.

Dean laid a hand on my back and rubbed circles between my shoulder blades. "We can make love as soon as I get home. I promise that the minute I walk in the door, I'll report straight to the bedroom."

I turned in the chair and looked up at him. "When will that be? Won't you have to stay overnight?"

"No," he quickly replied. "I'll tell Richard I need to fly straight back."

"But it's not always up to you," I reminded him. "Remember that time when Mike was late getting to the airport and it pushed you over your limit for maximum hours of flight time?"

Dean exhaled sharply and backed away from me. "Look, I'll say no if you want me to, but it's a good gig, and apparently, Mike requested me. If I don't do it, that'll put Richard in a bind. You know how he likes to deliver for the clients. Keep them happy."

"You don't want to keep your wife happy?"

Dean frowned. "That's not fair, Olivia. Come on. It's just one night. I'll be back before sunrise."

I realized intellectually that I was being unreasonable, but emotionally, I couldn't help myself. I was disappointed, but there was another side to this as well . . .

I waited for Dean to call Richard back, accept the job, and hang up. Then I watched him go silently into the bedroom.

"I just feel like maybe you're a bit starstruck!" I called out to him in the other room.

He reappeared in the bedroom doorway and leaned a shoulder against the jamb. "What are you talking about?"

I should have just bitten my tongue, but I didn't. "Mike Mitchell requested you personally, and you're thrilled because he's such a major star. You're flattered."

"You used the word *starstruck*," Dean replied.

"Yes. If it were any other client, you would have said no."

"But it's not any other client," he argued, disappearing into the bedroom again. "The guy's a major VIP for the company."

I sipped my juice and called out to him, "I'm sure that Richard could have found another pilot for tonight if you had said no!"

What was wrong with me? Why couldn't I just let it go?

"But I'm the one Mike requested," Dean replied, calmly. "And I don't want to let Richard down."

I stood up and went into the bedroom. Dean was at the closet, sifting through shirts on hangers.

"Just as long as he doesn't try and talk you into staying for one of his wild parties," I said. "Do you think that's what he's planning?"

"Is that what you *expect* will happen tonight?"

My eyes closed. "Please don't do that, Dean. I hate it when you do that."

"Do what?"

"Answer a question with a question."

He took a deep breath and let it out. "The party thing only happened a couple of times. And I told you . . . I'll come straight home."

I tried to accept his word, to not assume the worst.

He selected a shirt and checked it for wrinkles, then chose a jacket that had been recently dry-cleaned.

"I'm sorry," I said, running a hand through my hair. "I'm just disappointed, that's all."

"I know." He kept his back to me while he removed the cellophane wrap from the uniform.

I strode toward him and laid my hand on his shoulder. "See? This is exactly what I was talking about on the boat. I'm worried about scheduling sex and how it might affect us, and here we are, fighting already."

He faced me at last, moved closer and slid his arms around my waist, touched his forehead to mine. "I'm sorry too. It was supposed to be a romantic night, and it's a special anniversary. I should have thought of that."

"It's not your fault. It's me. I'm nervous about getting pregnant. I'm afraid it's not going to happen, and I've been thinking about it too much lately. Dreaming about what color to paint the nursery. I've even been looking at cribs, comparing all the brands." I drew back and looked him in the eye. "I need to relax about all that. I don't want to end up like that unhappy couple who got frustrated with each other and ended up in therapy."

Dean frowned a little. "You've been shopping for cribs? Why didn't you say anything?"

I shrugged. "I don't know. I didn't want to put pressure on you. And I know how much you hate it when I'm impatient."

"I didn't hate it when you were impatient to marry me."

I smiled as he pushed a lock of hair behind my ear. "I wanted to get you to the church before you realized what you were getting yourself into and changed your mind."

"Never." His lips touched mine, and we kissed tenderly.

"I'm sorry," he said, taking a step back, "but I really have to get going. Are we okay, though?"

I bit my lower lip and rocked back on my heels. "Hmm. Only if you're back in bed with me by sunrise. Otherwise, you'll be in the doghouse."

He tapped his forefinger on his temple. "Got it. Dawdling leads to doghouse."

I left him alone to get dressed and make his way to the airport.

Looking back on that conversation later, I wished I had behaved differently. I shouldn't have given Dean such a hard time about taking the job, nor should I have suggested that he was starstruck. That had always been a sore spot between us because my rich father had once told him—point-blank—that I was out of his league in every way and he was just starry eyed at the idea of being with me.

I disagreed, of course. I loved Dean for the man he was *because* of all the luxuries he never had growing up. It made me think more of him, not less. I was in awe of him, and I was grateful and amazed that he loved me.

But on the morning of his return flight from Saint Thomas, none of that would matter in the least. I didn't care what my father ever thought about Dean. All I wanted was to hear the sound of my husband's key in the door. And to feel his arms around me. Just one more time.

CHAPTER 2
OLIVIA

Miami, 1990

The phone rang in the middle of the night. I sat up in bed, stomach burning with panic, as if I already knew something terrible had happened. Maybe it was a premonition. Perhaps somehow, in the mysterious abyss of sleep, my soul had witnessed something.

"Hello?" I answered, glancing at the empty pillow beside me while I tried to convince myself that everything was fine. Dean had probably decided to stay overnight in Saint Thomas after all, and that's why he was calling.

"Is this Olivia?"

But it wasn't Dean. It was his boss, Richard. My breathing quickened as I switched on the lamp. "Yes, Richard, it's me. What's going on?"

There was a pause on the other end of the line, which sent a wave of nausea through my insides.

"I hate to be the one to tell you this," he said, "but Dean's plane is missing."

I tossed the covers aside and swung my feet to the floor. "What do you mean . . . missing? Did he crash?"

Silence again, and I immediately began to perspire.

"We don't know," Richard replied in a low, serious tone. "All I can say is that he made contact with air traffic control in San Juan shortly after leaving Saint Thomas, but then he just . . . disappeared."

I stood up and walked out of the bedroom. "I don't understand what you're saying to me. How could he just disappear?"

Another pause. "His plane vanished off the radar."

The words hit me like a brick, and I sank onto the sofa in the dark living room. For a moment I couldn't speak. All I could do was sit in a state of shock and disbelief.

"Olivia, are you still there?"

"Yes, I'm here. I'm just trying to digest this."

"I know it's difficult," Richard replied. "But rest assured, a search has already begun. The Coast Guard was summoned immediately, and we know exactly where Dean went off the radar. The Puerto Rican authorities are involved as well, and there's a navy ship in the area, so they've been alerted. It's a clear night with good weather, a near-perfect calm on the water, so that's a blessing, and the sun will be up soon."

"They'll be searching for wreckage," I mumbled, pushing my hair back.

"Yes, and for Dean. We're all praying."

I tried to comprehend this. "Was there anyone else on the plane with him?"

"No. There was supposed to be a flight attendant on the return trip, but she wanted to stay in Saint Thomas. I think there might be something going on between her and Mitchell, so Dean flew back on his own."

Oh God. I thought of how I had pressured him to come straight home to me and wished that instead I had given him the choice to stay and return in the morning.

"You mentioned he contacted air traffic control in San Juan," I said. "Was he having a problem? Was it a Mayday call?"

"That's unclear. From what I understand, he said he was having some trouble with his instruments, and he reported some fog."

"And then he just vanished?"

"That's what it sounds like."

"But that makes no sense. If he was having trouble with his instruments, wouldn't he have requested permission to land somewhere?"

"One would think."

"Maybe if his instruments were acting up, he lost radio contact. Maybe he'll land in Miami like he's supposed to." I looked out the window at the dark Atlantic Ocean sparkling brightly beneath a full moon. "Like you said, it's a clear night. He could find his way back, couldn't he? Even without his instruments?"

"He's an excellent pilot," Richard said. "But if he was out there, radar would be picking him up."

I began to feel a little shaky as I tried to imagine what might have occurred. "If he had to ditch over the water," I said, "there are life jackets on board, aren't there? He would know what to do to survive?"

Richard let out a breath. "I don't know, Olivia. Sometimes pilots can get disoriented, and they don't even realize they're going down until it's too late."

I pictured Dean's plane in a death spiral and felt like I was going to be physically ill.

"Are you all right?" Richard asked. "Is there anyone you want me to call?"

"No," I replied, wiping a tear from my cheek while my heart pounded like a jackhammer. "I'll call my mom. But please, can you keep me informed as soon as you hear anything?"

"Of course."

We hung up, and I sat for a moment in a state of terror-filled paralysis, staring straight ahead, seeing nothing but frightening images of my husband: Dean sitting in the cockpit and fighting to control the shaking throttle while the plane was going down. I imagined him fighting until the last second to lift the nose before finally giving up, squeezing his eyes shut, and crashing into the sea.

Something in my heart took flight, and my gaze shot to the full moon again.

No. It wasn't possible. Dean wasn't dead. If he were, I would feel it. I would feel darkness and despair. Hopelessness. But that's not what I felt at all. People were searching for him, and I believed they would find him. I believed my husband had landed that plane safely on the water. Someone would spot the wreckage and find him floating, alive, and he would come home to me. Because if there was one thing I knew about my husband—besides the fact that he loved me—it was that he was a survivor.

~

Shortly before dawn, my mother arrived. I buzzed her upstairs to the condo, where I had been pacing around the kitchen while finishing a third cup of coffee. When I let her in, she pulled me into her arms.

"There, there," she whispered as I broke down and wept on her shoulder. It was the first time I had given in to tears since Richard had called. I suppose I had been fighting to remain in a state of denial, which was much easier than accepting a potential reality where Dean would never come home to me.

I withdrew from the comfort of my mother's embrace, shut the door behind her, and followed her into the kitchen. Neither of us spoke while she set her pink Gucci bag down on a chair and stared out the massive wall of windows at the fiery sunrise over the Atlantic.

"He shouldn't have taken that job last night," she said, judgmentally. "He should have turned it down and come with you to dinner. Then none of this would be happening. But he just couldn't resist the brass ring, could he."

I stared numbly at my mother. "Seriously, Mom? That's what you want to say to me right now? You can't bite your tongue, just this once, and pretend that you care that my husband might be . . ."

I couldn't say the word. I couldn't even consider the possibility that he might be . . .

She turned to me with umbrage. "Of course I care. I'm just angry with him, that's all. I'm angry that he's put you in this position—that he's causing you such pain—when it all could have been avoided if he'd only just—"

"Stop it, Mom." I held up a hand. "You're not helping. He took the job because he's a great pilot. He's passionate about his work, and he's dedicated. And I hate it when you say those things about him, as if all he cares about is money and prestige. As if that's the only reason he married me. You'd think after four years of your daughter being blissfully happy, you might consider the possibility that you were wrong about him."

My mother held up a hand as well, but it was a gesture of surrender. I felt my shoulders relax slightly.

"You're right," she said. "I'm sorry. I know you love him, and now's not the time for me to be critical."

"No, it's not." Part of me wanted to continue singing Dean's praises until she finally admitted defeat, once and for all, but I was emotionally drained. Instead, I picked up my coffee cup, dumped what remained of the cold contents into the sink, and scrubbed it out with a long-handled bristle brush. I waited for my blood pressure to return to normal before I set the cup on the dish rack and faced my mother again.

"If your father were here," she said as she moved to the sofa in the living room, "he would be on the phone right now shouting at people. At least then we'd know something."

I moved into the living room as well and sat down beside her. "Richard promised he would call back as soon as he heard anything."

"Who's Richard?"

"Richard Walker. Dean's supervisor."

I reached for the remote control and switched on the television, then flipped channels from *Good Morning America* to the local morning news. After a while, the words *breaking news* appeared on the bottom of the screen, and a publicity shot of Mike Mitchell caught my attention.

"Here's something." I fumbled with the remote to increase the volume.

The anchorwoman read the report: *"Last night, a charter plane out of Miami went missing off the coast of Puerto Rico. It was returning from Saint Thomas after flying musician Mike Mitchell to his private home there. The plane belonged to Gibson Air, which operates a fleet of private luxury aircraft all over the world. A representative from Gibson has confirmed that Mitchell was not on board when the plane went down. A search is being conducted for the pilot. We will continue to follow this story as it unfolds."*

She transitioned to another news item, so I sat back against the couch cushions and hit the mute button.

"They're saying his plane went down," I mumbled in a low voice. "Richard didn't use those words. He just said he 'disappeared.'"

Mom reached for my hand and squeezed it. "Maybe he didn't want to upset you."

I knew she was trying to be helpful, but nothing she said made me feel any better. "Maybe." We sat in grim silence.

"Either way," Mom said, "no news is good news, right? If they haven't found any wreckage yet, you can still have hope. He could still be out there. Maybe he landed safely somewhere."

I stared blankly at the television screen. "He can't be dead, Mom. Wouldn't I feel it? Wouldn't I know?" I turned to her. "Did you feel it when Dad died?"

"Well, of course I did," she replied. "But I was in the room with him." She squeezed my hand tighter and turned her attention back to the TV.

~

A short while later, Richard called back. My stomach dropped as soon as I answered the telephone and recognized his voice. "What's happening? Have they found anything?"

"Not yet," he replied. "They're still searching, but I just got off the phone with the air traffic controller in San Juan, and he read me a transcript of Dean's radio communications before he disappeared from radar. I had them fax it over."

"What does it say?" My blood was now burning hotly with adrenaline.

"It's a bit strange," Richard replied, "and I hope we can find the black box to know exactly what was happening."

"What do you mean, strange?" I wished he would hurry up and spit it out, but it sounded like he was flipping through pages of notes. I tried to be patient.

"Before I read it to you," he said, "you should know that the controller mentioned a lot of radio interference—hazy reception and static that came and went—so it was difficult to decipher what Dean was saying, if he was actually calling for help. If it was a Mayday call, other stations or planes would have picked it up, but so far nothing has been reported about any distress signals. So that's a bit unusual."

"Go on," I said as I paced the length of the condo along the windows. Mom was still seated on the sofa, watching me intently.

Richard continued. "First, Dean identified himself and reported his location. He was about fifteen miles off the coast of Puerto Rico, flying at four thousand feet, when he requested a higher altitude. The controller sensed an urgency and granted it, then waited for a response, but there was no *roger* from Dean. The controller continued to try and make contact, then Dean finally responded. This is what he said, and I'll read it to you, exactly as it's written: 'Flight Seven Five Eight at six thousand feet. I'm inside a strange cloud. I don't know how to describe it. It rose up from the ocean. Very fast. I couldn't climb fast enough to avoid it, but everything is clear where I am now. It's like a tunnel. I can see for miles ahead of me, due north. Clear skies ahead. Maintaining speed of one hundred ninety miles per hour.'"

Richard paused and turned a page. "There was some more interference, and Dean was cutting in and out. Then he said: 'Compass is spinning. The cloud is swirling around me counterclockwise. I'm increasing speed to two hundred twenty miles per hour to make it out. Clear skies ahead . . . about a mile out.' Then the controller asked: 'Are you experiencing any turbulence?' Dean replied: 'No turbulence. No wind.' Then there was more static while the controller attempted to regain radio contact. Dean said: 'The tunnel is shrinking around me, but I can still see a door out of it. Maintaining current speed.'"

Richard paused again. "That was his last radio contact. After that, the controller continued to track him on radar for about a mile. The last sweep of the scope showed him heading northwest at one twenty-eight a.m. On the next sweep, the scope was blank."

My heart throbbed with grief and disbelief as I stood at the window, looking out at the vast ocean. There was a container ship in the distance, heading out to sea, and a number of small sailboats. I tried to take slow, deep, calming breaths as I considered what I'd just heard.

"Did he sound flustered to the controller?" I asked. "Did he act like he was in trouble or losing control of the aircraft?"

"No. The controller described him as calm and collected, totally at ease, which was why he was so surprised when the plane vanished."

My mother called out to me from the couch. "Olivia! There's something else on the news."

"Hang on a second," I said to Richard as I moved closer to the TV and increased the volume. "Richard, turn on *Good Morning America*, then call me right back."

I hung up and stood on the area rug, staring with wide eyes at the images displayed on the screen. There were photographs of the type of plane Dean had been flying, followed by a view of the luxurious interior with white leather seats and an attractive flight attendant in uniform. She held a tray of drinks. Then they switched to another photo of Mike Mitchell. The anchorwoman said she had him on the phone.

"How are you doing?" she asked. *"We're all glad you're safe."*

"Yes," Mitchell replied. *"I feel very fortunate this morning."*

"I'm sure you do. Can you describe to us what the flight was like on the way to Saint Thomas?"

"Yeah. The weather was perfect. Clear skies the whole way. Very smooth flight with no issues. And I've flown with that pilot many times. He's a real pro, so you can't help but wonder if something else was going on."

"What do you mean by 'something else'?" the anchorwoman pressed.

"Well, it's the Bermuda Triangle," Mitchell replied. *"This certainly isn't the first plane to go missing, and it makes you wonder what's really going on out there. People have been reporting seeing strange lights in the skies, time warps, and all sorts of things. You should look into Flight Nineteen in 1945. Five US Navy planes went missing during a routine training exercise, and no trace was ever found. A lot of really weird stuff happened during the search too. I'm telling you, there's something going on out there, and no one seems able to explain it."*

The anchorwoman nodded with concern. *"Let me ask you this, Mr. Mitchell. Have you ever seen any strange lights or unexplained objects in the sky?"*

"Oh, for pity's sake," my mother said, interrupting the broadcast. "They're going to turn this into a circus and start searching for little green men."

"Shh, Mom," I replied, sitting forward to listen.

"I haven't," Mike replied, *"but I know people who have. I just hope everyone out there searching will be okay and that they find the pilot. He was a good guy."*

The anchorwoman thanked Mike and showed video images of Coast Guard helicopters taking off while she described the search area.

The phone rang again. I rose quickly to my feet to answer it, and it was Richard.

"Did you see that?" I asked.

"Yes, but don't read too much into it, Olivia. That guy does too many drugs. And he probably wants to milk the publicity."

"Are you sure about that? Because that transcript you read to me was kind of strange, don't you think? I mean . . . what was Dean talking about? What sort of cloud forms a tunnel?"

"Clouds can move and shift in all sorts of ways."

"Yes, but he said there was no wind. And what about the compass spinning around?"

Richard was quiet for a moment. "Listen, Olivia, I don't want to crush your hopes, but the things Dean was saying . . . it makes sense if he was disoriented."

"How so?"

"If there was a problem with the compass, it's likely that other instruments were failing as well, and if his artificial horizon wasn't working—"

"What's that?"

"It's an instrument that shows where the horizon is so that the pilot can keep his wings level. If that's malfunctioning, even the smallest bank to the left or right can be imperceptible to a pilot, and without instruments to show that the plane is losing altitude, and without any points of reference from inside a cloud, a pilot can't possibly tell that he's spiraling until it's too late to recover. That might explain why Dean thought the cloud was rotating in a counterclockwise direction."

I found all this difficult to accept. "But he said he could see clear skies ahead, through a doorway at the end of the tunnel."

"Again," Richard gently replied, "he might have been looking at the ocean. It was dark, and there was a full moon. The reflections on the water might have looked like starlight."

At the thought of Dean's plane spiraling toward the dark sea, my throat constricted, and my eyes burned with tears. I took a moment to collect myself before I was able to speak. "Thank you, Richard. Will you promise to call me right away if you hear anything? I'll keep praying."

"I'll do the same," he replied.

I hung up and turned to my mother, who was staring at me with concern. "Are you all right?"

The walls seemed to be closing in all around me. How could this be happening? Yesterday, Dean and I were sailing, talking about starting a family. He was supposed to be home by now. He had promised to crawl into bed with me at sunrise, and we were going to make love.

But he hadn't come home. He was out there somewhere. Alone. Dead or alive, I didn't know. I continued to cling to the hope that he had survived, but when I met my mother's troubled gaze, my hopes plummeted. I felt odd, like my skin was tingling. Then I felt as if I were suffocating and needed an oxygen mask. My mother leaped to her feet and urged me to sit down.

CHAPTER 3
MELANIE

New York, 1986

The therapist's door was open, so I crossed the threshold, timidly. Outside the window, rain came down steadily, and the office seemed dark, lit only by a single standing lamp in the corner, though the curtains were open to a leafy outdoor view. My eyes went first to that small glimpse of nature before they settled on the therapist.

He was sitting behind an antique desk, but he soon stood and moved to greet me. "You must be Melanie," he said warmly. "I'm Dr. Robinson. Please come in."

Feeling slightly apprehensive—because it wasn't my normal habit to reveal my deepest secrets and insecurities to strangers, or to anyone for that matter—I slid my purse strap off my shoulder and approached a chocolate-brown leather sofa, which I presumed was intended for the patients. Dr. Robinson waited for me to sit down before he lowered himself into a large leather armchair and placed a notepad on his lap.

Neither of us spoke while I glanced around the room. I took in the red Persian carpet beneath my feet and the ornate dark wood paneling with impressive historic millwork. Books were everywhere, stacked on the fireplace mantel and stuffed at every angle on the shelves behind Dr. Robinson's desk. Above my head, a brass chandelier was in need of a good polish.

"This is a lovely room," I commented, still looking around without ever meeting the doctor's eyes. But was he really a doctor? I wondered passively. A psychiatrist? Or was he a PhD, like me? "It feels like something out of an Edith Wharton novel."

Dr. Robinson looked around as well. "I suppose that's true. Are you a fan of Edith Wharton?"

I shrugged. "I read *The Age of Innocence* in my first year of college when I had to get a writing course out of the way."

He folded his hands on his lap and inclined his head, waiting patiently for me to continue.

"I was a science major," I explained. "I had a lot of textbooks to read. Stuff to memorize. Equations to solve. Reading romantic novels felt like something I should be doing on summer vacation."

He nodded, and only then did I allow myself to truly look at him instead of the decor. How old was he? I wondered. Thirty perhaps? He had blue eyes and a strong jaw. I looked away again—this time at the throw pillows on the sofa. I straightened one of them and tried to fluff it up a little.

Dr. Robinson said nothing. He simply sat there, quietly watching me. I felt like a blood sample on a slide under a microscope.

"So what brings you here today, Melanie?" he asked, and I was grateful that he was finally taking charge of the conversation, because I had no idea what to say. The silences made me want to squirm.

"It wasn't my idea to come," I said, picking at a loose thread on my jeans. "It was the head of the physics department at Columbia who suggested it. Dr. Fielding? He said the cost of this would be covered?"

Dr. Robinson nodded. "Yes. And why did he suggest that you talk to someone?"

"Because I was late on a few things. I'm working on my dissertation for a PhD in particle physics," I explained, "but I seem to have lost interest lately. Dr. Fielding says he's worried about me." I looked away and rolled my eyes a little. "Or so he claims. I think he cares more about the research than he cares about me. There are some important donors funding the project."

"What's it about?"

I met Dr. Robinson's gaze directly. "I'm studying zero-point energy—the instance where all activity in an atom ceases—and the associated effects that a quantum vacuum might have on an airplane. Or in layman's terms, I'm trying to solve the mystery of why planes go missing over the Bermuda Triangle."

His head drew back slightly. "Wow. That sounds very interesting."

"I've always thought so," I replied. "Of course, planes go missing all the time, all over the world, but I did a search of the records at NTSB—that's the National Transportation Safety Board—and it showed a much higher frequency of aircraft going missing over the Triangle than in other places. And I'm not talking about regular crashes. Those can be explained. I'm talking about planes that vanish without a trace, and there's often unusual circumstances surrounding the disappearances that leave investigators baffled." I paused and sat back again. "Anyway, Dr. Fielding thought I needed to talk to someone about why I'm not motivated anymore."

My therapist waved a hand through the air as if he were conducting a symphony. "Why do *you* think you've lost interest?"

"Well . . ." I swallowed uneasily. "My mother died recently. That's why it was suggested that I talk to someone. To work through my grief."

Dr. Robinson stared at me again, as if I were something he was trying to identify from a great distance. "I'm sorry about your mother. Were you close to her?"

Without thinking, I sighed heavily and realized it sounded like I was disappointed by his question, which maybe I was. It was kind of predictable. "She died suddenly," I explained. "It was a shock. I'm sure you heard about the tornado in Oklahoma recently? It tore through a trailer park, and a bunch of people were killed?"

"Yes. Your mother was one of them?"

"Yes."

He frowned. "I'm sorry to hear that. Where were you when it happened?"

"Here in New York. I saw it on the news, then a police officer called to tell me that she was . . . well, you know . . . that she was dead."

He nodded sympathetically.

There was another long, uncomfortable silence.

"I hadn't been home in almost two years," I explained, feeling pressure to elaborate. "I can't even remember the last time we spoke on the phone."

When I started picking at that loose thread on my jeans again, he prompted me further. "Was there a reason you hadn't spoken?"

I was beginning to get the hang of this. It wasn't a conversational tennis match where the ball went back and forth over the net and both players contributed equally. It was just me, hitting the ball up against a wall that didn't say too much. That meant I had to keep talking—otherwise, we would just sit there, through those awkward silences.

Looking away toward the leafy view outside the window, I said, "When I left home to go to college, I didn't keep in touch. I just wanted to get away from there."

"Why?"

"Because I didn't have an ideal upbringing." I paused, looked at the doctor, and narrowed my eyes at him. "How am I doing? Is this what you're looking for? You want to use your handy-dandy therapist's shovel to dig into my childhood? I came fully prepared to talk about my mother."

He was completely unfazed by my condescending tone. He simply shrugged, and I felt an immediate twinge of remorse.

"Is that what you'd like me to do?" he asked. "Focus on your mother?"

I tried to relax. "It doesn't matter. My life is pretty boring, actually. I can give it to you in a nutshell, if you like. When I was a child, my mom was always bringing home a new man to live with us. There was a new 'dad' for me every year or two. Out with the old, in with the new. Most of them were horrible."

"And what about your real father?" Dr. Robinson asked. "Was he in the picture at all?"

"No. I never knew who he was. To be honest, I don't think my mother did either. Or if she did, she planned to take that secret to her grave. Which, as it turned out, she did." I paused and thought about that for a moment. "She was only seventeen when she had me. My grandmother didn't know the guy either. At least I don't think she did."

"Tell me about your grandmother."

I perked up at this question, perhaps because my grandmother was someone that I was proud of. "She was a force of nature. She lived in the trailer park, three doors down, so I could go there after school when I was little."

"Did your mother work?"

"Yes. She worked in a diner. They were open until midnight, so she worked a lot of nights. At least that's what my grandmother told me. Maybe she was out partying. I shouldn't judge her. She was barely twenty and saddled with a three-year-old. I don't know what she would have done without my grandmother to help out and take care of me."

"It sounds like your grandmother was an important part of your life. Where is she now?"

"She died when I was fifteen. Then it was just me and my mom and whatever guy was living with us at the time."

The doctor's brow furrowed with concern. I knew immediately what he was thinking, so I held up a hand. "No, no. I can tell by the way you're looking at me . . . I assure you, there was none of *that* going on. Nothing X rated. Most of them were okay. I just had to listen to a lot of yelling and screaming when they drank too much, which was pretty much every weekend. My mom liked her whiskey, and she had a talent for poking angry bears."

I scrutinized Dr. Robinson's face for a few seconds and felt rather overcome by the warmth in his eyes. It was remarkable how he could meet my gaze at length without looking away. It wasn't awkward for *him* at all.

"Is this really important?" I asked. "Talking about my mother's boyfriends? My goal here is to get back to work on my research. Figure out how to stop planes from disappearing in the Bahamas. And those boyfriends aren't the ones I'm supposed to be grieving about."

With his elbows perched on the armrests of the chair, his notepad on his lap, he steepled his forefingers. "I find it interesting that you use the words *supposed to be*. It brings me back to something you said earlier—that it wasn't your idea to come here. You also say that you came prepared. Perhaps you feel that coming here is a test that you have to pass?"

I laid my hand on my purse. "I don't know. Maybe."

"If it is a test, who's providing the grade? The head of the physics department? Or me? You?"

I chuckled. "You think that I'm here just to say the appropriate things that my professor would want me to say so that I don't flunk out of my program?"

"I didn't say that," Dr. Robinson replied. "Is that what you think I think?"

My head drew back slightly, and I laughed. "Wow. This line of questioning is making me feel a little dizzy, like we're going around in circles. What do you think I think about what you think I think?"

With a smile, he chuckled as well. "I apologize. I just want to get a sense of what you'd like to achieve from these sessions. What's your end goal, Melanie?"

"Well, that's an interesting question, Doctor," I replied with a touch of humor. "It's kind of existential, don't you think?"

He offered no response to that, so I was forced to answer him seriously. I tried to dig deep because I suspected that's what he wanted from me. Deep, important, profound thoughts.

"I guess I just want to know if I'm on the right path. I always thought this research project was my calling in life, but now I'm not so sure. Lately, I've started to wonder if I enrolled in this program just to escape my life at home with my mother. And my project seems . . . I don't know . . . it seems sort of childish to me now."

He inclined his head. "Pardon me. I'm just trying to understand. Do you think physics is childish?"

"No, of course not. Not as a whole. It's just my project that seems silly. I think it's too personal."

"How is it personal?"

"I'm sorry, I feel ridiculous talking about this. But I suppose I have to if you're going to help me figure out my life and tell me what I should be doing."

With a friendly, open smile, he said, "I'm not here to tell you how to live your life, Melanie. Only to help you reflect on where you are and why. And hopefully, that will help *you* to make good decisions moving forward."

"Okay," I said hesitantly. Then I glanced at the grandfather clock by the door. "I feel like I've been here awhile. Is our time almost up?"

He checked his wristwatch. "We still have a few minutes."

"All right . . . well then . . . sometimes I wonder if I'm just providing fodder for those awful supermarket tabloids that tell us about celebrities that were kidnapped by aliens or a pig from Arkansas that grew human feet. I worry that my work is silly."

"I don't think it's silly at all," he replied. "And if the head of the physics department at Columbia approved the topic . . . if he believes there could be a solid scientific explanation . . ."

"I suppose." I sat there, looking down at my hands. "But sometimes I wonder if I should just give it up and use my research for something else—like predicting severe weather systems."

"Like tornadoes that rip through trailer parks?" he asked.

My eyes lifted. He was very astute. "Maybe."

Dr. Robinson considered that for a moment, then checked his watch again. "It looks like we're out of time for today. But this is a very good place to pick up again next week. You'll come back? I'd like to hear more about why you feel the subject of airplanes vanishing into thin air is too personal for you. Would you be willing to talk about that?"

"Sure," I replied and felt a little kick from my old passion for the project. It came as a surprise because I had been so bored with it lately.

Besides that, I had enjoyed talking to Dr. Robinson, and I wanted to see him again. There were so many other things I could talk about on this sofa. But mostly, I wanted to know if my work was important or just a silly childhood fantasy.

CHAPTER 4
OLIVIA

Miami, 1990

By nightfall, the search for Dean and his missing aircraft was still ongoing. My sister, Sarah, and her husband, Leon, had arrived at noon to keep me and my mother company while we waited for news, but there were no calls from Richard or the Coast Guard. That's not to say the phone hadn't been ringing off the hook, but it was friends or family calling to check up on me or reporters asking questions: Whether I believed Mike Mitchell's alarming theories about the Bermuda Triangle, or if Dean had ever spoken to me about strange occurrences in the past. Unidentified flying objects? Sensations of zero gravity? Unexplained equipment malfunctions? Eventually, I just handed the phone to Leon, who asked them to respect my privacy during this difficult time and stop calling.

"Thank you for coming over," I said to Sarah as I walked her and Leon to the door after supper.

"Are you sure you'll be okay tonight?" Sarah asked as she hugged me. "We could stay longer if you want."

"I appreciate that, but I'll be fine. Mom's here."

Leon hugged me as well. "Stay strong. Let us know if you need anything."

"And we'll be back tomorrow," Sarah added as they made their way to the elevator.

I shut the door behind them and returned to the sofa to join my mother in front of the TV.

"I don't understand it," she said. "It's the top news story all over the country."

"Do you think it's because of who we are?" I asked. My late father had been no stranger to front-page headlines about his business activities. He'd even graced the cover of *Forbes* magazine once, in the late seventies. It hadn't taken long for the media to dig into Dean's personal life and make the connection.

"Maybe," she replied. "But mostly, I think it's because of what Mike Mitchell said on national TV this morning. It lit the whole thing on fire."

We had been watching CNN for hours. They had a reporter on the ground in San Juan covering the search from there, but now they were interviewing so-called experts about other unexplained paranormal phenomena over the Bermuda Triangle.

I sat forward on the sofa cushion and picked up the remote control to increase the volume. "What's this guy saying?"

He was a guest in the studio, a yachtsman who sailed regularly around the Bahamas.

"It was the most bizarre thing I ever experienced," he said. *"I was off the coast of Nassau with a crew of five, and it was a breezy day—the water was pretty choppy. We see a fogbank ahead, but it wasn't like a normal fog . . . it was thick like milk, and it seemed to be traveling toward us because we weren't going that fast. Then wham—we're inside it, like we passed through a wall, and I couldn't even see the water over the side. It was the same milk down there. I hear my first mate shouting from the bridge, so I run to see what the trouble is, and our compass is going crazy,*

spinning around and around. All the power goes out. The radio isn't working. We were in a bit of a panic until all of a sudden we emerge out of the fog and into the sunshine! But we weren't really out of it because it was like being in the hole of a donut. We were surrounded by that milk, in a perfect circle all around us. And there was no wind. It was a flat calm in there, and deadly quiet. It was kind of eerie, if I'm being honest. No one said a word. We were all stunned. We floated around for about a minute, then the milky wall came at us again, and just like that, we're back in choppy waters with high winds."

"Incredible," the anchorman replied. *"Did your instruments start working again?"*

"Yes, as soon as we were out of it, the power came back on. But later that day, we learned about a freighter that disappeared in the exact same area, not long after we'd had our strange experience. They lost radio contact and never found any wreckage or evidence of it sinking. There were no distress signals, so that remains a mystery to this day."

With a rush of panic, I grabbed hold of the remote control and switched off the television. "I can't take this anymore." I squeezed my eyes shut and pressed the heels of my hands to my forehead. "I don't want to hear about ships disappearing. I just want them to find my husband."

Mom slid close and laid a hand on my shoulder. "They're still searching," she said. "And maybe all this media attention is a good thing. The more people who know about it, the more eyes will be on the water, keeping watch."

I fought to regain my composure and sat back. "You're right. It might help." I turned the television back on.

CHAPTER 5
MELANIE

New York, 1986

"When we left off last week," Dr. Robinson said, "we were beginning to discuss your doctoral thesis about planes disappearing over the Bermuda Triangle."

I tried not to roll my eyes, because after a week of reflecting upon everything we had talked about, I was convinced that my therapist was just humoring me when he pretended to take my project seriously.

Avoiding his gaze, I admired the standing lamp in the corner of the room with fringe hanging from the shade. It was raining again, just like the previous week, and I felt a chill under my damp clothes.

"Another dreary day," I said, evading his question. "Here we are, sitting around in the middle of the afternoon with lamps on."

"On the bright side, they're calling for sun tomorrow." He smiled warmly at me.

"Do you like your job?" I asked.

"I do," he replied.

"You're lucky. I'm not sure what I'm going to do with this degree after I graduate. If I graduate."

"Does that worry you?" he asked, sitting forward slightly. "That you won't finish what you started?"

"I'm not sure."

When I didn't elaborate, he asked another question. "Last week you mentioned that you felt your project was too personal to you. Can you tell me why?"

I kicked off my wet shoes, tucked my legs up under myself on the sofa, and hugged one of the decorative cushions—the one with the tassels on it. I took my time formulating my answer while raindrops struck the windowpane like pebbles.

"When I was a little girl," I said, "I would sometimes stay overnight at my grandmother's trailer, which was very cozy. It was kind of like this room. She had books everywhere, toppling over in big piles, and a tall, standing lamp like the one you have over there."

I paused, and Dr. Robinson waited patiently for me to continue.

"She had this old black-and-white picture of my grandfather that hung on the wall in the living room. I never met him because he died long before I was born, but he looked so handsome and heroic in that photograph. He was a pilot during the Second World War, and he wore a leather bomber jacket and a smart-looking cap while he stood on the wing of an airplane with a confident smile. I used to stare at that photograph for what seemed like hours on end. I felt like he was smiling right at me."

"Did your grandmother ever talk about him?"

"Oh yes. All the time. She would tell me what a wonderful man he was. Decent and honorable. A real gentleman. Looking back on it now, I think she was trying to teach me something about what a husband and father was supposed to be like. She knew what I was seeing at home—all the losers my mother kept falling for, the guys who couldn't hold down a job and criticized the way she cooked. Or told her that she was useless and eventually smacked her around." I sighed and looked at Dr. Robinson directly. "She didn't want me to end up like my mother, obsessed with my looks, moving in with a guy just because he whistles at me in a bar. She wanted me to pursue my own dreams."

Dr. Robinson nodded. "Do you feel that you're pursuing them now?"

I inclined my head at him. "Isn't that why we're here? To figure that out?"

His hands were clasped together in front of him, but he opened them as if to say, *I don't know. Is that why we're here?*

I gave him a look. "Fine. If you're forcing me to answer every question that comes up—"

He quickly interrupted. "I'm not forcing you to do anything, Melanie. This is a safe space. There are no tests or grades here. We can talk about whatever you want to talk about. No pressure. No expectations. No judgment."

I considered that and realized I was relieved to hear it, because I had been putting a lot of pressure on myself lately—all my life, really—to not end up like my mother.

"Let's go back to that picture of your grandfather," Dr. Robinson said. "You mentioned that he was a pilot."

I was beginning to discover that I rather liked therapy. Where else could you talk about yourself for a whole hour to someone who hung on your every word?

"Yes. As it happens, the grandfather I never knew went missing off the coast of Florida in 1945. It was a routine training exercise with the navy and a big news story at the time. They called it Flight Nineteen. Five planes vanished without a trace. You should look it up."

"I already did," he replied.

My eyebrows lifted. "You did?"

"Yes. After you told me about your dissertation last week, I was curious. I've always had an interest in aviation." He left it at that, and I was disappointed. I wanted to learn more about him, but as usual, he brought the conversation back to me. "It's incredible that your grandfather was one of those pilots."

"My claim to fame," I said proudly, as if it were a party trick.

Dr. Robinson picked up his pen and jotted something down on his notepad, then returned his attention to me. "So you've been passionate about planes that vanish ever since you were a child, and you've dedicated your entire life and education to a field of science that could potentially solve a famous mystery, something that is also very personal to you. It's connected in a way to your family. Your grandmother in particular, who you respected and continue to hold in very high esteem. But lately, for some reason, you've lost interest. Your professors seem to think it has something to do with the death of your mother and the grief that you're experiencing. Let's talk about that."

"Do we really have to?" I asked.

"You don't want to?" He studied my expression intently. Whenever he did that, I experienced a swooping sensation in my belly, as if I were topping the high crest of a roller coaster, then dropping.

I twirled the pillow tassel around my finger. "I already told you what it was like growing up with her, with all the potential stepfathers coming and going. I'm sure you're looking at me and thinking that I'm an easy textbook case of a girl with mommy issues who needs to come to terms with the past and recognize that I'm not an extension of my mother, and I should learn to separate my feelings about her death from my work."

He sat back and regarded me with compassion. "Things are usually more complicated than that. But you do seem to have this therapy gig all figured out."

I laughed. "Do I?" Secretly, I was flattered and delighted that he had said that. "What can I say? I always did excel in the classroom. Otherwise, I'd still be back in Oklahoma. Or maybe I'd be following the yellow brick road with Dorothy and Toto." I chuckled and worried that it might appear that I was flirting with him. "That was a little bit of tornado humor," I explained.

He nodded and held up a hand. "I got it."

He said nothing more, and I had the distinct impression that he wanted to loosen the reins a bit and allow me to speak more freely about whatever I wanted to talk about, and it didn't have to be my mother. I began to feel very relaxed and unafraid about opening up about other things, which was new for me. Normally I was a closed-off person. I found it difficult to be intimate with people. Most of my friends were just acquaintances or colleagues from the physics program. That's why I lived alone.

My legs were still tucked up under me, and my right foot was falling asleep, so I shifted my body and set my feet on the floor, slipped my shoes back on. Then I found myself glancing toward Dr. Robinson's bookshelves.

"Would it be all right if I took a look at your books?" I asked. "I need to stretch my legs."

"Feel free," he answered amiably with a sweep of his hand, as if to say, *Welcome. Explore my world.*

He remained seated, watching me as I moved to the bookcase and looked over the spines, running a finger along each one. There were a number of psychology textbooks but also an impressive collection of self-help books with titles like *The Gifted Child*, *Children of Alcoholic Parents*, and *Surviving the Death of a Spouse*.

"Do you ever just read for pleasure?" I asked, glancing over my shoulder at him.

He laughed softly, then reached into a basket beside his chair and pulled out a copy of *The Talented Mr. Ripley*. Inwardly, I felt a surge of joy at the discovery that my therapist was actually human and he had a private life outside this room. I had noticed the previous week that he wore no wedding ring, and I found myself wondering if he had a significant other. Or was he like me? A loner whose main focus in life was academic in nature?

"I suppose every patient who comes in here is like a new project for you," I said. "A puzzle to solve. You must find it very challenging. And rewarding."

"I do, when it goes well."

I finished perusing his bookcase and returned to the sofa. "So where were we?" I asked.

He consulted the notepad on his lap and fiddled with his pen, like a tiny baton he twirled between his fingers. "We were talking about your grandfather the pilot, and I jumped the gun by attempting to solve your puzzle too quickly, when clearly there is still much more for me to learn about you."

His words delighted me, for he was stating that he believed I had interesting hidden depths. No one had ever wanted to take a deep dive into my soul before. Except for my grandmother, but she had been gone for a long time.

"You must be a high achiever," I said with a smile, "if you're willing to take on the challenge of other people's problems."

He gave me a conspiratorial look that told me I was correct, but he was my therapist, and we weren't here to talk about him. So he wrangled me back into the paddock.

"You mentioned you don't want to talk about your mother today," he said. "What would you like to talk about?"

"Gosh," I replied. "I don't know. I can talk about anything?"

"Anything you like."

"All right then." I thought about it. "Let's talk about my dissertation."

"Wonderful."

"What would you like to know? Because honestly, I don't know where to begin."

He gestured toward me. "You could tell me about your hypothesis. The science of what you're trying to prove."

"Okay. I see what you're doing here, Doctor. You're trying to reignite my passions. It's fine. I understand. Your goal is to get me motivated again, and the head of the physics department is the one who's funding these sessions."

"Does it matter to you what *my* goal is?" Dr. Robinson asked.

"A little," I replied. "I guess I just want to understand your intentions while you're drilling into me."

He chuckled. "I'm just trying to do my job. To help you look inward, be as self-aware as you can possibly be. Life is easier when you know yourself. When you can accept your past and your limitations and recognize your strengths and desires. When you really know who you are and what you want, and you don't try to be something you're not."

I let out a breath. "That's very inspiring." I felt my brow furrow with curiosity. "How old are you, if you don't mind my asking? You seem . . . I don't know . . . mature with the things you say, but you don't look that old."

He hesitated, and I sensed in him a twinge of discomfort.

"I'm sorry. Is that breaking the rules?" I asked. "Should I not have asked you that?"

His shoulders relaxed slightly. "It's fine. I'm twenty-eight."

I nearly fell off the sofa. "You're only twenty-eight?"

"Does that surprise you?"

"Well, yes. You seem so much older. Maybe it's the way you sit in that big armchair with your legs crossed, offering fatherly advice."

"Does it bother you that I'm young?"

"I don't think so."

"You're not sure?"

I thought about that for a few seconds. "No, really, it's fine. You have a PhD. Clearly, you're well qualified. And I'm sorry I said you seemed old. I didn't mean it as an insult. I'm sure if I saw you on the street, out kicking a soccer ball around, I'd see you differently."

He looked down at his notepad and scribbled a few lines.

"I wish I knew what you were writing about me," I said.

"It's nothing, really. I just want to remember the things we talk about in our sessions."

I grinned and looked away, sheepishly. "Now I'm embarrassed."

"Why is that?"

"Because I said you looked like a dad sitting in that armchair. I can just see your diagnosis now. *Patient desperately in need of a father figure.* Is that what you wrote down?"

He set his pen down and folded his hands. "No, Melanie, it's not. I just wrote simply that you were surprised to learn my age. But let's talk about that, if you don't mind. This isn't the first time you've tried to guess at how I am perceiving you. It's almost as if you want to be one step ahead of me."

"Maybe I missed my calling," I said. "Maybe I should have been a therapist instead of a physicist."

When he gave no reply, I groaned. "God, I'm such a cliché. I wanted a father figure, and I saw that picture of my grandfather and wished I could bring him back from the dead. So that's why I'm doing this."

"Slow down," Dr. Robinson said, raising a hand. "You're going to put me out of a job."

I laughed. "We're back here again. Maybe I really did miss my calling."

"Is that what you think?"

I shook my head. "I don't know. Maybe I just need to finish what I started and get my doctorate and then reevaluate. I'm only twenty-four. Maybe this is all happening exactly as it should. I can solve the Bermuda Triangle mystery that kept me going all through my childhood and teen years. I mean, I never would have gotten all those scholarships without my mad passion for science in school. It's what got me into the gifted program, where all the teachers looked at my sad, unfortunate life and wanted to help me succeed. So here I am, living in New York City, this close to becoming a doctor of particle physics. That's impressive, right? I was only sixteen when I started college. I should be proud of myself."

"Yes, you should," he replied with a flash of respect and admiration in his eyes. I was completely bowled over by it. No one had ever looked at me like that before.

Dr. Robinson glanced at his watch. "Our time is up," he said apologetically. "I'll make a note of where we left off, and we can continue next week."

"That sounds good." I gathered up my purse, and he escorted me to the door, where I paused for a moment. "I know it's only our second session, but I feel like it's helping. I just want you to know that. I feel like there's hope that I'll find my way out of this slump and finish my dissertation."

"I'm glad to hear that. Perhaps future pilots flying out of Bermuda will be grateful for that as well," he said and sent me on my way.

I descended the stairs to the reception area and retrieved my umbrella from the foyer. As I left the clinic, which was housed in a beautiful brownstone on the Upper West Side, I prepared to raise the umbrella over my head, but the rainstorm had passed, and hazy rays of sunshine were beaming through leaves on the trees, reflecting off puddles in the street.

I began to walk but had to squint at the blinding reflections in the pools of water on the pavement. Then I looked up.

There was something rather incredible about the floating mist that sparkled within those rays of light after the rainstorm. It reminded me of the grayish-white haze that was described in a flight report I had studied a while back. The pilot had mentioned long horizontal lines in an "electronic fog" that formed a vortex out of which he had flown at an impossible speed. He also mentioned a sensation of zero gravity when he emerged from the so-called tunnel.

I stopped on the sidewalk and thought about this. Was it possible that those clouds were composed of charged particles from a geomagnetic storm? Under the right circumstances, could this cause a hyperacceleration and g-forces that might be enough to break an airplane to pieces? Or even propel it through a traversable wormhole? Possibly into another time dimension?

Feeling exhilarated, I quickened my pace and walked briskly to catch the subway back to the lab.

CHAPTER 6
OLIVIA

Miami, 1990

Five days after I received Richard's middle-of-the-night phone call about Dean's disappearance, the Coast Guard called off the search. I was devastated because nothing had been found. Not a single trace of debris from the wreckage or a body. They had even expanded their search to cover a broader area, taking into account the currents and an object's drift in the water, but still, nothing.

I stood at the large window inside our condo and held a cup of tea. A sailboat was making its way from the marina toward open water. The sun was high in the sky and the winds were light, from the west. I envied those passengers—whoever they were—heading out to enjoy the day. Would I ever be able to do that again? Enjoy a day? Feel blessed and grateful for my wonderful, happy life?

My mother had gone home. She had stayed with me these past five days, sleeping in the guest room, leaving only briefly to pick up a few essentials from her beach house or to get snacks for us, though I had little interest in eating. I appreciated her presence and emotional support, but now, after learning about the end of the search, all I wanted was to be alone. I needed silence—raw, absolute silence—to try and accept what everyone was pushing me to accept: that Dean was lost forever.

It wasn't easy. It didn't help that the tabloids were printing outrageous stories like **GIANT SEA SERPENTS SPOTTED IN THE SEA OF DOOM! FLYING SAUCERS TERRIFY PASSENGERS OF LUXURY CRUISE SHIP! GOVERNMENT COVER-UP!**

I couldn't stop myself from thinking about what Mike Mitchell had said on the news—that there was "something going on out there." What if he was right? What if Dean's instruments had failed because of some unexplained supernatural force of nature? And what if he was still alive somewhere? It was still possible, wasn't it? I didn't believe in sea monsters or UFOs, but there was no wreckage where they had expected it to be. No body. Perhaps Dean had landed the plane safely somewhere, but he was hurt and had to recover before he could find his way home to me.

I couldn't give up hope. At least not yet. If he was alive, he would need me to keep a light on in the window.

The phone rang. I turned away from the bright sunlight at the glass and answered it. "Hello?"

It was Sarah. "Hey, sis. How are you doing?"

"As well as can be expected." I moved to the sofa and pictured Dean on the end of it with his feet up on the coffee table, watching a basketball game. Rather than sit down, I turned away and went back to the kitchen. "You heard they called off the search?"

"Yes. I'm so sorry."

"Me too." My tea was cold, so I set the cup in the sink. "But I can't give up hope. Tomorrow I'm going to call the regulatory board that does crash investigations and find out what their conclusion is, and I'm going to stay on top of them, because it all seems so suspicious, don't you think? It doesn't make sense that Dean could just vanish into thin air. Something's not right about this."

"Oh, Olivia," she said with a sigh. "I hope you're not buying into all those crazy stories they've been printing."

I shook my head with frustration. "I don't know. I mean . . . of course not. But how can an entire plane just disappear? I want to know how they're going to explain that."

Sarah spoke gently. "I understand that you need answers. I would need that, too, if it were Leon. I'm so sorry about the fact that you haven't gotten any closure."

My pulse quickened. "I hate that word, *closure*. People keep using it."

"Yes, well . . ."

"I know what you're trying to say. You want me to accept the fact that Dean's not coming back, but I have to be honest. I'm not entirely sure if that's true. I can still feel him here with me."

"I get it," she replied sympathetically, but I knew what she was thinking—that I needed to give it time, and eventually I would come to my senses and realize that Dean couldn't have survived a plane crash over the water, and the tabloids were just trying to cash in on the story.

"I have to go," I said, because I didn't want to think about closure. It was still too soon. I wasn't ready to move on.

We hung up, and I returned to the window to look out at the water. The sailboat was now a tiny speck on the horizon, barely visible. Soon I wouldn't be able to see it at all, but that didn't mean it would cease to exist.

~

The next morning, when I woke, I forgot, for a brief, fleeting second, that Dean was missing. The world felt normal as my eyes fluttered open, but then I took a breath, and I remembered.

The agony of loss slammed into me all over again, like a hot, heavy wind. It made my chest ache, my lungs constrict. *Oh God* . . . it was real. Everyone had given up. The search was over. No one was looking for Dean anymore. He was presumed dead.

I rolled to my side and stared at the vacant bed beside me. I laid my hand on the soft surface of Dean's pillow, then snuggled into it and squeezed it tight to my face, inhaling deeply, wanting desperately and frantically to breathe in the scent of him, to feel him inside my body. But I couldn't capture it—I couldn't feel him at all, which came as a shock. I began to panic and weep and scream into the soft feather down until the pillowcase was drenched with my tears.

Where was he? Alone somewhere in the vast, open sea?

Or was he somewhere else, in another dimension of the universe, still flying his airplane, thinking everything was fine?

Was he in heaven?

God. Please, not that.

My body shook with wrenching sobs in the dim, lonely room. *Please, Dean . . . if you're out there . . . if you can hear me . . . come home.*

~

Hours later, I turned on the television. There were no more news items about the crash—if that's what it was. The latest story involved a senator who had been caught shoplifting in Atlanta. There was nothing about Dean in the newspapers, either, not even a short piece on page ten or eleven.

I didn't know what to do with myself, so I closed my eyes and dreamed about all the Sunday mornings that Dean and I had sat at the kitchen table, trading sections of the newspaper while we sipped coffee and thought about what to make for breakfast. Eggs or pancakes? Both? Usually we had both, and it was always Dean who stood over the skillet flipping the pancakes while I scrambled the eggs. The thought of it made me smile, but then it filled me with grief. When I opened my eyes, I could barely see through my tears.

~

I tried to nap in the afternoon, but it was pointless because I couldn't stop staring at the telephone, waiting for it to ring, for someone to call me with news and tell me that Dean had been found.

Later, my eyes were fixed on the kitchen phone when it finally rang and interrupted the interminable silence. I jumped up and nearly knocked over a chair as I dashed around the table to answer it. I dropped the receiver when I picked it up. It bounced on the floor, and I fumbled to grab hold of the coiled cord and pull it back.

"Hello?" I said anxiously, afraid that I might have cut off the caller.

"Hello. Is this Olivia Hamilton?"

"Yes." I listened like a wild creature of the forest—alert and ready to act.

"This is Mike Mitchell," the caller said. "I was on the airplane with your husband a few hours before he disappeared."

My heart turned over in my chest. Not knowing what to expect, I leaned against the kitchen counter and rubbed the back of my neck.

"Yes, I know who you are," I replied, appreciating the fact that he had used the word *disappeared* instead of *crashed*.

"I heard they called off the search," Mike said. "I'm so sorry."

"Thank you."

There was an angry part of me that wanted to say: *You have a lot of nerve. This is all your fault. If you hadn't decided to fly off to your party mansion that night, Dean would still be here.*

But I didn't say that because it wasn't fair. I could just as easily blame Richard or the other pilot who got sick and needed to be replaced at the last minute. Or I could blame myself for putting pressure on Dean to fly straight home.

"How are you holding up?" Mike asked.

"Not that well, if you really want to know." I had to fight to keep my voice steady. "I just don't understand how they could give up the search when they didn't find anything. I mean, he has to be out there, right? An airplane can't just vanish."

"Well, that's up for debate," Mike said, "but I hear you."

I shook my head, willing myself to be rational, to resist all the strange, outlandish theories that had been circulating the past few days, but it wasn't easy.

Mike let out a deep breath. "I wasn't sure if I should even call you. People kept telling me I should leave you alone to grieve and that I shouldn't give you false hopes, but I at least had to offer my sympathies and tell you how sorry I am."

"Thank you. But what sorts of false hopes would you be giving me? Specifically?" This I needed to know.

He cleared his throat. "Well . . . listen." He paused. "I have a friend who has done some research on the Triangle. He's a smart guy with a science background, and he has some interesting ideas about what's going on."

A week ago, I would have rolled my eyes at this kind of talk, but since the search had been called off, I was desperate for new information.

"Go on." I pushed away from the counter and paced around my kitchen.

"Do you know about Flight Nineteen?" Mike asked.

"You mentioned it on the news," I replied.

"That's right, and that's not the only mysterious case out there. And I'm not talking about the rubbish the tabloids have been printing. Ignore that stuff."

"What are you talking about, then?"

"Well . . ." He paused. "In 1978, a plane disappeared while coming in for a landing in Saint Thomas. The aircraft was visible on the radar, and the air traffic controller could see it approaching—with his very own eyes. He estimated it was only about two miles away. He looked down at the radar for a second, and then boom! It was gone. They declared an emergency and a search began, but no trace was ever found. And that was two miles from the airport. That's a true story. You can look it up."

"How did they ever explain it?" I asked.

"They never did. And some of the official reports about other disappearances are highly redacted. There are other strange things, too, like they found a piece of a plane that had vanished, and there was a magnetic particle attached to it, but they couldn't identify what that magnetic particle was. So where did it come from? Where did the rest of the plane go?"

"Are you talking about UFOs?" I asked, and despite my desire to cling to any possible theory that supported the idea that Dean had not been killed in a crash, my brain couldn't rationalize that he had been abducted by aliens.

"I don't know," Mike said. "Maybe there are electromagnetic disturbances in our atmosphere that scientists have yet to identify. Think about it. Einstein's theory of relativity was only published this century. We're still learning, right? So imagine everything that physicists still haven't discovered yet about gravity and wormholes and time warps. We don't know what we don't know!"

I exhaled heavily. "I just want my husband back."

"I'm sorry. I didn't mean to go off like that. I just find it strange that this happened."

"I find it strange too." I twirled the phone cord around my index finger and thought about everything he had just told me. "Listen, would you mind sharing the name of your friend who's been studying those missing airplanes? I might like to pick his brain."

"Sure. He's a retired schoolteacher, and he lives outside Miami. His name is Brice Roberts. I already talked to him about this, so he won't be surprised to hear from you."

Mike gave me Mr. Roberts's phone number, which I jotted down on a notepad. "Thank you. I appreciate this."

"No problem. Good luck. And let me know if you ever need anything. I'd love to help. I'm obsessed with this stuff."

I hung up the phone and wondered what Dean would think about me calling a total stranger about wormholes and time warps. I was quite certain that he'd try to talk me out of it.

~

Mike Mitchell's friend, Brice Roberts, turned out to be an eccentric, which was a polite way to describe a man who slept every night in a bomb shelter in his backyard and boarded up his house to prevent the Russians from infiltrating his water system through satellite technology.

He believed that Dean's plane had been swallowed up by an alien mother ship. He suggested that I shouldn't give up hope because Dean was most likely alive and well, and he would return to me years from now, not having aged a day. If I loved him, Brice said, I should wait for him, even if I was an elderly woman when he returned, because he would need my support in a world that was vastly different from what he had left behind.

Things went downhill from there. Brice led me into his bunker and showed me his cork wall of newspaper articles that dated back to the 1947 Roswell crash cover-up. "And what about this?" He slapped his open palm on a black-and-white photo of a covered bridge, tacked to his corkboard. "In '69, at least forty people saw a UFO in Massachusetts, and one family in their car saw lights coming out of the woods near this bridge. The next thing they know, they're in a gigantic hangar with other people, in some otherworldly place, and then, like magic, they're back in their car two hours later, sitting in different seats."

Brice shared a few more alien-abduction stories. Then he turned and offered me a hit of LSD, which was when I decided it was time to leave.

I felt foolish during the two-hour drive home because I'd always considered myself to be a sensible person, but I didn't feel that way when I returned to the condo, parked the car in the garage, and burst into tears over the steering wheel.

I sat in my car and dug through my purse for a tissue, then blew my nose, got out, and started walking toward the elevator.

A short while later, I was back in the condo, gazing numbly out the window at yet another sailboat leaving the marina, heading out to open water. As I watched it, I began to feel nauseous and needed to sit down until the feeling passed.

~

"I think I might be depressed," I said to my mother later, when she called.

"You're devastated over the loss of your husband, which is completely normal. You need grief counseling," she suggested.

"Maybe," I replied as I warmed a can of chicken noodle soup on the stove and wondered what Dean would think of that suggestion. Would he recommend it for me?

"I suppose you want to say *I told you so*," I said to my mother.

"You mean about that crazy conspiracy theorist?" she replied. "Yes, that's exactly what I want to say, but I won't. I think you already know what you need to know."

"That I shouldn't go any further down this rabbit hole?" I replied, a little tersely.

"Exactly."

I thought about it for a moment and let out a sigh. "But I'm desperate for an explanation. I can't live forever in the dark, always wondering what happened to Dean, never getting any true closure."

It was the first time I had been the one to use the word *closure*, but my experience with Brice had felt like a glass of cold water in the face.

"I know it hurts," Mom said, "but eventually, you're going to have to accept that Dean is gone. I'm sorry, sweetheart."

My whole body tensed. "I don't want to accept anything until I see the crash investigation report from the NTSB. I don't know how long that will take, but I'll need to hear their official conclusion. And I'm going to do some more research on my own and look into missing planes in the Bermuda Triangle."

"I wish you wouldn't," my mother said.

"Why not? If nothing else, it'll give me something to focus on and keep my mind busy."

"You could always come home to New York and live with me for a while," she suggested. "Start fresh."

That's what Dean and I had wanted when we'd moved from New York to Miami four years earlier. A fresh start. It had certainly felt fresh for a while. At least until he agreed to fill in for another pilot who had the nerve to catch a stomach bug and miss a scheduled flight.

"I have to go," I said, looking down at the soup in the pot.

As soon as I hung up, I bent forward, inhaled the scent of chicken in the broth, and felt nauseous again. Then I blinked a few times with disbelief.

Could it be? Was it possible?

Sucking in a breath, I dropped the spoon onto the counter and went to find my address book in a drawer in the bedroom. I pulled it out and flipped through the pages like a maniac, searching alphabetically for the right number. At last, I found it.

I hurried back to the kitchen and called my doctor. She knew my situation and agreed to see me within the hour.

~

I'd always imagined that the day I found out I was pregnant would be cause for celebration. Dean would pick me up and swing me around and tell me how happy he was. We would spend the rest of the day calling family and friends and delivering the happy news. Then we would snuggle in bed, just the two of us, where we could bask privately in the joy of our creation together. A baby. A beautiful child growing in my womb. We would talk about names for a boy or a girl and discuss the possibility of buying a house of our own instead of continuing to live in the condo my mother provided for us, rent-free.

But Dean was not here to share this special moment with me. I was alone, sitting in my doctor's office, aware of her sympathetic expression as she delivered the results of my pregnancy test, as if it were something sad. It was, in a way. Maybe my doctor was simply reflecting my mood.

We discussed due dates, vitamin supplements, and morning sickness. Then she folded her hands on the desk. "I hope you can be happy about this."

I nodded, responsibly. "I am happy. It's what we always wanted."

She regarded me with compassion. "Do you have someone you can talk to about this?"

"I have my mother," I replied. "And my sister. And friends."

"No, I mean . . . a professional."

"A therapist?"

"Yes. They can be very helpful."

I lowered my gaze and shook my head. "I don't think so. But I'll let you know if I change my mind. In the meantime, I'm just going to go home, watch *Golden Girls*, and eat a gallon of ice cream."

She laughed, but I wasn't joking. I think she knew it.

CHAPTER 7
MELANIE

New York, 1986

"Thank you for suggesting I talk to someone," I said to Dr. Fielding as I walked with him out of the physics lab. "It's really helped. I think I was just stuck, in more ways than one. Obviously, I was upset about my mom, but I also think I hit a wall with my research. I couldn't seem to get past it, but Dr. Robinson has helped me with that too. I mean, he doesn't know much about particle physics, but he lets me talk about my work, and it feels like brainstorming. I've had some really good ideas come to me on that sofa in his office."

"That's wonderful," Dr. Fielding replied. "I'm champing at the bit to read your paper."

"And I'm eager to get it finished. Who knows what might come of it?"

He pressed the elevator button. "How is the writing coming, by the way? Will you be ready on time to present it?"

"I think so," I replied. "I'm almost halfway through the rough draft."

"Excellent." The elevator doors opened, and he stepped inside. "We'll talk again next week."

As soon as he was gone, I hurried back to the lab to collect my things, because I had a session with Dr. Robinson in less than an hour.

It had been six weeks since I had begun my treatment, and I couldn't deny that I looked forward to our weekly sessions with a fervor I'd never felt before. Often, while I worked in the lab, I replayed our previous conversations in my mind and made a mental note of all the things I wanted to talk to him about—like discoveries I had made with my experiments or the unusual things that happened to pilots just before they disappeared, which always fascinated him.

I also enjoyed talking about personal things—a delicious meal I had prepared, a good book I was reading, and of course, my relationship with my mother. It was all about me, which was what made it so intoxicating, to be listened to like that. I couldn't help but wonder if this was what it felt like to meet your perfect match. Whatever I said—even if it was mundane—he would listen with interest and inquire further, always appearing completely rapt. Those hours with Dr. Robinson had become the most electrifying hours of my entire adult life.

Gathering up my things, I went to the ladies' room to freshen up and apply some makeup, which I had purchased at Walgreens that morning. Face powder, mascara, and lip gloss. It felt strange because I never wore makeup.

After I put it on, however, I studied my reflection in the mirror and hated what I saw. A wave of nausea crept up from the pit of my stomach, so I grabbed some tissue from one of the stalls and quickly scrubbed at my face. Then I stuffed everything back into my bag and hurried out the door.

~

"I'd like to talk about something that just happened," I said to Dr. Robinson when I sat down on the sofa in his office. He sat across from me in the big armchair, his notepad on his lap, hands upon it, clasped together.

It was a bold and daring request I was making. I had struggled with the idea of bringing it up during the subway ride, and I had rehearsed a few different ways of communicating the issue. I also debated with myself about whether I should introduce a topic that could completely backfire on me. But Dr. Robinson had become my most intimate confidant, and he had proved to me that this room was a safe space where I could say anything without fear of judgment. I felt close to him now, I trusted him, and it seemed wrong not to bare my soul in this matter. He was my therapist after all. It was his role in my life to help me gain better self-awareness and learn not to bury my feelings. To truly understand myself.

"We can talk about whatever you like," he replied in his usual warm, magnanimous manner that broke down all my walls and filled me with courage.

"All right." I paused and lowered my gaze as I spoke. "Just before I came over here, I put on some makeup." I swallowed uneasily, kept my eyes fixed on the floor. "I wanted to look nice, so I powdered my nose and applied lipstick. I'm only mentioning it because it feels significant. Because I *never* wear makeup."

I looked across at Dr. Robinson. I'm not sure what sort of response I was expecting, but he watched me with concern, his expression serious. I waited for him to say something, but of course he didn't.

Suddenly we were back to the early days of our sessions together, where he would wait patiently for me to lead our conversation somewhere that suited me, and long silences would arise until I filled them.

"But then I looked at myself," I continued, "and I felt totally pathetic. I mean . . . what was I trying to do? Make myself sexy and attractive? For you? My therapist? That's crazy, right?"

He shifted in his chair, and the awkwardness caused me to lose my nerve, so I dropped my gaze and fiddled with my thumbnail. "All I could think about was my mother and how she used to get all gussied up to go out at night, looking for a man. She would curl her hair like Farrah Fawcett. I remember she had these green satin shorts that she called 'hot pants.' She'd wear them with shiny black patent leather go-go boots. It never failed. She always managed to bring some guy home from the bar, and it would last for a while. Until it didn't."

Dr. Robinson touched the pads of his fingertips together and waited for me to continue.

"That's why I felt nauseous in the bathroom. It was the lipstick. I had to rub it all off." I sighed heavily. "I think the point is that . . . I'm still doing it."

"Doing what?" he asked.

"Living in fear that I'm going to end up like my mother." This time I stared at him and waited for *him* to speak.

"And that's why you washed off the makeup?" he asked.

I nodded, tipped my head back against the sofa cushion, and slouched down low. "I always dreamed that one day a man would love me for who I was on the inside, not because of my cleavage or my big hair. And he would love me forever and he wouldn't leave. And lately . . ."

I swallowed hard and tried to summon my courage again, but it was gone.

Dr. Robinson remained quiet. I wished he would say something. I wanted him to recognize what I was really trying to explain—that he had awakened a desire in me. A desire to feel sexually attractive. I wanted him to understand that I was falling in love with him.

I sat up again. "So what do you think about that, Doctor?"

I realized this had become a mildly flirtatious pet name I liked to use whenever I felt a spark flicker between us. It represented a deeper attraction that neither of us would ever dare to acknowledge because there were professional ethics to consider here. His, not mine. Of course, I would never do anything to jeopardize his reputation or career. I respected him too much for that, and I cared about his happiness.

Dr. Robinson cleared his throat. "Well," he finally said, after taking a moment to think before he spoke. "It's been quite clear to me . . . and I believe you already know this yourself, Melanie. You knew it long before you started seeing me. You know that you carry a resentment toward your mother for not providing you with a traditional family life and a steady father figure."

I felt my brow furrow. Where was he going with this?

"This is why your feelings around her death were so confusing to you," he continued. "You didn't know whether to be sad or indifferent or to feel guilty because you hadn't spoken to her in so long. And that confusion spilled over into all the other aspects of your life, including your work. It made you question your choices in the past and made you doubt who you really are. If you want to wear makeup, you should be able to wear makeup. It should have nothing to do with your mother. Yet it does, so clearly we still have some work to do."

I couldn't help but wonder if this was just a way of changing the subject, a redirection to usher me away from the true point I was trying to make. I had already lost my nerve about that, so I followed his lead.

"We've gotten sidetracked lately, haven't we," I said, "talking about my dissertation. But that's been helpful too. Your interest in the subject made me remember why I was always so fascinated by it. And that was my goal when I came here. To figure out if I was on the right path."

"I'm glad our sessions have been helpful," he said. "But if it's all right with you, I'd like to go back to what you were saying earlier, when you were describing your mother to me."

Not knowing what to expect, I shifted my position on the sofa. "You have a theory?" I asked.

"Possibly." He set his notebook aside on the small table beside him and sat forward with his elbows on his knees. "Of course, it's important that you feel good about your academic and professional life, Melanie, and that you are fulfilled in that area. But your personal life matters, too, and I'd like to address that, if we could make that our next area of focus."

As always, I felt comfortable putting myself in his hands. "All right."

Dr. Robinson inched a little closer. "Have you ever tried to think about your mother as a young woman like you, with hopes and dreams, similar to what you mentioned to me earlier?"

I frowned a little. "What did I say earlier?"

"You said that you always imagined—and I believe you used the word *dreamed*—that one day someone would love you forever and would never leave."

I watched him warily, with laser-like focus. "Yes?"

"I think perhaps you may have some abandonment issues that we should explore, but before we discuss that, I'd like you to consider something else, if you will."

"Okay."

"Isn't it possible that your mother wanted the same thing you want today? And when she got 'all gussied up,' as you put it, that she was going out in search of a partner. A mate. Someone who would love her forever and be a good father to you? Maybe that's what she wanted more than anything, to give you that."

Something welled up inside of me and lodged thickly in my throat. "But she never stayed with any of those men. Nothing ever lasted. She always fought with them and eventually kicked them out."

He sat back again. "Why do you think that was?"

"Because they were losers."

"What else? Think about what would happen before she asked them to leave."

"The fights would get really bad," I replied, "and she would tell me to stay in my bedroom. I think she was afraid that they might yell at me, too, or do something worse."

He inclined his head, in that way he had of encouraging me to think more broadly about something.

"That's when she kicked them out," I said, blinking slowly a few times as a new realization dawned. Then I looked toward the window. "Oh . . ."

Dr. Robinson said nothing for a while. We simply sat there together in the quiet of the afternoon, watching the leaves on the oak tree blow gently outside the window.

Eventually, I returned my attention to him. "I think what you're suggesting is that my mother was trying to do her best. She wanted to give me a normal family life. That's why she went out on the prowl. She was looking for a husband and father."

"I do think all of that is true," he replied, "and I like where we're going with this, but I also want you to be realistic. I'm not trying to paint your mother as a saint, and I don't think you should either. Just try to think of her as a normal human being, a young woman who you might be able to relate to and understand. She was only seventeen when she had you, so when she went out, she was probably looking for something—not just for you but for herself as well. But there's nothing wrong with that. It doesn't make her an irresponsible person. It's part of the human condition to want love and to be loved in return. Most of us want a true, deep connection with others."

"A soul mate," I said.

He stared at me for a moment, then held up a hand. "Let's not overly romanticize what I'm suggesting here."

"You don't believe in soul mates?" I asked.

He hesitated and blinked a few times, appearing unsettled. Then he glanced at his wristwatch. "I'm afraid we've gone over our time."

I looked up at the grandfather clock. "I hope you don't have another patient waiting."

"It's fine. You're the last one today. But we really should stop here."

Disappointed, because I wanted desperately to hear him answer my question, I bent forward and pulled on my shoes, reached for my tote bag on the floor, and stood up. "This was a really good session," I said. "Sometimes I can't believe the things we talk about. You keep making light bulbs come on in my head."

He smiled warmly. "I'll see you next week?"

"Of course," I replied.

Nothing could keep me away.

He followed me to the door and said goodbye before he closed it softly behind me.

As I made my way down the creaky staircase to the empty reception area and outside to the sunny afternoon, I felt a thrill in my heart and found myself thinking of my mother and how she was always so happy in the early days of a new relationship. That's when the baseball games and camping trips happened, and she was the best mother in the world, smiling and laughing and baking cookies that made the house smell good when I came home from school.

That was also when I dared to believe that my world could be different. All I'd ever wanted was for us to be happy and secure, but my mother's happiness seemed to hinge on the success or failure of whatever current relationship she was in. It was all so volatile and unpredictable. Everything depended on the man and how good he was to us and how hopeful my mother was about the future.

This was why I had never wanted to rely on someone else to make my dreams come true. I wanted to be self-reliant.

But did that mean I had to be alone? Wasn't it possible to love someone who wouldn't turn out to be a disaster? To find a good, decent man like my grandfather? A man I could rely upon and trust?

I didn't know the answer to that question, but it was something I wanted to discuss next week with Dr. Robinson. I couldn't wait to pick up exactly where we had left off. Maybe next time I wouldn't lose my nerve, and I would tell him exactly how I felt.

CHAPTER 8
OLIVIA

Miami, 1990

Six months into my pregnancy, I slammed the phone onto the cradle after another frustrating conversation with someone at the National Transportation Safety Board. They still hadn't concluded the report about Dean's so-called crash, and the woman on the phone was pithy with me, making it clear that she was tired of answering my calls.

I was disappointed because she'd been compassionate at first. Understanding of my loss. She'd handled me with the utmost care and kindness. But her tone had changed recently, which was why I thought maybe I needed to consider what my doctor had suggested eons ago and arrange to see a therapist. Because maybe the clerk at the NTSB wasn't the problem. Maybe I was.

I stared at the stack of crash reports I had been reading for the past six months, copies I had attained from the Federal Aviation Administration Library on a research trip to Washington. I was mostly interested in flights that had vanished over the Bermuda Triangle, and I learned some incredible things, which weren't that far off from some of the wild tales that Brice Roberts had talked about.

There were a number of investigations that cited unexplained radio interference and blackouts, disappearances without any distress signals, flights that vanished in perfect weather with no engine trouble, no fires or explosions reported. In addition, no wreckage, debris, or bodies were ever found.

One report offered a disturbing conclusion that the aircraft must have met with a "sudden and violent force that rendered the aircraft no longer airworthy and was thereby beyond the scope of human endeavor to control." The force that rendered the aircraft uncontrollable was unknown.

Another report from a similar disappearance said that "no more baffling problem has ever been presented for investigation."

It was obvious to me that my research into the subject of missing planes had become an obsession, which had everyone concerned, because the media frenzy was over. The public's fascination with the Bermuda Triangle had passed. I was the only one still fixated on it. One friend suggested it was pregnancy hormones, but Sarah thought I had lost touch with reality. A week ago, she'd begged me, yet again, to see a therapist.

As I sat at the kitchen table, I felt the sweet sensation of my baby moving in my belly. It was like a flutter of butterfly wings. Was he kicking or rolling over? Or was he a she?

I sat back and stared at those crash reports and realized how quiet the condo was. There was no music or television, laughter or conversation. It was just me, alone with the sound of pages turning. It wasn't so bad in the daytime, but at night, in the darkness, with only one lamp at my desk or with the cold glare of the fluorescent light bulb over the kitchen table and the unbearable silence, I recognized how desperately I missed Dean. There was no joy left in my life, only a terrible sorrow born out of an unfathomable loss. Sometimes my body ached from the grief in my heart, and I couldn't sleep. Night after night, I would get up and read crash investigation reports until dawn, searching for a clue. Anything that might have happened in the past. Something that might give me insight into what had become of Dean or if there was any possibility that he was still out there, alive somewhere. But night after night, the result was the same. I found nothing.

My baby kicked again, so I rubbed tiny circles just above my belly button. "Hi there," I softly said. "It's too quiet in here, don't you think? Maybe you'd like to hear some music?"

He or she didn't respond, which only made me want to try harder to impress. I stood up, went to the shelf over the stereo, and withdrew Van Morrison's *Moondance* album, which was one of Dean's favorites. We used to listen to it when we were first married, living in the tiny studio apartment close to the flight school. My father had still been alive at the time, but we were cut off completely from my family, which had brought us closer together. It was only after Dad died that Mom finally reached out to us and suggested we move into the condo.

As I lowered the needle onto the vinyl record and heard the familiar guitar chords and jazzy rhythms, I wondered if I should think about a trip home to New York. Mom had been suggesting it ever since she found out I was expecting, but I always said no. I suppose I wanted to keep that proverbial light on in the window for Dean. And New York didn't hold much appeal for me these days, because that's where I'd had the terrible falling-out with my father. But Dad was gone now, and my mother was looking forward to becoming a grandmother.

I walked to the window, looked out at the sailboats in the marina below. Every time I saw them, I thought of Dean, and all I felt was a great big gaping hole in my heart and in my life. This condo was beginning to feel like a tomb. Was this the place I wanted to raise my child?

The phone rang, and as always, with a flash of hope, I hurried to answer it. "Hello?"

"Hello, is this the wife of the missing pilot?" the caller asked.

"Yes," I replied. "Who, may I ask, is calling?"

There was a long pause, then a screeching sound like static from an old walkie-talkie. "This is your husband calling from outer space. I won't be coming home tonight because I met a hot alien and we're in love!"

Laughter ensued, and I understood right away that it was a prank call, probably some teenagers in the building.

"Grow up, will you?" I sternly replied and slammed the phone down, hard.

My heart pounded raucously, and my stomach churned with anger. Clenching my hands into fists, I returned to my chair and took a few deep breaths, laboring to calm myself. I laid my hands on my belly, closed my eyes for a moment, and listened to the silence.

When I opened my eyes, I found myself staring at the toppling pile of crash reports and wondered what the devil I was searching for, exactly. I heard the voice of the prank caller in my mind. *This is your husband . . . calling from outer space . . .*

I slid my hands across my belly and felt a sudden momentous shift in my emotions. What was I doing here? Alone in a condo in Miami when I had a baby on the way. Dean's baby. At long last, I began to consider the possibility that it was time for me to call my mother and talk about my return to New York.

CHAPTER 9
OLIVIA

New York, 1990

Six days before Christmas, my blood pressure skyrocketed, and I fell into a frightful panic. I had swelling in my legs and ankles, which the doctor called "edema." A dipstick test showed protein in my urine. Taken together, these were signs of preeclampsia, which was a danger to the health of me and my baby. The doctors wanted to keep an eye on me until they could get my blood pressure under control, so I was admitted to the hospital for a few days, where I couldn't shake the fear that something terrible might happen and I would lose my baby. The baby Dean and I had created together. Before I lost him.

It was Christmas Eve when I was finally discharged and prescribed complete bed rest until the day of my delivery. Maria, our housekeeper, brought me a chicken dinner on a tray, and Mom was very attentive. After dinner, we watched *A Christmas Carol* with George C. Scott.

I tried to be cheerful the next morning when my mother wheeled a cart, piled high with gifts for me and the baby, into the room. I thanked her as I opened them, but it wasn't easy to get through the day. I was in a constant state of anxiety, and there weren't even any pretty snowflakes outside my window to lift my spirits. Just a curtain of cold, hard rain. My bedroom was a forbidding shade of gray, as if I were living inside a thundercloud where only bad things could happen.

I prayed heartily for good things because surely I had suffered enough loss this year.

On Boxing Day, my mother woke me up by marching into my bedroom. She ripped the curtains wide open and said, "Look! Snow!"

I sat up and squinted at the whiteness beyond the glass. Big fat snowflakes turned to slush as they slid slowly down the windowpane.

"That's lovely," I replied, feeling my baby kick, which gave my mood a lift.

Mom sat on the edge of my bed. "Maria will be in soon with some oatmeal and blueberries, and then you'll have to take a shower and get dressed because you're having visitors today."

"Visitors," I said with a frown. "Who?"

"Cassie, Rachel, Amanda, Kevin, and Gabriel. I called Todd, but he's in Barbados for the holidays."

These were my oldest and dearest friends from college, which included my ex.

"Mom, why did you invite Gabriel? That's going to be awkward."

"No, it won't be. It's been five years, and you've each moved on. He's been seeing someone for over a year now. She's a nurse, I'm told."

"But I haven't seen him since . . ."

I didn't have the energy to explain that the last time I'd spoken to Gabriel was at a coffeehouse in SoHo, when he'd invited me to watch him play his saxophone. We were broken up at the time, but he wanted to get back together, so I showed up with Dean. It was my way of telling Gabriel that we were over for good, and I had always felt guilty about that. It was cruel and cowardly of me, to flaunt my new boyfriend in front of Gabriel like that.

"I'm supposed to be resting," I told my mother, grasping at any excuse not to see people. "You shouldn't have done that."

"Don't worry. They won't expect you to get up and do a jig. I explained the doctor's orders, and they just want to come by and see you. To cheer you up a little."

I looked at the snow piling up on the windowsill outside and decided I could use a little bit of cheer. "Okay, fine," I said. "But I'll definitely need to take a shower and get out of this old nightgown."

My mother bounced happily off the bed and went to check on my breakfast.

~

I was sitting up in bed rereading *What to Expect When You're Expecting* when I heard a commotion in the front hall and knew that my friends had arrived. I marked my page, set the book aside, and listened to my mother's welcoming laughter. This group of friends had been like second children to her when we were all together in college. After graduation, we went our separate ways, so there was plenty of catching up to do.

I waited in bed, but they took their time, and I wondered if my mother had commandeered them into the living room for her own little social gathering, but the next moment, Rachel appeared in the doorway with a bouquet of helium balloons, followed by Cassie and Amanda, who carried flowers and gifts. They took one look at me and burst into tears, but they were happy tears.

"Look at you," Rachel cried. She approached the bed and wrapped her arms around me. The others gushed about how well I looked and how long it had been since we'd seen each other.

Kevin walked in next and gave me a less emotional greeting, a kiss on the cheek and a high five. "Congratulations on the bun in the oven," he said.

"Thank you," I replied and looked at each of them in turn. "It's so good to see you guys. I can't believe it. Sit down. Tell me how you've been."

The ladies set the flowers, balloons, and gifts on the floor and climbed onto the bed, while Kevin sat on the upholstered chair by the window.

I looked at all of them with wonder, then realized someone important was missing. "Did Gabriel not come?" I asked.

Kevin gestured toward the door with his thumb as if he were hitching a ride. "He's in the kitchen with your mom, talking about his parents' fiftieth-wedding-anniversary party."

Rachel gave me a look, because she remembered all the ups and downs of our relationship and how my parents had adored Gabriel, which was half the reason why we'd broken up. I just couldn't take the pressure to hurry up and marry him.

"You smell great," I said to Cassie. "What is that perfume?"

She rolled up her sleeve and held out her wrist. "It's Opium. Yves Saint Laurent."

"I love it."

"That's good, because I got you a bottle."

"Oh!" I exclaimed.

"You never could keep a secret," Rachel said. "Just don't tell her what I got her."

"I would never," Cassie replied with a coy grin.

A light knock sounded at the door, and Gabriel walked in. He wore a navy cable-knit sweater over a crisp white collared shirt and loose-fitting jeans. His hair was longer than I'd ever seen it. He crossed the threshold and regarded me with a friendly, affectionate smile. "Hey there," he said. "Long time no see."

"Too long," I replied as he approached, bent over the bed, and kissed me on the cheek.

"I'm really sorry about Dean," he said in a soft voice.

"Thank you. I appreciate that."

He stood back and took in my belly bulge. "You look well."

"Big as a barn," I said, trying to sound lighthearted as I cupped my belly with both hands. "And how are you all?" I asked, not wanting to be in the spotlight the entire time.

Rachel launched into a dramatic tale of the holiday dinner with her gigantic family, which transitioned into a full hour of catching up on everyone's careers and personal relationships. Only then did they broach the topic of Dean and his high-profile disappearance off the coast of Puerto Rico.

I told them what had happened that night, and Rachel held my hand.

"We were planning to start a family," I said. "We talked about it that very day, but I had no idea I was already pregnant. I wish he could have known."

Cassie rubbed my knee.

"That's rough," Kevin said. "I hope you know that we're here for you if you need anything."

"Thank you," I replied, sitting up straighter. "You guys are the best."

But even as I spoke the words, I knew we couldn't be what we once were to each other when we were young and single and attending college. Rachel, Cassie, and Amanda were married now, and Kevin was living in California, still single but running a business that kept him tied down geographically. As for Gabriel . . . he was still in New York, but there was too much water under the bridge where he was concerned. Things still felt awkward between us, and a casual friendship with an ex-boyfriend wasn't something I wanted. I only wanted Dean.

"So when are you going to open these gifts?" Kevin asked, kicking at one of them with his toe and breaking the tension. "And when can we pop those balloons?"

"We're not popping them," Cassie replied, feigning outrage. "That would scare the baby." She leaned closer and spoke to my belly. "Don't worry, little darling. I've got your back."

I squeezed Cassie's hand. How wonderful it was to be with good friends after so many months of solitude.

Kevin passed me a present, and I expressed my delight with a boxful of baby shoes in all shapes and sizes. "This should take us all the way to kindergarten," I said.

Later, when it was time for them to go, they each kissed me on the cheek and said goodbye.

"Don't worry. You're going to be fine," Rachel whispered in my ear. "And I'm going to call you." I wondered if she would.

Gabriel was the last to say goodbye. "Let me know if you ever need anything," he said. "I'm still here in the city."

"Thank you," I replied and watched him go.

A week later, Rachel did call, and she came again to visit—this time to tell me that she was expecting a baby as well. We had plenty to talk about, and from that moment on, we called each other every day.

My world changed after that. For the first time, I could see a light at the end of my tunnel of grief. My due date was only days away, and the doctors were assuring me that my prognosis was good. On top of that, I had stopped reading crash reports, and I no longer went looking for stories about the Bermuda Triangle. It seemed as if I was finally ready to give up my search for answers. What was the point, after all, when no answers existed?

CHAPTER 10
MELANIE

New York, 1986

I found it difficult to concentrate on my work the week after my light bulb moment in Dr. Robinson's office. Mostly, I thought about Dr. Robinson and how brilliant and insightful he was. I imagined all sorts of scenarios where we might run into each other somewhere coincidentally, outside the office, and go for coffee or a walk in the park. I lay in bed each night imagining our conversations and all the things we would talk about. My dreams of those encounters soon evolved into elaborate fantasies about a courtship with dinners in restaurants and going away for a romantic weekend. A brief engagement. A wedding at city hall. A child on the way.

Needless to say, I fell behind in my work and spent a lot of time sitting at my typewriter, staring at the wall. I couldn't wait to see Dr. Robinson again, and when I woke up on the morning of our next appointment, it felt like Christmas.

I rose from bed and opened the curtains, then made coffee and tried to write about zero-point energy. I wanted to expand on the Hutchison

Effect and prove, through my lab experiments with high-voltage equipment, that if nature's electromagnetic wavelengths and frequencies were sufficiently disrupted, it could cause an aircraft to disintegrate in a microsecond. Perhaps even disappear into another dimension. But the words just wouldn't come. I couldn't think about Tesla coils and electrical induction when I was in such a heightened state of anticipation about my four o'clock appointment. Adrenaline sizzled through my veins at the speed of light.

Eventually, I gave up and went out shopping for something new to wear. I found a blazer on sale and a smart-looking tweed pencil skirt. After lunch, I took a long shower and later spent time in front of the mirror curling my hair. I even applied makeup and didn't allow myself to rub it off.

Dear, wonderful Dr. Robinson . . . he was helping me to become the woman I was meant to be, free of fears and inhibitions.

I arrived early for my appointment and sat in the waiting room while my stomach fluttered with excitement. When at last Jane, the receptionist, called my name, I stood and made my way up the plush red carpet on the mahogany staircase, then took a deep, calming breath before I knocked on Dr. Robinson's door.

Just the sound of his footsteps as he moved to answer it was enough to send me into an emotional uproar. This was always the highlight of my week—the beginning of a session, when I could look forward to an entire hour alone with him.

The door opened, and there he stood, the object of my dreams, in the flesh. He wore tan-colored trousers and a chocolate-brown turtleneck sweater. He was so devastatingly handsome I felt faint.

"Hello, Melanie," he said with that familiar warm smile that filled me with joy. "Come in."

He stepped aside, and I entered the office, moving casually toward my usual spot on the sofa.

He sat down across from me, reached for his notepad, and placed it on his lap. "How was your week?"

I was disappointed that he didn't seem to notice anything different about me—that for the first time, I had made a significant effort with my appearance.

Or perhaps he did notice and felt it would be inappropriate to comment.

"It was good," I replied. "Better than good, actually."

"Really? Why is that?"

I hesitated because this was the moment I had been rehearsing continuously in my mind. The moment when I would open the lid on my affection for him and tell him how I felt. "Because of what we talked about last week."

He didn't need to consult the notes on his lap. He remembered. "About you being able to relate to your mother in a different way?"

"Yes, that exactly. I don't know if you can tell, but I'm wearing makeup today."

"I did notice," he said with an almost congratulatory nod, as if to say *well done*. "And how did you feel when you put it on? Was it different from how you felt last week?"

"Very much so, yes. I felt . . ." After a pause, I said, "Hopeful."

"Hopeful in what way?" he asked, writing that down.

I wondered if he knew what I wanted to say to him and that was why he had posed the question—to hear me admit my feelings and finally, confidently unleash them.

"I felt hopeful because I began to imagine myself—I mean *really* imagine myself—finding happiness with someone." I paused and forced myself to maintain direct eye contact with him. Then the words finally spilled past my lips. "With you, actually."

His eyes lifted, and he stared at me for a second. "I'm sorry. Did you just say . . . with me?"

"Yes." I stared at him unwaveringly, giving him some time to absorb my confession. Then I began again. "This past week, I could see the sort of life we could have together, and it wasn't dysfunctional like all my mother's relationships. It was healthy and happy. I thought about what you said about it being a normal part of the human condition to want to feel a connection with someone. To be loved. That's how I feel. I mean . . . I've been coming here for weeks, and we've done nothing but talk about personal things. You know me better than anyone has ever known me in my entire life."

He shifted uncomfortably in his chair. "But Melanie, I'm afraid that's a one-way street, because you don't know anything about *me*."

"I know everything I need to know," I told him. "Everything that matters. I know that you're kind and compassionate, understanding and forgiving. You're patient and always calm. I can't imagine you ever yelling or becoming violent like those men my mother used to bring home. You're the exact opposite. You're not from my world, and that's a gift."

I noticed a bit of color in his cheeks. He began to click his pen and consult his notes. Then at last he cleared his throat, looked up, and responded. "I'm glad you told me about this. It's important that we talk about everything that you're feeling. But I also think it's important that you understand the boundaries that exist between us. I'm your therapist, and any sort of personal relationship between us would be completely inappropriate. Professionally unethical."

I felt a little sick to my stomach suddenly, because this wasn't what I'd imagined he would say. I had pictured this conversation many times, and though I'd expected him to be professional and tell me that we couldn't become romantically involved because he was my therapist and I was his patient, I'd still believed that something in his expression would contradict that fact. We would keep talking, and eventually he wouldn't be able to deny how he felt about me, and we would figure out a way to be together.

But that's not what was happening. It wasn't what I saw in his eyes. All I saw was fear.

I lowered my gaze and cupped my forehead in a hand.

"Are you okay?" he asked. "Can you tell me what you're feeling right now?"

"Mortified," I replied. "Embarrassed."

"Don't be embarrassed. Remember this room is a safe space for you. You can tell me anything, and we'll work through it. And if it makes you feel any better, what you're feeling is completely normal and very common. I've become a person in your life who is caring and attentive. It's not atypical for patients to mistake their feelings of well-being for romantic love. But that's not what this is."

I forced myself to look up at him. "How do you know? Because it feels very real to me. Our conversations about my work have been incredibly exciting, don't you think? I know you've enjoyed that as much as I have."

"I do enjoy talking about your work," he agreed, "because I'm interested in the subject. But that doesn't mean there's a romantic relationship here. I'm your therapist, and I'm interested in everything you have to say, Melanie, but only in the context of your treatment, and only in this room. Outside of it, there can never be anything between us."

I felt my breaths coming faster, as if I were being rushed down a flight of stairs because the building was on fire. "What if I wasn't your patient anymore?" I asked. "What if I quit therapy and then we could—"

He quickly shook his head. "No. There are rules about that too. It still wouldn't be permitted. Therapists can lose their license over things like that. Or worse. It's illegal."

His voice was firm, leaving no room for doubt on my end. All of a sudden, I couldn't speak. It was as if I had been hit by a truck, so I just sat there in somber silence.

He watched me for a moment. "How are you feeling right now?"

I laughed with disbelief. "You want me to tell you how I'm feeling? Maybe you're in this line of work because you enjoy torturing people."

He said nothing in response to that, so I was forced to answer his question.

"Fine. If you want me to be honest, I will be. I'm terrified because I've never felt this way before. About anyone. Lately, I can't think of anything but you. It's gotten in the way of my work because I can't concentrate. So much for solving the mystery of the Bermuda Triangle, because all I can think about is you, even though I've tried to talk myself out of it. Believe me, I have." I paused and exhaled sharply. "I love coming here every week and talking to you about my work. About everything. I love how you listen to me. How you look at me. But now I'm afraid that I've messed everything up, and you're going to tell me you can't treat me anymore because you're afraid I'll go off the deep end and make you lose your job. Please don't do that. Please don't stop our sessions. I don't know what I would do if I couldn't talk to you anymore."

Dr. Robinson looked down at his notes and spoke gently. "I'm not going to stop treating you, Melanie, unless you want to be transferred to someone else, in which case I would honor that request." He looked up again. "What I would prefer to do is use this opportunity to help you overcome some deep-rooted fears that you may have about intimacy and commitment and, from there, help you learn to have healthy relationships with others in the future. I think you've made some real progress in that area already—by opening yourself up to the possibility of entering into an intimate relationship with someone you respect and admire. That person just can't be me. So the first thing you need to do is accept that what you feel for me is not real because you don't know me as a person in a reciprocal relationship. What's happening here is something called erotic transference."

I nodded in agreement because I had studied psychology during my undergraduate degree, and I knew what erotic transference was. I'd also known that he would put that label on this today. That didn't mean I believed it was true.

What I did know was that I was completely shattered. He seemed so sure. He was unwavering, unwilling to admit that there was something special between us and not just erotic transference.

Perhaps I was arrogant to think this way, but I believed I was far too smart to be confused about what was real and what wasn't. Certainly, Dr. Robinson was brilliant, and there were many things he was correct about when he analyzed my feelings and behaviors, but not this. He wasn't just a fantasy prince to me. And I didn't need to know what kind of car he drove or what his favorite food was in order to know him on a deeper level. I believed I could see into his soul and that we were meant to be together.

If only he would allow us to explore that. If only his job weren't in the way.

He checked his watch. "I'm afraid we've run out of time for today."

I glanced up at the clock. Then I met his gaze. It was very strange. When our eyes met, I felt almost sorry for him. All I saw was a lonely man, trapped by the strict code of ethics of his profession.

"Can we continue this next week?" he asked, and I realized that he looked a little shaken.

"I think we have to," I replied, "because we can't leave it like this. We need to talk more about it. At least I do."

He nodded, stood up, and walked me to the door. I stopped at the threshold.

"I have only one request," I said, looking up at his handsome face and wishing I could lay my hand on his cheek. "If we're going to continue our sessions together, could I at least call you by your first name?

Dr. Robinson seems so formal to me, and you've always called me Melanie. You've never called me Miss Brown."

He hesitated a moment, and then his expression softened. "All right, Melanie. If you like, from now on, you can use my first name. Starting next week, you can call me Dean."

I felt a jolt of excitement run through me and left the clinic in a state of rapture.

CHAPTER 11
DEAN

New York, 1986

I had been a practicing clinician for quite some time, and this was not my first encounter with erotic transference. Often, I was the only caring male figure in a female patient's life, and it was not uncommon for that patient to mistake her feelings toward me for something resembling love. But as I watched Melanie walk down the stairs and then closed my office door behind her, I realized that my hands were shaking. I cupped them together and tried to control my response, but the trembling was overpowering. I was gripped by a feeling of dread for where our next session might lead, because she was correct about something. The attraction was mutual, and all I could see ahead of me was disaster.

Closing my eyes, I took a few deep, calming breaths, then returned to my chair and reminded myself of my training. There were protocols in place for this sort of thing. First, I had to recognize that this feeling of connection was countertransference, nothing more. It was my own emotional baggage that was causing me to relate to my patient in an intimate way. We shared similar pasts, and I was, quite heartily, fascinated and intrigued by her work on airplanes that disappeared over the Bermuda Triangle. When I was a boy, I had dreamed of becoming an astronaut or a pilot, but I had majored in psychology because it was my best subject and it offered the greatest opportunity for scholarships and fellowships, which were a necessity for me to continue my education. Like Melanie, I did not come from money, and my childhood was not ideal. I had done everything I possibly could to escape the world from which I came. We had that in common, she and I, and because of that, I felt a kinship.

But again . . . this was my own past kicking around inside me, and I had to keep my issues separate from hers.

Sitting back, I looked across at the sofa and thought of her sitting there, confessing her love for me, looking so vulnerable and shockingly self-aware. Frankly, I was in awe of her.

Recognizing that this was a complex case unlike any other I'd experienced before, I rose from my chair and went to my desk to look up the number of one of my colleagues and a mentor, Dr. John Matthews. He had supervised one of my projects during my master's degree, and he had taught me an important lesson: that clinicians who failed to deal with countertransference issues often ended up in front of disciplinary boards for inappropriate relations with clients. We'd all seen it many times, so I understood the importance of discussing these transference dynamics with a colleague and ensuring that I maintained a helpful and professional therapeutic relationship with my client.

I found John's contact information in my Rolodex, picked up the phone, and quickly punched in the number. Before it had a chance to ring, something stopped me. With a rush of panic, I slammed the receiver back down in the cradle.

I stood, moved around the desk, and walked to the window to think this through. What would it mean if I began sessions with Dr. Matthews? Where would it lead?

I was the youngest, newest therapist in this prestigious Manhattan practice, hired less than a year ago, and I had lofty ambitions for a partnership at some point in the future.

My boss, the owner of the practice, was a woman. What if she found out about this and discovered my history? All the other clinicians here had spotless reputations and Ivy League credentials. I had come out of a state college in the Midwest, and as for my reputation . . . well, there were a few blemishes. If she knew about that, would she lose confidence in my abilities?

I returned to my desk, sat down, and considered the situation further. At least I was aware of the danger and impropriety of what I was feeling for my client. Did I really need to discuss all that with another therapist, only to have him tell me what I already knew? That I felt an intimacy with Melanie because she dredged up uncomfortable memories and realities from my own life, while at the same time she stirred my boyhood dreams of aviation? I already knew this was what drew me to her, so what was there to learn from my own therapeutic treatment?

The answer was clear. She was a patient, and it was my job to help her, not harm her. At the same time, knowing her history, the worst thing I could do presently was abandon her.

So there it was. A course of action. Decided upon.

I would continue to treat Melanie and guide her through this issue of her erotic transference, and I would look inward and rely on my training to manage my own. If I had trouble coping with the situation in the coming weeks, I would do the responsible thing and contact my mentor, Dr. Matthews, and whether Melanie liked it or not, I would move her to another therapist.

~

The train was crowded during my evening commute to my apartment in New Jersey that evening. I had to stand for most of it while fighting not to think about Melanie Brown as I bumped up against other passengers in the hot, sweaty confines.

What a relief it was to finally reach my station, step onto the platform, and breathe in the cool evening air. I walked to my car, a 1971 Ford Pinto with a persistent and rather concerning rust problem.

Twenty minutes later, I entered my studio apartment on the second floor of a building that overlooked a used-car lot. It had been my home since I finished my degree and in time accepted the position at Wentworth Wellness Clinic, with high hopes and big dreams for a brighter future. I had always imagined this would be a temporary living arrangement until I could afford something better, ideally in Manhattan, where I could give up my car before it died unexpectedly on me. But each year, when I was faced with the end of my lease agreement, nothing had changed. I still couldn't afford anything better, so I signed on for another twelve months of long commutes and noisy neighbors who played the television too loudly in the evenings.

Dropping my car keys onto the kitchen table, I glanced at the mess I had left in the sink the night before, then checked the cupboard for food. I found peanut butter and crackers and a can of beef stew, which would have to do, because it had been a long day. I couldn't face getting back in my car for a grocery run.

I dug around the cutlery drawer for the can opener, then noticed the little red light on the answering machine was blinking. I pressed the button to listen to the messages, but as soon as I heard that foul, guttural voice, I froze, my stomach clenching instantly with stress.

"It's your father. You'd best come home if you want to see your aunt again. They moved her to hospice care today. They said it could be a few days. Not much more."

Click.

My muscles went rigid, and I dropped the can opener onto the countertop with a clatter. What had my father just said? Hospice care? I hadn't even known Auntie Lynn was in the hospital. The last time we spoke, two weeks ago, she told me she was doing well with the chemo and the doctor said she was in remission.

I made a dash for the phone and called the farmhouse, but there was no answer. Dad and Gram were probably at the hospital with Auntie Lynn, or Dad was at the bar. God, I should be there too. At the hospital. Not the bar. Why hadn't anyone called me?

Maybe Auntie Lynn hadn't wanted them to. She hated to burden me with her troubles, even though I told her she could never be a burden to me. I owed her everything. If it weren't for her, who knows where I would be at this stage in my life? Probably in prison with my brother, because he was the person I had clung to after Mom died. I'd followed him around like a shadow until Auntie Lynn swooped in from Arizona and took me away to live with her and her husband. She'd arrived just in the nick of time too. I was thirteen and on a dark path with my brother, but she pulled me out and managed my upbringing and schooling from there. She steered me away from the drinking and partying. It's unfortunate that she couldn't have taken my brother, too, but it was too late for him. He was seventeen and had already quit school to pump gas and move in with his buddies.

Auntie Lynn saved my life. She had tried to save Gram's life, too, when Gram fell down the steep farmhouse stairs and broke her hip. Auntie Lynn was a widow by then, so she left everything behind in Arizona to return to Wisconsin and care for her elderly mother. But dear Auntie Lynn hadn't expected the greater challenge to be caring for her alcoholic brother at the same time.

It was too much for her. It would have been too much for anyone. No wonder she got cancer.

I stood up and went to my desk to find my address book, then called my boss at home and explained that I had a family emergency. She agreed that I should cancel all my appointments for the next few days and book a flight.

A half hour later, I was climbing into a taxi and making my way to the airport.

~

My flight to Madison, Wisconsin, landed late the following morning, and I was worn out from two long layovers and the stress of not knowing how Auntie Lynn was doing. I didn't even know what hospital she was in. Every time I had a chance to call the house, no one answered.

I hurried out of the airport, found a cab, and made my way home. As soon as the driver pulled into the front yard, I paid him, got out, but waited for him to drive off before I approached the door.

Pausing a moment, I took in my surroundings. The place looked different. Empty and deserted. The toolshed looked like it was about to topple over. A rusty old barrel was full of stagnant water, and the door to the screened porch was wide open, banging against the outside wall whenever a gust of wind took hold of it. Off to the side, piles of brush from last season waited to be burned.

Swallowing over a bitter sense of dread at the mere notion of climbing those stairs, I instead wandered around the side of the house to see if my father's truck was in the yard.

There it was. Older and more broken down than I remembered.

Was he home? And what about Gram?

Enough stalling. I needed to know how Auntie Lynn was doing, so I went to the back door and walked into the kitchen without knocking.

The house was quiet. I set my bag down, removed my jacket, and hung it on the coat tree. "Is anyone here?"

No one replied, so I made my way to the front parlor but found it empty. The drapes were closed, and all the rooms were dark. I felt a little sickened by the stench of ashtrays full of cigarette butts and the sight of grungy, cigarette-stained paint on the walls.

Poor Aunt Lynn. I shouldn't have stayed away so long. God, I needed to see her. I needed her to know how grateful I was for her presence in my life. I needed her to know that she had made a difference. She had performed a miracle, really.

"Hello?"

There was no response to my call up the stairs, so I climbed them heavily, with a sinking feeling in my gut as the odors of the old house brought back memories of my mother shouting at my brother and me when we caused a ruckus in the living room, wrestling and roughhousing while Dad was passed out drunk on the sofa. She didn't want us to wake him because he'd invariably blame her for the noise, and then she would commit the cardinal sin of talking back to our father, and the situation would escalate. Over time, we learned the hard way to stay out of earshot. Mostly to protect our mother, not ourselves.

Upstairs, all the bedrooms were unoccupied, beds unmade. I found Auntie Lynn's room at the end of the hall, and it was just as cluttered and dirty as the others, which came as a surprise because she'd always been a tidy person. She must have been very sick and weak from the chemo, unable to bear all the responsibilities of homemaker in this grim, desolate place.

My heart tightened with regret, and I sat down on the edge of her bed. I shouldn't have listened when she insisted that everything was fine. I should have come home to check on things, especially because I knew, deep down, that my father and grandmother together were a handful.

I realized I had been in denial about that, willing to stick my head in the sand and be selfish while I pursued my own dreams of a better life. I wanted it for myself, but in my defense, I'd also wanted to make Auntie Lynn proud. And I wanted to make enough money to provide for her. I'd often dreamed of setting her up in her own apartment anywhere she liked. Perhaps near me in New Jersey and eventually Manhattan. If only she hadn't gotten sick. I never expected to lose her so soon. Before I'd finished what I'd started.

I checked my watch. It was past noon. I needed to call around and find out where they had taken Auntie Lynn so that I could visit her.

Just then, a car pulled into the yard and brought me to my feet. I moved to the window and looked out. My father and grandmother were getting out of Auntie Lynn's old Toyota Camry. They shut the car doors and stomped up the front porch steps.

By the time they walked in, I was halfway down the stairs. They stopped short at the sight of me.

"Well, look what the cat dragged in," my father said.

My grandmother scowled at me. It was shocking how much she had aged since the last time I had come to visit. She looked thin and frail, almost skeletal. Her color wasn't good.

"You're too late," my father added. "She's gone. Died this morning."

His words shot out of him like a cannonball and shook all the walls in the house. I grabbed onto the staircase banister. "What?"

"You heard me," he replied.

I felt like I had been sucker punched in the gut. I still couldn't believe it was true. It couldn't be. "Why didn't anyone call me? I would have come. I could have been here." I stared at them both, waiting for an explanation.

My father ignored the question and lumbered into the kitchen. I descended the rest of the stairs and heard the sound of the fridge opening and a beer cap snapping off a bottle. Then the sound of the metal cap missing the garbage can and landing on the dirty linoleum floor.

I observed all of this in a state of paralysis and numb silence. My grandmother tossed her purse onto the small table in the entry hall and dragged herself into the darkened living room. I followed her in and opened the curtains while she sank onto the upholstered easy chair and lit up a cigarette. She took a deep drag and savored it before she spoke.

"I told him to call you," she said in a raspy voice, "but you know what he's like."

"Don't talk about me like I'm not here!" my father shouted from the kitchen.

Gram and I ignored him because we both knew better than to talk back.

Feeling weak and sick, I moved to the sofa and sank onto it, bowed my head, and squeezed great clumps of my hair in both hands. "What happened? I thought she was doing okay."

"She was," Gram replied. "They said she was in remission, but it was some other infection that did her in. Then she got pneumonia."

I forced myself to look up while my eyes burned with tears, which I fought with all my might because I couldn't let myself cry. Not here, in front of my father, in case he walked in. "Did she suffer?"

My grandmother looked away. "She suffered plenty. At least they were generous with the morphine. So even if you had come yesterday, she wouldn't have known it."

I rocked back and forth and squeezed my eyes shut in a despairing attempt to manage my grief. I couldn't let it rise to the surface. Not here. Never here. *God, oh God. Why?* Inside, my heart was sobbing.

"It's not natural for a parent to outlive a child," Gram said. "It ain't fair. She was so good. The best of all of us."

I lifted my head and nodded, then heard my father shout, "Well, she's gone now, ain't she! So you better get used to it!" He stormed out the back door, and I heard the truck door open and slam shut. The engine roared to life, and he sped out of the yard.

"We won't see him again till tomorrow," Gram said. She took another drag of her cigarette. "He'll be at the bar all night. He'll probably sleep in a ditch somewhere. Or in the drunk tank."

I sat back and wiped a hand down my face. "We should call the police and let them know so they can pick him up later before he gets behind the wheel and kills someone."

I should have said "before he kills someone *else*," because he'd already taken my mother from me. It would be a terrible thing if he killed another child's mother that night.

"What happens now?" I asked Gram. "Will there be a funeral?"

"No. Lynn didn't want any fuss. She made us promise to spread her ashes in the wind. That's all." Gram paused. "I suspect that had something to do with the money they charge for funerals these days. You know how tight things are around here."

When I didn't respond, she added, "This is a big house, you know. It takes a lot of upkeep."

She gave me a pointed, accusing look—as if I were a stranger she loathed. Someone who was not a part of this family because I had dared to leave. I had insulted and denigrated them by wanting a better life.

Her sinister eyes narrowed, and I wondered if she knew that I had been sending monthly checks to Auntie Lynn over the past few years to help with the grocery and medical bills. That's why I had no extra money left over to reduce my monstrous student debt.

I suspected that if Gram knew about those checks, she'd want me to continue sending them. But I knew that if I sent money now, it would go straight to booze and cigarettes. That's why Auntie Lynn had kept it secret from them.

I tried to change the subject. "Did she ask for me at all?"

"She was too drugged up."

"Before that?"

Gram tapped her cigarette on the ashtray and spoke callously. "She wrote you a letter the other day. She asked your father to put it in the mailbox."

My heart nearly beat out of my chest. "What happened to it? Did he post it? Or is it still here somewhere?"

Reading that letter would give me one final, private moment of connection with her. It would provide me with the closure I would undoubtedly need over the coming months and years.

"He threw it out," Gram said flatly.

I blinked a few times in disbelief. "He did what?"

"He tossed it."

I glanced searchingly around the room. "Where? Here?" I stood up to go and rifle through the trash can in the kitchen, but Gram stopped me.

"Don't waste your time looking for it. He threw it out at the hospital."

"Why in God's name would he do that?" I whirled around, my emotions running high.

"He didn't think it mattered much because you never came to visit. He didn't think you'd care."

"And you let him do that?"

She merely shrugged.

"What were you thinking?" I asked. "He threw out the last letter from his dying sister? Your daughter. Did you read it? Or did he? Is that why he threw it out? Because you didn't like what it said?"

She shrugged again, and all my training and education as a psychologist sailed out the window. All I wanted to do was throttle her. I couldn't think of what I would say if she were one of my patients and this were a therapy session. I had no desire to unravel her as a person or help her reach a deeper level of understanding about herself and the roots of her choices and behaviors. I just wanted to get out of there, go back to New York, and never, ever return.

But something in me fell to pieces, and I couldn't leave. All I could do was crumple onto the sofa and bury my head in my hands. "I can't believe he threw it out. I can't believe I didn't get to see her."

"It's your own fault. You should have come sooner," she said cruelly.

My eyes lifted, and I gaped at her. "I would have come if someone had called me."

"Oh, stop whining. Don't be such a baby. Go and get me a drink, and get one for yourself too. You look like you need a stiff one."

My grandmother had never been a warm or loving person in the past, but this was too much. I couldn't bear to look at her. I couldn't even be in the same room with her. I felt like I was choking.

"I need some air." I pushed myself off the sofa and got to my feet. "I'm going for a walk."

She tapped the ashes off her cigarette again and said nothing as I turned and left the room.

~

I stayed long enough to view Auntie Lynn's remains at the funeral home before she was cremated. The sight of her in the temporary wooden box nearly broke me. She was emaciated after her long illness and looked much older than the youthful woman I remembered.

I requested a few moments alone with her to tell her how much I loved her, but it wasn't enough. I derived no closure or comfort from it because I knew she couldn't hear me. It was too late. She was truly gone from this world, and she would never know how much she had meant to me. I had failed to show her my love in the end.

My regret was immeasurable. My guilt was immense, and I knew it would never leave me. It would burrow deep into my bones and stay there forever.

After the cremation, my grandmother insisted on keeping the ashes in an urn at the house, again defying Auntie Lynn's final wishes to be scattered in the wind. I tried to argue on her behalf, but I was outnumbered, so I said goodbye and called a cab to take me to the airport.

Naturally, my father was drunk as I was leaving, and he shoved me up against the wall. "You think you're too good for us? Is that it?" he shouted.

He was a large man, taller than me, and I was lucky that he was drunk because when I pushed him away, he staggered sideways and fell into the stairs.

"If you walk out of here, don't you ever come back!" he bellowed as I picked up my bag and made for the door.

My grandmother simply watched all of this with indifference, from that ratty old chair in the darkened living room, smoking her cigarette.

I slept for over an hour on the flight out of Wisconsin. When I woke, I was groggy. I sat with my forehead resting against the window while I looked down at the fluffy white clouds below the aircraft.

In those moments, I wondered if heaven existed. If it did, I hoped Auntie Lynn was enjoying herself in some way. She loved to paint. Maybe she was standing at an easel with a colorful palette. The thought brought me some comfort, but then, in a flash, an image of her unkempt bedroom, the smell of the dirty sheets, hit me like a cold, hard wind. I imagined her final days with my father and grandmother, who were cruel and hateful with their words. What comfort or love had they offered her in her final hours? None, most assuredly. They would not have been kind. My heart ached for Auntie Lynn. I could barely breathe through my sorrow.

Then guilt launched into me again like a brutal punch, and I shuddered agonizingly. I should have been there. She must have thought I didn't care. That I had deserted her. *I had.* That's exactly what I had done, and I hated myself for it. I kept my head turned toward the glass so no one would see me weeping.

Later, after the meal, I was in a daze and found myself staring at the clouds again and thinking of Melanie Brown and her project about airplanes that vanished over the Bermuda Triangle. Where did they go?

I thought of our many conversations about her life in Oklahoma and her feelings of guilt about the death of her mother. How ridiculous it was for me to sit in that chair in my office and tell her how to cope with her emotions when I was completely wrecked over the death of my aunt and could barely cope with my own abandonment issues.

Who was I to offer advice? I was a fraud.

When I arrived back at my apartment, there was no food in the refrigerator or cupboards, so I used my credit card to purchase a few essentials at the supermarket. When I reached the cash register, I let out a breath of relief when the card wasn't declined, because I'd been certain the balance must be over the lending limit, considering the cost of that plane ticket home.

That evening, I couldn't bear to sit alone in my apartment, so I went for a long walk. I strolled for hours and thought of Auntie Lynn and the idyllic life she had given me in Arizona. We'd never had much money. It was a middle-class existence, but to me it was paradise compared to my life with an abusive, alcoholic father, a drug addict for a brother, and a bitter, apathetic grandmother who said cruel things.

I tried to remind myself that it hadn't always been so terrible. Not when my mother was alive. Wistfully, I recalled a day when she had wrapped two plastic garbage bags around my winter boots to keep my feet dry because we couldn't afford a new pair. She had secured them with an elastic band. Then she kissed me on the top of my head. I felt loved that day.

But then she died, and no one cared if my feet got wet. Until Auntie Lynn arrived.

As I walked with my head down, farther west, away from the industrial sector where I lived, I stepped on some broken glass and was shaken out of my depressing reveries. Looking around, I found myself in a derelict neighborhood. Everywhere I looked, I saw graffiti. Parked cars were stripped of their tires, and apartment buildings had broken or boarded-up windows. I heard angry voices from people inside those deteriorated buildings and quickly turned around and retraced my steps back toward my own neighborhood.

Afterward, the sight of that poverty and social misery left me distressed and disheartened for hours, especially after my trip home—seeing how little had changed. My father was still an angry alcoholic who had killed my mother in a drunk driving accident and gone to jail for it.

My grandmother was still cold and uncaring, and though my aunt had tried to help them, she had been swallowed up too. Just like my mother.

How many patients came to me because they couldn't bear the stress of their difficult upbringings or their money troubles? My grandmother always dismissed my father's drinking. She blamed it on the fact that we were poor.

That never made sense to me. Wouldn't we have been less poor if he spent less money on booze?

My brother went to prison for burglary. Again, my grandmother blamed his criminal behavior on the fact that we were poor and he was desperate. I blamed it on the drugs, but I also understood that it was a vicious cycle. He did drugs because he was depressed and had no hope. No dreams of anything better that might be attainable for him. The only life he knew was a life of poverty and neglect, while I had been rescued from all that.

Why me? Why was I the lucky one?

Maybe that's why I became a therapist. Maybe I needed to feel like I was doing for others what Auntie Lynn had done for me.

When I finally reached my neighborhood, entered my building, and climbed the steps to my apartment, I felt no better about my life. I couldn't stop thinking about Auntie Lynn's bedroom, the smell of those ashtrays in the living room, the garbage bins in the kitchen that needed to be emptied, and the dirty, ripped linoleum floors with rotten wood beneath.

If only I'd had more time to pay off my student debt and open a practice of my own. If only Auntie Lynn had lived long enough to see me succeed.

As I lay in bed that night, I was overcome by a profound feeling of loneliness and a deep sense of failure.

Who was I to anyone? What did my dreams matter now?

CHAPTER 12
MELANIE

New York, 1986

"It's good to see you," I said as I entered Dr. Robinson's office and headed for my usual spot on the sofa, reminding myself that I could call him Dean now.

Our conversations never began until we were both comfortably seated, so I waited for him to get settled and pull his notebook onto his lap. Then at last he asked, "How were things for you this week?"

Part of me wanted to unload all my woes and tell him how miserable I had been since our last session—how I'd missed him and longed for him, *dreamed of him!*—but another part of me wanted to be strong and put on a brave face. The last thing I wanted was to be pathetic in his eyes. Or make him feel that he had to transfer me to another therapist because I couldn't keep my emotions in check.

"To be honest, I've had better weeks," I replied. "I'm not even sure where to begin."

"Where would you like to begin?" he asked. "Take your time."

I stared at him and studied his beautiful pale-blue eyes. There was something different about them today. There was a problem. I felt it in my core.

Oh God. What if he was going to end our therapeutic relationship, and this was to be our last session? An almost debilitating sense of dread rose up in me, and I had to look away, toward the window.

"I still don't believe you," I said.

"About what?" he asked.

I should have exercised some self-restraint or at least spoken in a tactful, roundabout way, but I couldn't stop myself from spewing out my true feelings.

"About this being a clinical thing. Erotic transference. I tried to convince myself of that all week, but it was hopeless. All I felt was heartache because of your rejection. It was like someone had died."

"It wasn't a rejection," he said. "Try not to look at it that way."

I met his gaze. "How else can I look at it? I'm in love with you, and you don't return my feelings. You don't want to be with me. At least that's what you say. So I have to accept that. I have to try and move on. To bury my feelings, like a corpse in the ground."

"I don't want you to bury anything," he said. "To the contrary, it's best to lay things out in the open so that we can work through them together."

"But I don't want to work through them if the end result is the same—that we can never be together. That will be too painful. Maybe it would be best if I transferred to another therapist so that I could work through it with that person. Because it's going to take a lot for me to get over you."

No! I didn't mean it! I didn't want to transfer to another therapist! What was I saying?

He twirled his pen around his fingers and regarded me closely and carefully. "If that's what you want, Melanie, I'd be happy to recommend someone."

I shook my head and looked down at the floor. "I didn't expect you to call my bluff."

"I didn't realize it was a bluff," he replied. "And what *did* you expect?"

"I don't know." I sighed, dejectedly. "You're an excellent therapist. You're not taking advantage of me because that would be unethical. You're doing the right thing, referring me to someone else. But maybe that's what makes this harder to bear, because you're so decent and honorable. You don't have a temper like those men in my mother's life. You're caring and responsible and so unbelievably perfect."

He set his notepad aside and shook his head at me in a disapproving way.

"What?" I asked.

His expression changed. For the first time he seemed impatient with me. "This is exactly why you need to recognize that what you're feeling for me isn't real."

"I don't understand."

"I'm not perfect. Far from it. As I said before, you don't know the first thing about me."

"Then tell me," I pleaded, sitting forward on the edge of my seat. "*Please.* Isn't this what you said I need to do? Recognize the difference between what's real and what's fantasy? Help me separate the two. If you want things out in the open, then don't be a hypocrite. Consider it your parting gift to me so that I can have better luck with my next therapist."

"That's not how this works."

"Seriously? You can't share anything with me? Last week you said you wanted to help me learn how to have healthier relationships with people, but you're like a brick wall, and all this is doing is making me feel more certain that I don't want to get involved with anyone. Ever. That it's not possible to really know someone, and I'm better off alone because people are either mean and nasty or . . ." I gestured toward him with my hand. "They're totally closed off and impenetrable, and either way, they break your heart."

I sat back and folded my arms, seething inside.

The room was quiet except for the pendulum on the grandfather clock, swinging back and forth while we both waited for me to recover my composure.

At last, Dr. Robinson—*Dean*—spoke. His voice was soft and resigned as our eyes met.

"I drive a crappy car," he told me. "It's in the shop right now getting fixed, but I can barely afford the repair because I'm broke. I'm always broke. I'm in debt up to my eyeballs, so when you see me sitting here in this elegant leather armchair in this upscale Manhattan brownstone . . . well, that has nothing to do with me. I live in New Jersey. On top of that, my father went to prison for manslaughter after killing my mother in a drunk driving accident. Drove straight into a tree. He's still a drunk, and my brother is currently serving a five-year sentence for burglary and assault. It's a wonder I didn't end up in prison myself, because I stole a car once, and I torched it with a bunch of juvenile delinquents. I just never got caught. No one I work with knows any of that, by the way. So I'd appreciate it if you respected the rule of confidentiality in this room." Dean spread his hands wide. "So there you have it. Not so perfect after all."

I stared at him in silence. Part of me was surprised, but not really. I should have been stunned by everything he had just told me, but for some reason, I wasn't. I suppose I had always felt an inexplicable understanding between us—that we were the same. The only thing that surprised me was that he had shared it all in one single, uninhibited flood of truth and emotion.

I was delighted. And still absorbing it all.

We sat quietly, our eyes fixed on each other's. He was waiting for me to respond, as he often did with those practiced pauses, which were meant to draw me out and force me to articulate my thoughts and feelings. But something about this moment was different. The therapist was gone from the room. He was looking at me like a normal human being, a friend, asking me what I thought of everything I had just heard.

"How old were you when your mother died?" I asked.

"Twelve."

"And what happened to you after your father went to prison?"

"After I torched the car? I got lucky. My aunt came and got me, but she didn't take my brother. He was older than me and doing his own thing. It was too late for him, but my aunt was a positive influence and helped me do well in school, encouraged me to go to college, and rallied to get me some scholarships."

I sat back against the sofa cushions and regarded Dean with wonder. A strange inner excitement flowed through me. A gratifying sense of vindication.

"I always knew we were the same," I said. "No wonder you understood me so well."

He looked off into the distance and shook his head, and I felt him pull away again, emotionally.

"Don't do that," I said. "Please don't try and tell me that you were just doing your job, that you revealed yourself to me today only because you want to analyze my response, as if I were some object in an experiment. Over the past eight weeks, you've understood everything I was going through because you had gone through the same things yourself. Did you ever feel guilty for not saving your mother somehow? For not being there to protect her? Maybe if you had convinced her not to go with your father that day when the accident happened . . ."

He gave me a look and chuckled bitterly. "Please don't get me started on guilt, Melanie," he said, holding up a hand. "Because this is your session, not mine. Besides, we've already crossed a line. Remember when we talked about professional boundaries?"

I bowed my head and closed my eyes. "There it is. The brick wall again. And it's not professional ethics. What's going on here is not that black and white."

I heard him shift in his chair, and I lifted my gaze. He was now sitting forward with his elbows on his knees, wringing his hands together, looking at me intensely.

"I did what you asked," he said. "I told you something about who I am. Now I think you owe me the same courtesy in return. Do what I ask of you."

"And what is that?" My heart began to race.

"I think it would be best if we did what you suggested earlier and move you to another therapist."

My stomach burned with alarm, and I responded instinctively, without filters. "No, we can't do that. Not now. I finally feel like I know who you are."

"But that's not the goal here," he replied. "Who I am is irrelevant. These sessions are about you, and the way you're feeling about me is only going to get in the way of your treatment."

"But I don't want these sessions to just be about me."

He tipped his head back and stared up at the ceiling. "This is exactly what I am trying to convey to you. I shouldn't have shared all that. Now the boundaries are breached, and we can't go back."

"I disagree. Wasn't that the goal in this room? Truth? Honesty? Openness? Now we understand each other, and won't that be good for me? To learn how to relate better to others?"

When he didn't reply, I felt a surge of panic. "Please don't send me to someone else."

"I think I have to. This is . . ." He made a back-and-forth gesture with his hands. "What's going on here is dangerous. It could get me fired or worse."

I should have been heartbroken that he was trying to end our sessions together, but instead my heart soared, because he had just admitted that there was something between us—an intimate connection. Perhaps even sexual desire?

"Okay," I said in total submission to what he was asking of me, but only because I didn't want to be his patient anymore. I wanted to be something else to him.

He rose abruptly from his chair and went to his desk, flipped through his Rolodex, and wrote something down on a notepad. Then he tore off the sheet and returned to me. "This is who you should see."

I accepted the slip of paper and read the name and address. "Dr. Sandra Hood?"

"Yes. She's excellent, and she's in a good location for you. I'll tell her that I'm referring you."

I swallowed uneasily because I wasn't sure what was happening here. Was he telling me that he never wanted to see me again, as a patient or otherwise? Or was this a first step to a different sort of relationship? If so, how were we supposed to get there?

I cleared my throat and felt slightly intimidated because he was standing over me, waiting for me to collect my things and leave. I looked up at him.

"So that's it? You want me to go now?"

"I think that would be best."

I felt like I was getting kicked out of a department store for shoplifting.

"You seem angry," I said as I gathered up my purse.

"Not at all," he replied, turning away and moving back to his desk.

I stood up and watched him. He refused to look at me.

"I'm sorry," he said.

Those two words, coming from him, spoken with such tenderness, shocked and terrified me. I was petrified that this might be the end—that he truly didn't want to see me again, ever, in any capacity. But not because he didn't care. I felt as if I had been pushed off the edge of a cliff. I was plummeting to the ground, and my emotions were in turmoil. I didn't know what to say. I just wanted to flee, to escape this excruciating pain of him leaving me.

I flung my purse strap over my shoulder and strode to the door.

"I should go then," I said. "Goodbye."

The word flew out of my mouth like a spear, and my stomach burned sickeningly as I walked out and shut the door behind me. I raced down the stairs and said nothing to Jane as I passed through the reception area and ran outside.

Down the steps I fled, sucking in a few deep breaths as I hurried along the street toward the subway. When I reached the intersection, I stopped at the lights and fought to comprehend what had just occurred.

Dean had opened up to me. He had tried to put an end to my romantic feelings by revealing his imperfections, but it had the opposite effect. What he told me only made me love him more. He was just like me—wounded, lost, and alone, just trying to get by.

The light turned green, the walk signal appeared, but I couldn't move my feet. All I could do was stand in a daze while busy New Yorkers rushed past me, bumping me repeatedly.

How could I have left Dean's office like that? I hadn't even thanked him or told him how much our time together had helped me. If this was the end, so be it. But I couldn't leave it like this.

I checked my watch. There were still ten minutes left in our appointment. I had never left early before. Could I go back and make it right? Tell him how much he meant to me and promise that I wouldn't make his life difficult? Was that what he was afraid of? That I would cling on for dear life and start showing up at his house, begging for him to love me?

No, I wouldn't let myself do that. He had explained the boundaries, and I would do my best to respect them. But I still needed him to know that I was okay and that I understood his decision.

Before I knew what I was doing, I had turned around and was running back to the clinic. I sprinted up the steps and forced myself to pause and catch my breath so that I could walk in calm and collected.

Jane was packing up for the day. She smiled at me questioningly, and I said, "Sorry, I forgot something upstairs. I left my notebook . . ."

"Oh," she replied. "I think he's still up there. Hurry and you'll catch him. I'm just heading out. See you next week."

"Have a great weekend," I replied as I climbed the stairs to the second floor. When I reached the top, I hesitated and rested my hand on the decorative newel post.

Maybe this was a mistake. What was I going to say when I knocked on the door and he opened it? He would probably wonder if he should call the police and get a restraining order. He would worry that I was out of control. But I just wanted to tell him that I was grateful. And that I thought he was wonderful. And that I didn't want him to think badly of me. I wanted him to know that I was okay, that I was going to see the other therapist he recommended, that I had great respect for him and I thought he was brilliant and good at his job, and that he didn't need to worry about anything. I wasn't a crazy person, and I understood the boundaries, and everything was fine.

I reached his office door, raised my fist, and knocked.

His footsteps tapped across the floor, and my belly did a cartwheel. The door opened. I met his gaze and sucked in a breath. He was so handsome. Those eyes . . . I felt myself dissolving into atoms and molecules, vanishing into another world where only the two of us existed.

I don't know how long we stood there like that, staring at each other in a state of pounding emotional mayhem.

Dean was frowning, his chest heaving, and I thought for a moment that he was furious with me. But then he extended a hand, pulled me into the room and into his arms. As he pushed the door closed behind us, I fell into a state of pure and perfect rapture in his embrace.

CHAPTER 13
MELANIE

New York, 1986

That hour in Dr. Robinson's office, after he locked the door and held me close in his arms, was the most thrilling hour of my life. Certainly, I had been kissed before. I'd had sex many times, but it was never anything special, at least not for me.

But Dr. Robinson . . . *Dean* . . .

Oh, he was nothing like anyone in my past. He was caring, sophisticated, and worldly, and every cell in my body reacted to him physically. When he kissed me and led me to the sofa and eased me onto the soft cushions, my heart thundered in my chest and burst open with love and desire. My body seemed to mold perfectly into the contours of his, and there was great compassion and tenderness in the way we touched each other.

I felt his uneven breathing on my cheek and the movement of his hand across my hip, but then he quickly drew back.

"We shouldn't be doing this," he said.

"Please don't stop." I clung to him, my limbs trembling from my heightened emotions.

"But this is wrong."

"I don't care. I just want to be with you. And you want to be with me too. I can tell. It's not just transference. It's much more than that. You know that, don't you?"

He sat up on the end of the sofa. I sat up, too, and hugged my knees to my chest.

"I do," he replied, and I exhaled with relief. "But that still doesn't make it okay. There are rules in my profession, and this isn't allowed."

I swung my legs to the floor, inched closer to him, and clasped his hand. "But if I wasn't your patient anymore, we could see each other, couldn't we?"

"We'd have to wait awhile." He bowed his head in defeat and sat forward, elbows on knees. "This has been a hellish week for me. You have no idea."

"Why?" I rubbed his back. "What happened?"

For a moment, he didn't respond. Then he shook his head. "My aunt died."

"Oh God. I'm so sorry. The one who raised you?"

"Yes. She had cancer, and we thought she was in remission, but she got sick with some kind of infection, and no one called to tell me. I didn't get to see her. She wrote me a letter, but my father threw it away."

"You're joking."

"His cruelty knows no bounds."

We sat for a while in the quiet office. Then Dean stood and walked to the window. Not knowing what to expect from all this, I waited for him to come to terms with what we had just done and what we were to each other. I didn't see how he could deny that there was an intangible bond between us now.

At last, he faced me. "I could lose my entire career over this."

My belly churned with fear that he was going to resist what was clearly meant to be. "I'll never tell," I said. "I promise. No one will ever know."

He thought about that, then returned to the sofa, sat down beside me, and took my hand. "Can I trust you?" he asked.

"Of course you can. No matter what happens between us, I would never do anything to jeopardize your career. Ever. I just want to be with you."

"I want to be with you too," he said.

They were the loveliest words anyone had ever spoken to me. My heart swelled with joy as we sat there, contemplating what this meant and what a future together might look like.

"You can come to my place," I suggested. "I live in an apartment above an insurance broker's office. It closes at five every day, and they're not open on weekends. The entrance is at the back, so no one would see you coming and going after hours. If I stop coming here as your patient, we could keep things secret for a while. As long as we need to."

He nodded and pulled me close, held me in his arms and kissed the top of my head. "We'll have to avoid public places until some time passes."

"We'll get takeout," I cheerfully replied, "when we're hiding out at my apartment."

The sun was setting, and I noticed how dark the office had become. Dean checked his watch. "I hate to say this, but you should probably go."

"Of course. I understand."

We both stood, and I watched him move to pick up my purse and hand it to me. His wavy hair was tousled, and his shirt collar was askew. I felt my blood grow warm in my veins. "Would you like to come over tonight?" I asked, tentatively. "I could leave now, and then you could follow later. Separately."

Our eyes locked and held, and there was a conscious but unspoken awareness of our intense physical attraction, our deep longing to be alone together. After weeks and weeks of yearning, of fighting a constant battle with our forbidden desires, it was impossible for either of us to ignore it.

"All right," he said. "I'll need half an hour to catch up on a few things here. Then I'll come over."

"I'll leave the porch light on for you." I smiled and felt a surge of exultation as I slung my purse over my shoulder, kissed him on the cheek, and walked out.

CHAPTER 14

DEAN

New York, 1986

Five months after I began my affair with Melanie Brown, my boss, Dr. Caroline Weaver, knocked on my office door. She held a coffee in her hand, her leather briefcase at her side. It was a Wednesday, 8:45 a.m., and the practice had not yet opened for appointments. I was seated at my desk reading over a report from a social worker regarding a new patient I was to meet that morning—a troubled youth in a foster home situation. The court had requested a psychological analysis regarding a violent crime he had committed in the spring.

"You're in early today," Caroline said.

Normally, I began appointments at ten on Wednesdays and took evening appointments.

I tapped the open file on my desk. "I wanted to prepare for my session with the Abbott boy."

"That's today?"

"Yes. In fifteen minutes."

She hesitated in the doorway, then took a few steps into my office and looked around at the sofa, the bookcase, the grandfather clock. She pursed her lips, and I sensed she was displeased about something.

"I'd like to see you in my office later when you have a chance," she said. "There's something I need to talk to you about."

I sat back with a tremulous feeling in my gut. "All right."

She looked around again, as if she were redecorating the office in her mind, and I feared suddenly that she knew about my transgression and was about to have me fired or, worse, brought up on criminal charges. She said nothing more as she turned and walked out.

~

I had a hard time concentrating that morning. I'm not sure if my patients were aware of how distracted I was, but at one point, I had to excuse myself and leave the room, lock myself in the bathroom, and take a few deep breaths to calm my stress levels. When I returned to my chair and my patient resumed talking about his late brother, I sat in a heightened state of terror that my relationship with Melanie had been discovered.

Oh God, what had I been thinking, becoming involved with a patient? It was an unconscionable abuse of power, and I'd known it was wrong at the time—of course I had—but I was weak and lonely and broken up inside after the death of Auntie Lynn. I should have called John Matthews immediately and begun sessions with him. I should have followed the proper protocols. But I didn't. And now, here I was.

At lunchtime, I said goodbye to my last patient of the morning and braced myself to go upstairs and face Caroline.

~

"Come in. Have a seat," Caroline said without looking up from the notes she was writing at her desk. She waved her hand impatiently, as if I had disturbed her train of thought and she needed me to be quiet until she finished.

I sat down. She ignored me while she continued to write. Then she slammed down her pen, shut the file, and folded both hands together, facing me squarely from across the large desk.

"Last night," she said, "I was at Lincoln Center, and I was introduced to someone who asked a favor of me."

I let out a small breath. Was this something else? Or was it a roundabout way of broaching an awkward subject?

"A favor?" I repeated.

"Yes." She stood up, moved around her desk, and leaned on it, directly in front of me, so that I was forced to look up at her. Carolyn certainly had a talent for asserting her professional power as owner of the practice and making everyone feel intimidated.

"That someone just happened to be Oscar Hamilton," she told me.

I felt my shoulders relax slightly because anything to do with Oscar Hamilton, one of the richest business moguls in New York, could have nothing to do with me and my lowly indiscretions.

"It turns out that one of his daughters is a film student at Tisch, and she's making a documentary about how people deal with grief after the loss of a loved one."

I shifted in my chair, waiting for Caroline to explain what the favor had to do with me.

"Mr. Hamilton asked if his daughter could come here to interview a therapist who could shed light on the psychology of grief, and since that was the subject of your very well-received doctoral thesis, I thought you'd be the perfect person." Caroline stood and returned to her chair behind the desk. "On top of that, you're easy on the eyes. You'll look good on camera."

I laughed uncomfortably and lowered my gaze to the floor. "I don't know about that."

"You're too modest, Dean. Maybe that's what makes you so attractive." She studied my face for a moment. "Anyway, I just got off the phone with Oscar's daughter—Olivia is her name—and she'd like to come tomorrow afternoon. She said it would take an hour, possibly two, so I already told Jane to reschedule your afternoon appointments."

I drew back slightly. "I see. So . . ." I paused. "I guess that means I'm about to make my film debut." I spoke amiably, though I was miffed that she hadn't asked me first.

"You'll be great," she said. "I really appreciate it." She picked up her pen, signaling that she wanted to get back to work.

I got up, returned to my own office, and collapsed with relief onto my chair.

~

It was dark by the time I arrived at Melanie's apartment that night. I had stayed late at work to write long, in-depth notes about the boy from the foster home, who had been breaking into neighbors' houses to snoop around while they were sleeping. When he was finally caught in the act by a homeowner, who had risen in the night to get a snack, the boy had lashed out and thrown a large carving knife at him.

I wasn't ready to form a conclusion yet. I would require more sessions with the boy because he was determined not to talk about what had happened or how he felt about it. It was like trying to squeeze water out of a stone.

The empty parking lot behind the insurance broker's office was dimly lit by a single lamppost that flickered and crackled, but the steps on the outside of the building, which led to Melanie's apartment on the second floor, were well lit by her outdoor light. I climbed the long set of stairs and rapped lightly on the glass window.

She took her time answering, and when the door finally opened, she had a sour look on her face. "You're late," she said.

My spirits sank because it had been a long day—first with the stress of my paranoia about getting fired, then with a difficult afternoon session where I'd been yelled at, cursed at, and called a few unpleasant names by a patient with anger issues.

"Sorry. I had to write up a report that's due tomorrow."

"Then you should have called." She turned away but left the door open for me to enter. "I cooked supper, but now the chicken's dry and the broccoli's limp. It's all ruined."

I closed the door behind me and noticed a white tablecloth, candles, and a bottle of wine, even though she knew I didn't drink. "I didn't know you had something special planned."

She usually worked on her thesis paper until I arrived and never minded if I was late.

She went to the oven, removed a pan with two chicken breasts she'd been keeping warm, and served up the vegetables and rice to go with it. She dropped both plates onto the table with a clatter, then picked up the wine bottle and emptied the last of it into her glass. She pitched the bottle into the garbage can and said, "Well, go ahead. Sit."

She dragged her chair across the floor and plunked herself onto it, picked up her fork and knife, and carved angrily into her meat. "And don't blame me if it tastes like leather."

"I'm sure it will be delicious," I replied, taking a seat across from her.

We ate in silence until I attempted to smooth things over. "It's wonderful, Melanie. You must have spent a lot of time on this."

"Obviously."

The chicken was indeed tough and dry, and I tried not to wrestle too violently with it. "But you're angry with me."

"No, I'm not." She refused to look at me as she guzzled half her glass of wine.

"Do you want to talk about it?"

"Not really."

"Why not?"

She dropped her cutlery onto her plate. "Fine. I'll tell you why I'm angry. I finished writing my dissertation today, and that's why I wanted this dinner to be special."

I set my fork down as well and gave her my full attention. "That's wonderful. Congratulations."

She ignored my comment and resumed eating. "Don't even bother."

"Don't bother to do what? Tell you how happy I am for you? Because I am."

"Then you should have been here on time."

I tried to be patient and understanding. "I didn't know you finished today. I had no idea you were even close."

"Oh, but that's the point, isn't it? You *should* have known."

This was not the first time Melanie had become irate over something she felt I should have noticed or understood. Usually, I talked her through her anger by using therapeutic techniques, but tonight I was mentally exhausted, and I didn't want to be her therapist. I just wanted to eat my supper.

"I'm not a mind reader," I replied and immediately regretted it because I had learned early in life not to talk back. I knew where it would lead.

She looked up from her plate and glared at me with piercing contempt. "I beg your pardon?"

Here we go.

I made every effort to speak in a soothing, tender tone. "How am I supposed to know what you're thinking if you don't tell me?"

"You used to know," she replied. "You'd always know, sometimes even before I knew it myself. You'd ask me questions and draw things out of me."

"If you're referring to the conversations we used to have in my office, that was different."

"How? We were talking, just like we should be talking now."

"Yes, but I was acting as your therapist," I tried to explain. "When I spend time with you outside of work, I don't want to work so hard at . . . drawing things out of you."

She scoffed bitterly. "What are you saying? That I'm high maintenance? Is that it?" She chugged the rest of her wine, and suddenly I was disgusted by the drunken, sleepy look in her eyes. It was all too familiar.

"That's not what I'm saying," I said, scrambling to think of a way to pull her back from the abyss. But she didn't give me a chance. She rose from the table, stormed into the bedroom, and slammed the door behind her.

Weary and frustrated, I rubbed at my temples, then forced myself to get up. I followed and knocked softly on her door.

"Get the hell out!" she shouted from inside. "I don't want to talk to you!"

I remained outside her door and thought of all the times she had listened to her mother fighting with her boyfriends. I wished Melanie had had another example from which to model her behavior. It was unfortunate that she never knew her grandfather, the pilot. If he had survived, what would her life look like today?

Inhaling deeply, I told myself that this was an opportunity to help her learn how to communicate more effectively with me, because everything didn't always have to end in a screaming match.

"I understand that you're angry," I said, "and I'm sorry if I hurt your feelings. Will you let me come in so we can talk about it?"

"No. Stay out. I'm sick of this."

For a brief, iridescent moment, I thought she might tell me that she wanted to end things between us, that our relationship hadn't turned out the way she'd imagined and I wasn't what she wanted after all. My spirits took flight at the possibility of it—that this could all be over and I would no longer have to live in fear of the unearthing of our affair and the shame and dishonor that would result.

"What are you sick of?" I asked.

She didn't answer, so I decided to wait quietly until she was ready to talk. After a moment, I heard the bed creak, her footsteps across the floor. The door opened.

Her cheeks were wet, and her makeup was smudged under her eyes. "Are you ashamed of me?" she asked miserably, sobbing. "Am I not sophisticated enough for you? Is that why you refuse to be seen with me?"

"Of course not," I gently assured her.

We had gone over this before. It was a conversation we'd had many times.

"You know why we have to be discreet," I added.

"But it's been five months!" She wiped her nose with a balled-up tissue. "I want to be able to go places with you and do things. And now that I'm finished with my paper, I want us to spend more time together."

I knew her well enough to understand what that meant. She wanted me to become her new obsession, to be the focus of all her dreams for the future. I was her means of escape from her deep, inherent unhappiness.

But I was not the cure for what ailed her. Mostly, I was the problem, because I had been in a position of power when we'd first become involved. She had placed her trust in me as a professional, and I had betrayed that trust. I had taken advantage of her vulnerability. And even though I'd tried to tell myself it was consensual, deep down I knew it was not, because it was never an equal relationship. Now she felt stuck and powerless, and rightly so. What she really needed was to return to therapy. But that would most certainly expose our relationship if she spoke to someone else, so it was left to me, and me alone, to help her heal.

She shuddered with a woeful sob and said, "And things have been different lately. You don't call me as often as you used to."

"I call you every day at lunch."

"You used to call me more."

Sadly, there was no defense or winning for me with this line of questioning. All I could offer was appeasement.

"I just wish you could stay with me every night!" she sobbed. "I don't know why you insist on going back to your place when you could easily come here."

"You know why," I explained. "We have to keep up appearances. If we don't, I could lose my job, and then where would we be?"

She darted forward and wrapped her arms around my waist, buried her tearstained face in my shoulder. "I know. I'm so sorry. You're right. I'm just so miserable without you, and I hate being alone, and I want you to make it all better, like you always do."

It was a heavy load to bear: the total and complete responsibility for Melanie's happiness. I felt the weight of it like a house on my back, and I wished I could undo what I had done.

She looked up at me with pleading eyes, then pulled me down for a kiss. Her nose was running, and the taste of alcohol on her breath rattled me. It took me back to my childhood, and I became instantly repulsed, but I knew I couldn't reject her. Not in that moment.

"Come and lie down with me," she implored, dragging me by the hand. "I want you to hold me and promise me that everything's going to be all right."

I was tired and hungry, I hadn't finished my supper, but I knew I couldn't refuse. She was in a fragile state, and it would take some time for me to talk her out of her miseries. Perhaps she would fall asleep quickly after consuming that entire bottle of wine. I hoped that would be the case, because I was mentally and emotionally exhausted.

~

The following day, I saw patients in the morning, then spent my lunch hour tidying my desk and bookcases for the student film crew that was scheduled to arrive at one. Caroline popped in shortly beforehand.

"Everything looks good," she said. "And thanks for doing this. It could be huge for us."

I wasn't sure what she meant by that but assumed it had something to do with the favor she was doing for one of the richest families in New York. Caroline was ambitious and sometimes talked about expanding the practice to Brooklyn or even Connecticut, where she lived. Finding an investor with deep pockets was probably part of her master plan.

"It's no problem," I replied.

I rather liked the idea of an afternoon where I didn't have to sit in that chair and listen to other people's problems. I was having enough trouble coping with my own lately.

The clock struck one, and my phone rang, as if on cue.

"That must be them." Caroline tucked a few stray tendrils of hair behind her ear. "I'll go downstairs and greet them and show them up. And don't be nervous. They're just college students," she added, but I suspected the reminder was for herself, not me. "I'm sure they'll love whatever you have to say. Good luck. Break a leg."

"I'll try not to," I replied with a laugh.

A short while later, there was a knock at my door, and Caroline walked in with the film crew, which was smaller than I'd expected. It was just a young woman with a backpack, hugging a binder to her chest, and a tall, thin, bearded guy lugging a large camera case and tripod.

My eyes settled on the woman just as the sun came out from behind a cloud and shone through the oak leaves outside the window. She was slender and blonde, rather Nordic looking. She smiled at me, and it was a smile so dazzling it almost knocked me out of my chair.

I quickly stood. "Hello. Welcome."

Caroline gestured toward me with an outstretched hand. "This is Dr. Dean Robinson, one of the most up-and-coming psychologists in New York when it comes to grief counseling. We feel very lucky to have him with us."

The young woman strode forward confidently and extended her hand. "I appreciate you doing this. I'm Olivia Hamilton, and this is Brendan Davies."

I shook hands with them.

"I'll leave you to it, then," Caroline said cheerfully as she moved to the door. "Let me know if there's anything else you need. My office is just upstairs."

"Thank you so much," Olivia said. Then she faced me again. We stared at each other for a few seconds, and I noticed a small scar on her left cheek, which did nothing to detract from her natural beauty. In fact, it added to it. She struck me as someone who was probably quite adventurous.

"Let's get started." She glanced around the room, and her eyes settled on my big leather armchair across from the sofa. "Is this where you usually sit?"

"Yes."

She glanced at the window and seemed to be evaluating the angle of the light and the backdrop of bookcases on the far wall.

"Would it be okay if we moved the chair over here? Closer to the bookcases? We'll put it back when we're done."

"Of course. Whatever you think is best."

She and Brendan set to work arranging the furniture and setting up the camera and a few lights, while I sat at my desk working on a file. Olivia asked Brendan to get some B-roll footage of the office and me working at my desk. Then she said, "I think we're ready now, Dr. Robinson."

"You can call me Dean," I said as I stood and followed her.

She circled around the furniture. "Here's what's going to happen," she said. "I'll sit across from you and ask you some questions. The camera will be on you the entire time, but don't look into the lens. Just try and forget about it. Focus all your attention on me. Pretend it's just the two of us having a private conversation."

"That shouldn't be too difficult," I replied.

She moved to the small chair opposite mine, about six feet away, sat down, and began flipping through her notes.

"You can start rolling anytime," she said to Brendan, who was positioned behind her, manning the camera on the tripod. She regarded me with a friendly expression and said, "Let's start by talking about how you became a therapist. What attracted you to the profession?" She leaned a little closer and spoke in an intimate tone. "I just want to chat for a bit so that you can get used to the camera and feel comfortable with me."

"Okay." I rather liked the prospect of being on the receiving end of the questions for once.

"Great." She blushed a little and looked down at her notes. "So. Let's begin. Tell me about your interest in psychology."

I spent the first few minutes describing my education and how I was grateful for the scholarships that had made it possible for me to pursue a higher education. Normally I tried to hide my past from patients and colleagues, but for some reason, I was inclined to be honest and share the facts of my upbringing—the extreme poverty and the loss of my mother at an early age.

"What an incredible life you've lived." Her blue-eyed gaze settled on mine. "I would think that having experiences like that would give you some valuable insight into the emotional pain that other people might be going through."

"Perhaps. I also lost my aunt recently, so . . ."

"I'm sorry to hear that."

"Thank you."

"Were you close?"

"Very."

She was quiet for a moment, then regarded me with kindness. "Is that what you find rewarding in your job? Helping other people who have had it rough?"

"Sometimes. But to be honest, I think maybe the reason I gravitated toward this profession was because I wanted to learn about human behavior so that I wouldn't repeat the mistakes my father made. Or maybe I just wanted to feel like I'd won a losing battle in some way. That I was able to break the cycle." I told her about my brother in prison and how I was lucky to have escaped that path.

Olivia stared at me, nodding, and I felt suddenly self-conscious.

"I'm sorry," I said. "That was probably too much information. How much film did we just waste?" I laughed softly as I looked at Brendan.

"Please don't worry about that," Olivia replied. "It was all wonderful. I could listen to you talk about your life all day. But I'm sure you have patients to see, so we should probably get to the interview questions." She seemed suddenly flustered as she looked down at her notes again. "Okay, so . . . let me ask you this . . ." She met my gaze with that same absorbing stare that made something inside me come alive. "Have you ever treated a patient who had trouble letting go of a loved one?"

"I've treated many," I replied. "Of course, I can't talk about specific cases, but what would you like to know, generally?"

She sat forward. "Can you tell me about people who believe that their loved one is still present in their life? As a spirit? What makes them entertain an idea like that?"

"Well, let me see. From a psychological perspective, they are most likely having trouble moving through the stages of grief. They become stuck in the denial stage, which is where they continue to resist the reality that their loved one is truly gone. Are you familiar with the stages of grief?"

"Yes."

"Good. So it's my job to help them navigate through those stages to reach acceptance. Then they can finally let go and move on and find happiness again. In time."

"Have you ever thought that maybe it might be true?" Olivia asked. "That the lost loved one is actually hanging around, and maybe *they're* the ones having trouble moving on?"

I smiled at her. "Are you suggesting that I should be treating the ghost?"

She laughed and lowered her gaze. "That's funny. Okay . . . let me ask you this, if you don't mind. Do you believe in the afterlife?"

I shifted in my chair. "That's a question I wasn't expecting to be asked today."

She apologized and tried to backpedal.

"No, it's fine," I said. "I'll do my best to answer that." I paused and thought about it. "I'm afraid I can't give you a definitive answer, because there's no real scientific evidence, so . . ." I gave her an apologetic look. "I'm sorry. That's not very helpful for your film, is it?"

Was her film really about grief? I wondered.

"It's perfectly fine," she said. "I get what you're saying. How about we talk about dreams instead. They can feel very real. What can you tell me about patients who believe that their loved one is visiting them in their sleep?"

"That's a very common occurrence, actually," I replied, relieved to be back on familiar ground. "It's been widely studied. Those types of dreams can be pleasant and comforting, especially when the deceased loved one is free from illness or is young again. But sometimes they can be disturbing. Either way, they usually have an impact on the grieving process, which can include increased sadness or also provide comfort. Both of those things ultimately bring the bereaved closer to the stage of acceptance of the loved one's passing."

Olivia watched me for a moment, then inclined her head. "Have you had any dreams about your aunt who passed away recently?"

The question made me pause and reflect upon my life over the past few months. "Strangely, no."

It was surprising, in fact, considering the stress of it all, and I found myself looking inward and thinking of how I had been consumed by my complicated and confusing feelings about Melanie. I had been on a roller-coaster ride of emotions lately—at first desire, then guilt, shame, regret, and always an intense fear of our relationship being discovered. I had not often thought about Auntie Lynn.

"Statistically," I said, "only about sixty percent of bereaved individuals experience vivid dreams of the lost loved one, and that is likely related to the fact that we only remember five percent of our dreams on any given night anyway. So maybe I have dreamed about her. I just don't remember."

Olivia nodded and consulted her notes. "Can you tell me anything about prophetic dreams that involve the death of a loved one?"

"What do you mean exactly?"

She sat back and tried to explain. "This is just one of many examples, but I read about a woman who was napping in the afternoon, and she dreamed that her sister was banging at the door and shouting her name. She woke up and ran to the door, but no one was there. An hour later, her brother-in-law called to say that her sister just had a heart attack at the shopping mall and died."

I nodded. "I've also read accounts of people having experiences like that."

"And how would you explain it?" she pressed.

I considered it for a moment. "Well. Think of it this way. There are just under five billion people in the world, and millions die every year. Dreams like that happen all the time, but not always when someone has died. The chances of those two events happening on the same day are not out of the realm of possibility."

"So you think it's a coincidence."

"Probably."

She studied me intently. "Do patients ever get frustrated that you don't believe them? Or suggest that you should have a more open mind?"

"Quite often, as a matter of fact," I replied. "But have you ever heard that old expression that if you open your mind too much, your brain might fall out?"

She threw her head back and laughed, while Brendan bent over the camera to check his focus and make sure he was getting the shot.

Next, Olivia asked me about end-of-life visions, where people in hospice care reported seeing their deceased loved ones appear in the room. "Sometimes it happens weeks or even months leading up to a death," Olivia said. "Do you believe that this is truly a visit from someone who has already crossed over, or is it something else?"

I inhaled deeply and let it out. "In my professional opinion, it's exactly what the term suggests. It's a *vision* of a loved one. Something derived from the person's imagination as a coping mechanism to help them deal with their fear of dying."

"Interesting," Olivia said. She asked me a few more questions about what sorts of therapeutic methods I would employ to help the patient move through the grieving process, then looked at Brendan and said, "Did you get everything?"

"Yep. Got it all."

"Great. Well, I think that covers everything I wanted to ask you about." Olivia closed her binder and rose to her feet. "I can't thank you enough. This was really terrific."

"Are you sure?" I asked as I stood. "Maybe you were looking for something more conclusive or inspiring about life and death and what lies beyond."

"No, not at all," she replied. "Not from you. What I was looking for today was a more grounded scientific approach to the subject of bereavement. I've already interviewed plenty of psychics and mediums and people who say they saw a pink haze over their bed after coming home from a funeral. You gave me exactly what I needed to balance it out."

"Ah." I was relieved. "That's good to hear. And I enjoyed it."

"I'm glad." Olivia glanced at the clock. "It shouldn't take us very long to pack up this equipment and get out of here. Do you have more patients to see today?"

"None at all," I replied. "Dr. Weaver canceled all my afternoon appointments, so take your time. Can I help you with anything?"

"That's very kind, but we're okay."

While she and Brendan packed up their camera and lights and moved the furniture back to where it belonged, I asked her about her film. "When do you expect to have it 'in the can,' so to speak?"

"It's going to make up most of my grade for this semester, so I'll need to turn in the final cut in a few weeks. This is my last year."

"You're graduating?"

"Yes. Then it's off to the world of independent filmmaking."

"Will you continue making documentaries?" I asked.

"I'm not sure. I have a job offer from a studio in LA, but it's for TV stuff, and to be honest, I'm not that keen about moving out West. I've got time to figure things out. I'm only twenty-four. For the time being, I'd like to hang on to some independence and creative freedom with projects of my own choosing."

If it were anyone else, I would have said, *Sometimes you have to make sacrifices to pay the bills,* but I doubted that would be an issue for her.

She and Brendan finished packing up and made their way to the door.

"Thank you again," Olivia said.

We shook hands in the hall, and I was conscious of the warmth of her hand in mine. It caused a rush of regret in me when I realized I was not free to pursue any sort of acquaintance with this woman beyond today. I was trapped by the morally wrong thing I had done when I had become involved with Melanie. Yet Olivia was looking at me with admiration, as if I were above her somehow in intelligence and life experience.

I'd never felt more like a fraud.

"Goodbye," she said, and I closed the door behind her, returned to my desk, sank onto my chair, and stared up at the ceiling.

What was to become of me? I wondered wretchedly. Would my unethical behavior as a therapist be discovered if Melanie continued to feel unhappy or unloved? How would I even be able to prevent such an outcome, short of making constant grand gestures to prove to her that everything was as she dreamed it would be—that I would love her forever and never leave her. Her growing insecurities had become deeply troubling lately, and her behavior suggested that nothing would satisfy her outside of a marriage proposal, even if it required the engagement to be a long one to avoid any punitive action from the disciplinary boards. She only seemed happy when I was showering her with affection and desire, which had come naturally at first when everything was new and exciting, but lately I had woken up to the wrongness of what we had done, and I feared I couldn't continue the charade of those early passions.

My phone rang just then, and my stomach dropped because I knew it would be Melanie, calling to ask why I had neglected to telephone her during my lunch hour. With a tightening knot of dread in my core, I picked up the phone and said, "Hello. Dr. Robinson speaking."

"Hi there."

It was a woman's voice. But it wasn't Melanie. It was Olivia Hamilton.

CHAPTER 15
DEAN

New York, 1986

At the sound of Olivia's voice on the phone, a feeling of lightness practically lifted me off my chair.

"I'm sorry to bother you again," she said, "but I forgot to get you to sign a release form."

"A release form," I replied. "What is that? Permission for you to use my image and voice?"

"Yes, exactly. It's also where you sign away your right to approve or disapprove of the final project."

"I see. And I assume I won't be able to demand a cut of the box office proceeds later if it becomes a huge hit?"

She laughed softly and seductively into the phone, though I'm sure she hadn't intended to sound seductive. I was just so wildly delighted to hear her voice again that it affected me that way.

"Wouldn't that be nice," she said. "Something to dream about, right?"

"Right," I replied.

"So listen," she said without missing a beat, "I can swing by on Monday during your office hours. But if you're free right now, you could meet me in the park. I'm just heading out to walk my dog."

"A walk?"

"Yes. You said your afternoon appointments were canceled? It's a gorgeous day."

There was a sudden flash of heat in my bloodstream as I was tempted to say yes. I wanted to, but it would feel like cheating. If Melanie were a fly on the wall right now, she'd hit the ceiling.

When I didn't respond to the invitation, Olivia began to retreat. "I'm so sorry. Maybe I'm overstepping. Are you seeing someone? I didn't see a ring on your finger, so I assumed it would be okay for me to ask."

I admired how open and direct she was.

A reply tumbled past my lips all too quickly. "No, I'm not seeing anyone."

In my defense, it was a well-rehearsed response because my relationship with Melanie was intended to be a secret. Even she understood that.

"I can meet you right now," I said. "Where are you?"

"At my parents' place. It's directly across the park from your office. How about we meet at the corner of Fifth Avenue and Seventy-Ninth. There's a soft-serve ice cream truck there. You can't miss it. It's red and yellow. Let's say twenty minutes?"

"Sure. I'll see you in a bit."

I hung up the phone, tidied my desk, and locked up.

~

Olivia was waiting for me when I arrived at the ice cream truck on Fifth Avenue. She wore the same white shirt, jeans, and backpack that she had worn for the interview, and she was leaning against the park wall. A large black dog sat patiently on the sidewalk in front of her. Olivia's head was turned in the other direction, her attention caught up in the chaos of an ambulance blaring its siren and trying to push its way through the traffic. She jumped when I said hello.

"I didn't mean to startle you," I said.

Her face filled with pleasure at the sight of me, and she pushed away from the wall. Her dog stood as well, in tune with her change in energy, and he began to wag his tail.

"You didn't," she replied. "It's just so noisy here. I was distracted. Glad you made it."

"Me too." We smiled warmly at each other for several seconds until it felt a bit awkward, so I looked down at her furry friend. "Who might this be?"

"Pardon my rudeness." Olivia patted her dog on the head. "This is Ziggy. Ziggy, this is Dean."

I knelt down and scratched behind his soft ears and under his collar. He lapped at my chin, and I laughed. "Yes, you're adorable."

"He likes you," Olivia said.

"I like him too. What kind of dog is he?" I asked, getting to my feet.

"I have no idea," she replied. "I got him from an animal shelter last year. He's some kind of mutt, maybe a mix with a lab, I think? Whatever he is, he's very smart."

"I see that." I turned toward the street. "Did you want to get an ice cream cone?"

"Absolutely. Ziggy has been staring at that truck since we got here. He'd be devastated if we didn't."

We moved across the wide sidewalk, and I dug into my back pocket for my wallet. "What would you like? Or should I ask what Ziggy would like?"

She smiled. "He prefers vanilla."

I paid for the cones, and we made our way into the park toward the Ramble.

"Do you live around here?" I asked, licking my ice cream and watching Ziggy trot happily ahead of us.

"My parents do," she replied. "I have an apartment with some friends in Greenwich Village, but they don't allow dogs there, so Mom and Dad are looking after him until I finish out the year."

"That's good of them."

"Yes, but Mom said she only agreed to it because it meant I'd have to come by every day to walk him and spend time with him. Not that I don't enjoy spending time with my parents, but it felt like extortion when they agreed to keep him."

I laughed.

"What about you?" she asked. "Where do you hang your hat?"

"I'm a Jersey boy," I replied, leaving out the part about me dreaming about moving to Manhattan one day.

By this time, Olivia was nearly finished with her ice cream cone. "Ziggy! Treat!"

He stopped and turned, and she knelt on the path to let him gobble up what was left.

"What a good boy you are," she said, rubbing the top of his head. She stood again, and we resumed walking. "Before I forget, I should get you to sign that release form." She handed me Ziggy's leash so that she could retrieve it from her backpack, along with a pen. "Have a look," she said. "Read it over carefully, and if you're okay with it . . ." She held out the pen and gave me a hopeful grin. "I really appreciate this."

It was a short, one-page document that took me thirty seconds to read and sign. "It looks fine to me."

"Excellent." She stuffed everything into her backpack and slung it over her shoulder again, and off we went.

"I have a question for you," I said.

"Ask away. Oh, Ziggy! Put that down. That's disgusting." She darted forward to pull a plastic burger wrapper from his jaws. He growled for a second but surrendered it. "I'm sorry about that. You were saying?"

I got a whiff of her fragrance as she flicked her hair. She smelled clean, like Ivory soap.

"When you were asking me all those questions for your documentary," I said, "you seemed focused on ghosts and spirits. You asked me if I believed in the afterlife."

"Yes?"

We were now deep in the wooded area, wandering leisurely beneath the shade of the trees.

"Is that something that interests you?" I asked, genuinely curious. "Is that the real theme of your film?"

She chuckled softly as she walked. "Unlike you, I do try to keep an open mind about all that, and I want my film to leave it up to the audience to decide. But if I'm being perfectly honest, despite the fact that my parents are regular churchgoers, I have to say no, that I don't think there's anything else after we go. When we're dead, we're dead, and that's the end. Our bodies become part of the earth again—ashes to ashes, dust to dust—and maybe we'll fertilize a tree or some grass and that's how we live on, but I don't expect to be floating in paradise after I'm gone, however you want to define paradise. Are you shocked?"

"Not at all," I replied. "There is something earthy about you. Natural, I mean. Feet on the ground."

She grinned at me. "I think that's a compliment, I hope?"

"Absolutely."

"And yet," she continued, "I like to consider myself to be a spiritual person. When I'm out on the ocean, away from the city lights, I could stargaze for hours. Just sit there and contemplate the miracle of the universe. I confuse myself sometimes."

We came upon some broken glass on the path, and I took hold of Olivia's elbow and guided her around it. "Watch yourself."

She was light on her feet and followed me like a floating feather off to the side. "Thank you."

The happy, appreciative look in her eye caused something to light up inside me. Or catch fire. She was very beautiful, although it wasn't just a physical beauty. There was something else—something deeply joyful about her.

I thought of Auntie Lynn in that moment. I recalled my first night in her house in Arizona after she had come to collect me when my father was sent to prison. She had asked if I was too old for bedtime stories because she had something she could read to me if I liked. I replied grumpily that I wasn't a baby.

"Well, that's a relief," she had said. "How about this then?" She pulled an entire box of *Mad* magazines out from under the bed, and we looked at them together. I went to sleep laughing.

In a flash, I was back in my father's house in Wisconsin, in the gloomy bedroom where Auntie Lynn had spent the final years of her life. A thick mass of regret spread through my stomach.

Olivia touched my arm. "Are you okay? You look lost in thought."

"I'm fine," I replied, pulling myself back from the abyss. "Just thinking about my aunt."

"The one who died?"

I nodded, and she looked at me as we walked.

"I'm sorry about that," she said. "She must have been very important to you."

"She was." I turned to look at Olivia's profile. "Have you ever lost someone close to you?"

"No," she replied. "Just distant relatives that I didn't know very well. That's crazy, isn't it? How lucky am I?"

"Very lucky indeed."

"I'm sure my luck won't last forever," she added, "because death comes to us all. One day, I will probably mourn someone terribly, and for a very long time." She turned to me. "You must have to deal with that every day in your work."

"I do. It's not always easy."

Olivia, Ziggy, and I found our way through the woods to a secluded section of rock on the edge of the lake. Olivia took Ziggy off the leash, removed her backpack, and withdrew a bright-yellow tennis ball.

"Go get it!" she shouted as she pitched the ball into the water. Ziggy jumped in with abandon and caused a tremendous splash. His excitement helped to distract me from thoughts of Auntie Lynn.

"I hope you're not in a hurry," Olivia said to me. "He could do this for hours if I let him."

We sat on the water's edge and talked at length about politics and other current events while she threw the ball. She asked how I managed to keep the emotional demands of my work from interfering with my leisure time, and I was forthcoming about the pressures and challenges, without ever mentioning anything to do with Melanie.

I enjoyed Olivia's questions and her genuine interest in my work, and it excited me that she didn't try to tell me about any of her own personal problems. Maybe she didn't have any. She seemed so relaxed. Happy and positive about the future. It was rather miraculous—how a trauma-free life could be so full of lightness and joy. Even Ziggy seemed inspired by Olivia's positive spirit. He leaped out of the water, dropped the sopping-wet ball in front of her, and waited excitedly for her to pick it up and throw it again. She laughed and smiled with affection every time he dived back into the water, as if she hadn't a care in the world.

It was past five when she put Ziggy back on the leash and we made our way out of the Ramble to the open paths.

As we walked, I felt strangely as if I were floating in some kind of waking dream, as if this weren't really my life. It was someone else's. Again, the fraud. The imposter. I didn't want these moments with Olivia to come to an end because then I would walk to the nearest subway station, descend the steps, and travel back to my own reality. To Melanie's apartment. If Melanie had called the office that afternoon, she would most certainly be angry with me because I wasn't there and I hadn't told her I would be leaving early. She would want to know where I had been, who I was with. I would be forced to explain myself. What would I say?

Olivia and I reached the corner of Fifth and Seventy-Ninth, where we had begun our walk, and she held out her hand to shake mine.

"Thank you again for meeting me and for signing the form. Now the film can proceed. I'll be editing all day tomorrow and probably all weekend."

"I wish you luck," I said as I continued to shake her hand for longer than was customary, but I didn't want to let go of this feeling. This happy, hopeful lightness of being. This strange, undiscovered joy. "But I'm sure you won't need luck."

Her eyes glimmered with playfulness, or maybe it was flirtation. Was it?

The ground seemed to shift beneath my feet, as if I had just stood up in a small, unsteady rowboat. Suddenly, everything felt very precarious, and I was certain I was about to lose my balance and topple over the side, then sink into the dark, cold depths, where I would be alone, unable to breathe. Not because of Olivia. The suffocating sensation came from Melanie and the terrible mistake I had made.

~

Thankfully, while I had been walking in Central Park, Melanie was at the library editing her thesis paper. She'd had a productive day and had not called my office.

The following day, I sat in my armchair at work and listened attentively to my morning patients. But between appointments, when I sat hunched over my desk completing session notes, I admitted to myself that I was in great danger because I couldn't stop thinking about Olivia Hamilton—a woman I had only just met and had spent very little time with. It was what . . . ? A few hours at most? We had walked her dog in the park. I'd signed a form she needed. And yet . . . I couldn't stop thinking about her. I thought of her athletic figure, her deep, blue, long-lashed eyes, and how she had smiled with such a zest for life as she'd watched Ziggy leap into the lake. That energy took my breath away. And then I went to see Melanie, and she was depressed and negative about her work, and I had to thrust all that beautiful wonder from my mind. I was still fighting to forget about Olivia.

At the end of the day, just as I was packing up my desk for the weekend, Caroline knocked lightly on my door and entered. She must have been on her way out, because she carried her briefcase in one hand and her trench coat draped over the other arm.

"Oh, good," she said. "I caught you."

I locked my desk drawer and rolled my chair back. "Red handed," I said with a friendly smile.

She smirked and leaned a shoulder against the doorjamb. "I have another favor to ask, but please don't feel pressured to say yes. I understand it's the weekend and you might already have plans."

"What's the favor?" I asked.

She moved fully into my office and set her briefcase on the back of my armchair. "I've been invited to a dinner at the Hamiltons' tonight, and Liz suggested that you come as well."

"Liz?"

"You really aren't a New Yorker, are you? Liz is Oscar Hamilton's second wife. Much younger than the first, who passed away quite some time ago. She's Olivia's mother."

"I see." I found myself suddenly curious about the family's history.

"Dinner is at seven at their penthouse on Fifth Avenue. I'm not sure who else will be there, but I got the impression it'll be a small gathering. Are you free?"

I wondered why I had been added to the guest list at the last minute. Was this a polite way to thank me for helping their daughter with her school project? Or had Olivia suggested it?

Naturally, I thought of Melanie. We had no firm plans, but this was a Friday. She would expect me to come over. I would need to give her a call.

"Yes, I do happen to be free," I said.

"Excellent. I'll ring Liz back right now and let her know that you're coming." Caroline approached my desk and wrote the address on a slip of paper. "I'll see you there. And you should probably wear a suit and tie."

"No problem," I replied with a sudden attack of nerves because the only suit I owned was a decade old. I supposed that meant I had some shopping to do in the next hour.

As soon as Caroline was gone, I picked up the phone and dialed Melanie's number.

"Hello?" she said.

"Hi, it's me."

"Hi, you." She sounded upbeat, which was a relief.

Nevertheless, I paused and tapped my finger a few times on the desk before I spoke. "So listen," I said. "I'm not going to make it over to your place tonight after work. Something's come up."

My announcement was met with silence, so I forced myself to continue.

"My boss, Caroline, just came in and asked if I could go to a dinner. She thinks it might help with her expansion plans, and she wants me there."

"Where is it?" Melanie asked. "At a restaurant?"

I loosened my collar a little. "No, it's a private dinner party at someone's house."

"Whose house?"

I swiveled my chair around to face the bookcase. "Do you know who Oscar Hamilton is?"

"Of course. I'm not an idiot. You can't live in New York City and not know about the Hamiltons."

"Right. Okay, so . . ." I pinched the bridge of my nose because I hated this feeling of having to explain myself, this fear that I was going to send Melanie into a funk and I would need to spend the next hour pulling her out of it or not go to the dinner at all. "So Caroline was at Lincoln Center the other night, and she met Oscar Hamilton and his wife, and they asked if they could send their daughter over to the clinic to do some interviews for a film she's working on. Caroline said yes, so now they invited her to dinner, as a thank-you, I guess, and me as well."

Silence again. "Which daughter?"

I closed my eyes as I answered. "The youngest."

"Olivia?"

"Yes."

"I see." Melanie paused. "Did you meet her? Did she interview *you*?"

"Yes. She just had some basic questions about grief counseling. It only took a few minutes."

More silence. "Why didn't you tell me about that?"

With a heavy sigh of defeat, I leaned back in my chair. "It only happened yesterday, and last night, we were talking about your thesis paper. I guess I forgot about it."

"Dean . . ."

I didn't respond. I just waited with burning dread for the axe to fall.

"Fine," she said, coolly, surprising me. "So the dinner's at their house tonight? They live on Fifth Avenue, right?"

I sat forward again. "Yes. That's the address Caroline gave me."

"Will Olivia be there?"

"I'm not sure."

Melanie grew quiet and spoke despondently. "I guess it's okay, but I was hoping to watch a movie with you tonight. What time do you think you'll be done?"

"I don't know. It's hard to say."

"Can you come over afterward? Please? It'll save you from driving all the way home to New Jersey in the dark."

There was no good reason for me to refuse her request, so I agreed, partly because I was in a hurry to leave the office and get myself a new suit. But mostly because I couldn't handle an argument and a free therapy session right now. I didn't have the energy for it.

CHAPTER 16
DEAN

New York, 1986

I arrived at the Hamilton residence fifteen minutes early but waited from a distance, across the street, a block away, so as not to appear too eager. Looking up at the tall building in the light of the setting sun, I wondered how many of the top floors the Hamilton family occupied. There were terraces with greenery spilling over the railings on three levels. At street level, a doorman in a smart-looking uniform stood under a maroon awning. He greeted an older couple who stepped out of a black limousine and entered the building. The woman wore a fur coat, even though it was a comfortably warm evening.

I checked my watch continuously, and when I saw Caroline step out of a yellow cab with her husband and enter the building, I decided it was time to make my entrance as well. I walked to the intersection, crossed over, and approached the doorman.

"Hi. I'm here for dinner with the Hamiltons. Do I just go inside or . . ."

"What's your name, sir?"

"Dean Robinson."

"Yes. Good evening, Dr. Robinson. They're expecting you. Right this way, please."

He held the glass door open for me, and I walked into a wide, white-marble foyer the size of a ballroom. A circular upholstered settee was positioned directly below an enormous crystal chandelier, and at the sight of all that wealth, I had to resist the urge to turn around and leave on the grounds that I didn't belong there.

My stomach tightened with nervous knots as the doorman spoke to the man seated at the concierge desk. "This is Dr. Robinson for the Hamiltons."

The concierge stood. "Welcome, sir. The elevator is just there."

"Thank you." I walked stiffly to the open elevator and stepped inside. It was luxurious with a clean red carpet, a shiny brass rail, and brass buttons. The doors closed in front of me, and up I went, all the way to the top.

When the bell dinged and the doors opened, I stepped off, into a huge private vestibule with black-and-white marble walls, a large vase of roses on an enormous display table, and only one door in front of me. I swallowed nervously, then approached and rang the bell. The door opened, and a man in a black-and-white tuxedo greeted me.

"Good evening," he said. "You must be Dr. Robinson. May I take your coat?"

I slipped out of it, handed it over, and tried not to look dazed as I took in the wide entrance hall with fresh flowers on two matching mahogany tables to my left and right. Directly in front of me, an ornate stone staircase led to another floor, and classical music played from speakers that were hidden from view.

An attractive blonde woman approached me. She wore a fashionable broad-shouldered magenta dress and a pearl choker at her neck. She came clicking across the floor in high-heeled shoes, smiling broadly. "Hello, Dr. Robinson. Welcome. I'm Liz. Olivia's mother. We are so pleased you could join us."

"I appreciate the invitation. But please call me Dean."

"I will. Come with me, this way."

She linked her arm through mine and led me through a large living room with Victorian furnishings, then into a smaller parlor with an enormous fireplace and cozy groupings of sofas and chairs. There were about ten people standing around with drinks in hand, chatting casually. I saw Caroline, and she nodded at me. I looked around for Olivia, but I seemed to be the youngest person in the room.

"Let me introduce you to a few people," Liz said. "You obviously know Dr. Weaver and her husband." She led me to another group of two couples, who turned out to be family members. One woman was a child from Oscar Hamilton's first marriage. "This is Olivia's half sister, Sarah, and her husband, Leon. And this is my brother, James, and his wife, Jan. They're visiting us from Miami."

I shook everyone's hands and discovered that Liz had grown up in Miami. Her father was a renowned architect who designed glass skyscrapers and was responsible for half the city's modern skyline of hotels and condominiums.

Liz asked me what I'd like to drink, and I requested a Coca-Cola. It arrived in a crystal tumbler with ice and a slice of lemon, brought to me on a sterling-silver tray by a young man in a tuxedo and white gloves. I thanked him, and he said, "You're very welcome, sir."

While the others chatted, I couldn't help but glance discreetly at the spectacular view of Central Park in the fading evening light. I found my mind wandering to the image of Olivia throwing the ball into the lake and the sound of Ziggy's thunderous splash as he chased after it. I thought of her stopping to kneel on the path and feed him what was left of her ice cream cone.

Where was she tonight? Not dining at home, obviously. My disappointment was palpable.

My attention then turned to the arrival of another person, Mr. Hamilton. He was older than I'd expected. Quite elderly looking, in fact. Liz hurried to kiss him on the cheek and whisper something in his ear. Then she led him to Caroline and her husband, while I took a moment to straighten my tie and try to relax. After a moment, Mr. Hamilton turned to me and said, "You must be Dr. Robinson."

"It's a pleasure to meet you, sir."

We made small talk for a few minutes. Then a servant entered the room and announced that supper was served.

As a group, we strolled into the formal dining room, which was lit by gentle wall sconces and silver candelabras on a white-clothed table. It was at that moment Olivia appeared in the doorway, out of breath and pulling a silk scarf from around her neck. "I'm so sorry. Am I too late? I'm not dressed."

Everyone froze before taking their seats, including Mr. Hamilton, who regarded her with a look of censure.

"You're not too late, sweetheart," her mother replied. "Go and get changed. We'll wait for you. Hurry up now."

Olivia dashed off.

"Young people these days," Mr. Hamilton said, and everyone chuckled nervously and agreed.

We sat down, and conversation resumed while we waited for Olivia to return. When she finally walked into the room, I nearly lost my breath at the sight of her in a slim-fitting, off-the-shoulder white cocktail dress. She sat beside me and apologized again for being late, and everyone was riveted and entertained by her excuse, which involved some heavy edits of footage of a psychic medium who claimed to speak to the dead.

"It's a good thing I have Dr. Robinson's brilliant interview to keep me from being categorized as a horror film," she said, charmingly.

Everyone laughed, and the first course arrived.

~

When coffee was served with dessert, Olivia turned to me and spoke quietly. "Do you have plans later?"

"I'm not sure," I replied. "What usually happens after dinner at your parents' house? Are the gentlemen expected to smoke cigars together while the ladies retire to the drawing room for tea?"

She chuckled softly. "Thankfully, no. My father will want to go to bed early. He's not as young as he used to be."

"How old is he?" I whispered.

"Just turned eighty," she whispered back, "but my mother is only fifty-five, so she tires him out."

I refrained from asking any more questions about that.

"Dad is usually accommodating on weekends," Olivia continued, "when I want to take off and go somewhere. Do you like jazz?"

"Um . . ."

"A friend of mine plays the saxophone with a quartet, and they have a gig tonight at a coffeehouse in SoHo. I'm going to see them. Would you like to come?"

I thought of Melanie and wondered if she was waiting by the phone or listening for my car in the back parking lot. But the notion of spending a few more hours with Olivia Hamilton was impossible to resist, so I said yes.

After the table was cleared, Mr. Hamilton offered to bring out a bottle of a fifty-year-old Madeira port, but Olivia said, "If you don't mind, Daddy, I'd like to take Dean to see Gabriel play saxophone tonight. Would that be okay?"

Mr. Hamilton sat back in his chair. "I wish I had the energy to keep up with you young people. I'd go along if I could, but I need my beauty sleep. Off you go, then. Have a good time."

"Thank you, Daddy." She rose from her chair, wrapped her arms around his neck, and kissed him on the cheek. Then she turned to me. "I'll just be a few minutes. I have to change."

I couldn't help but notice that rich people changed their clothes a lot.

When the bottle of port arrived, I politely declined but enjoyed an interesting and deep discussion with Mr. Hamilton about the psychological effects of grief. He asked me all sorts of questions relating to his late mother, who had been unhappy for years after the death of his father in 1961. I was conscious of Caroline listening discreetly from the far end of the table.

When Olivia entered the room, my heart stopped yet again at the sight of her in a black turtleneck, large hoop earrings, and a long black pencil skirt with flat shoes.

"Are you ready?" she asked as she tucked a leather clutch purse under her arm.

I rose to my feet, thanked Mr. and Mrs. Hamilton for the wonderful meal, and followed her to the door. Olivia and I were just donning our coats when Mrs. Hamilton hurried toward us, her heels clicking noisily across the expansive entrance hall.

"Dean . . . before you go . . . if you're free on Sunday, we'd love for you to join us on the yacht. We're heading out around noon. We've invited Caroline and her husband as well."

Slightly flustered, because Melanie had made plans for us to drive to Long Island on Sunday, I turned to Olivia, who was tying the belt on her cashmere coat. "Will you be going?" I asked, not forgetting that she had a documentary film to edit.

"I'll go if you go," she replied.

How could I possibly refuse? Caroline would be displeased if I declined the invitation. She would want to know why, and what would I say?

"I'd be delighted," I said to Mrs. Hamilton, who furnished me with the details.

A moment later, Olivia and I stepped off the elevator on the ground floor and made our way across the luxurious lobby, where the doorman was quick to escort us to a shiny black Rolls-Royce at the curb.

I had expected that we would hail a cab, and I'd worried briefly about how much cash I had in my wallet after the purchase of the suit earlier that evening, but clearly there would be no charge for this. We climbed into the back seat, and while Olivia greeted the chauffeur in a friendly, familiar manner, I tried not to appear too wonder struck, because this was not a world I knew. I felt completely out of my depth.

~

I barely knew this woman, and she was not from my world, but for some inexplicable reason, I felt a connection to Olivia that was mind boggling and far more powerful than my ability to resist it. There were moments when we sat together in the dimly lit coffeehouse, listening to the jazz quartet and chatting quietly between sets, when I felt as if nothing existed in the world outside of our intimate conversations. It was just the two of us, leaning close.

During a break in the music, I met her friend Gabriel and the other members of the quartet. Later, when the lights came on and the coffeehouse was about to close, Gabriel invited us to a party somewhere nearby, but Olivia declined and said that she had to pull an all-nighter and get back to her film editing.

As soon as Gabriel was gone, I paid our bill with my nearly maxed-out credit card. "I hope I didn't keep you from your work tonight," I said. "I feel like a bad influence."

"Not at all," she replied. "And it's not even true that I have to pull an all-nighter. I just didn't want to go to that party, and it was the only excuse I could think of."

I helped her with her coat, and then she asked to use the telephone to call for the car. After she hung up, she turned to me. "How are you getting home? Benjamin could drive you, if you like."

"Thank you, but that's not necessary," I quickly replied as we walked outside. "My car is parked a few blocks from your parents' place."

We stood on the sidewalk talking until Benjamin pulled up. When we climbed into the back seat, we both grew quiet. It was late, and I sensed that Olivia was tired, or perhaps it was something else.

At last, she turned to me. "I should probably tell you that Gabriel is my ex."

My eyebrows lifted, and I felt a small pang of jealousy. "Oh. I didn't realize . . ."

"No, of course you wouldn't. I shouldn't have taken you there. I don't know why I did. It wasn't because I wanted to make him jealous or anything. I wasn't trying to play games to get him back. It was quite the opposite, actually."

"What do you mean?" My heart began to race.

Olivia reached for my hand and held it, and her touch sent an electric current through me. "I wanted him to know that it was over between us and there's no hope and that he should move on. It's difficult when we're still friends and we run in the same group. But that sounds like I was using you for something, and that's not the case either."

I didn't know what to say. All I could do was sit and watch her in the darkness of the car with only brief flashes of city lights to illuminate her lovely face.

"I don't want to presume anything," I finally said. "But I'm not sure what's going on here."

"Really?" She laughed a little and seemed charmingly vulnerable to me. "I feel like you must. I've been so painfully obvious, forgetting the release form after the interview, then getting my parents to invite you to dinner tonight. You look surprised. Now I feel foolish."

"Don't feel foolish," I said, secretly delighted. *More* than delighted. I was over the moon. "When you were late, I thought you weren't coming. Then, when you walked into the room, I was so happy to see you."

I heard her breath catch in her throat. We drove under a streetlight, and her face lit up with a smile. She leaned close and touched her lips to mine. They were soft and warm, and she tasted like sweet cream and caramel. I cupped her chin in my hand, and we kissed briefly as the car pulled to a halt in front of her building.

I felt dazed as we slid apart. The doorman appeared at the window and opened the door for Olivia.

"Good evening, Ms. Hamilton," he said. "Dr. Robinson."

We both got out and stood for a moment on the sidewalk grinning at each other until the doorman recognized that his services were no longer required. He tactfully disappeared inside, and the Rolls-Royce pulled away from the curb.

"I'll see you Sunday," she said and gave me further instructions on how to find the yacht at the marina. Then she kissed me on the cheek and walked into the building.

Part of me wanted to stand there and watch from outside as she stepped onto the elevator, because I couldn't take my eyes off her, but I forced myself to turn and walk away, toward my car. I smiled as I walked down the street. I'd never felt such euphoria.

But then I checked my watch. It was well past midnight. Melanie must be wondering what had become of me. My body went cold, and my smile died away as I imagined the look on her face when I arrived. She would be in a very unhappy state. I quickened my pace and dug into my pocket for my keys.

CHAPTER 17
MELANIE

New York, 1986

You mustn't fall apart, I said to myself when Dean finally pulled into the parking lot and got out of his car. *Stop crying.*

But this was unbearable. I had been waiting all night for him to arrive. I had been checking the clock since ten, getting up from the sofa every fifteen minutes to look out the window and watch for him.

Why did he keep doing this to me? He knew how his absence brought me down. But for weeks now, he had been distant and detached, even though I'd done everything in my power to make him see how much I loved him and needed him. Surely he understood that he was the source of all my happiness, that the time we spent apart was meaningless to me. It was as if the earth stopped spinning and the sun grew dark—until the moment he walked through my door and smiled at me. Then all was right with the world, and the sun would come out again.

Why, then, had he not called to let me know that he would be late? Or at least to let me know that he was thinking of me?

Backing away from the door, I took a few deep breaths and reminded myself that he had been with rich, beautiful people tonight. *Do not shout at him. Be supportive. Or he might leave you.*

He knocked, and I tried to pat down the puffiness under my eyes, but what was the point? My whole body was puffy. All I'd done over the past month was stuff my face with ice cream and potato chips. I hated myself. I hated the way I looked, and I had to force myself to move forward, release the dead bolt, and open the door.

There he stood on the landing with his hands in the pockets of a brand-new dark suit and tie, shiny new shoes as well. The sight of him looking so elegant and handsome filled my head with distressing thoughts of the glamorous dinner party and the socializing and all the stylish women who must have been there. I imagined them in Gucci gowns, high heels, and expensive French perfume. Meanwhile, there I stood in my small kitchen wearing old cotton pajamas with a stretchy waistband and a shabby old bathrobe. Was it any wonder that I was struggling? That I feared Dean was going to desert me?

"Hi," he said, looking sheepish.

Suddenly and overwhelmingly, I wanted to grab hold of his lapels and shake him violently, plead with him to never do this to me again. He couldn't stay out late and keep me waiting and wondering what he was doing or who he was with.

"Come in," I said and took a step back.

He entered, and I shut the door behind him, secured the dead bolt. "That was a late dinner. Is this a new suit?"

"Yes. Caroline wouldn't have been happy if I'd shown up in the rumpled suit I wore to my high school graduation, so I had to rush out after work and get something."

"You look handsome."

"Thank you." He shrugged out of the jacket, hung it on the back of a kitchen chair, and moved to kiss me on the cheek. "How was your night?"

He seemed tired. Listless.

Oh God! What's happening?

I couldn't bear his quiet manner. He seemed indifferent toward me. He was bored. Unhappy.

"Fine," I replied as I fought to conceal my panic and sudden rising anger. "How was yours?"

He followed me to the sofa, sat down, and loosened his tie, as if he were relieved to be home at last. But I didn't believe it for one second, because he refused to look me in the eye. He kept his gaze fixed on the television, even though the volume was turned down.

"It was interesting," he replied and began to speak in a more animated fashion. "You should have seen the place. The lobby was all marble, and there was a doorman in a uniform. The family owns three of the top floors of the building with separate outdoor terraces and views of Central Park, and there was a butler who answered the door and a bunch of servants. Everyone was dressed up like it was a formal event, but apparently, they dress up for dinner every night." Finally, he met my gaze. "What a strange way to live, don't you think?"

I studied his expression carefully. "Yes, that is strange. But you had a good time?"

"I did." I sensed he was trying to play it down. "Caroline was happy. She wants to impress Mr. Hamilton, and I had a good conversation with him about grief counseling. Who knows what might come of it?" Dean shrugged a shoulder, making light of everything, but I could see right through him. I wasn't a fool. I knew he was impressed by that world.

"If Caroline opens a few new clinics," he added, "she might put me in charge of one of them. That could be a game changer for me."

"For us," I firmly reminded him.

"Of course." But he kept his gaze fixed on the television.

My blood began to boil. I watched him intensely, willing him to look at me, but he just kept staring at the stupid TV. I hated him for it. I loathed him with every cell in my body.

"What's going on?" I asked desperately, taking hold of his arm and shaking him. "Why won't you talk to me? I feel like something's wrong."

His chest heaved with a sigh of defeat or frustration—I wasn't sure, but either way, it only exasperated me further. I clenched my jaw and squeezed my hand into a fist while I fought the raging desire to howl and cry and hit him and shout accusations. *Why did you stay out so late? Were you with someone? Someone rich and beautiful? Olivia Hamilton?*

"There is something," he said, "and I'm sorry. I hope you won't be too disappointed. But they invited me to go on their yacht on Sunday. For a cruise up the Hudson River. I know we made plans to go for a drive to Long Island, but I just couldn't say no."

"Why couldn't you?" I asked miserably, expelling the words on an inconsolable sob.

At long last, he comprehended the level of my anxiety and faced me on the sofa. "I couldn't say no because it's for work. And Caroline wants me there. I told you why."

"Yes, but . . ."

Why is this happening? Why is life so unfair to me? Nothing ever goes my way!

"But I was so looking forward to Sunday." I was desperate to appeal to his sense of responsibility, to his concern for my well-being. If he truly cared for me, it would matter to him, wouldn't it? "I wanted us to spend the day together."

"I wanted that too," he replied, "but this is important. These are important people."

I glared at him. "And *I'm* not important? Is that what you're saying?"

"Of course that's not what I'm saying."

"It sounds like it."

I didn't understand how he could be so willing to break our date on Sunday. We had planned it over a week ago. I had been dreaming of it every day, imagining all the things we would do, what we would say to each other. I thought it would be my chance to recapture the passion we'd had in the beginning.

But now this. He wanted to cruise up the Hudson River on a luxury yacht with the Hamiltons of New York. What other young women would be there? The daughter, Olivia? Wealthy and sophisticated and confident. She had everything to offer Dean, and I had nothing. Of course he would prefer her dazzling wealth and refined beauty over someone like me. Drab, unhappy, and colorless. I wanted to scream.

I stood abruptly and went to the kitchen. Dean didn't get up. He just sat there on the sofa, sitting forward with his head bowed low. Why wasn't he following? How could he let me feel this way and not care?

I burst into tears.

Suddenly, he was there, holding me in his arms, speaking in tender tones, uttering words of comfort and reassurance. "Please don't cry. We'll go another time," he said. "Besides, you're not done polishing your thesis paper yet. You can work on it on Sunday, and then we'll go for a nice long drive when you're finished. We'll have something to celebrate then. We'll have a much better time, don't you think?"

I wanted to believe him, but I could sense his detachment. This wasn't genuine. He wasn't the least bit disappointed about our Sunday drive. He only wanted to spend the day with the Hamiltons.

"Will she be there?" I asked, wiping the tears from my cheeks.

"Who?"

"You know who. The daughter. Olivia."

He stepped back. "I don't know. Probably."

"Is that why you want to go? To see her again?"

"No," he replied, his cheeks flushing. "I told you, it's for work. Melanie, please stop . . ."

"I just want you to love me!" I sobbed. "I don't know what I'll do if you don't. Please, Dean. You can't leave me. You promised me you wouldn't."

But had he really promised? I wasn't sure.

His eyes flashed with something—concern or fear or possibly resignation. I found myself letting out a breath of relief because that meant he was still mine, that he understood that he couldn't end this. He couldn't just walk away from me—from this great love that existed between us. I had never loved anyone like this before. Never in my life. We were meant to be. He was everything I'd ever dreamed of.

"Promise me you'll come over as soon as you get off the boat," I pleaded.

"I promise," he said. "But you have to promise me something as well. You won't spend the day doing nothing but missing me and working yourself into a state of anxiety like you did tonight. Focus on your work. It's an important project, Melanie. It's important to *you*."

I wiped under my nose and sniffed. "Okay, I promise. I'll go to the library. I won't sit by the phone."

"That's a good plan," he said. "Now come back to the living room." He took a step in that direction, urging me along. "We'll watch some television together."

Feeling somewhat better, I took his hand and followed him back to the sofa.

CHAPTER 18
DEAN

New York, 1986

When my alarm went off on Sunday morning, there was a part of me that thought I shouldn't go. I seriously considered calling my boss and claiming that I had come down with a stomach bug that might be contagious. That would get me out of it, and Melanie would never know that I had kissed another woman, and she would continue to keep our relationship a secret. But who was I trying to fool? I couldn't stop thinking about Olivia. It was a yearning that had begun the first moment we met, and though I tried to banish her from my thoughts, the effort was futile. I was falling in love, and I was falling hard.

Consequently, a few hours later, I walked up the gangplank to the main deck of a seventy-five-foot luxury yacht. It was not a sailboat, as I had imagined, but something that resembled a small cruise ship.

As soon as I stepped aboard, I was met by a crew member with a tray of champagne flutes. I took one, just to be polite, and was shown into the spacious main salon where everyone was gathered. It was the same crowd from the dinner party, and when my gaze connected with Olivia's, the whole world, and everyone in it, disappeared.

She made her way toward me. "Hi. I'm glad you made it."

"Me too." The euphoria was back. The blissful, thrilling euphoria.

Her parents approached, and her father shook my hand and welcomed me aboard. "I hope you like seafood," he said. "We're having shellfish for lunch. No allergies we need to know about?"

I turned to look at the dining area with a large oval table set with crystal stemware, floral decorations, and stylish leather chairs all around. "I love seafood," I replied. "Everything looks wonderful."

We chatted for a while until I heard the engine roar. As we slid smoothly away from the dock, the deck shivered beneath our feet.

~

A few miles up the Hudson River, we sat down for a delicious lunch of lobster and snow crab clusters served with roasted potatoes and a colorful salad. I wondered if the seating arrangements were prearranged, because this time, I was shown to a seat beside Olivia's half sister, Sarah, while Olivia sat at the far end of the table, across from me diagonally. Her sister was a gifted conversationalist, and I enjoyed getting to know her.

After lunch, Mr. Hamilton took Caroline's husband and me up to the raised pilothouse to meet the captain and view the state-of-the-art electronics suite. Mr. Hamilton seemed to enjoy explaining every bell and whistle to us. I couldn't hide my amazement, for I had never seen anything like it.

Later, when we returned to the main salon, the ladies were engaged in a fast card game that had them laughing and shrieking as they battled it out. If there was one thing my father had done well—and only one thing—it was to teach me how to play cards. At the end of the first hand, Olivia insisted that I join in, and I began to feel more comfortable in my surroundings, less like a fish out of water.

The boat eventually docked in Tarrytown, where we disembarked to visit a few antique shops and get some ice cream. While the others continued shopping, Olivia and I found a bench on the waterfront and talked about our very different upbringings and how they had shaped us into the people we had become.

I held nothing back. I told her everything there was to know about my family, including my father's and brother's prison incarcerations. It was the opposite of what she had experienced—both financially and emotionally—yet somehow, we had emerged with similar temperaments and core values that matched up in every way. She was impressed that I had survived so many hardships yet carried no bitterness in my heart, which was mostly true. The fact that I was optimistic about my future and wanted to spend my life helping others to find a similar sense of optimism within themselves made her lean close and kiss me.

"I love that you believe that people can overcome any obstacle, no matter how dire, and find happiness."

"I do believe that. I have to believe it."

She raised my hand to her lips and kissed it. "What's amazing to me is that so many of my friends—who have everything to be grateful for—don't share your optimism. They can be so spoiled and selfish, and it drives me mad when they complain about things that aren't laid out perfectly to their liking."

"Like what?" I asked.

She thought about it for a few seconds. "Oh . . . I hate it when they're rude to waiters if the food isn't cooked or presented exactly how they want it. And then they leave without tipping. Sometimes I'm ashamed to be a part of this world when so many people are struggling."

I sat with my arm along the back of the bench, my body turned slightly toward hers, and she rested her head on my shoulder.

"Is that what Gabriel was like?" I asked, tentatively. "Is that why you broke up with him?"

"No, actually," she replied, lifting her head. "He was a good guy. He came from money, but his parents were very conscious of social injustice. His father was a human rights lawyer."

"How long were you with him?"

"Two years." She looked up at me and smiled. "But why are we talking about this?"

I paused, then ran my finger down a long tendril of her hair. "I just want to know everything about you. And maybe I'm a little jealous that he's known you longer than I have."

"A little jealous" was an understatement. I hated to think of her with anyone else, especially a talented saxophone player who was clearly still in love with her.

"Was he your first love?" I asked.

She looked down at our joined hands and took a moment to form her reply. "No."

I inclined my head. "Your pause makes me curious. If he wasn't your first love, who was?"

"A bad boy from high school," she explained with a sheepish sigh. "He smoked cigarettes and hosted wild parties when his parents were out of town. My father tried to forbid me from seeing him, which only made me want him more. I used to sneak out and lie about where I was. Normal teenage stuff, I guess. We dated for about six months until he cheated on me, which I simply could not forgive. That's when I realized he was a jerk and I kicked him hard and fast to the curb." She leaned close again and nuzzled my cheek with her nose. "What about you? You must have had a first love."

I told her about a girl named Robin from high school. "It was all very dull and run of the mill," I explained. "She was nice, but we grew apart when we went to separate colleges."

Olivia and I talked more about how those early relationships had taught us things about ourselves and what we wanted out of future relationships. Most importantly, they taught us that we could survive and move on when those relationships ended, despite the fact that we once believed we could never live without that person.

It turned out that we could. And we were better off too.

When it was time to return to the yacht, we stood and walked hand in hand to the gangplank, just in time for the departure. Soon, we were cruising away from the marina, and hot hors d'oeuvres were served on the top deck while the sun began its slow descent toward the horizon. Seabirds soared above us and called out to one another.

From a distance on the open deck, I watched Olivia speak intimately and affectionately with her mother. Almost instantly, I was caught up in a powerful undercurrent, a longing that I feared would carry me away and drown me if I weren't careful. But there was no stopping it, I realized. Not while I was lost in the magic of the setting sun and the sweet perfume of the evening on the river. I was certain that something monumental was happening here. For better or worse, I was falling in love.

When we finally reached the city, it was past dark, and I was overcome by a perilous desire to be with a woman who was beyond my reach for so many reasons. As we made our way toward the gangplank, I was trying to convince myself that I should back away from this when Olivia asked me a question.

"Are you doing anything for dinner tonight?"

I should have told her I had plans. I should have said that I was meeting a friend or I had work to do. But my passionate desire knew no bounds. I wanted to spend more time with her. The feeling was unshakable, no matter how hard I tried to break free of it.

"Not really," I replied.

"Would you like to come over to my place?" she asked. "My roommates are probably there, but they won't mind. I could cook us some spaghetti."

"Spaghetti sounds delicious," I replied, feeling happy and wretched all at once and horribly conflicted as we said goodbye to the others.

~

It was obvious to both of us how we felt about each other. Even while Olivia and I cooked together, we burned to be closer. We ate across from each other at the small kitchen table, and there were silences that had nothing to do with awkwardness or a shortage of conversation and everything to do with our racing hearts and heated blood. I couldn't look at Olivia without wanting to touch her and hold her and confess that I was falling head over heels in love with her, after only a few days.

Later, as we stood side by side at the sink washing dishes, I glanced at my watch and realized it was almost 10:00 p.m. As was so often the case, Melanie drove into my thoughts like a battering ram.

I shuddered with dread, and I hated myself for what I had done—for surrendering to my grief and loneliness, and for betraying my integrity as a therapist and as a decent human being.

At the same time, I resented Melanie for pushing so hard, for not taking no for an answer, and for continuing to lay all her emotional issues on me, as if it were my job—not professionally but personally—to prop her up and cure all her woes.

I was trapped, like a prisoner in a locked room where Melanie held the only key. I was completely at her mercy, but it was my own fault because I had wanted her, in the wrong way.

And here I was again, desiring a woman who was forbidden to me.

"Is something wrong?" Olivia gently asked, putting away the last of the dishes we had washed together. "I feel like you're somewhere else."

I shook my head to try and wake myself up from a nightmare. "I'm sorry. I guess I'm more tired than I realized."

She studied my expression with a look of concern, then reached out, took my hand, and led me to the sofa in the living room. "Come and sit down with me."

I sank onto the soft sofa cushion beside her and wanted overwhelmingly to tell her everything—that there was a woman named Melanie who was in love with me and I had made a terrible mistake by becoming involved with her because she was a patient. As a result, she had the power to destroy me. She was waiting for me at that very moment. It was an impossible situation. I didn't love Melanie. I don't think I ever had, but I didn't know how to get out of it.

But no . . . I couldn't tell Olivia that. She would be disappointed. Possibly disgusted. She had been cheated on once before, by her first love. Naturally, she would be wary of a man who had done what I had done. Of course she would. And then she would turn away from me. She would leave. I would never see her again, and I would be left alone. Alone with more regret.

There was a sudden ringing in my ears, and I felt light headed. There was no one I could turn to, no one who could fix this.

"What's wrong?" she asked. "You can tell me."

"No, I can't."

"Yes, you can. I want to know. Please . . ."

I was too ashamed to look at her. "You shouldn't be with me. You're too good for me."

"Please don't say that. I'm not so special. I'm just lucky to have been born into a rich family. I don't deserve all the blessings in my life. I didn't earn them. But you've worked hard for what you have. You fought your way out of a rough life. You're strong, Dean. I'm not half the person you are."

Suddenly she was kissing me, and her lips were moist and warm, and I couldn't resist the love and tenderness she offered. How was it possible that she could turn this darkness into light? All the obstacles between us fell away like a crumbling wall of stone. I pushed Melanie from my thoughts and embraced the beautiful woman in my arms and wished we could leave New York and run away together, even if we had to live as paupers. I would do anything to be with Olivia and escape what I had done.

I knew in that moment that I had to find a way to end my relationship with Melanie, and I couldn't delay because it was clear that Olivia's passion matched mine. To her, I was good, decent, and strong. I sat on a pedestal.

That was the man I wanted to be, and perhaps I could be . . .

I had come so far. I had pulled myself out of a wretched childhood. I couldn't let anything drag me back there.

Just then, a key turned in the lock. Olivia and I quickly sat up on the sofa. We straightened our disheveled clothes and pretended to be engaged in conversation as two young women walked in.

Olivia greeted them. "These are my roommates and best friends, Rachel and Cassie."

We chatted briefly, and I was grateful for the excuse to say good night, because Melanie was waiting for me. It was time I put an end to this painful charade.

CHAPTER 19
DEAN

New York, 1986

The hour was late when I drove into the back parking lot at Melanie's apartment. The lights were still on in her kitchen window, so I suspected she'd heard me arrive. I glanced up at the door at the top of the stairs and saw her move the curtain aside to look out, but she didn't wave at me. She simply stared.

The curtain fell closed, and I knew I was in for it.

With a knot of dread the size of a football in my gut, I got out of the car, climbed the long, steep steps to the second level, and knocked.

She took her time answering, which I recognized as an attempt to make me sweat. It was passive-aggressive behavior on her part, and it was not unusual. She often exhibited behaviors that put her in a position of power over me. It was what she needed in order to feel safe and valued, and I despised myself for allowing it to become the foundation of our relationship.

"Melanie. I know that you're home," I said, "and I understand that you're angry. I'm very sorry I'm late, but I had no control over that.

The boat went halfway up the Hudson River Valley. We were gone for hours."

I left out the part about having dinner with Olivia afterward, and I felt like a heel, but I needed Melanie to open the door so that I could begin to pave the way toward a resolution to this problem.

I continued to stand outside on the landing, knocking and pleading with her to open the door, but she wouldn't budge. Finally, I bowed my head in defeat. I had no idea how I was going to make her understand that we couldn't go on like this. How could I convince her that things weren't healthy between us and she needed to see another therapist? She was going to be devastated. It would kill her.

I felt a sudden, intense surge of guilt. My leaving, deserting her, not loving her, was her worst fear.

Was I sure?

I knocked again and spoke more firmly this time. "Melanie, open the door."

At last, I heard the heavy pounding of her footsteps across the kitchen floor. The dead bolt was unlocked, and the door swung open.

There she stood, in her red terry cloth bathrobe, her eyes puffy from crying. She didn't speak a word. She simply turned and walked away, back to the living room. I heard the television blaring, so I entered the apartment, closed the door behind me, and followed. She lay down and curled up in a fetal position on the sofa, clenching a crumpled tissue in her fist.

I noticed the empty wine bottle on the floor beside the sofa and felt sick to my stomach. I was angry with myself, to be sure, but I was also disgusted by the person she became when she drank. She was so much like my grandmother and my father, and I couldn't go back to that life. I wanted nothing to do with it.

At the same time, I understood why Melanie had this problem, and I knew that I had failed as her therapist and as her lover and friend. She needed help, but I couldn't be the person to help her. Not after what we had become to each other.

I moved closer, got to my knees on the floor in front of her, and brushed a lock of hair away from her forehead.

"Hey," I said in a gentle voice. "I'm sorry I was late. I should have called."

"How could you call me if you were on a boat?" she asked. "With such important people?" Her speech was slurred, and she smelled of alcohol.

"Fair point," I replied, then considered what to do. "I'm going to get you a glass of water," I said. "Then we can talk."

Even as I spoke the words, I knew it was the wrong time to have this conversation. She needed to be sober so that we could talk calmly and sensibly.

I rose to my feet, went to the kitchen, found a glass in the cupboard, and filled it at the sink. When I turned around, she was standing by the kitchen table, glaring at me with a mixture of rage and despair. A vein throbbed visibly at her temple, and her cheeks were flame red.

"I saw you," she said. "I went to the marina, and I saw you get off the boat with her. I saw you holding hands."

I couldn't seem to form words. All I could do was stand there, speechless and immobile. I looked down at the floor. "Let's go into the living room where we can talk."

Her cheeks flushed with color. "No. I don't want to go anywhere with you. I know you don't love me. I don't think you ever did. I was never good enough for you. You're too ambitious, and don't pretend it's not true. You were just using me because you were lonely, and I was weak and vulnerable, and you knew I was easy prey."

"That's not true." It was an honest answer because I had never wanted to take advantage of her or hurt her in any way. I had fought against it as best I could. And I had been weak and vulnerable too.

"If you don't want me, you should get the hell out," she said.

I set the glass of water on the table and carefully approached her. "Please, let's just talk, okay? I don't want to end things like this. Let's sit down."

She swayed on her feet, and I wondered if she'd had more than just one bottle of wine.

She pointed at the door. "Get out of here. I want you out of my life."

It was what I wanted as well. I couldn't deny it. But not like this. There was too much at stake. We needed to part ways as amicably as possible, and I believed that I could help her get there—to accept that our relationship had never been a healthy one outside of therapy. I wanted to talk about it and agree to a plan where we could both get the help we needed and move on.

"Melanie . . ." I took a few steps forward, but she screamed at me.

"Get out!" She grabbed hold of my arm, marched me to the door, opened it, and shoved me out onto the landing. "I never want to see you again!"

"Wait," I said, whirling around to face her because I still wanted to talk this through. But she came barreling toward me until I fell back against the rail. Then she slapped me across the face.

It had been many years since I had been struck like that. I had forgotten the shock of it, how much it burned.

Before I could recover my senses, she screamed, *"Get out!"* and tried to push me down the stairs.

I grabbed hold of her shoulders, only to keep myself from falling, which was the wrong thing to do. We both lost our balance and tumbled down the steps together in a violent cacophony of grunts and groans and a tangle of limbs and flesh striking wood and steel. Pain shot through my body, and I thought this might be it, that I would die. Then I struck the asphalt and the world stopped spinning.

For a moment I was paralyzed. I couldn't breathe and my heart hammered. My skull throbbed. Slowly, groggily, I managed to lift my trembling hand to my scalp.

Blood. There was a lot of it. I groaned in agony and writhed until I rolled over. Somehow, I managed to get to my hands and knees. I didn't think anything was broken.

Then I threw up.

Pain was everywhere.

I looked to my left and saw Melanie lying facedown on the asphalt. I couldn't make sense of what had happened. Was she okay?

I was bruised and battered, but I managed to crawl to her.

"Melanie . . ."

I rolled her over. Her eyes were wide open with fright, and I knew immediately that she was dead.

Blind terror slammed into me. I forgot my own pain and searched for a pulse at her neck, hoping desperately that I was wrong. But there was no pulse. I pressed my ear to her chest and heard nothing.

I knew CPR. I thought perhaps I could revive her, but as soon as I pushed her robe open and began chest compressions, blood spurted out of her mouth, and I was horror struck. I fell backward and scrambled away like a crab. Then I collapsed on my back and stared up at the night sky in a daze.

I don't know how long I lay there like that, beaten, blinking up at the sky. A raindrop struck my forehead. Another hit my cheek . . . my hand. Suddenly it was sheeting down. Cold, hard raindrops woke me from my stupor, and I realized I was shaking uncontrollably. I was in shock. I needed to call 911. I sat up and crawled back to Melanie. Only then did I become cognizant of the fact that she was naked beneath the terry cloth robe, which I had pushed open to perform CPR.

Help me. Please, someone . . .

But if an ambulance came, they would ask what had happened.

What is your relationship to this woman? the police would ask.

I would be compelled to explain that I was her therapist. They would find evidence that we were lovers. The story would make headlines. Caroline would be shocked and disappointed, and I would be fired and most certainly arrested. And Olivia . . . *oh no . . . not Olivia.* She would learn what I had done, and she would never want to see me again. She would think me the worst villain she had ever known, and her sense of betrayal and hatred would burn deep and without forgiveness.

I sat back on my haunches and began to sob. *Why . . . why did this happen?* I would go to jail, and everyone would say I deserved it. It was where I belonged. No one would care enough to hope for my release or help me prove my innocence, because I was not innocent. I was guilty. I had done a terrible thing. It was my fault that Melanie was dead.

Suddenly, the world began to spin in dizzying circles before my eyes, and I panicked. Everything was a blur after that. I barely remember carrying Melanie to my car and setting her inside the trunk. Or running back up to her apartment to make sure there was no evidence of our relationship. I only remember that I closed her robe because it was raining and she was getting wet.

When the night was finally over and I crawled into my bed at dawn, I understood that the image of Melanie, lifeless on the pavement in that bright-red terry cloth robe, would haunt me for the rest of my life.

CHAPTER 20
DEAN

New York, 1986

The next few days passed in a blinding haze of shock and fear and guilt and night terrors. I woke up in a sweat on numerous occasions and wanted to call the police. Surely, turning myself in would be better than this—better than the painful, debilitating fear of being discovered. At night, alone in my apartment, I sobbed and cried for poor Melanie. What had I done? I felt nothing but bleakness and doom.

Later that week, Caroline knocked on my office door. She looked concerned. "Two detectives are downstairs," she said. "They want to ask you some questions."

I broke out in a sweat. "What about?"

"A former patient of yours," she replied. "They're coming up now."

She met them in the hallway and escorted them into my office. There were two of them. A man and a woman. Caroline left me alone with them, but as she closed the door behind her, she looked displeased, and I suspected she didn't want other clients to see a crime squad in the building and not feel safe.

I set aside the file I was working on and took a few slow, deep breaths before I stood up to face whatever they had to say.

"You're Dr. Robinson?" the male detective asked, while the woman glanced around my office as if she were taking an inventory with her eyes.

"Yes." My heart pummeled the inside of my rib cage, and I felt certain that my face had gone stark white. "What's this about?"

"I'm Detective Smith, and this is Detective Mason. We're investigating a missing person, and we were told that she was seeing you for therapy?"

"That's possible. What's her name?"

"Melanie Brown."

I tried to look surprised, then frowned with concern. "Yes. Melanie was a patient of mine, but she stopped coming months ago."

"Why was that?"

I shrugged, because it happened all the time. "She felt that she'd gotten what she needed out of her treatment, and maybe she was tired of coming. She was busy with school, as I recall."

"Yes, that's why it was discovered that she was missing. She was supposed to present a physics dissertation a few days ago, but she didn't show up. People are concerned."

Detective Smith watched me intently for a moment, and I was certain he knew everything. Any second now, he was going to tell me I had the right to remain silent.

"Did you feel she was ready to stop treatment?" Detective Mason asked.

I turned to her, then let out a heavy sigh. "Honestly? No. She was under a lot of pressure with school, and she had quite a few personal issues we were working on."

"Like what?"

I hesitated. "I'm afraid that's confidential."

Detective Smith nodded, as if he had expected me to say that. "Is there anything you can tell us that might help us locate her? Did she ever talk about a boyfriend, or did she mention a reason she might want to leave town?"

I folded my arms and rocked back on my heels. "I know that she was nervous about presenting her research project. She was worried it wasn't serious enough."

"It was about the Bermuda Triangle, is that correct? Planes that go missing? Sounds pretty interesting to me."

Detective Mason nodded in agreement.

My heart pounded faster because I had Melanie's typed and bound dissertation at home in my apartment. I had taken it on the night she died because she had thanked me in her acknowledgments and revealed far too much about our relationship. If they were looking for incriminating evidence, that's where they would find it. I hoped they weren't in the process of getting a search warrant.

"No mention of a boyfriend?" Detective Smith asked. "One of her classmates said she mentioned a guy once, a few months ago. 'Lovesick' was the word she used. She said Melanie was happy for a while, but then she seemed depressed and wouldn't talk about it. Sounds like something didn't work out."

I prayed that they weren't just trying to bait me. "I don't know anything about that," I said. "It might have been someone she met after she stopped coming to see me."

"Her classmate also said that she had a drinking problem and that she was promiscuous. The phrase she used was . . ." He consulted his notepad. "'Queen of the one-night stands.' Is that why you were working with her? Because of a sex addiction?"

This was all news to me. Melanie had never revealed a tendency toward one-night stands during our sessions together. In fact, it was the opposite. She was critical of her mother for that behavior.

Perhaps I didn't know Melanie as well as I thought I did. Another failure on my part.

I cleared my throat and looked from one detective to the other. "As I said, what we talked about in her sessions is confidential, but if that's what her classmate said . . . I won't contradict it."

"Got it. So she never mentioned anyone specific who we might want to question? It would be helpful if you gave us something . . . anything?"

"I'm sorry," I said, shaking my head. "I don't recall that she ever mentioned names or told me any specifics. And for me to divulge that kind of information, legally, you'd have to subpoena my session notes, which you're welcome to do if you feel it might help."

Detective Smith pulled a card from his shirt pocket. "My next question was going to be if she was suicidal. But you're not going to answer that, are you?"

"Um . . ."

"Didn't think so. In that case . . ." He handed me his card. "Thanks for your time today. If you think of anything you can tell us that might help us find Ms. Brown, please give us a call. Day or night."

"I will," I replied and waited for them to leave before I went to the sofa, sat down, and buried my head in my hands.

Within seconds, I felt sick and faint and had to lie down with my feet elevated. I looked up at the grandfather clock and saw that I had ten minutes before my next patient arrived, so I forced myself to get up and dig out my session notes from Melanie's visits. Before that moment, I hadn't been able to look at them, but it was a necessity now. I needed to make sure that there was nothing incriminating in those files. And I had to get rid of her dissertation.

~

Shortly before I left the office for the day, my telephone rang. Since it was past 5:00 p.m., I considered letting it ring and making a clean getaway, but I decided at the last second to pick it up.

"Hello. Dr. Robinson here."

There was a soft chuckle on the other end of the line, and I knew at once that it was Olivia. "You sound so official. It's only me."

I hadn't spoken to her all week, though I had called her apartment a few times and left messages. Luckily for me, she was busy editing her film, so I'd had time to pull myself together after what happened.

"Hi, you," I said. "It's nice to hear your voice."

"Yours too. I missed you this week. I'm sorry I was so busy."

"No need to apologize. I was busy as well. How is your editing going?"

"That's why I'm calling, actually. I finished it this afternoon, so I feel like celebrating. Freedom at last."

"That's wonderful. Congratulations. Did it turn out the way you hoped it would?"

"Yes. Better than I hoped. It really came together nicely over the past few days. I think I'm going to get a good grade. But enough about that. Are you free this weekend? Because I have a proposal for you."

I sat down at my desk. "I'm listening."

"Well . . ." She paused in a playful way to draw out the suspense. "My mother is flying down to Miami to visit her family, and she wants me to come with her. I told her I would, and we're leaving tonight. But I haven't seen you all week, so I was wondering if you'd like to come with us. I'm sorry it's such short notice."

"To Miami?" I asked, surprised by the suggestion. I checked my watch. "Could I even get a flight this late?"

"You wouldn't have to worry about that," she replied. "We're taking the private jet, and we'll be staying in my mother's condo. There's a guest room for you to use. And it's my grandfather's birthday on Sunday, so we'd be expected to go to an afternoon party there. But

Saturday we can do whatever we want. Go to the beach. Go sailing with Sarah and Leon. Go shopping. Dancing. Movie."

I tried to absorb what she was suggesting—that we could fly to Miami on a private jet and spend an entire weekend together. I'd never even flown first class before.

"Um . . ."

"If you have plans, I understand," she said. "Like I said, it's short notice."

"It's not that. I'm just . . ." *Just what?* "I don't have plans," I said.

"Great," she replied. "Could you meet us on the tarmac at eight thirty? We're leaving from Newark. I can tell you how to find us."

"Sure." She gave me the details and suggested I bring a dress shirt for the party on Sunday.

We hung up. Five minutes later, Caroline knocked on my door.

"Hi. Come in," I said as I locked my desk.

She strolled in and sat on the arm of my sofa. "I hear you're jetting off to Miami tonight."

Taken aback, I shook my head with surprise. "News travels fast. I only just got off the phone with Olivia five minutes ago. Are you going as well?"

"No, that's a family thing. I was just chatting with Liz, and she told me that Olivia asked to invite you."

I stood up and retrieved my jacket from the coat tree. Caroline watched me put it on, and I wondered what she wanted.

"Listen," she finally said, rising from the sofa. "It was pretty obvious last weekend on the boat that there was an attraction between the two of you. And it looked like you left with her afterward. Did you?"

I met Caroline's gaze directly. "I might have."

Her eyes narrowed, and she paused. "It's really none of my business, but I just want you to know that I've been spending some time with Liz, and she's interested in helping me expand the practice. It turns out her brother had some mental health issues and therapy really made a difference for him, so . . ."

Not entirely sure where Caroline was going with this, I buttoned my jacket and waited for her to continue.

"Just don't screw this up for me, okay?"

"What do you mean?"

"I mean . . . I don't know what's going on between you and Olivia, but if you break her heart, that could be the end of my negotiations." She stared at me for a moment, her gaze unwavering.

"I see."

"I hope you do." Everything about her tone and body language felt like a stern warning or perhaps even a threat. "On the other hand, if things go well between you and Olivia and it turns out to be something lasting . . . well. If that becomes the case, I'd want to talk to you about becoming a partner and possibly taking charge of one of the other locations. I think we could build something really great together."

Suddenly I understood everything, and all I could do was nod to let her know that I received her message, loud and clear. "That sounds interesting," I said. "A lot to think about."

She was telling me, in no uncertain terms, that I would be rewarded for making Oscar Hamilton's daughter happy. Or the opposite could happen. Caroline was a ruthless businesswoman. She wouldn't think twice about throwing me under the bus if I got in the way of her lofty ambitions.

Something in me grew weary. There I was, again at the mercy of a woman who wanted something from me. And again, I was handed the responsibility and pressure to make someone happy.

Caroline moved to the door. "Sounds like it's going to be a fun weekend for you." She winked at me. "You lucky devil. I'll want to hear all about that private jet on Monday."

I didn't comment on that. I simply gathered up my things and tried to focus on Olivia and nothing else as I walked out. All I wanted was to be with her again so I could feel the euphoria. I didn't care if we were on a luxury jet or sleeping in a dumpster. Anything would be better than this hell I was living.

CHAPTER 21
OLIVIA

New York, 1986

It had been almost a full week since I had kissed Dean Robinson goodbye in my apartment stairwell after our cruise up the Hudson River and our romantic spaghetti dinner afterward. I'd had a student film to edit by the due date, so I had forced myself to stay focused and get the job done, when all I wanted was to see Dean again. I couldn't even begin to fathom my delight when my mother finally consented to let me invite him to join us in Miami for the weekend.

Dean had agreed to meet us on the jet, where I sat in breathless anticipation. The pilots were doing their safety checks, and the flight attendant had already served drinks. She would be closing the main cabin door in the next few minutes. I was seated at a window, watching for Dean and praying that he hadn't changed his mind and wasn't running late for some reason. We were scheduled to depart at 9:15 p.m., and once the doors were closed, that would be it. We would leave without him.

Finally, I spotted him walking toward the airplane with that attractive manly swagger, a blue Adidas duffel bag slung over his shoulder. A shiver of elation tingled through my body, and I turned to my mother, who was seated in the white leather seat across from me. "I see him. He's coming."

"Well, that's what I call cutting it close," she replied, flipping through a glossy magazine and reaching for her glass of chilled pinot grigio.

I still wasn't entirely sure that she and my father approved of my budding relationship with Dean. They had always liked Gabriel, and for a while they assumed we would get engaged. For that reason, they had opened their hearts to him and considered him part of the family. When we broke up, they were surprised and dismayed. My mother cried actual tears and said I had just tossed a match into my beautiful house and burned it down.

Indeed, it was a painful breakup. To soften the blow, I had told Gabriel to give me six months on my own to figure things out. But six months had passed quite some time ago. Then Dean appeared—the most attractive man I'd ever met, exactly my type with golden hair and blue eyes, an athletic build, and a smile that made my heart bounce around inside my chest like a soft rubber ball. But it wasn't just his looks. Whenever I was with him, I felt a perfect sense of harmony, and all seemed right with the world.

It was still early days, of course, and I knew he had feelings for me, but I wasn't entirely confident that the depth of his passion equaled mine. I was ready and eager to leap fearlessly into a committed relationship with him, but I sensed something was holding him back from that sort of impulsiveness. I suspected it stemmed from his upbringing. More specifically, the death of his mother and a deep-rooted fear of future abandonment. But who was I to make such judgments? I wasn't a psychologist. That was his department.

I continued to watch out the window as he climbed the gangway steps and entered the plane. Our flight attendant, Serena, met him at the door.

"Welcome aboard, Dr. Robinson," she said. "May I stow your bag for you? And would you like anything to drink?"

"Do you have orange juice?" he asked.

"We have everything."

Serena disappeared into the galley while I stood up and kissed Dean on the cheek. "I'm so glad you made it. I was starting to worry."

"Sorry about that. Traffic was bad." He followed me to the pair of leather seats across from my mother, who sat in a single.

"Hello, Dean," she said. "It's nice to see you again."

"It's nice to see you too," he replied, then looked all around the cabin. "This is really something."

My mother ignored his comment while I breathed in the scent of him and admired the way his open collar stood up at his neck and how his wavy hair curled around it. My whole being seemed to lift off the chair and float, and we hadn't even taken off yet.

I linked my arm through his and asked how his day had gone.

"It was all right," he replied, sitting forward and looking down at his shoes.

I felt a twinge of unease, a sense that something was off. But then he looked into my eyes and said, "I'm so happy to see you. You have no idea."

My heart swelled at the intimacy I felt when he spoke to me, and I felt warm all over.

Serena appeared with a glass of orange juice on a tray. Then she closed the cabin door, and the captain spoke over the intercom.

"Good evening, ladies and gentlemen. It should be a smooth flight to Miami. Clear skies all the way. Please go ahead and get comfortable and prepare for takeoff."

We all buckled our seat belts, the engine roared beneath us, and the plane began taxiing toward the runway.

~

Not long after we reached cruising altitude, I leaned close to Dean and whispered in his ear, "I have a surprise for you."

Our faces were mere inches apart, and all I wanted to do was kiss those beautiful, soft lips. I was dizzy with desire, but I resisted the urge because my mother sat two feet away, looking bored with her magazine. She would certainly notice if we started making out like lovesick teenagers.

"What's the surprise?" he asked. The small space between us seemed electrified.

"You told me on the boat last week that you had an obsession with airplanes when you were a child and that you once thought about becoming a pilot."

"Yes."

"Before you got here, I asked the captain if you could check out the cockpit, and he said yes. He even said you could sit in the copilot's chair if you want to."

Dean shook his head with disbelief. "Seriously?"

"Yes. Do you want to do that?"

"Do you even have to ask?"

I laughed and turned in my seat to wave at Serena.

She approached and leaned close. "What can I get for you?"

"Nothing, but could you let Captain Taylor know that Dean would like to visit the cockpit and ask when it's okay for him to do that?"

"Certainly." She went forward to speak to him.

A moment later, she returned. "The captain says now is a good time. I can take you, if you'd like?"

Dean turned to me. "You're amazing. Do you know that? I feel like I'm living in a fantasy world."

I blew on my fingernails and pretended to polish them on my shoulder. "Just call me dream weaver."

He laughed, unbuckled his seat belt, and followed Serena to the cockpit.

For the next few minutes, I sat and watched him talk to the pilots and felt an enormous sense of pride and satisfaction. It thrilled me to see him experience something that he'd always dreamed about.

The first officer got up and invited Dean to take his seat. The three of them talked and pointed at the instruments, and I wished I were a fly on the wall, until my mother interrupted my reverie and spoke cynically.

"I hope he doesn't crash the plane."

I turned to her. "Mom. Don't say that. He's not going to crash the plane."

She shrugged a shoulder, and I recognized that it was a subtle dig at me for breaking up with Gabriel.

I leaned across the aisle. "Please give Dean a chance. I'm begging you. Because I really like him."

"I like him too," she replied, cheerfully but unconvincingly.

"Mom." I looked her straight in the eye. "He could be the one."

She stared at me for a moment, unblinking. Then she let out a breath. "Fine. I'll give him a chance. I just want you to be happy, that's all."

"I am happy. I'm *very* happy."

Sitting back in my seat, I squeezed the armrests and wished my mother could just let me live my own life and choose the man I wanted for myself. She had no idea what was in my heart.

Dean remained in the cockpit for almost the entire flight to Miami, but when it was time to begin the final descent, he returned to his seat.

"That was amazing." He buckled his seat belt. "I can't believe that just happened. Thank you."

"I'm happy you enjoyed it. What was it like?"

He squeezed my hand. "They shut off the autopilot function and let me take control of the yoke. Did you notice when we climbed in altitude?"

"Yes."

"That was me. Then I leveled it out again. What a feeling. It was like I died and went to heaven."

I was entranced by his elation, and in that moment, I realized that his joy was my joy. I also realized that I was wildly, passionately in love, but it was a deep, soulful love. An unselfish love.

Twenty minutes later, we touched down in Miami, and I couldn't wait to get off the plane and spend the entire weekend with this man I absolutely adored. I could barely contain myself.

~

The following day, my sister's sailboat charged through heavy, roaring swells on the open water, as if on a warpath. Gulls coasted on the wind above us, and on the distant horizon, the Miami skyline seemed to bob up and down with every rise and fall of the bowsprit. The day was bright, the sky clear, and the whitecapped waves shimmered gorgeously under the hot yellow sun.

Sarah and her husband, Leon, had invited Dean and me to sail with them while my mother went shopping, which was always her preference. Dean had never been on a sailboat before, but he was eager to learn about blocks, rigging, and wind direction. He was a quick study, and it was obvious to me that Sarah and Leon approved of him. For that, I was grateful. Perhaps they could wield some influence over other members of my family.

Late in the afternoon on the homeward run, as Dean and I stood at the starboard rail, I spotted a pod of bottlenose dolphins. They swam fast alongside the boat, leaping above the waves.

"Look at that!" I shouted, pointing at them as they kept pace with us. "Dolphins!"

I laughed with delight at the spectacle, but when I turned to Dean, he was staring morosely at his left hand on the rail. His eyes were wide, his expression blank, as if he were in a trance. I touched his shoulder and shook him a little. His eyes lifted, and it was a few seconds before he seemed to recognize me.

"Hey," I said.

"Hey," he replied, as if he had just woken up.

"Did you see the dolphins?"

He glanced across the water and spotted them veering away from us. "Oh, wow. Look at that." He wrapped his arm around my waist and pulled me close.

I wasn't sure if he was aware that he had been somewhere else just then. I felt a twinge of concern, but I let it go and kissed him on the cheek. Then we stood together in the brisk wind, gazing toward Miami in the distance.

~

That night, we went to dinner on our own. I had reserved a small, private corner booth for us in my favorite Italian restaurant with red leather upholstery on the seats, red-and-white checkered tablecloths, and a gigantic mural of the Roman Colosseum on the wall. The owner knew me well because I had been going there for years with my parents, ever since I was a young girl and loved cheesy macaroni. He was delighted to see me, and he treated us like family.

Dean looked handsome in the candlelight, suntanned after our thrilling day on the water. I laid my hand on his knee.

"Did you have a good time on the boat?" I asked.

He leaned close, and his breath swept across my lips. "It was wonderful. Everything about this weekend has been amazing. And it's not just about flying a jet or going sailing for the first time. The best part has been spending time with you. I feel like the luckiest man on Earth."

"I feel the same way," I said. "I don't want this weekend to end."

It was a good thing we had a private booth because he kissed me softly and tenderly, lingeringly, which only left me wanting more. I nuzzled his clean-shaven jaw with my lips and nose and hugged his arm as he laid his hand on my bare knee beneath the table.

We talked a bit about what to expect at my grandfather's birthday party the following afternoon. Then the first course arrived, and we slid apart on the red leather seat.

Later, after we finished our pasta, I reached for Dean's hand. "I have to ask . . . where were you today?"

I was referring to the moment when he'd almost missed the dolphins.

Dean's Adam's apple bobbed. He turned away from me slightly and shook his head with frustration.

I sensed he was displeased with himself, not the question I was asking, so I soldiered on. "Dean?"

"I'm sorry about that," he said. "I was lost in thought."

"Do you want to talk about it?"

He turned to me, and I rubbed the top of his thigh. "I wish I could," he replied, "but I can't."

"Why not? Whatever it is, you can tell me. Maybe I can help."

"I don't think so." He flicked some bread crumbs off the tablecloth.

"I'm a good listener. Try me."

He sat forward, folded his arms on the tabletop, and looked intently into my eyes, down at my lips, then back up at my eyes again. I thought for a moment that he was going to confess all his woes and share everything with me, but I was disappointed when he sat back and let out a casual sigh. "I'm afraid it's confidential. Professional ethics. That sort of thing."

I sat back as well. "I see. It's a patient." We both gazed for a moment at the mural of the Colosseum on the far side of the restaurant. "It must be difficult to work intimately with people and not be able to fix their problems right away. It must take a lot of time and patience."

"Yes."

"Do you have anyone you can talk to?" I asked. "I mean, sometimes it's necessary to brainstorm a problem with friends or, in your case, colleagues who might have good ideas."

He nodded and lowered his gaze. "I can discuss things with Caroline. And other therapists in the office."

I sensed he was not sharing everything, so I rubbed his thigh again. "That doesn't always help?"

"No."

"I'm sorry."

We sat for a while in silence, and all I wanted to do was pull him out of his obvious gloom.

"What's wrong?" I asked. "Please tell me."

At long last, his eyes lifted, and I sensed a deep fear in him. It bordered on panic.

"If you really want to know," he said, "I don't always enjoy my work."

"How so?"

He sat back and touched the handle of his fork. He slid it sideways, to the left, then moved it back again. "It's not easy to sit for eight hours a day, listening to people's problems and regrets, trying to steer them out of their own private version of hell. There's a tremendous pressure in that. It's exhausting, actually."

I understood. "I don't doubt it. And I don't think I could do what you do, which is why I admire you so much."

Our waiter arrived with our next course and set both plates down in front of us. He carried a pepper mill under his arm, which he offered to us.

A moment later, Dean and I were alone again. I tried to pick up where we had left off. "On the day we went walking in the park with Ziggy—"

"That was a great day," he said, interrupting me.

"Yes, it was," I replied with a smile, then continued. "When we were sitting at the lake, you told me you majored in psychology because it was your best subject and that you knew you could get scholarships if you chose that path."

"Yes."

"But you've also told me that it was your boyhood dream to be a pilot. Do you ever think that maybe you might be happier doing that?"

He sliced at the tender duck on his plate and considered what I was suggesting. "I think about it all the time."

Something inside of me felt an immense satisfaction. I wasn't sure what caused it. Maybe I was pleased with myself because I had opened a lid for him. I had presented the possibility that he could escape his stresses and soar to a place that would make him happier than he was now. A place where he wouldn't miss any more dolphins leaping out of the water right in front of him.

"Anything's possible, you know," I said, tasting the tender roast duck.

"I'm not sure about that," he replied.

"Why not? If you wanted to be a pilot, you're certainly smart enough. You can be anything you want to be."

He looked at me with affection and something that resembled awe. "You're such a dreamer."

"I suppose I am. If there are obstacles in front of me, I just see them as hurdles that require a bit of a jump. Easily done, most of the time."

"You think it's easy because you've never encountered a hurdle that rises up and slams you onto your back and knocks the wind out of you."

I considered that for a moment, reflected upon my privileged life, and felt embarrassed. "You're right. I've lived a pretty cushy life. Maybe I don't know what I'm talking about. I'm just a spoiled rich girl who thinks every dream is just a wish away. Ripe for the picking."

He placed his hand on mine. "No, that's not what I meant. I don't think you're a spoiled rich girl. I think you're a beautiful person, and you just want others to be happy."

I sipped my water and finished my duck. "Thank you for saying that. I appreciate it."

"And I appreciate what you see in me," he replied. "You have no idea how much it means to me—to be seen as someone who deserves to be happy. I'm not always so sure about that."

I regarded him with disbelief. "Of course you deserve to be happy. You can't let events of the past dictate where you go from here. And I'm referring to where you come from—your difficult childhood and the things your father and brother did. None of that was your fault. You're a good person, and you should follow your dreams."

"Sometimes it's easier said than done," he replied. "I have a mountain of student debt to pay off. And Caroline dangled a carrot in front of me this week. She said she might make me a full partner if she expands her practice. It would be completely irresponsible of me to walk away from an opportunity like that after everything I've invested in this career."

I sipped my water. "It's obvious that she thinks highly of you."

He shrugged a shoulder, as if to suggest that he didn't know why Caroline would feel that way.

He was very modest, I was discovering, which was one of the things I loved about him. He wasn't arrogant like so many of the young men in my social circle. It only made me want to help him more. I wanted to lift Dean up as high as possible so that the sun could shine on him. If there was an empty hole inside of him—which I believed there was because of his work pressures and the emotional wounds from his childhood—I wanted to fill it up with happiness in every possible way.

Wasn't that the true meaning of love? Wanting a sense of well-being for the person you cared about? And if a bomb was dropped into that person's life, wasn't it necessary to do everything in your power to defuse that bomb? Or throw yourself on top of it if you had to?

That was my version of love. And what I felt for Dean was pure and deep and everlasting. I believed it with every inch of my soul, and I decided, that night in the restaurant, that I would do everything in my power to ensure his happiness and to keep him in my life forever.

CHAPTER 22
OLIVIA

New York, 1986

A month after my weekend in Miami with Dean, my mother called and asked that I come over right away. "Your father wants to speak to you," she said.

I recognized an urgency in her voice and worried that something terrible had happened. "It's not Ziggy, is it?"

"No. Ziggy's fine. It's something else."

"Okay," I said warily. "I'll be there in half an hour."

As I rode the elevator up seventeen floors to their Fifth Avenue penthouse, I couldn't shake the sickening sensation of dread in my belly. I wasn't sure why, but I felt like I was going to the gallows. Perhaps it was the fact that my father was involved, and he usually left most parenting or personal issues to my mother. This had to be serious.

The elevator doors opened, and I began to wonder if this "talk" involved Dean. Frankly, I was surprised it had taken them this long to sit me down for a heart-to-heart conversation about him, because it was obvious to me that after the boat cruise, they had decided he wasn't good enough for me. They never said so, exactly, but they were reluctant to invite us to dinner, and Mom continued to ask me about Gabriel. Lately, I had to beg for every invitation they extended to Dean.

I paused a few seconds to steady my nerves before I walked in the door. When I finally stepped across the threshold, my mother was already waiting in the entrance hall.

"I thought you'd never get here," she said impatiently. "Your father is in a state."

"What do you mean?" I asked as I handed over my purse and sweater to Maria, our housekeeper.

Ziggy galloped out of the kitchen just then, and I made a fuss over him, scratching behind his ears and kissing his furry cheeks. I was grateful for his excitement. It helped to bolster my courage.

"He's in the library," Mom explained without answering my question. "Let's go and see him."

I braced myself and followed, while Ziggy trotted jauntily behind us. We moved through the living room, past the main dining area, and across the long gallery. The door to the library was closed, and my mother knocked lightly before she opened it. When we walked in, my father rose from his enormous armchair.

"Hi, Dad," I said, feeling skittish as I moved toward him. He was a giant of a man—tall and big boned—and I never felt the force of his intimidating presence as severely as I did in that moment when he pulled me into his arms for a hug and kissed the top of my head, which was his usual habit.

"Hello, sweet pea," he replied lovingly, as if he were about to tell me that my dog had died, which wasn't the case because Ziggy was fine, sniffing around the room.

I withdrew from my father's embrace and craned my neck to look up at him. "Mom said you wanted to talk to me?"

"Yes. Come and sit down."

I moved to the chair that faced his, and my mother sat on the sofa.

"We have something to tell you about Dean, and it's not good, I'm afraid."

My breath caught. "Is he all right?"

"Oh yes," my father replied, as if Dean's well-being were some sort of injustice. "He's fine, but . . . this is difficult to say to you, my darling, but it's important that you know the truth." My father sat forward slightly. "He's been keeping something from us. He's not who he says he is."

"What do you mean?"

My father leaned back again and crossed one long leg over the other. "To begin with, his family is not . . ." Dad paused. "They are not the sort of people you should associate with."

My back went up, and I spoke with anger. "What are you trying to say?"

"I'm telling you that the man you are seeing has a dark past, and I don't think you can fully trust him."

I scoffed. "Are you being serious right now? If you're talking about the fact that he grew up in poverty and his mother died in a drunk driving accident when he was twelve, I already know about that, and that's why I love him. Because he managed to emerge from all that as a kind, decent person, and he built something good out of his life, helping others. That took courage and intelligence."

My father frowned. "I don't think you know everything."

I laughed at his incredible arrogance. "I think I do."

Dad sat forward again, wanting to test me, it appeared. "Did you know that his father spent time in prison for manslaughter? That he's the one who killed Dean's mother?"

"Yes, I know that."

My father drew back as if surprised. "And his brother is in prison at this very moment for aggravated assault and burglary and a slew of other crimes?"

"I know about that too."

Dad let out a breath and fell silent. "You never told us any of that. You made it seem like Dean was an Ivy Leaguer."

I shook my head in disbelief. "Who even cares where he went to school? And you're surprised that I would hide these things from you? Clearly, my instincts were spot on, because you are doing exactly what I feared you would. You're judging him based on his social class and his financial situation."

"It's not about money," my father insisted. "It's about character. And I'm not judging anyone. I'm just trying to protect you."

"Protect me from what? True love?"

"No. From a man who is trying to better himself and raise himself out of his low and unfortunate circumstances. Have you seen his apartment? Do you know what kind of car he drives?"

I sat stiffly, breathing faster and harder as my anger burned. "You think he only wants me for my money?"

I was enraged by this suggestion because I knew it was ludicrous. Dean loved me for me. There was not a single doubt in my mind about that. What made me angry was my father's heedless, pompous assumptions and his belief that a man could never fall in love with me without having an ulterior motive. That Dean couldn't just love me for *me*.

I stood up. "I don't want to talk about this anymore. And I'm very disappointed in you, Dad."

He looked at me with outrage. "I beg your pardon?"

I froze suddenly, realizing that I had insulted him deeply.

"There's more," he blasted. "Sit back down."

He spoke harshly, and I found myself dropping obediently onto the seat cushion.

"Dean's father was arrested again last night," my father said. "Another DUI offense. This time he killed an entire family. Two parents with two young children. A boy and a girl, ages five and nine."

Shock caused my breath to come short. I could barely get words out. "Oh my God." I couldn't bear to think of that poor family. And Dean . . . *oh no* . . . poor Dean.

My thoughts returned to the situation at hand, and rancor hardened my voice. "How do you know all this?"

"It doesn't matter how I know it."

"You hired someone, didn't you? Someone to investigate Dean and keep tabs on him and his family?"

My father hesitated, and then he finally confessed without the smallest indication of remorse. "Yes. But only because I've had a bad feeling about him. I've always suspected he was hiding something from us."

"He was!" I shouted. "And so was I, because I knew you wouldn't think he was good enough if you knew where he came from. And guess what? I was completely right. But he *is* good enough, Dad. I know what's inside his heart, and he's a kind, smart, decent person. The best I've ever known, and if I can make his dreams come true, then why not? He deserves to be happy, and I don't need a rich man to take care of me. I don't need all this luxury. I'm not that materialistic, but obviously you are if you think that I would let Dean's financial circumstances get in the way of our relationship. It doesn't matter to me what his father has done. Dean is not his father. He's the opposite. All he wants to do is live a better life, to be a better person than his father was. And if you can't see that, I don't want to be your daughter anymore."

I stood up again, this time determined to leave. My mother stood up also.

"Olivia, please wait." She and Ziggy followed me out of the library. "Don't go."

"I have to," I replied as I reached the entrance hall. "I love Dean, and I want no part of this."

I heard my father's heavy footsteps raging across the living room. Suddenly he was shouting at me. "I am not wrong! He only wants you for your money. That's how he wants to better himself."

This was it. The last straw. I couldn't take it anymore. "You are completely wrong," I insisted. "And I don't care what you think anyway! I'd marry Dean today if I could."

"Don't be a fool, Olivia." He strode forward.

"I'll be as foolish as I want to be," I replied. "It's a free country."

"Fine. If you don't care about money, then you won't care if I cut you off. Because I'm telling you, I won't have a gold digger in this family. If you want him, you're on your own."

"He's not a gold digger!" I shouted. "Oh God, Dad! How could you even think that? He loves me. Is it that hard for you to imagine that someone might actually love me for who I am?"

I grabbed Ziggy's leash off the coat tree and strode to the door. Ziggy followed, tail wagging, bless his sweet, innocent heart. I hooked the leash to his collar.

"Olivia, please don't go," my mother pleaded, following me out of the apartment, into the vestibule.

I pressed the elevator button repeatedly. "I have to, Mom. I love him."

"Please, understand that your father just wants to protect you."

"I don't need protecting. I can think for myself. And I don't care about my allowance. Dean matters more to me."

The elevator doors opened, and I stepped on with Ziggy. My mother fingered the pendant around her neck, and her eyes grew wet with tears. As the doors closed, I watched my father step into the vestibule, take hold of my mother's arm, and try to lead her back into the apartment, but she slapped his hand away.

The last thing he said was, "Don't worry, she'll come around."

The floor shuddered beneath my feet, and the elevator began its descent.

~

An hour later, I stood on a New Jersey sidewalk with Ziggy at my side, blinking up at the front of Dean's apartment building. After I'd left my parents' place, I hadn't known what to do. I couldn't go back to my own apartment because they didn't allow dogs, and besides that, I was fit to be tied. Furious and frantic about what to do next . . . where to go. Naturally, the first thing I did was call Dean from a pay phone and tell him what had happened with my father. He told me to come straight over, so there I stood, still shaky from being cast adrift by my family.

At least I had Dean. He was my life raft now.

I gave Ziggy a pat on the head, entered Dean's building, walked up to his apartment, and knocked on the door. He opened it immediately and invited me inside.

While Dean hugged me, Ziggy was impatient to be greeted as well. He pawed at Dean's thigh and turned circles with excitement. It was a much-needed tension breaker, and we laughed as Dean got down on his knees and let Ziggy lick his chin. Ziggy cried and whimpered with happiness at the sight and smell of Dean. I couldn't blame him. I felt the same sense of relief.

"I don't think he likes anyone as much as you," I said. "Obviously, he's a good judge of character."

"I don't know about that," Dean replied, rising to his feet. "Maybe it's that can of beef stew I gave him last week. He's probably been dreaming about it ever since."

Dean gave me a meaningful look, took hold of my hand, and led me to the sofa. Ziggy followed and lay down at our feet.

"Rough day for you," he said as he pushed a lock of hair behind my ear. "Are you okay?"

With that simple question, all my anger drained away. I let my head fall forward onto his shoulder. "I am now," I replied, closing my eyes.

"Do you want to talk about it? Tell me what happened?"

My thoughts went immediately to Dean's father, the death of that young family, and the new drunk driving charge, which was what had sparked my father into action.

I sat back and took hold of Dean's hand. "It was horrible. The worst conversation we've ever had."

"I'm so sorry. I feel like it's my fault. I don't want to cause a permanent rift between you and your dad."

"It's not your fault. He's always looked down on anyone who wasn't born into privilege. But I never thought he would be that way with someone I cared so much about."

We both slouched low on the sofa and snuggled close.

"I have to tell you something," I said hesitantly as I thought of Dean's father and the latest DUI. "Have you spoken to your family today?"

Dean shook his head and rubbed my shoulder.

I sat up and laid my open palm on his chest. "There was a reason my father wanted to speak to me today, because of something that happened last night. I don't know how to tell you this, but you're going to hear about it sooner or later, so . . ." I swallowed over a thick lump in my throat. "Your father got into another car accident last night when he was drinking. He was arrested and . . ." I paused. "It was a very bad accident. A family was killed. Both parents and two children."

Dean stared at me with wide eyes. He blinked a few times, expressionless, and then his face went white as a bone. "Where did you hear this? From your father?"

"Yes. Apparently, he's been snooping around your personal life, looking for a reason to make me stop seeing you. But I don't care about that, Dean. I mean, I do care, but I know it's not your fault that your father is an alcoholic or that he's probably going to prison again. You're not him. You're *you*. And you're a good person."

With a pained expression, Dean struggled to stand up.

"Are you okay?" I asked.

"I need some water."

Ziggy's ears perked up when Dean stood. Ziggy followed Dean into the kitchen, where he filled a glass of water at the sink, took a few sips, then filled a bowl with water for Ziggy and set it on the floor.

"I always knew this would happen again," Dean said. "Dad got behind the wheel all the time after he'd been drinking. I should have done something. I'm a therapist, for crying out loud. I could have helped him or at least kept an eye on him."

"Only if you had stayed there," I replied, rising from the sofa and joining him in the kitchen. "And even then, it might not have made a difference. You don't know."

Dean bent forward with his hands on his knees, looking as if he was going to be sick.

"Can I get you anything?" I asked, rubbing his back.

"No." He breathed with intentional control, deep and slow. "No wonder your father doesn't want you to be with me. I can't blame him. I'm bad news."

"No, he's wrong," I replied. "I need to be with you because . . . because I love you."

Dean went still. Then he straightened and looked at me with something that resembled despair. "I love you too."

I wished I saw joy in his eyes, but I saw only uncertainty and regret. It sent a cold shiver of dread down my spine.

"Please don't do that," I said. "Don't think for one second that you're not good enough for me or that I'd be better off without you. I wouldn't be. I'm in love with you, and I need to be with you." I laid both my hands on his chest. "I have my own money that my father has no control over. Quite a bit of it, actually. My mother gave it to me when I was eighteen. It's enough to live on, at least for a while. So it doesn't matter what my father thinks or if he cuts me off. We'd be okay."

Ziggy drank all the water in the bowl, then looked up at each of us in turn, water dripping from his jowls.

"You know . . . ," I carefully suggested, "if you think you're always going to be unhappy in your job, you could make a change. It's never too late to start fresh with something new."

Dean nodded, but he seemed unable to form words. I think he was still in shock from the news about his father.

"We could go away together," I suggested. "I know someone who just finished flight school in Miami. You could do that, too, if you wanted. It's what you've always dreamed about, right?"

He nodded again.

"And I'm sick of New York," I added. "There's no way to avoid my family. They're everywhere, and I finished my degree. I'm ready for a change."

"What are you saying?" Dean asked.

"I'm saying that we could take off and start fresh somewhere else. Together. I just want to be with you, and I told my father that I would marry you today if you asked. Not that I expect that," I quickly added. "I just want you to know how sure I am. I'm so happy when I'm with you."

He was nodding at me, encouraging me to continue talking, as if he needed me to work harder to convince him.

"I know it seems like a lot," I said. "But when you know, you know."

"Yes," he repeated.

He looked at me intensely while Ziggy began to wag his tail. Then Dean pulled me into his arms and held me tightly. I felt his ragged breathing on my neck, and I clung to him, wanting nothing more than to run away with him that very moment and start a new life together. Anywhere but here.

Dean drew back and cupped my face in his hands. "Let's do it," he said. "Let's go to Miami."

"Really?" I laughed with disbelief. "Are you sure?"

"Positive."

Then he dropped to one knee in the kitchen and kissed the backs of my hands over and over, as if I had just delivered him from the fires of hell.

"Marry me," he said.

Ziggy backed up excitedly and barked. I ignored him and covered my face with both hands. My whole body was vibrating. All I could do was pull Dean to his feet, kiss him passionately on the mouth, and revel in the joy of what was to come—a long life with this man I worshipped. He was everything I could ever dream of, and in the deepest, most romantic corners of my heart, I knew he could do no wrong.

1993
NEW YORK

CHAPTER 23
OLIVIA

I stood at the edge of the lake in Central Park, just past the Ramble, where Dean and I had walked on the first day we met. I did the math. It had been two years, eleven months, and one day since I said goodbye to Dean in Miami, watched him get on the elevator and go to work. Little did I know that it would be the last time I would ever see him.

Turning to check on Rose, who had fallen asleep in her stroller, I thought about the NTSB report that had finally been published. The investigators concluded that the plane had most likely crashed into the sea due to pilot disorientation, which had occurred because of instrument failure. The cause of the instrument failure was undetermined, and it would likely remain a mystery forever.

As for the wreckage—or absence of it—they claimed that the plane had impacted the ocean with such speed and force that it was completely obliterated, and the currents had scattered the small bits of debris over a wide geographical area, making it impossible to pinpoint during the search.

I was told by friends that Dean would have died instantly and without pain. They were trying to offer comfort, but comfort was not something I felt. In the weeks following the publication of the report, I continued to find it difficult to understand that nothing had ever been retrieved, not even a small fragment of the aircraft.

But then the death certificate arrived. I had a daughter to support, so I took the payout from the insurance company and decided, once and for all, that it was time to let go of my obsession with the Bermuda Triangle and focus on Rose. Dean's parting gift to me.

But even now, still, in the darkest moments of the night, I dreamed of him coming home. Always, he was on a sailboat, standing at the helm with wild, windblown hair and sun-bronzed skin after almost three years at sea. I would stand on the dock at the marina in Miami, wave at him, and shout from across the distance, *Welcome home!* He would throw me the ropes, and I would secure the boat. Then he would step onto the dock, wrap his arms around me and kiss me hard, and tell me all about his adventures.

As I stood looking at the quiet, calm lake in Central Park, I exhaled heavily. At least, with the death certificate in my possession, there was some relief in knowing that I could stop trying to solve the mystery of Dean's disappearance and simply get on with living. Everyone in my life had urged me to let go of him, and eventually I'd understood that they were right. It was important for Rose to grow up with a mother who was emotionally present, not searching for something unreachable in the great beyond.

Rose was everything to me now, and I had resolved that the best way to honor Dean was to be a good mother to the child he had left behind.

Rose stirred in the stroller, woke up, and looked around groggily. I smiled and rubbed the back of my index finger across her soft, pudgy cheek. "Hey there, sleepyhead. Are you ready to go home?"

She nodded, so I whistled to Ziggy and turned the stroller around.

These days we had a small apartment of our own because I had wanted my own space, something less lavish than the Fifth Avenue penthouse where my mother liked to entertain on weekends. I wanted a more normal upbringing for Rose. It was important to me that she learned the true value of a dollar and understood that she had to work for the things she wanted. It was what her father had always done, and it was one of the many reasons why I had fallen in love with him.

~

On the way home from our walk, I decided to get a couple of videos for the weekend. I tied Ziggy to the lamppost outside our local Blockbuster and told him to stay.

It was almost 5:00 p.m., and the store was crawling with customers. Most of the new releases were already rented, but I was in the mood for an old classic, which I would watch after Rose went to bed.

As usual, the classics section was the road less traveled. I browsed around and picked up *The Last Time I Saw Paris* with Elizabeth Taylor and Van Johnson. I was reading the description on the back of the box when I felt the presence of someone next to me, glancing at me repeatedly. Feeling uneasy, I lifted my gaze and saw that it was Gabriel.

"Hey," he said, relaxing slightly. "I thought it was you. I was over in the thriller section and had to come over and check."

I placed the movie back on the shelf. "Yes, it's me. Oh my gosh. It's so nice to see you." I moved out from behind Rose's stroller, and we hugged. "What are you doing here?" I laughed at myself. "Looking for a movie, obviously."

He tapped the video he held in his hand. "Busted. And who is this? It can't be Rose." He squatted down to say hello to her. "Look how big you are."

"Rose, this is my friend Gabriel," I said. "Say hello to him."

She grinned adorably. "Hello."

"And who is this purple guy?" he asked, pointing at her fuzzy dinosaur doll, which came everywhere with us.

"Barney!" She held him out.

Gabriel spoke in a deep voice. "Hello there, Barney. It's very nice to meet you." He shook Barney's hand or paw or whatever it was, which made Rose giggle.

Gabriel stood up and smiled at me. "Charming and gorgeous. Just like her mother."

"Oh, stop," I replied, slapping him on the arm.

"You never could take a compliment," he warmly replied, and there was an awkward pause. "So what are you doing here?" he asked. "These aren't your usual stomping grounds."

"No, they're not. I'm still getting my bearings, actually. I just moved into an apartment a few blocks away. A two-bedroom for me and Rose."

We both turned our attention to the movies on the shelves and pretended to browse as we talked.

"Let me guess," Gabriel said. "You couldn't take any more of your mother's weekend soirees?"

I chuckled. "You know me too well. And did you also know that she's dating a senator? She started seeing him last month."

"Go, Liz," Gabriel said. "How do you feel about that?"

I shrugged. "He seems like a nice man, and she deserves to be happy. But he's quite a bit older. I suppose that's nothing new for my mom."

"Whatever floats her boat," Gabriel said.

"Or pops her cork."

We both laughed and continued to browse the classics section.

"What do you have there?" I asked, indicating the video he'd already selected.

He handed it to me. "I thought it looked interesting."

"*Jacob's Ladder.*" I flipped it over and read the description. "It does sound interesting. Is this the only copy?"

"No, there's still quite a few over there."

"I might get it," I said. "A thriller would be a nice change after *The Little Mermaid.*"

"For sure." He glanced down at Rose. "What time does this little one go to bed?" He rubbed the top of her head and made her giggle and squirm and offer Barney up to him again.

"Seven o'clock sharp," I replied. "Right, Rose?"

"Right!" she replied.

Gabriel accepted the Barney doll and made him toddle across the top of the video shelves. Then he leaned close, as if Barney were telling him a secret.

"Barney says he wants to watch *The Little Mermaid* tonight," Gabriel said. "Is that what you're going to watch?" he asked Rose.

"Yes!" She held out her arms. Gabriel walked Barney across the safety bar of her stroller and plopped him onto her lap. She hugged him and stretched out her little legs.

"Home?" she asked.

"Yes," I replied. "We should get going. I left Ziggy outside, and he's probably getting impatient."

Gabriel handed me the *Jacob's Ladder* video. "Here, you take this one. I'll go grab another. But it was really nice to see you."

"You too," I replied.

He disappeared around another aisle.

As I stood in line for the cash register, I found myself glancing about and wondering if he was still around, but I didn't see him again after that.

When Rose and I finally left the store and joined up with Ziggy, the sun was setting, and there was a hazy, almost magical glow in the air. I began to jog behind her stroller, and we sang songs the rest of the way home.

~

"So you just went your separate ways?" Rachel asked when we met in the playground the following morning with our coffees. We stood side by side, pushing Rose and Amelia in the baby swings. "On a Friday night?"

"Of course," I replied. "I was on my way home to put Rose in the bathtub, and I assume he was going home to watch *Jacob's Ladder* with his lady friend."

Rachel laughed. "His lady friend? That's funny. You do know they broke up, right?"

I felt a little jolt of surprise and an unexpected rush of satisfaction, even though I had no designs on Gabriel or anyone else. But he had been my territory once, so my ego couldn't help but feel some sense of gratification that he hadn't committed wholeheartedly to another woman.

"I didn't know that," I said. "What happened?"

"She was an OR nurse, and she started seeing an anesthesiology resident behind Gabriel's back. Then she announced out of the blue that she was moving to Japan with him."

"Wow, that's rough."

"Not really," Rachel said. "I don't think Gabriel was all that surprised or disappointed. At least that's what Kevin told me. Kevin never really liked her. He said she had no sense of humor, and I think Gabriel was looking for a way out."

I listened to this with interest. "Did you ever meet her?"

"No. I haven't kept in touch with Gabriel at all. I swear I didn't know he was living in your neighborhood. I would have told you when you were apartment hunting."

I let out a sigh. "Well, it's a big city. We probably won't run into each other much."

Rachel was quiet for a moment while we pushed our daughters in their swings. "Maybe we should do something about that," she finally said.

"What do you mean?"

"Maybe we should all get together."

"How can we get together?" I asked. "We're scattered all over the country."

"I don't mean *all* of us. I mean you, me, Thomas, and Gabriel. Thomas plays the bass guitar. He and Gabriel would probably hit it off and plan a jam session."

I considered this. "That sounds like a lot of fun, but I don't know. I'm not looking to get involved with anyone, and I treated Gabriel terribly before. I still feel guilty about that, and I don't want to lead him on and have to break his heart again."

"Why do you assume that's what would happen?"

"It's the most likely scenario, don't you think? I'm still not over Dean, and I'm not sure I ever will be."

We pushed our girls harder in their swings, and they raised their hands in the air.

"Maybe don't look at it that way," Rachel suggested. "I could be the one to invite him over to our place, and I would tell him that you're still going through stuff, and you're not over Dean, but we want to hang out as friends. He's a grown-up. He'll get it, and he can say no if he wants to."

"I'm sure that's what he'll do," I replied. "Self-preservation will take over, and he'll run for the hills rather than subject himself to the drama and emotional turmoil that would surely ensue if he became involved with his selfish ex-girlfriend again."

"You're not selfish," Rachel insisted. "It's not like you cheated on him. You were broken up for months before you started dating Dean."

"But then I brought him to Gabriel's jazz gig and sat there snuggling at the table, right in front of his face. I would hate me if I were in his shoes."

Little Amelia started to screech, so we grabbed hold of the chains and stopped the swings.

"Want to go play in the sandbox?" Rachel asked, and the girls shouted with approval.

We released them from the baby swings and set them on the ground to run.

"Please don't call him," I said as we pushed the empty strollers to the sandbox. "My life is complicated enough. I'm not interested in romance right now."

"Who said it would be a romance? He's an old friend. And you need to get out and have some adult conversations. Your brain can't survive on Disney cartoons alone. Believe me, I know."

I laughed. "I won't disagree with that, but still . . . promise me you won't set anything up. I just want to be a grieving widow right now. I'm content with that."

Rachel sighed. "Fine. I'll let it go."

"Thank you. I appreciate that."

We dug juice boxes out of our lunch bags and called the girls over for drinks and snacks.

~

The following Wednesday, about an hour after I put Rose to bed, the telephone rang. I was on my knees at the coffee table, inserting pictures into a photo album.

I leaped to my feet and hurried to answer the phone before it woke her up. "Hello?"

"Hi, Olivia?"

I recognized the caller's voice immediately and blinked a few times. "Yes."

"It's Gabriel. I hope I'm not catching you at a bad time."

I paused and slowly began to twirl the telephone cord around my index finger. "No, not at all. I put Rose to bed an hour ago, and I was just . . ." I glanced at the mess of pictures spread all over the floor in the living room. "I was tidying up."

He said nothing for a few seconds, and I pulled a chair out at the kitchen table and sat down.

"How did you get my number?" I asked.

"I called your mother, and she gave it to me. I hope that's okay."

"Of course. It's fine," I replied, remembering how my mother had kept in touch with him for a long time after we broke up.

"How did you enjoy that movie the other night?" he asked. "Did you watch it?"

"*Jacob's Ladder*? Yes, I watched it. It was terrific. The ending took me by surprise."

"Me too," he replied. "I wasn't expecting that."

"Thanks for recommending it," I said.

"You're most welcome."

He was quiet again, and I began to chew on my thumbnail.

"The reason I'm calling," he finally said, "is to ask if you'd like to have dinner with me this week. Maybe Thursday or Friday?"

I didn't respond right away, so he added, "No pressure. Just as friends."

"Oh . . ." My belly turned over with unease. I hated this. He was such a good person, and I didn't want to hurt his feelings, but I wasn't interested in any sort of relationship—platonic or otherwise.

"Now I'm embarrassed," he said. "I've put you on the spot."

"No, you haven't. I'm so sorry. You just caught me off guard. I'm not used to getting dinner invitations. I've been keeping a low profile lately. Not really interested in having a social life these days."

Neither of us spoke for a moment. It was painfully awkward.

"I understand," he said, and I felt a rush of guilt.

"Please don't think I'm trying to brush you off, Gabriel. It's not that at all. It's just . . ."

"Yes?"

"I live a very boring life. I give Rose a bath every night, and I read her a story, and I put her to bed. That's my routine, and I'm comfortable with it. I like the boredom."

He paused. "And I'm too exciting?"

I laughed. "Yes, I suppose you could say that."

Silence. Awkwardness again.

"That's unfortunate," he said.

"I'm so sorry."

"No, no, don't feel bad," he replied, "and I know you do. I can hear it in your voice. Honestly. I just thought, since we live in the same neighborhood and we're both on our own, that we could have a meal together. But I understand. It's okay."

I didn't know what to say. "Gabriel . . ."

"No, it's fine, Olivia. Please. Don't worry, okay? It's all good. But if you ever change your mind and just want to get out of the apartment for some food or to see a movie or whatever, call me, okay? We're friends. I'll leave you my phone number."

"Okay. Let me grab a pen."

I found a small notepad, jotted down his number, thanked him for calling, and hung up.

For a moment I sat there, staring at the magnets on the refrigerator door and the jar of crayons on the counter. The living room floor was still strewn with photographs, and they weren't going to insert themselves into the photo album, so I returned to the coffee table, sat down on the floor, and continued my task.

A half hour later, it was done. But as I put everything away, I couldn't stop thinking about my conversation with Gabriel. I felt bad about it—as if I had rejected him all over again when he was just calling to be a Good Samaritan and get together as friends.

Maybe I was resisting his friendship because a part of me still believed he wanted more. It was why I had taken Dean with me to the coffeehouse that night when Gabriel was playing his saxophone. It had seemed like the only way I could make him see that I was moving on and he needed to do the same. I couldn't let him go on waiting for me forever. And when he came to visit me the Christmas when I was pregnant with Rose, I was relieved to hear that he was dating someone. It took the pressure off. At last, I didn't need to feel guilty anymore about breaking his heart.

But here we were, both single again, and I didn't know how to make him understand that I didn't want to start anything. I just wanted to be on my own.

On the other hand, maybe I was utterly conceited to imagine that he wanted me back. Maybe he had no interest in me romantically whatsoever, and he felt sorry for me—a single mother who spent every day pushing a stroller around the streets of New York and renting Disney cartoons at Blockbuster, then watching old classics at home alone on Friday nights.

It was true. That's all I ever did. Rose was my entire life, the center of my existence. Sometimes I worried that I wouldn't even remember how to have an intelligent conversation with grown-ups at a formal dinner party. What would I talk about? Diaper rash? Hopscotch?

For a while, I stood in my kitchen with a cup of chamomile tea, and before I could change my mind, I grabbed the notepad with Gabriel's phone number on it and called him back.

"Hello?" he said, answering after the third ring.

"Hi, it's Olivia. I hope I'm not calling too late?"

"Not at all." There was a coolness in his voice, and I suspected he wasn't keen on playing a game of hot and cold.

"Listen," I said, "I just want to apologize for being so . . . I don't know . . . standoffish earlier. I know you were just trying to be a good friend."

"You don't have to apologize," he said. "I get it."

"No, I don't think you do. It's not that I don't appreciate my friends. It means a lot to me that you called. You're very special to me, and I hate how things ended with us, back in college. That night at the coffeehouse in SoHo . . . I'm so sorry about that. I shouldn't have brought Dean there, and I've always regretted that."

He cleared his throat. "It's no big deal, Olivia. Apology accepted."

I sank down onto the kitchen chair. "You must have hated me."

"*Hate*'s a strong word."

"Is it?"

"Well . . . ," he replied.

I laughed. "I can hardly blame you."

Gabriel laughed too. "We were young. Life is very dramatic for twentysomethings. And if it makes you feel any better, I eventually understood where you were coming from. You needed to hit me over the head with a crowbar to get me to hear what you were saying to me—that you wanted your freedom, and I just wasn't the one."

It was true. Gabriel hadn't been the one. Dean was the one. He would always be the one.

"I was a slow learner," Gabriel added.

"No, you weren't. It was my fault too. I think a part of me was scared about venturing out into the world without you. I wanted to feel that you'd always be there for me. Because you were my best friend."

"Until Dean came along," he said.

I exhaled. "Yes."

I could have said so much more—that when I met Dean, I felt as if I'd found the person who would be there for me until my dying day. Our love was instantaneous and passionate and mutual, and not even the disapproval of my family and the withdrawal of their financial support could stop me from running away with him. I would have given up everything to be with him.

But I didn't say those things to Gabriel because it would only rub salt in an old wound.

"I'm glad you called," he said, "because I want us to be friends. You still mean a lot to me, and I hope you know that I'm here for you if you ever need anything. I'm not trying to make romantic overtures or win you back. I swear, when I called you, I just wanted to go out for a nice meal and hear about your life."

"I'd like to hear about your life too," I replied. "I'm curious about the nurse. Rachel told me about her. And your job. How you ended up in the school music program when you once had big plans to start a record label."

He laughed. "Those were the dreams of a nineteen-year-old."

"Then you grew up," I replied.

"Yes, and I have no regrets. I love what I do. Kids today need more jazz in their lives."

I felt a warm glow inside of me. "I would like to hear more about that. Is it too late to accept your dinner invitation? I could get Mom to take Rose for an evening. She'd love that."

"How about Friday?" Gabriel suggested. "I'll make a reservation somewhere."

"That sounds great."

I told him my address, and he said he would come by at 7:00 p.m. Then I hung up the phone and felt a surprising surge of excitement—something I hadn't felt in a very long time. Already, I was starting to think about what I might wear.

But then I felt guilty and disloyal, as if I were cheating on Dean. Or the memory of Dean.

I tried to remind myself that he was truly gone, and he wasn't coming home—ever—and surely, he would want me to go on living. To be happy somehow. But the thought of him coming home to me blossomed again in my imagination, and I found myself thinking of him on that sailboat with the wind in his hair, waving to me as he arrived at the marina, eager to tell me all about the life he had been living at sea.

Maybe I was crazy, but I just couldn't bring myself to turn off that light in the window. I wasn't sure I would ever be able to do that.

Then I heard my mother's voice in my head. *Just give it time,* she always told me. I was trying . . . but how long was it going to take?

CHAPTER 24
OLIVIA

It wasn't a date, I told myself when Gabriel knocked on my door at 7:00 p.m. I had dropped Rose off at my mother's apartment earlier in the afternoon, which allowed me time to enjoy a leisurely shower and get dressed. I didn't want to look like I was trying too hard, so I chose pants and flat shoes with a plain silk blouse, though I dressed everything up with a necklace and hoop earrings.

"Hi. Come in," I said, stepping back to invite him inside. "I just need to grab my purse and coat."

Gabriel walked in and patted Ziggy, who had trotted to the door. "Nice place."

"Thanks. Although you didn't see it an hour ago. Everywhere you looked—toys, toys, toys."

"Sorry I missed that." He waited patiently while I pulled on my trench coat and watched Ziggy turn circles over his bed in the living room before lying down. Then Gabriel and I made our way to the elevator.

"I'm glad we're doing this," he said as he pushed the down button. "And I'm surprised, to be honest. I half expected you to change your mind at the last minute."

"I expected that too. But here we are. It's seven o'clock, and we made it across the finish line."

"Or at least out of the starting gate," he replied with a smile.

We chatted about the weather, of all things, as we rode the elevator down and walked out of the building. It was a beautiful June evening, humid but breezy. I caught the fragrance of lilacs in someone's front garden and stopped to take hold of a fresh bloom. "That's lovely."

"The smell of lilacs always reminds me of my childhood," Gabriel said.

"The house in Connecticut? With the rabbits?"

"That's the one."

We started walking again.

"That was such a wonderful house," I said. "I loved going there. Are you sorry your parents sold it?"

"Sometimes. But mostly I'm glad they're in a smaller place now. Easier to maintain."

I turned to him and smiled. "Did you know that your mother sent me a gift when Rose was born? It was the most adorable little blue velvet dress with white lace trimming. She wore it on her first birthday."

"That sounds like my mom," Gabriel said.

We continued to catch up as we walked the six blocks to a Greek restaurant I had never been to before. Inside, the walls were painted white with bright-blue trim, and the floor was flagstone. The hostess showed us to our table at the back, nestled beneath an artificial olive tree. Tiny lights on the black ceiling glimmered like stars.

Gabriel held my chair out for me. "Sorry for this," he said. "I didn't know it was going to be so romantic. Please ignore."

I laughed. "Don't apologize. This is marvelous. I feel like I'm on a patio in Santorini."

The waiter arrived to take our drink orders, and Gabriel selected a bottle of red wine from Zakynthos. Then we spent time reminiscing about our trip to Europe after our freshman year of college when we backpacked through France, Austria, and Germany with our friends.

"We were a tight group back then," I said, also remembering how Gabriel and I had become a couple that summer. It was an exciting time.

Our wine arrived, and we paused to look over the menu. We began with an appetizer platter of grilled vegetables, Halloumi, olives, and crispy toasted bread. Then I ordered pastitsio with a Greek salad, and Gabriel ordered the halibut.

"This is heaven," I said with a sigh. "You have no idea. Thank you."

"It's my pleasure. Truly."

There was a note of affection in his eyes, and I felt a twinge of discomfort—perhaps because it felt like not a moment had passed since we were a young couple, devoted to each other and on the same path. Then I remembered something I had once told Dean—that my first love was a bad boy in high school who smoked cigarettes and cheated on me. That had been a white lie. Gabriel was my first *true* love, but I hadn't wanted Dean to feel insecure after I took him to the coffeehouse to watch Gabriel play in the quartet.

Our appetizer arrived, and we talked about Gabriel's work as a music teacher and school band conductor, and he asked if I ever thought about filmmaking, which had once been my passion.

"When I was in school, if someone had told me I would drop the ball on my film career after graduation, I wouldn't have believed it."

"Why did you?" he asked.

I dipped a bread crisp into the hummus and shrugged a shoulder. "After I left New York, other things became more important to me. All I wanted to do was support Dean in his new career. It wasn't easy for him to start over completely. But it was the right thing. Or it would have been if he hadn't . . . well, you know."

"I have to applaud the guy," Gabriel said, reaching for an olive. "After spending all those years in school to become a therapist . . . then to leave it all behind to follow your childhood dream . . . that must have taken a lot of courage."

"It did," I replied, as I recalled the nights Dean woke up from nightmares when he was reliving the stress of his sessions with patients who were abusive or on the brink of doing terrible things.

"It was difficult for him to walk away from it," I added. "He hated leaving his clients when many of them depended on him."

Gabriel nodded with understanding.

"I'm sorry," I said, sitting back in my chair. "I'm sure you didn't ask me out to dinner to hear me talk about my late husband."

"It's fine. He was a big part of your life, and losing him must have been rough. I can't even imagine it."

I sat forward again. "Thank you."

Gabriel picked up his wine and took a sip. "Would you like to tell me what happened that night? When he disappeared?"

Surprisingly, I did want to talk about it. So I told Gabriel everything, starting with the argument Dean and I had in the condo before he left and ending with the late-night phone call that upended my entire world. I also admitted that I had driven halfway across the state of Florida to visit a man who believed that alien abductions were responsible for all the missing ships and planes over the Bermuda Triangle.

"When I was pregnant with Rose," I said, "I couldn't stop reading crash investigation reports. That's all I did for weeks. I'm not sure what I was looking for exactly. Maybe some reference to a scientific explanation for why compasses would start spinning around, or why so many other pilots reported strange mists. I wished there was a book about it, but I never found anything like that. Just sensational articles in the grocery store tabloids."

I sipped my wine and took a bite of my dinner.

"Then one night," I explained, "when I felt Rose kick inside my belly, it was like she was trying to tell me something—that I needed to stop obsessing about Dean's disappearance and think about becoming a mother. That's when I realized how alone I was in Miami, so I decided to move back to New York and live with Mom for a while. It turned out to be the right decision. Brought me back to reality. Helped me let go of the life Dean and I had together in Florida."

"Have you been back there since?" Gabriel asked.

"Only once," I replied, "for my grandmother's birthday party last fall. It was strange to walk into the condo after all that time. Kind of depressing, actually."

"I'm sorry," he said.

I picked up my wine and tried to appear laid back about it all. "What can you do? Mom wants to sell the condo now and buy a new one in a different building. Maybe it's time I let her do that."

Gabriel set his fork down and pushed his plate aside.

"Are you finished?" I asked.

"Yes."

I watched him for a moment. "You regret asking me about Dean, don't you? Maybe we should have stuck to reminiscing."

"It's fine," he replied. "I don't regret anything. I'm glad you told me all that because I thought about you a lot. We all did. I mean . . . it was on the news and everything. That must have been a nightmare."

"It was. Having a rock star involved made it difficult to go to the grocery store without seeing pictures of Dean and the airplane in the newspapers. There was so much speculation about what went wrong and if there were drugs involved. I don't even want to think about that."

"No," Gabriel replied, agreeing with me. "It's horrible to imagine."

The waiter arrived and took our plates away, and we ordered coffee. While we waited for it to arrive, I sat forward and rested my forearms on the table. "Let's not talk about Dean anymore. Tell me about the musical you've been directing."

"I was going to get to that, actually," Gabriel said, also leaning forward. "It's next weekend, and you should bring Rose. There's an afternoon performance for children on Saturday. Bring your mom, and if Rachel wants to bring her daughter, she's welcome too."

"That sounds like fun."

"We'll stop by my place on the way home," Gabriel said, "and I'll give you tickets."

We spent the rest of the evening discussing state education and local politics. What a pleasure it was to talk about grown-up things and linger over coffee.

~

The following weekend, we attended *Cinderella, the Musical.* The high school auditorium was packed with crying babies and noisy, restless toddlers, but Gabriel took it all in stride. At one point, he sent the mice from the chorus into the aisles to dance with the children.

Later, after two enthusiastic curtain calls, we waited in the crowded lobby to congratulate him. When he finally emerged from backstage, Rose and Amelia had fallen asleep in their strollers, and my mother was expressing her desire for a dry martini.

"Well done," I said with enthusiasm as he approached.

Rachel hugged him. "That was incredible, Gabriel. Amelia loved it. Just look at her. She swooned when the prince walked by a few minutes ago, and now she's passed out cold."

Gabriel laughed. "I'm glad you enjoyed it. The students did a terrific job, didn't they?"

"They certainly did," my mother gushed. "And that boy who played the prince? What a voice. He'll have a Tony on his mantel one day, mark my words. You did a wonderful job, Gabriel."

"Thank you, Liz. That's very kind." He stepped forward and kissed her on the cheek.

"On that note," my mother added, "what is everyone doing for dinner this evening? Gabriel, are you free? Rachel? What is your charming husband up to?"

"No plans," Rachel replied.

"Then we should all get together and have some pasta at my place. The girls can come in their pajamas and fall asleep on my bed." She turned to Gabriel. "Please say you'll come. I'll have Maria prepare seafood linguine, which was always your favorite, if I recall."

"I'd be mad to pass up Maria's seafood linguine," Gabriel replied.

My mother wrapped her arm around his waist. "You are such a darling."

A family approached Gabriel to shake his hand and discuss music class, so we said goodbye and pushed the strollers toward the exit. I don't know why, but when we reached the door, I looked back at him. He looked back at me, too, and we watched each other for a moment before I walked out of the school, where I had to squint from the shock of the bright sunshine.

~

At my mother's request, Gabriel and Thomas brought their instruments to the dinner party. Gabriel also brought a bag of maracas and tambourines for the girls, which he presented to Rachel and me as he walked in the door.

"Noisemakers. Yippee," Rachel said with a laugh, inclining her head at me. "Maybe we should hide these until after dinner?"

"Good plan. Thanks for bringing them, though," I said to Gabriel. "It'll be fun."

The smell of seafood and cream wafted across the air, and my mother greeted Gabriel with a kiss on the cheek. She linked her arm through his and led him into the living room.

Rachel whispered in my ear. "You do realize that she'd give anything to see you two back together. And he looks awfully good in that black shirt."

I nudged her with my elbow. "Don't *you* start."

We followed them into the living room, where Rose and Amelia were sitting on the floor with Thomas, playing with a musical toy clock. As soon as Rose spotted Gabriel, she leaped to her feet, ran to him, and presented her Barney doll.

"Hello, Barney," he said as he knelt. "And hello, Rose. How are you?"

"Good." She wrapped her tiny hand around Gabriel's thumb and dragged him toward my mother's grand piano.

"Oh dear," I said to Rachel. "I should go rescue him."

Rachel clasped my arm. "No, don't. He's fine."

Gabriel picked Rose up under the arms, sat her gently on the piano bench, took a seat beside her, and played "Twinkle, Twinkle, Little Star." She tried to play a few keys, and he managed to accompany her rather nicely. It was a pleasure to watch.

~

The following day, Rachel and I took Rose and Amelia to the playground.

"That was fun last night," Rachel said as she pushed Amelia in the baby swing. "Thomas and Gabriel certainly hit it off."

After the girls had fallen asleep in my mother's room, Gabriel and Thomas set up their instruments and played old jazz standards until midnight.

"They sounded good together," I replied. "Mom loved it."

"What about you? Did *you* love it?"

I slid her a glance. "Of course. Gabriel's saxophone is so . . ."

"Sexy?"

I laughed. "Okay, we'll go with that."

Rose yelled, "Faster!"

"How is that man still single?" Rachel asked. "That's what I want to know."

I pushed Rose harder in her swing. "I don't know, but I had to admit . . . I didn't feel right, enjoying myself so much."

"Let me guess. You felt disloyal to Dean?"

"Yes. I know it's crazy, because he's not here, but it felt like a betrayal—to let our daughter sit at the piano with my ex-boyfriend. And when I watched them play the maracas after supper, I was kind of . . ." I paused.

"Kind of what?"

"I don't know. Enraptured? Is that wrong?"

Rachel pushed Amelia a few times and seemed hesitant about what to say next. "You know, I find it interesting that you always talk about Dean as if he's just gone away on a trip or like he got lost somewhere. You never use the word *died* or *passed*."

"I'm aware."

She looked at me. "Is that what you believe? That he might still come home? And that's why you don't feel like you can have feelings for another man?"

I thought about it for a moment. "Mom thinks I should see a therapist to help me accept that he's gone. Funny. That used to be Dean's job, helping people through the stages of grief. Maybe that's why I don't see the point in it. I did a documentary film on this very subject, so I already understand what's going on here. I can't reach acceptance because I never saw a body, and I'm still in denial. I don't see how a therapist is going to change that. Unless they can locate the wreckage."

"Maybe you just need to fall in love again," Rachel suggested. "Maybe that's what's happening now."

I shook my head. "No. I'm not ready for that."

"You say you're not ready, but you also said you were enraptured by the sight of Gabriel playing the maracas with Rose last night."

"Yes, but I don't think I was enraptured by Gabriel, specifically. I'm just dreaming of a father figure for my daughter. If Dean walked onto the playground right now, the problem would be solved."

"But Dean isn't coming back," Rachel reminded me. "Ever. So if you want a father figure for Rose, you need to consider someone who actually exists." Rachel slowed Amelia's swing. "Want to get down?" she asked.

"Yes!"

We pulled both swings to a halt, lifted the safety bars, and set the girls on the ground. Rose took off toward the baby slides, and we all followed.

"I understand that you're just trying to help," I said to Rachel as we helped our daughters up the little ladder and held on to them as they slid to the ground. "Because you want me to be happy, and I want that too. But Gabriel and I are just friends, and I don't want to wreck that by leading him on and hurting him again."

"I see." She let out a sigh of defeat. "Just don't forget that it's a miracle he's still single, and he won't be for long, so don't take it for granted that he'll wait around forever."

"I don't want him to wait around," I insisted. "That's exactly what happened before, and I felt bad about it. For years."

Rachel shook her head at me. "There's no arguing with you, is there?"

"Not about this. I'll be ready when I'm ready, and that time is not now. Whatever is meant to be will be."

She helped Amelia up the ladder again. "Sometimes I think it will take an act of God to make you let another man into your life."

"Maybe," I replied. Then I called out to Rose, "Who wants ice cream?"

She ran to me, eager to get back in her stroller.

~

Two weeks passed, and the subject of Gabriel did not come up again. Neither Rachel nor my mother mentioned him once. And he didn't call.

After a month, I began to wonder why. Had I talked about Dean too much when we had dinner together in the Greek restaurant?

Probably.

When another Friday night rolled around, I found myself at Blockbuster again, browsing the classics section after a walk with Rose and Ziggy through Central Park. It was crowded, as usual, and I couldn't help but glance around at the other customers, wondering if I might bump into Gabriel.

I began to imagine what I would do if I did. Maybe this time, I would invite him to my place to watch something together after Rose was asleep. He only lived a few blocks away. It seemed strange that we never got together, even as friends.

I picked up a movie with Rosalind Russell and read the back-cover description, then replaced it on the shelf and continued looking. Finally, I realized I was being ridiculous, lingering in the store and trying to conjure Gabriel somehow with the force of my imagination. But he didn't appear. Eventually, I stood in line and rented three movies for the weekend.

After we returned home, I gave Rose a bath and read her a story. When she was finally asleep, I made popcorn and watched Alfred Hitchcock's first color film, *Rope*—the story of a sinister murder amid a group of college students.

When I went to bed, I wished I had chosen something lighter, because I couldn't stop thinking about the dead body that was hidden in a chest beneath the buffet table, right under everyone's noses as they sampled the food. I had a hard time sleeping that night.

CHAPTER 25
OLIVIA

The September air was cool and crisp the morning I dropped Rose off for her first day at Kinder Social Time. She was signed up for three sessions a week at a children's center in Greenwich Village, which promised arts and crafts, games, and sing-alongs. I was excited for her to learn new social skills, but when it came time to leave her, she cried and clung to my leg, and I almost changed my mind about the program, thinking she was too young. Thankfully, a teacher stepped in and lured Rose into the classroom with the promise of finger painting. When I was certain that she was comfortable, I left the building and walked to a little coffee shop I used to frequent when I lived in the neighborhood. I ordered a large latte with a chocolate chip muffin and was on my way out when I bumped into an old friend who was on his way in.

"Olivia! How are you?"

It was Brendan, from Tisch. He was sporting a trendy new haircut and a brown leather jacket and jeans.

"I'm okay," I replied as we hugged. "It's good to see you. What have you been up to?"

"I'm working on a TV series for NBC," he explained as we moved out of the doorway and spoke on the sidewalk. "We're shooting some scenes around the corner. How about you?"

I adjusted my purse strap on my shoulder and pointed in the direction of the play center. "I just dropped my daughter off at preschool."

His cheeks flushed a little. "Oh. Listen . . . I heard about what happened to your husband. I'm really sorry. I was going to send a card, but I didn't have your address . . ."

I waved a hand dismissively. "Please, it's fine. It's been a few years now. All is well."

It was an awkward conversation, so I changed the subject. "I thought you went to LA after graduation?"

"I did. I worked on a bunch of shows for NBC, but when they needed someone in New York, I was quick to volunteer."

"You're enjoying it?"

"A hundred percent. What about you? Working on anything?"

"Just motherhood."

He shifted uneasily as if he wasn't quite sure what to say in response.

I was annoyed with myself for saying "*just* motherhood," as if it were less important than what he was doing.

"Hey, listen," he said. "I'm about to grab a coffee and head back. Would you like to see the set? I can get you past the barricades. Maybe it'll inspire you."

I tried not to be offended by the suggestion that I was suffering from a lack of inspiration or motivation. Rose was the center of my world. She kept me busy and inspired enough, and I liked being a full-time mother. I was happy with my life.

"I wish I could," I replied, checking my watch, "but I have a bunch of errands to run before I pick up my daughter. But thank you for the invitation. It was really good to see you."

His shoulders drooped a little, as if he was surprised and disappointed that I had not leaped at the chance to go with him. "It was good to see you too."

There was another awkward pause as we stood on the sidewalk.

"Bye, Brendan." I watched him enter the coffee shop. Then I turned and walked back to my car.

~

"I think it might have been a pickup line," I said to Rachel when I called her that afternoon.

"I'm sure most women would fall over backward to get on a film set and see some TV stars," Rachel replied. "That line probably works wonders for him normally. But you're not most women."

"No, I'm not," I said with a sigh. Rose was down for a nap, so I sat at the kitchen table with a cup of Earl Grey tea. "Maybe there's something wrong with me. Wouldn't most women in my situation be open to a relationship by now? It's been more than three years, and I act like I'm still married." I held my hand up and looked at my wedding ring, which I had not yet removed.

"You're the one who said you'll be ready when you're ready, and whatever will be will be."

"I said that when I felt like everyone was pressuring me to get back together with Gabriel."

"No one was pressuring you," she argued. "Your mother invited him for dinner as a thank-you for the tickets to see *Cinderella*. That's all."

"Mmm." I tugged at the string attached to my tea bag and bobbed it up and down in the mug. "But why didn't he call me after that? I never heard from him after that dinner."

"Did you want to hear from him?" Rachel asked. "I seem to recall that you didn't."

I sat back in my chair. "Well, I wasn't ready for anything serious."

"But you're ready now?"

"No, I'm not saying that. But I do think about him sometimes." I sat forward as a thought came to me. "Is he seeing someone? Is that why he hasn't called and why everyone stopped pushing him on me?"

Rachel laughed. "For the hundredth time, no one was pushing him on you. But now that you ask, yes, I did hear that he went out on a few dates."

My stomach clenched a little. "With whom?"

"I don't know her name or anything about her, only that they were fixed up on a blind date."

"Who fixed them up?" Surely not Rachel or Thomas.

"Someone at his school," Rachel told me. "One of the other teachers, I think. But don't worry. It didn't work out."

"I'm not worried," I assured her, though I wasn't sorry to hear that it hadn't developed into anything. "He has every right to date people, and so do I. If I was so inclined, that's exactly what I would do."

Rachel laughed into the phone. "Sure. Listen, I have to go. I'm not even close to being packed for our trip, and Amelia just woke up."

"Let me know if you need a ride to the airport," I offered. "I don't mind. I have nothing else on the go."

"Thank you, but Thomas already has a car arranged. So if I don't talk to you before we leave, I might call you from Atlanta. Thomas will be busy with the conference, and I might get bored."

"I'm sure you'll have a wonderful time."

~

The next night, I watched *Seinfeld* and began to feel a vague pain in the right side of my lower belly. I suspected it had something to do with the fact that I hadn't eaten much that day, so I forced myself to make a piece of toast and force it down.

By midnight, the pain had worsened, and I was growing concerned. I went to check on Rose, but the sight of her resting peacefully in her toddler bed made me wonder what would happen if my abdominal pain was something serious and I collapsed or dropped dead. What if I was deathly ill? My mother was in Europe, and Rachel was in Atlanta with Thomas. Who would look after Rose?

When the pain became so excruciating that I threw up in the bathroom toilet, I decided I needed to go to the hospital. Feeling panicked, I hurried to my desk, pulled open the drawer, and located my address book. I flipped through the pages until I found Gabriel's phone number.

He answered after the second ring. "Hello?"

"Gabriel? It's Olivia. I'm sorry to bother you at this hour, but I'm in a bind." I clutched my stomach and doubled over in agony.

"What's wrong?" he asked with concern.

"I don't know, but I'm having terrible abdominal pains. I didn't know who else to call."

"Do you need to go to the hospital?" he asked.

"Yes. But my mother's away, and it's the middle of the night. I'm afraid to bring Rose with me in case it's something serious like appendicitis and they need to admit me. You're only a few blocks away, so I thought maybe . . ."

"How long have you been in pain?" he asked.

"It started tonight, after I put Rose to bed."

"You should definitely get checked out," he said. "I'll be right there."

"Thank you." I hung up the phone and waited.

~

"Maybe you should call an ambulance," Gabriel suggested when he walked in the door and saw me wincing and squirming.

"A cab will be faster," I replied. "I just need to get to the ER."

"Do you want me to go with you? I could bring Rose and look after her there."

"No. She'll be better off here." I pointed at the kitchen and told him what to feed Rose if she woke up hungry during the night. "And you can sleep in my bed."

"Don't worry about anything," he replied. "I'll take tomorrow off work in case you do get admitted."

"Are you sure?"

"Yes, it's no problem. They'll get a substitute."

"Thank you so much, Gabriel. I can't tell you how much I appreciate this."

He walked me to the elevator and pushed the down button. The doors opened right away, and I stepped inside.

"I'll call as soon as I know what's going on," I told him.

I couldn't say anything more because I was in too much pain as the doors slid closed between us.

~

Six hours later, I used a pay phone in the hospital to call my apartment. Gabriel answered immediately, as if he had been waiting by the phone.

"Olivia?"

"Yes, it's me. I'm all done here, and everything's okay. They're sending me home. Is Rose awake yet?"

"No, she's still sleeping. But what happened? What was it?"

"It was something called mittelschmerz," I explained.

"Mittelschmerz. I've never heard of it."

"Me neither. But it has something to do with ovulation, where fluid from the ovary leaks into the abdominal cavity, which is what causes the pain. In my case it was severe. But it just kind of . . . resolved itself, I guess."

Gabriel was quiet for a moment. "Are they sure that's all it was? I hope they didn't miss anything, that it's not something more serious."

"Me too. But they did all sorts of tests. The doctor ordered blood work and did an ultrasound. They even did a pregnancy test. I insisted that it wasn't necessary—that it wasn't even remotely possible that I could be pregnant. Guess what the doctor said."

"Tell me."

"He asked me if I had a uterus. I said, 'Yes, I do,' and his response was, 'Then we are doing a pregnancy test.'"

Gabriel chuckled softly. "I guess they had to cover all their bases. But as long as you're feeling better and they're certain it's not something else . . ."

"I do feel better," I told him. "The pain started to go away about an hour after I arrived at the hospital, but they still did the tests. I thought for sure it was appendicitis. I'm so glad I'm not in surgery right now."

"So am I." He let out a breath of relief. "So does this mean you're coming home now?"

"Yes," I replied. "I'll take a cab and see you in about fifteen minutes."

~

It was 6:30 a.m. when I walked through the door and smelled fresh coffee brewing. Gabriel was in the kitchen stirring something on the stove. When he heard me come in, he met me at the door with Ziggy at his side. "Welcome home."

"Thank you." I patted Ziggy on the head. "I don't know what I would have done if you weren't here. I would have taken Rose to the hospital with me, I suppose, which would have been difficult."

He rested his hands on my shoulders. "Are you hungry? I'm making porridge."

"Starved. And that sounds wonderful." I hung my purse and jacket in the hall closet and joined Gabriel and Ziggy in the kitchen. "You could probably still make it to work now," I mentioned, glancing at the clock on the microwave.

He shook his head. "No, they've already arranged for a substitute, so I'll just take the day off. You must be exhausted. You haven't slept all night."

"I probably look like death warmed over," I replied, making a futile attempt to fluff my hair.

He went to the fridge and took out some milk. "Have a seat. And after we eat, you should go back to bed. I'll stay here until you wake up."

I felt both pleased and flustered because I wasn't accustomed to being pampered at home. It was always just Rose and me, and I was the one doing the pampering. "Are you sure? I feel like I've imposed enough already."

"It's no imposition," he replied. "And didn't you mention something about Rose having preschool this morning? I could take her to that while you sleep. Just tell me where it is and what time."

"Oh my gosh." I yawned. "You are the cat's meow."

He laughed at that and served me some porridge. "Would you like blueberries or sliced bananas with that?"

"Both would be amazing."

"Coming right up." He peeled a banana, sliced it, then sprinkled some fresh blueberries on my serving and poured milk on it. He set it on the table in front of me. "What else do you need? A spoon. One second . . ."

Just then, we heard the pitter-patter of little feet down the hall. Rose, wearing her pink nightgown with the unicorn on it, appeared in the kitchen doorway, rubbing her eyes. She looked up at Gabriel, and her lips parted slightly.

"Good morning, Miss Rose," he said in a friendly voice. "And good morning to you as well, Master Barney."

Rose scratched her bum. "We just woke up."

"I see that," Gabriel replied. "It's going to be a beautiful day. Does Barney like porridge?"

Rose walked to the chair opposite mine at the table and climbed onto it. "We like Cheerios."

"All right then." Gabriel turned to me. "Do we have Cheerios?"

With a mouth full of porridge and blueberries, I pointed at the cupboard over the dishwasher. "Up there."

"Got it."

A short while later, we were all seated at the table enjoying our breakfasts. Gabriel asked Rose how she liked her preschool.

She pointed at her artwork on the fridge. "We go today?"

"I'd love to take you," Gabriel replied, "if that's all right with your mom?"

He looked at me, and I nodded with enthusiasm. "I think that sounds like great fun. Rose, will you show Gabriel how to buckle you into your car seat?"

She nodded.

"Perfect!" Gabriel held up his hand for a high five. Rose slapped her little palm against his and giggled adorably.

After breakfast, Rose went into the living room to play with her dolls, and Gabriel turned to me. "What time does her preschool finish?"

"Noon."

"And does Rose usually nap?"

"Yes, after lunch, around two o'clock."

For a moment, we watched her in the living room. Then Gabriel made a suggestion. "What if I pack a lunch, pick her up at noon, and take her to the park for a picnic with Ziggy? I could bring her back here for her nap at two, and you could get some sleep until then."

I let out a sigh of absolute rapture. "Oh my gosh. That sounds heavenly, because my eyelids feel like sandpaper right now."

"Then you should definitely go straight to bed."

"I will. Just let me get Rose dressed, and I'll see you off." I stood up from the table and called to her. "Rose, let's go brush your teeth and get ready for preschool."

"Okay!" She scrambled to her feet.

As I led her to her bedroom, Gabriel was already clearing off the table and tidying the kitchen. I couldn't even begin to fathom how much I appreciated all that.

~

I woke to the sound of Rose's quiet voice in the living room. My eyes fluttered open, and it took a few seconds for me to remember that Gabriel had taken her to Kinder Social Time and then for a picnic in the park. What time was it? I rolled over to check the alarm clock next to the bed and discovered it was 1:45 p.m. They must have just gotten home.

My first instinct was to leap out of bed and assume my motherly duties, because it was difficult for me to turn that "mother button" off. But when I heard Rose chatting quietly and comfortably with Gabriel—as if he had already coached her to keep her voice low—I decided to lay my head back down on the pillow and relax for a bit.

Fifteen minutes later, when I was more fully awake, I got up and went to see how their day had gone. Still in the same outfit I'd worn to the hospital the night before, I shuffled to the living room, where Rose and Gabriel were sitting on the sofa with a large picture book on their laps. Ziggy was stretched out on the floor in front of the coffee table.

Rose saw me and jumped up. "Mommy!" She ran to me and hugged my knees. "We had a picnic. Ziggy chased a Fwisbee!"

"That sounds like fun," I replied and looked across at Gabriel, who was sitting easily on the sofa. "Thanks again for spending the day with her."

"It was my pleasure. We had a great time, didn't we, Rose?"

She returned to the sofa and snuggled next to him. "Finish story," she said. "Then nap."

"That's right," he replied. "It'll be nap time. And look, Ziggy's already asleep."

"He's tired," she said, her mouth spreading open with a wide yawn.

I quietly backed away toward the kitchen. "I'll let you finish the book."

Coffee was what I needed. I moved to the cupboard and focused on brewing a fresh pot. A few minutes later, while the coffee was dripping, Rose came out to see me. "Gabriel put me in bed? Read story?"

"Of course," I replied. "As long as he doesn't mind."

Gabriel walked into the kitchen just then. "He doesn't mind at all. Let's go pick out another book. Just a short one this time."

Off they went, which gave me time to pour myself a cup of coffee and sip it at the table.

About twenty minutes later, he returned to the kitchen. "She's almost asleep."

"That's wonderful," I said in a low voice. "Would you like some coffee?"

"Sure."

I stood up and poured him a cup. "Black?"

"Yes."

We decided to move into the living room, where we sat down on the sofa.

"Did you sleep this morning?" he asked.

"Like a baby. As soon as you left, I was out like a light. Did everything go okay? She didn't make a fuss when you dropped her off?"

"Not at all," he replied. "She was very proud to show me how brave and grown up she was."

I laughed at that. "You didn't see her on the first day. She clung to me like Velcro. But I'm glad she's used to it now."

"She did great. She's a wonderful little girl. You should be very proud."

I laid my hand over my heart. "That's the best compliment you could ever give me. Because sometimes I worry."

"About what?"

I waved a hand about. "Oh, you know, raising her on my own. It's tough sometimes."

"It must be." Gabriel sipped his coffee, and we sat quietly in the stillness of the afternoon.

"But enough about that," I said, not wanting the conversation to spin off, yet again, into the territory of my tragic widowhood. "Tell me about your picnic. I think that's the first time Rose ever saw a Frisbee. We always throw a ball for Ziggy."

At the sound of his name, Ziggy lifted his head, looked at me, then closed his eyes again and lowered his chin to his paws.

"She loved the Frisbee," Gabriel said. "She asked if we could do it again tomorrow. I told her she'd have to ask you about that." He paused. "You can have my Frisbee if you like. I've got a few of them."

"Oh. That's very generous. Thank you." Strangely, I was disappointed by his offer because I interpreted it to mean that he didn't want to join us. I could hardly blame him. It had been a long day.

"You must be exhausted," I said. "Did you at least get some sleep here last night while I was at the hospital?"

"I slept about four hours on your sofa."

We sipped our coffees, and for the first time in my life, I felt an awkwardness between us. I had the distinct feeling that Gabriel wanted to leave.

Sure enough, he finished his coffee in a single gulp and set the empty cup on the table. "I should probably get going." He stood up.

"There's no need to rush off." I rose to my feet as well and walked him to the door.

"It was a lot of fun today," he said with a smile. "I enjoyed playing hooky."

"I'm glad about that, at least." I watched him pull on his jacket.

"I'm just glad you're okay." He turned and opened the door to leave. "Say goodbye to Rose for me."

"I will. Thanks again, Gabriel."

He walked out, but instead of taking the elevator, he disappeared into the stairwell.

I shut the door behind him and stood for a second, baffled. Why had he been in such a hurry to leave? I wondered if he had a date later.

For the next few minutes, I tidied the living room and pondered the confusing state of my emotions. Gabriel was a good man. There was no doubt about that. It wasn't a huge eye-opener for me. I'd always considered him to be the most gentlemanly of all my male friends. Rose was certainly enamored with him, and she enjoyed his company. And he looked better than ever before. He was more confident, more of a man, compared to that young, lanky boy I'd dated in college.

As I knelt and picked at some crumbs on the carpet, I thought of the moment when I'd come out of my bedroom and seen this mature version of my old boyfriend sitting on the sofa with Rose, a large picture book on their laps. Something inside me had shaken, and I'd felt a release of some kind, followed by an unexpected surge of excitement. I sat back on my heels because I recognized exactly what it was, and I was surprised by it. I hadn't felt anything like it in years.

It was the thrill of physical attraction.

Goodness. I had thought that part of me was permanently closed for business. Shut down forever. Maybe I wasn't as dead inside as I thought.

With that revelation, I waited ten minutes for Gabriel to reach his apartment. Then I went to the phone in the kitchen, and I called him.

"You're probably tired of hearing from me," I said in a light and breezy tone, "but I was wondering if you're free tomorrow afternoon, because I'd love for you to come with us to the park. If you want to, that is."

He was quiet for a moment, and my tummy exploded with nervous knots because I sensed rejection in the offing.

"I don't know, Olivia," he said. "I'd like to, but . . ."

That was the moment I knew. I had feelings for this man, and not just feelings of friendship. Today they had morphed into something else.

All I wanted was for Gabriel to say yes and take a chance on me. To forgive me for the heartbreak in the past and start over, fresh. How could I convince him that I was ready to move past the loss of Dean and that I wouldn't toy with his affections again?

"I hope you know how much I care about you," Gabriel said.

"Of course I do." *But you don't want me.* I felt an acute sense of loss.

He spoke in a low, solemn voice. "I know I said that I wanted us to be friends, Olivia, and I thought that maybe we could be. But the truth is . . ."

He stopped talking, and I worried that my heart was about to be crushed.

"I find it difficult to be around you," he continued. "Because I want more than just friendship. I always have. And every time I see you, it just piles on more torture."

I should have felt sympathy or guilt as I usually did whenever I thought of how I had hurt him when we were younger. But this time, my heart soared.

"I find it difficult to be friends with you too," I told him. "I've always regretted what happened between us. I regretted how I hurt you. But there's more to it than that, Gabriel." I paused.

"Yes?"

I cleared my throat, nervously. "There's a love that's always been there. It never went away, but I needed to keep it buried and avoid you because I met someone else and I married him, and now I've been grieving for that man, because he died."

There it was. The word I hadn't been able to speak aloud. Until now.

"But I don't want to grieve forever," I continued, "and I . . ." I swallowed uncomfortably. "I miss you."

"I miss you too," he said. "But I don't want to feel like I'm your backup plan. That if Dean walked through your door tomorrow, I'd be second choice."

He was quiet for a moment, so I sat down. "You're not second choice. Not now."

Besides, that was never going to happen. Dean was never going to walk through my door. He was gone. That part of my life was over forever.

The clock ticked steadily on the wall, and the air conditioner switched on.

Finally, Gabriel spoke. "So what are we going to do about this?"

I considered that carefully. "I don't know. I think that's up to you."

I waited anxiously for him to respond.

"Maybe we could take things slow," he finally said. "See how it goes. Or maybe we should just relax and play Frisbee tomorrow."

I felt a tremendous rush of joy. "I'd like that."

Neither of us seemed like we wanted to hang up, so I tossed out another suggestion. "Unless you want to come back over and just hang out? I could cook us dinner later." I paused. "Or maybe you already have plans?"

"I don't have plans," he quickly replied, "and I'd love to come over. When?"

I bit my lower lip, feeling shy. "Is now too soon?"

"Not too soon at all."

No hesitation there. I giggled inwardly, and we said goodbye and hung up the phone.

For the next few minutes, I could do nothing but pace around my apartment impatiently, waiting for Gabriel to arrive. When I finally heard the elevator bell go *ding*, I ran out to the hall.

Gabriel stepped off the elevator. He saw me standing there, smiling. Everything slowed. My joy was immeasurable. For a few seconds, I felt as if I were floating, that we were the only two people left in the universe. My heart swelled with happiness, and I wanted to laugh and cry at the same time.

Gabriel walked slowly toward me until no distance between us remained.

"Hi," he gently said and took hold of my hand. Our fingers wove together, and I felt his warmth. I reveled in that small physical connection as our eyes met.

The corner of my mouth curled up in a tentative smile. "I'm so glad you came back."

"Me too."

Slowly, cautiously, he drew me into his arms and held me, and I realized that the sensation of floating had been the blissful release of the past. It was the sweet and splendid mercy of finally letting go.

1997
NEW YORK

CHAPTER 26

OLIVIA

There were moments, in the early years of my second marriage, when I felt as if I had been blessed with not one but two great loves. The first was filled with promise, but that life was cut short. For a while, I lost faith in future happiness. I crawled into a dark cave, curled up in a ball, and stayed there for ages. But somehow, miraculously, I'd been offered a second chance, and I was so very grateful that I had accepted that gift.

As I sat in the high school gymnasium listening to the children's choir perform a jazzy rendition of "Have Yourself a Merry Little Christmas," I hugged my two-year-old son, Joel, on my lap, while Rose, now six, sat primly on her chair beside me. Gabriel was up front conducting the choir, and the baby in my belly was kicking with a steady rhythm, like a future drummer destined for stardom.

Earlier in the week, I'd told Gabriel that this was going to be the best Christmas ever.

"Really?" he'd asked uncertainly, as if he still couldn't quite believe that I liked this life better than the previous one.

I raised his hand to my lips and kissed the back of it. "Yes, really, you goof." I spoke in a playful tone, making fun of him for having any doubts, because there was no need for him to question anything.

I loved him with every inch of my soul, I was grateful for his presence in my life, and I was as happy as any woman could be. We'd built a beautiful life together, surrounded by family, good friends, music, children we loved, and a new baby on the way. What more could any woman ask for?

And now it was Christmas. My favorite time of the year.

After the concert, snow began to fall. The weatherman had predicted a severe winter storm, so we drove home and settled in for the night, cozy in our warm town house on the Upper West Side. The city was quiet and peaceful with gently falling snow. Colorful Christmas lights flickered in all the windows on our street. Our own Christmas tree was lit, and presents were piled high on the carpet beneath it.

We watched *Home Alone* with Rose and Joel, while Ziggy, now a senior dog who no longer chased Frisbees, slept soundly on the floor at my feet.

Later, we put the children to bed and tidied up the living room.

"Tomorrow's the last day of school before the holiday break," I said, "and it's probably going to be a snow day."

"Looks that way," Gabriel replied. "I suspect there are children all over the city of New York hoping that will be the case."

"Teachers too," I mentioned with a smile.

He moved toward me, took my face in his hands, and I melted at his touch and the way he looked at me. "You're beautiful. Do you know that?"

"I think beauty, in this case, is in the eye of the beholder." I felt as big as a hot-air balloon.

He chuckled softly as he kissed me, and my body responded with desire. "Should we go to bed now?" he asked.

"You read my mind."

He took my hand, switched off the tree lights, and led me up the stairs.

We were quiet as we undressed because we didn't want to wake the children. When Gabriel slid into bed beside me, he whispered, "I love you," and the touch of his lips caused a fever in my blood. I turned to him and sighed softly with rapture as he held me in the precious warmth of his embrace.

~

I was dreaming about a unicorn galloping across a frozen lake and barreling toward me when Joel leaped onto the bed and shouted, "Snow!"

Barely awake, I glanced at the clock. "It's past eight." With a flash of panic, I sat up. "We slept in."

"No, we didn't," Gabriel replied. "And do you know why?" He tossed Joel onto the mattress like a wrestler and started tickling him. "It's a snow day!"

I got out of bed and pulled on my bathrobe just as Rose sauntered into the room, rubbing her eyes. "Is school canceled?"

"It sure is," Gabriel replied. "Who wants pancakes?"

"Me!" Joel shouted.

Rose leaped onto the bed. "Me too!"

"Not before you both get tickled!" Gabriel pulled Rose into the fray. She laughed and squealed, and Joel started a pillow fight.

"I'll go start the coffee," I said, leaving them behind to duke it out in their pajamas.

Downstairs, I opened the drapes to look out at the street. The sun was shining, and neighbors were outside clearing off their steps. I heard the scrape of a shovel on the sidewalk next door and the roar of a snowplow on the main road. There was at least a foot of snow down, and our car was buried.

"Guess we're not going anywhere today," I said to myself. Then I set to work preparing breakfast—pancakes, bacon, and a big bowl of fruit salad.

The children bounded down the stairs just as I was pouring the batter onto the skillet. They ran to the front window.

"Can we build a snowman?" Rose asked.

"That's a great idea." But I knew it would have to be Gabriel's activity because I was in no condition to push a giant snowball around.

He came downstairs, found me in front of the stove flipping bacon, and wrapped his arms around my enormous waist. "That smells terrific."

I set the spatula down, faced him, and slid my hands up his chest. "Good morning, husband."

"Good morning, wife."

Rose walked into the kitchen just then. "Ew, gross."

Gabriel chuckled and backed away from me. "Did I hear someone say they wanted to build a snowman?"

I returned to the bacon sizzling in the hot pan while Gabriel opened the fridge and took out a carton of orange juice.

"Me!" Rose replied.

"Help me set the table then," he said, "and we'll go out after breakfast."

The baby kicked in my belly, and I pressed my hand to that energetic foot. "I hear you. You can't wait to join the fun. It won't be long now."

"Who are you talking to?" Rose asked as she laid napkins on the table.

"Your brother or sister, whatever the case may be."

She approached and shouted at my belly button. "We're going to build a snowman today! But don't worry! We'll build another one for you when you get here!"

I rubbed the top of her head. "That's very sweet. You're going to be a wonderful sister."

An hour later, I bundled Rose and Joel up in snowsuits, scarves, mittens, and snow boots, and Gabriel took them out to the backyard. While they rolled giant snowballs around, clearing long swaths of green grass in the process, I went upstairs to shower and get dressed.

By the time I returned to the kitchen, the snowplow had gone by. Out back, the snowman was complete, and the children were packing extra snow into the gaps.

I opened the back door and called out to them. "Do you need a carrot for his nose?"

"Yes!" Rose replied. "And a scarf and hat!"

"Coming right up!" I went to the refrigerator and hunted around the vegetable drawer for the perfect nose for Frosty, then opened the bench in the front hall to search for an old hat and scarf. I was down on my knees, rifling through piles of mismatched mittens, when the doorbell rang. Assuming it was Rose's friend Mary Beth from two doors down, I leaned on the bench as I rose heavily to my feet and made my way to the door.

I opened it with a smile, but it wasn't Mary Beth on my front step. It was two men in dark overcoats. One of them flashed a badge at me, and my initial fear was that something had happened to my mother.

"Good morning," the taller man said. "Are you Olivia Hamilton?"

"Yes, but it's Olivia Morrison now."

They both glanced at my belly, then met my gaze again. "I'm Detective Johnson, and this is Detective Russo. We'd like to ask you a few questions. Could we come in?"

"Of course," I replied and stepped aside. They removed their snow boots on the welcome mat, then followed me into the living room.

"Please have a seat. Can I get you anything? A cup of coffee or tea?"

"That's very kind," Detective Russo replied, "but we're fine, thank you."

They both sat on the sofa while I sat on the upholstered chair across from them, next to the Christmas tree. "What's this about?"

Detective Russo pulled a small notepad and pen from his jacket pocket, while Detective Johnson leaned forward slightly.

"Not long ago," Detective Johnson said, "the body of a young woman was discovered in New Jersey, in the forest just north of Oakland. You might have heard about it on the news?"

I suddenly felt a little sick to my stomach because I couldn't imagine how that grisly discovery could have anything to do with me, but obviously it did, or they wouldn't be sitting in my living room.

"I did hear about that," I replied. "It's horrible."

"Yes, it is," Detective Johnson replied. "We've identified the victim as Melanie Brown. Does that name ring a bell for you?"

They both studied my expression intently.

"Should it?" I asked. "I mean . . . no. Who was she?"

The detectives shared a look, and then Russo answered my question with candor. "Until last week, Melanie Brown was considered a missing person. She disappeared in 1986. She was a student at Columbia, aged twenty-four at the time." They continued to watch me, as if they expected me to suddenly remember something, but nothing about that sounded familiar to me.

I shook my head. "I'm sorry. I don't know anything about her."

Detective Russo regarded me with laser-like focus. "What about your late husband? Dean Robinson. Did he ever mention her?"

I drew back. "No, never. Why?" They couldn't possibly think that Dean had anything to do with this. "When did you say she went missing?"

"October fourteenth, 1986."

Again, I shook my head. "We had just started dating around that time."

"Yes, that's why we're here. As it turns out, Melanie was one of your husband's clients at the Wentworth Wellness Clinic."

"I see." I sat back and pondered this. "I'm afraid he never shared anything with me about his clients. He was very conscious about confidentiality issues. Have you talked to Dr. Caroline Weaver? She owned the practice—and still does, I believe. She might know something. Or maybe she still has Melanie's file."

"We've already spoken to her," Detective Johnson told me, "which is why we're here. Dr. Weaver couldn't locate Ms. Brown's file. It went missing, and she didn't know why. So now we need to rule out the possibility that your husband might have had something to do with her disappearance or death."

I laughed dismissively. "No. That's not possible. Dean would never do anything like that."

The two detectives glanced at each other, as if they were considering how much information to share with me. Then Detective Johnson spoke with candor.

"Your husband was questioned in 1986, shortly after Ms. Brown disappeared. At the time, it was just a missing person case, but now that we have a body, it's been ruled a homicide, and we're going back over everything with a fine-tooth comb. Can you tell us why your husband quit his job at the clinic and moved to Miami with you shortly after Ms. Brown went missing?"

I blinked a few times. "We moved to Miami to get married, and he quit his job because he wasn't happy in his work. He'd always dreamed of being a pilot ever since he was a boy, so I was supportive of that, and I encouraged him. It was my idea, actually, for him to quit and move to Miami with me. I'm the one who suggested it."

They stared at me for a moment, so I felt compelled to explain myself further. "I was having some issues with my family. With my father, specifically. He was a bit controlling, so I wanted to leave New York. I suggested a fresh start for both of us."

"So it was *your* idea," Detective Russo repeated, seeming surprised.

"Yes." I paused and felt a flicker of unease. "Should I be calling my lawyer?"

He held up a hand. "No, that's not necessary. We're just gathering information, and we appreciate your help. I don't suppose your husband—"

"My *late* husband," I said, correcting him. "I've remarried."

"Of course. Apologies." He cleared his throat and continued. "I don't suppose Dean left any papers behind that you might have kept?"

"Are you looking for the patient file?" I asked.

"Yes, or anything else that might be of help to us. Even if it seems irrelevant, it might tell us something."

I shook my head. "No, I didn't keep any of his work-related papers, and I would certainly remember a patient file, because after his plane went missing, I went through all of his things very carefully. There was never anything like that. And I've since shredded most of it that wasn't a personal keepsake. I'm sorry."

Detective Johnson nodded. "All right then. So . . . is there anything else you can think of that might shed light on this?"

"I don't think so, except to say that I'm sure you're wasting your time on Dean because he would never be involved in anything like that. He was a kind, loving person."

Both detectives stared at me fixedly.

"Okay," Russo said. "One last thing. Did you keep anything at all that belonged to him? A personal memento? Something like a hairbrush or an article of clothing?"

"Why would you need that?"

"For DNA testing," he explained.

I shook my head. "I don't understand."

They both shifted uncomfortably on the sofa. "The autopsy showed that Ms. Brown was pregnant at the time of her death."

The floor seemed to give way under my feet. I remained quiet for a few seconds, trying to digest the implications of what this man was asking for—and suggesting.

"We could get a warrant," he informed me, "if you're not willing to—"

"No, it's fine," I said. "I want to help in any way I can, and I'm sure that DNA testing will rule Dean out as a suspect, because there's no way he could have been . . ." I stopped myself, because my pulse was accelerating, and I decided it would be best not to say anything more.

"I just need to think about what I might have. I kept a box of some things. Would a pair of gloves work?"

Detective Johnson sat back. "Yes. That would be perfect. Could you get that for us?"

"Yes." I stood up. "Just give me a moment. The box is upstairs."

The back door opened, and Rose walked into the kitchen. "Mom! Where's the carrot?"

I turned to the detectives. "They're building a snowman out back. It's for his nose. Could you wait one second?"

"Certainly. Take your time."

I picked up the hat and scarf from the bench and returned to the kitchen, where the carrot was sitting on the counter. "Here you go," I said to Rose as I handed everything over.

"Thanks, Mom." She went outside again, and I was relieved that she hadn't seen the two strange men in our living room. I wasn't sure how I would explain what they were doing there.

I hurried up the stairs to my bedroom, where I kept a small cedar chest on the top shelf at the back corner of my closet. I needed a chair to reach it, and when I pulled it down, it was covered in dust. I hadn't touched it since Gabriel and I moved into the house shortly after we were married. At that time, when I packed up my apartment, I forced myself to part with most of the mementos from my marriage to Dean, keeping only what would fit in this cedar box.

I carefully got down from the chair, set the box on the bed, and raised the lid.

My heart squeezed like a fist at the sight of what was inside—some photographs, a few love letters Dean had written to me, his diploma from flight school, a copy of my student film with his interview, my wedding ring, and leather gloves I had given to him on our last Christmas together. These were cherished items—it was a box full of love—but now two men were sitting in my living room, waiting for me to give them a personal item with Dean's DNA on it to prove that he wasn't a killer.

It wasn't true. There was no possible way. Dean would never hurt anyone. I was certain of that.

I heard the back door open and close, followed by the sound of Gabriel and the children kicking snow off their boots in the mudroom. Quickly, I pulled the cards and letters out to reach the gloves beneath, and I left the box open on the bed.

"Here they are," I said to Detective Johnson when I returned to the living room.

He stood and took them from me. "Thank you. This will be very helpful." He reached into his jacket pocket for his card. "If you think of anything else, even if it seems unimportant, please give me a call."

"I will."

I walked them to the door.

As soon as they were gone, Gabriel emerged from the kitchen. "Who was that?" he asked with a note of concern.

"Detectives," I replied, glancing at him only briefly as I handed him the business card.

He read it, and his eyes lifted. "What did they want?"

Rose and Joel emerged from the kitchen as well. Rose wrapped her arms around my hips and looked up at me with a smile. "Daddy says we can have hot chocolate."

"Sure." I took her by the hand. "Let's go make some."

As I passed Gabriel, I said, "I'll explain later. Would you and Joel like to watch a movie?" I asked Rose.

"Can we watch *George of the Jungle*?"

I found the hot chocolate mix in the cupboard. "Of course."

Gabriel watched me with a frown, and I was so afraid of sliding away from him, down that gradual slope, into the cave where memories lived and breathed. To the place where Dean had once occupied all my thoughts.

Heaven help me. I didn't want to return to that darkness where unanswered questions could snowball into obsessions. My place was here, in the present, in the light, where happiness lived.

~

As soon as the children were settled on the sofa with the movie, I climbed the stairs to my bedroom and found Gabriel standing over the cedar box on the bed. The lid was open as I had left it, and the contents were spread all over the down comforter. He was flipping through a stack of photographs.

When he noticed me in the doorway, he set the pictures back inside the box and gestured toward the cards and letters that were scattered about. "I didn't know you kept all this. Though I'm not surprised. He was your husband. You had a life together. A life I don't know much about because you don't talk about that. You only ever talked about how he disappeared. But to see all this . . ."

I approached and stood beside him, and we each looked down at everything. "That box has been at the back corner of my closet since we moved in here," I explained. "I haven't opened it since." I glanced at a bunch of holiday and birthday cards that were tied together with a black ribbon. I was relieved that Gabriel hadn't looked at those, because Dean always wrote something very intimate and adoring. "I just thought I should keep some of these things in case Rose ever wanted to know about her biological father."

Gabriel reached for my hand and squeezed it, but his mood seemed low. "What did the detectives want? I assume it had something to do with Dean?"

"Yes. Let's sit down."

We moved to the two reading chairs near the window, and Gabriel sat on the edge of the cushion with his hands clasped together, his head bowed. It broke my heart to see him like that, looking so defeated.

"It's not what you're thinking," I said. "They didn't find the wreckage or anything like that."

His eyes lifted, and I wasn't sure if he was relieved or disappointed. "What did they want?"

I drew in a deep breath. "You know that Jane Doe they found in the woods in New Jersey recently?"

"Yes."

"Well, it turns out that she was one of Dean's clients when he was a therapist."

Gabriel blinked a few times. "Oh." He paused. "But what did they want from *you*? Because you wouldn't know anything about his former patients. Would you? Isn't that confidential?"

"It is. And he never shared anything with me."

"And they know Dean is dead, right?"

"Yes, they know. But this woman has been missing for a while, ever since around the time I started dating Dean. Apparently, they questioned him back then, but whatever he told them didn't help because they never found her. Not until now. But when they went back to the clinic—to revisit that part of her life, I suppose—they discovered that her patient file had gone missing, and his old boss has no idea what happened to it. Dean just happened to quit his job and leave the practice not long after the woman disappeared. He moved to Miami with me. So I guess that's why they're suspicious all of a sudden."

Gabriel sat back, dumbfounded. "My God. They don't think that Dean . . ."

I shrugged. "I don't know. But I can't blame them for looking into it. The situation does make it look a bit suspect. But I'm sure that Dean had nothing to do with her death. That file probably just got misplaced."

"Right," Gabriel replied, not looking entirely convinced. He glanced back at the bed. "So what were they looking for? Was there some piece of evidence that . . . ?"

"They want to do some DNA testing," I explained. "You know it's a thing now? They're solving crimes with it."

"Yes," Gabriel said. "I read about that. Apparently, the FBI has a growing database."

We sat in silence, listening to the faint music from the movie playing downstairs. Then Gabriel sat forward and took both my hands in his. "You don't actually think . . ."

Tears threatened, but I fought to suppress them and keep my voice steady as I spoke. "Of course not. But there's something else." Gabriel's brow furrowed with concern as he waited for me to continue. "The detectives said the woman was pregnant. That's why they want Dean's DNA. For paternity testing, basically."

"Oh God. That's horrible." I could see the wheels turning in Gabriel's mind. "But if he turns out to be the father, that would give him a motive."

"What? No!" I shook my head.

Gabriel sat back. "Think about it. If he was just starting to date you at the time, and he got one of his patients pregnant, he wouldn't want anyone to find out about that. He would know that he could lose you, and you're . . ."

My whole body tensed. "I'm what?"

"You're *you*."

"What is that supposed to mean?" I asked. "Are you talking about how rich I am? Are you suggesting that he was motivated to kill off an ex-girlfriend because he wanted my money?"

"No, no . . . ," Gabriel replied defensively. "Of course that's not what I'm suggesting." He went suddenly pale.

"That's what my father thought," I added. "It's why he cut me off. And you know how I felt about that. I never believed for a second that Dean just wanted me for my money, and I still don't. I never forgave my father for saying that."

Gabriel raised his hands in surrender, understanding that it was a sore spot with me. "I just meant that if he was in love with you, he wouldn't want to lose you."

I tried not to let myself get worked up. The last thing I wanted was to create tension with Gabriel. It wasn't fair, and I knew it.

"I'm sure everything will be fine," he said. "They'll do the test and discover that he's not the father, and maybe they'll find a match with someone else that she was involved with. Someone with a criminal record."

"Yes," I said. "I'm sure that's what will happen." I began to chew on my thumbnail.

Rose called up the stairs. "Mom? Can we have some popcorn?"

"I'll go," Gabriel quickly said. "You should rest." He stood up and looked at the collection of memorabilia on the bed. "Would you like me to help you put this away?"

I stared at it for a moment. "No, I'll do it."

Gabriel seemed reluctant to leave, but when Rose called up a second time, he walked out to take care of her and Joel.

CHAPTER 27
OLIVIA

Two days before Christmas, a warm front moved across the state of New York. It rained steadily, which melted all the snow and caused flooding in the streets of Manhattan. Shoppers with boxes and bags skipped over puddles, and the snowman in our backyard was reduced to a small white blob on the grass, as if he had never been there at all.

A week had passed since the detectives came to the door, and we heard nothing. A few times, I considered calling Caroline Weaver to ask what she knew, but I resisted the urge because it was the holiday season, I was seven months pregnant, and I didn't want to think about my first husband being a killer. It was totally incomprehensible to me, like something out of a bad dream, so I stuck my head in the sand and didn't discuss it with Gabriel either. I did my best to maintain a sense of normalcy by baking sugar cookies and wrapping gifts, visiting friends, and singing Christmas carols at dinner parties.

On Christmas Eve, after Gabriel and I placed the toys under the tree and ate the milk and cookies that the children had set out for Santa, we went to bed to the sound of ice pellets striking our window as the temperature dropped rapidly.

By sunrise, the freezing rain had stopped, and the city was eerily quiet. I slipped out of bed and looked out the window. All the trees on our street were silver, cloaked in ice, and the sidewalk was a skating rink.

I glanced back at Gabriel, who opened his eyes briefly. "It looks slippery out there," I told him.

"I'll put salt out," he replied, but he made no move to rise. He rolled to his side and fell back to sleep.

A few minutes later, after I brushed my teeth and pulled on my bathrobe, I heard Joel's bedroom door open. He toddled out sleepily, and I took hold of his small hand. "Merry Christmas," I whispered.

"Did Santa come?" he asked.

"I don't know. I haven't been downstairs yet. Should we go and wake up Rose?"

"Okay," he replied.

Together, we knocked on her door, and then I quietly opened it. She sat up in bed. "Is it Christmas?"

"Yes," I whispered in the stillness of the dawn. "Go wake up your father."

Rose tossed the covers aside and sprang out of bed. She and Joel dashed down the hall. Gabriel groaned as they dragged the covers off him.

"Wake up!" Rose shouted with delight, and the house was no longer quiet.

Joel mimicked her. "Wake up! Wake up!"

Gabriel covered his face with a pillow. "Can't I be Scrooge today?"

Rose laughed and screeched. "No, you can't be Scrooge! Get up, Daddy! Don't be a lazybones!"

He threw the pillow aside and sat up. "Did someone just call me lazybones?"

"Yes!" She laughed hysterically while Joel bounced up and down on the bed.

"Then I must prove you wrong," he replied. "Let's go! Chop-chop! Go brush your teeth because those gifts aren't going to open themselves!"

He rose from bed and pulled on his New York Yankees sweatshirt, which clashed with his green plaid pajama bottoms. The children ran past me in the doorway, and he stood for a moment, looking at me sleepily. "Merry Christmas."

"Merry Christmas to you too."

For several seconds, I felt the weight of what hung between us—the question of what had happened to that young woman who was found dead in a New Jersey forest.

"I'll make coffee," I said, sweeping those thoughts aside for yet another day, because it was Christmas.

Gabriel scratched the back of his head and sauntered into the bathroom. I went to check on Rose and Joel. Then we all ventured downstairs to see what Santa had brought.

~

Later, after we opened our gifts and enjoyed a decadent feast of waffles, strawberries, and fresh whipped cream, I called Rachel.

"Merry Christmas," I said. "Is this a good time? Did you finish opening all your gifts?"

"Oh yes, hours ago. Amelia was up at the crack of dawn. How about you? Was Santa good to you?"

I touched the gold necklace at my neck. "Yes. Gabriel gave me an elegant diamond pendant. I love it."

We chatted for a few minutes about the gifts we received and of course the weather.

"Will you still go to your mother's place for turkey dinner?" Rachel asked. "They're calling for snow on top of all this ice. Thomas thinks we might lose power."

"Let's hope not. And we should be home before it starts anyway."

Rose came upstairs from the basement. "Dad got the train set working!"

"That's wonderful, sweetheart," I replied, covering the mouthpiece. "I'll come down as soon as I'm off the phone. I'm talking to Rachel."

"Okay!" She disappeared back down the stairs, and I returned to our conversation. "Sorry about that."

"No worries." Rachel paused. "So have you told your mother yet? About you-know-what?"

I sat down at the table. "No. I'm just not up for hearing her say *I told you so*. You know how she always felt about Dean. I hate to say it, but I think she would actually take some pleasure in hearing about it."

"Best to keep her on a need-to-know basis then," Rachel replied. "Otherwise . . . I don't suppose you've heard anything?"

"No." I straightened the napkin holder and moved the salt and pepper shakers closer together. "Nothing yet. Gabriel said it could take weeks for DNA results to come back. Other than that, we haven't talked about it much. We basically avoid the subject altogether."

"Really? I'm surprised. You usually talk about everything."

"Yes, but this is ugly. The thought of Dean having anything to do with that woman's murder is horrendous to me. I know it's not true, but either way, I don't think Gabriel wants to listen to me defending Dean, which is probably what would happen."

Rachel considered that. "I'll be glad when you learn the results so that you can put it behind you. Or deal with it. What will you do if it turns out to be incriminating?"

I cupped my forehead in my hand and closed my eyes. "I'm sure that it won't be." Sitting back in the chair, I laid a hand on my belly. "But I have to admit something. Ever since the detectives told me the date that the woman went missing, I started to remember my first few weeks with Dean. Melanie disappeared only days after our cruise up the Hudson River, when things were starting to get serious between us very quickly. Remember when I cooked him spaghetti at our apartment?"

"Yes. That was the first time I met him," she said.

"And then I didn't see him for a week because I was finishing my film, and the following weekend I invited him to go to Miami with Mom and me. Do you remember that?"

"I do."

I took a moment to reflect upon those events. "It was all so romantic because I was completely infatuated. But he was distracted that weekend, and he seemed very . . . I don't know . . . sad, I guess. Sometimes he would gaze off into space as if he was somewhere else. He told me it was stress from work, and that's why I encouraged him to leave that career and become a pilot. But he was awfully quick to say yes, even when his boss was grooming him for a partnership. He wanted to leave New York as much as I did, but I was running from something."

"Your father's iron fist."

"Yes. That's right. I was looking for an escape. But maybe he was too." I exhaled heavily. "Oh, this is ridiculous. I'm sure he had nothing to do with whatever happened to that woman. I don't know why I'm even thinking about this stuff. It's like I'm *trying* to make a connection."

We were both quiet as we pondered that fact.

"I think you should share those thoughts with Gabriel," Rachel said. "He would want to hear it."

"Would he? I'm not so sure."

"Of course he would. You shouldn't keep anything from him. He loves you, and he understands what you went through back then. Dean was your husband, and he died in a plane crash. That's traumatic."

I sighed with resignation. "I suppose you're right. I don't know why I've been so cagey about it. Maybe I don't like the idea of talking about Dean at all, because it shows that I'm still thinking about him, and I don't want Gabriel to worry that I'm still in love with him. The poor guy knows how obsessed I was, needing to know what caused the crash. But there were no answers, and there never will be."

"Yes," Rachel replied. "And you've accepted that. You're over it now. You've put it behind you."

"Have I?" I asked. "I hope so. Part of me still has doubts about so many things."

I heard heavy footsteps pounding up the stairs and knew it was Gabriel. He opened the door to the basement and poked his head out. "We got the trains running. You should come and see."

I cupped the mouthpiece with my hand. "I'll be right there."

He stared at me for a moment, then went back down.

"I have to go," I said. "They want me to see the trains in the basement."

"That sounds like fun," Rachel replied. "And I should go too. I need to baste the turkey and start peeling potatoes."

"We'll talk about this again?" I asked.

"Yes. But promise me you'll bring it up with Gabriel."

"I'll try." We said goodbye and hung up. Then I went downstairs to watch the trains go round and round.

~

That night, after a delicious turkey dinner at my mother's apartment, we returned home and switched on the tree lights. While Gabriel gave Joel a quick bath, I read a story to Rose, who could barely keep her eyes open. When we finished the book, I sat on the edge of her bed and watched her fall asleep.

How beautiful she was, in every way—from the shape of her sweet little nose to her adorable freckles and her crooked smile that contained a charm all its own. There were moments when I looked at her and saw Dean. She had the same full lips and arresting blue eyes.

I never mentioned the resemblance to Gabriel, but he had met Dean once, and he had seen enough pictures. Surely he must see the likeness as well. Yet he loved Rose as his own.

I adored Gabriel for that, and I was grateful to have him in my life. I loved him with all my heart. But it was a quieter love. A more sensible love, perhaps . . .

Gently, I ran the pad of my thumb across Rose's eyebrows.

Half-asleep, she whispered, "That feels nice."

I used to stroke Dean's eyebrows as well, usually when he returned home after a long flight. The memory of those intimate moments we'd shared in bed together—when it felt as if our bodies and souls were connected—was like someone pouring salt on a fresh wound on my heart.

But it wasn't fresh. It was an old wound that had finally healed over. Or so I'd thought.

Rose fell asleep. I switched off the lamp, kissed her good night, and pushed thoughts of Dean from my mind.

By this time, Gabriel was downstairs watching television, lounging on the sofa with his feet up. Ziggy was stretched out beside him, his head resting on Gabriel's thigh.

"My two favorite men," I said wistfully, moving past the Christmas tree. "What are you watching?"

Gabriel lowered the volume. "*Die Hard*. Come and have a seat." He gave Ziggy a gentle nudge. "Down you go. That's a good boy."

Ziggy plodded to his bed in front of the fire while Gabriel patted the empty sofa cushion beside him. I sank onto it and snuggled close.

"Would you like a foot rub?" Gabriel asked.

"That would be amazing."

He waited for me to remove my new Christmas slippers and get comfortable with my feet on his lap. Then he began to perform his magic.

"You have the best hands," I said as he kneaded the arch of my foot.

"And you have the loveliest feet."

I laughed. "Despite my swollen ankles?"

"Your ankles are perfect."

We sat in the colored light from the Christmas tree, while Ziggy snored loudly on his doggy bed.

"It started snowing already," Gabriel said. "Maybe tomorrow we could take a drive out of the city and go tobogganing."

"That sounds like fun, but I don't think I should be doing anything that involves speeding down a steep hill and flying into a snowbank. I'd be a beached whale. I wouldn't be able to get up."

"You're right," he replied. "Krazy Karpets would be unwise."

"By the sound of things," I said, "we might be snowed in without power anyway. We might need to stay close to home."

"Good thing we have a working fireplace."

"We could roast marshmallows," I suggested, regarding him with affection.

He continued to rub my feet while he watched the movie.

"I love you," I said.

He looked down at me with a glimmer of sadness in his eyes. "I hope so."

My stomach turned over with regret, and I leaned up on my elbows. "What do you mean, you hope so?"

"You've been distant the past week, ever since the detectives came."

"I'm sorry about that."

He nodded. "Has he been on your mind a lot?"

I lay down again. "I think it's important that I'm honest with you. So the answer is . . . yes."

Gabriel said nothing. He simply moved his hands to my other foot, and his silence convinced me to open up about everything I had told Rachel on the phone that morning. I confessed how I was frustrated that I still didn't know what had happened to Dean.

Then I thought of something. I rose up on my elbows again.

"Obviously, the detectives would love to identify Dean as the killer because then they could close the Melanie Brown file once and for all, because he's not here to be arrested. And if they could pin it on *him*, they wouldn't have to keep searching for another killer. But what if he's still out there somewhere?"

Gabriel's gaze shot to mine. "Who? Another killer?"

"No. Dean."

One corner of Gabriel's mouth twitched slightly. "What are you talking about?"

"There was never a body recovered," I reminded him.

Gabriel shook his head. "There's no evidence to suggest that he's still alive."

"No, but what evidence is there to prove that he's actually dead?"

Gabriel stared at me. "A death certificate."

"Based on what? The *assumption* that his plane went down and crashed into the ocean. But if they pin the murder on him, they won't be searching for the real killer."

Gabriel's hands went still. "You're not making any sense, Olivia. He's not still out there."

"But what if he was? I'm not saying I believe that. Just hypothetically speaking. They wouldn't be able to question him, but they'd find him guilty, and then the real killer would go free."

Gabriel's eyebrows drew together in a frown. "It sounds like you're still imagining that he's alive."

"No . . . I swear I'm not."

"Are you sure about that? Because it sounds like you're still hanging on. Or you're searching for an answer about why he left or where he went." Gabriel pushed my foot aside and stood. "If only it hadn't been the Bermuda Triangle."

"It has nothing to do with that," I said defensively. "I don't think he was abducted by aliens."

"Then what *do* you think?" he asked, looking down at me. "Or maybe that's not the right question. No one can say for sure what happened to Dean's plane. I just want to know . . ." Gabriel paused.

"Know what?"

"I want to know what you're searching for. What's missing in your life that makes you entertain the idea that he might still be out there?"

I stared at Gabriel for several seconds while my heart pummeled my rib cage. I hated the fact that he thought he wasn't enough for me, that I was still in love with a ghost, and that my love for Dean would always be more passionate or enduring. None of that was true.

Or maybe there was a nugget of truth to it, because Dean and I never had a chance to move past the honeymoon phase. But I was wise enough and mature enough to understand that that kind of youthful passion couldn't last, nor could it compete with a deep and lifelong love or with the kind of respect that was earned and built upon day after day.

When I didn't answer—because I was reflecting upon my love for the man who was standing in front of me—Gabriel asked again.

"Olivia. What are you searching for? What do you want?"

I blinked a few times. "I want you. And I want closure. That's all. Just closure."

His shoulders relaxed slightly, and he spoke in a gentler voice. "I want to believe you."

"Then believe me. You're my husband and the father of my children, including Rose. I love you. I don't want anyone but you."

A shadow of dismay swept across his face. "Sometimes, I fear that if he ever came back, you'd run off with him somewhere, and I'd never see you again."

I swung my legs to the floor, stood up, and wrapped my arms tightly around his neck. "That would never happen. Not in a thousand years."

He buried his face in my neck. "I don't know what I would do if I lost you a second time. You're the only woman I've ever loved."

In that moment, I wished I could say the same, but I couldn't because I had loved Dean deeply and passionately for the short time that we were together.

But that was a different life. Today, I was no longer the woman I had been when I met him, years ago—when I was light enough, untroubled enough, to be swept off my feet. I'd had no experience with grief or mistrust. Those were feelings I had come to know only after I was cut off from my family and after Dean disappeared. It was why I would never take my happiness for granted again. Gabriel was my joy now. Gabriel, Rose, Joel, and the unborn baby I carried.

"I'll never leave you," I promised as I cupped his face in my hands. "I love our life together. I don't want anything else or anyone else. I promise you that. You're everything to me."

He hugged me tighter still, as if he could shield us both physically from the unwelcome, surfacing past.

CHAPTER 28

OLIVIA

Two weeks later, not long after Gabriel returned to work and began auditions for a new spring musical, I was at home alone with Joel on a Wednesday morning. The doorbell rang. I thought it was my mother, who had promised to drop off a ballet costume for Rose, but it wasn't my mother. It was Detectives Johnson and Russo.

"Do you have a moment to talk?" Detective Johnson asked, and my heart plummeted to the pit of my stomach. I invited them both inside, then moved into the living room, where Joel and I had been building a large fort out of wooden blocks. It was intended to keep out a herd of dinosaurs.

"Joel, these nice men need to have a chat with me in the kitchen. Can you play on your own for a few minutes?"

He glanced up at the detectives with a wary expression, shrank away from them slightly, and said, "Uh-huh."

My stomach churned with nervous knots as I led them to the kitchen and quickly cleared off the table. I removed Joel's cereal bowl from breakfast and his plastic drink cup. Then I grabbed the red dish-cloth from the sink to give the table a wipe.

"Have a seat," I suggested when it was clean.

A moment later we were gathered around the table, facing each other.

"I assume you got the results from the DNA test?" I said apprehensively.

Detective Russo spoke matter-of-factly. "Yes. And I'm sorry to be the one to tell you this, but your late husband was the father of Melanie Brown's unborn child."

For a moment I couldn't breathe. My stomach was burning and my mind was frozen in limbo while I tried to process what he'd just said. "That's not . . . I don't . . . wait a second." I held up a hand and closed my eyes for a few seconds. "That can't be right." I took a deep breath and regarded the detectives fixedly. "Are you sure?"

"Yes," he replied. "There's no doubt."

I looked away toward the refrigerator and felt physically paralyzed as I tried to comprehend what this meant.

"Are you all right, Mrs. Morrison?" Detective Johnson asked.

I forced myself to meet his gaze. "I don't know. This is a shock. I feel a little light headed."

He stood up. "I'll get you some water. Where do you keep your drinking glasses?"

I pointed. "In that cupboard next to the microwave."

He found a glass and filled it at the sink, then set it down in front of me. I picked it up and took a few sips, which was mostly a way to stall this from going any further. To give myself a chance to digest what the detectives had already told me.

When I set the glass down on the table, Detective Russo said, "We do have some additional questions for you, if you don't mind."

"That's fine," I replied, still dazed and feeling a little nauseous while I tried to make sense of what I'd just been told.

"According to the autopsy, Ms. Brown was at least twenty weeks pregnant when she died. Can you tell us exactly when you began your relationship with Dean Robinson?"

"Yes." I felt disoriented as I told them everything about the first time I'd met Dean at the clinic and the reason why we met. "I was making a student film, and he was an interview subject."

"You wouldn't happen to have a copy of that film, would you?"

"I do. Upstairs on videotape. And I kept the raw footage as well, the stuff that ended up on the cutting-room floor, so to speak. You might find that more helpful than the final film."

"How so?"

I mulled over that day in his office, when I'd been insanely attracted to him. Until that moment, I hadn't really believed in love at first sight. Then everything changed for me. My whole world was transformed. "In the raw footage, he talks about his family and his upbringing. Is that what you're looking for?"

"We'll be looking at everything," he replied. "There might be some piece of physical evidence in the background, for instance."

"I see." But physical evidence of what, exactly?

Detective Johnson consulted his notes, but I had a question of my own.

"Obviously," I said, "the DNA proves that Dean was involved with Ms. Brown if she was pregnant with his child. But it sounds like they were seeing each other before he and I met. And the fact that she was pregnant . . . that doesn't necessarily mean he killed her. It could have been someone else. A jealous lover who was angry about her past relationships. I mean, it's not a crime to get someone pregnant."

"No, it's not," he agreed. "But your husband was Ms. Brown's therapist, and that's a separate crime altogether because it's illegal for a therapist to have a sexual relationship with a client."

My stomach burned hotter. "Oh." This couldn't be Dean. Not my Dean.

For a few seconds, I stared down at the table. Then I looked up again. "What other evidence do you have to link Dean to the murder, if that's what it was?" I squeezed my eyes shut. "How did she die, exactly?"

Detective Johnson leaned forward over the table. "It was most likely a head injury that killed her, but she also had a broken spine and a few other bone fractures. From what we've been able to piece together, it was probably a bad fall, possibly down some stairs."

"So an accident, then," I said.

"Possibly. Or she could have been pushed. Either way, someone dumped her body in the woods, and that definitely wasn't an accident."

I felt sadness, deep in the marrow of my bones. "Right."

Joel walked into the kitchen just then, and I pasted on a smile. "Hey, sweetie. What's up?"

He hugged my arm. "TV?"

"Of course." I stood up and said to the detectives, "If you could excuse me for one second. I'll be right back."

"Take your time," Detective Russo replied.

I took Joel by the hand and led him back to the living room, got him settled on the sofa. "How about *George of the Jungle*?" It was his favorite.

"Okay," he replied, and I glanced at the clock. It was almost noon.

"We'll have lunch soon," I said after I pressed play on the VCR.

He became immediately engrossed in the movie, so I returned to the kitchen and sat down. "Where were we?"

"We were talking about how Ms. Brown died," Detective Russo replied, "possibly from a fall."

"Yes." I swallowed over the sick feeling in my stomach. "You said you had other questions for me?"

Detective Johnson glanced at his notes. "We'd like to know if Dean ever talked to you about the Bermuda Triangle."

I chuckled a little with disbelief. "That's not a question I was expecting."

They stared at me without humor and waited for me to respond.

"No," I told them. "He never talked about it, even though he flew over those waters almost every day. We lived in Miami, and he often took clients to the Bahamas."

"But he never talked about how or why things go missing in that area? Did he seem concerned about it?"

"No. Why? Do you know something about that?" My lips parted slightly, and I felt a tingling sensation in all my extremities. For a long time after Dean's disappearance, I had wanted only to believe that there was some magic involved and that he would miraculously return to me. More recently, I had let go of those irrational hopes and dreams, but now, two professional detectives were sitting at my kitchen table and poking at my old obsession.

Detective Russo sat back. "I wish we *did* know something. It's one of those unsolved mysteries that keeps people up at night, imagining all sorts of otherworldly things."

"Not me," Detective Johnson remarked, giving him a look.

I regarded them both, one at a time. "Why are you asking me about this?"

Detective Russo spoke frankly. "Because Melanie Brown was working on a PhD in particle physics. Her dissertation was about planes that go missing over the Bermuda Triangle, and according to her friends and supervisors in the physics department, she was quite brilliant and used to make things levitate in the lab. I don't understand the science of it myself. It has to do with atoms and molecules and electromagnetism—way above my pay grade—but the point is . . ." He sat forward and rested his elbows on the table, wove his fingers together. "She finished her research paper and was preparing to present it just before she disappeared."

My cheeks felt hot. "Did she solve it?" I asked. "The mystery of why planes go missing? Or where they go?"

If only I had known about this woman's dissertation when I was reading those crash investigation reports. I would have devoured it.

He shrugged. "No idea. Because her paper was never presented, nor was it ever found. It wasn't with her things in her apartment when she disappeared or anywhere at the university. So that links your late husband to her death, because he disappeared, quite sensationally, over the Bermuda Triangle, and we can't help but wonder if he was somehow inspired by her research and used it to . . ."

"To do what?" I asked with shock about where this line of reasoning was going.

"To make himself disappear."

I stared at them both with astonishment. "Are you kidding me? You do realize this is insane. You think he made his plane vanish on purpose?"

Detective Johnson held up a hand. "I assure you, we're not looking for proof of little green men, and we're not suggesting that he figured out a way to say *Beam me up, Scotty*."

"Then what are you suggesting?" I asked.

Detective Johnson regarded me intently. "We need to consider the possibility that he was looking for a means of escape, a way to disappear, and something in Ms. Brown's research might have given him certain ideas—that his death could be attributed to . . . whatever people think is going on out there."

I considered this carefully. "You think it was a distraction? From what?"

"To be clear, we don't think anything at the moment. We're just here to ask questions. What we need to know is if he ever talked about the Bermuda Triangle or if you ever came across Ms. Brown's typed papers, perhaps when you were cleaning out your condo in Miami. Did you come across anything like that?"

"No. If I had, I would have paid a lot of attention to it because I read everything that I could get my hands on about the so-called Devil's Triangle. If that paper existed, even in a library somewhere, I would have found it."

They glanced at each other and looked down at their notes.

"So where does this leave us?" I asked. "Does any of this link Dean to her death? I don't see how it does."

"You're correct," Detective Johnson said. "It doesn't prove that he killed her. And we don't have a lot to go on otherwise. He's been officially declared dead, so it's not as if this is a manhunt."

I watched them both and couldn't help but wonder what they really thought. "Are you supposing that he crashed his plane on purpose out of guilt? And that he did it over the Bermuda Triangle because he didn't want anyone to suspect that he was suicidal and then question why?"

Detective Russo inclined his head gravely. "We can't rule it out."

"But this happened *four years* after Melanie died. Why would he suddenly want to disappear then? I don't see how it can be connected."

I felt anxious and restless and couldn't sit still.

Detective Russo continued to question me. "Let me ask you this. Have you ever received any notes or calls that might suggest that he was still alive somewhere?"

I laughed with disbelief. "Now you're suggesting that he *faked* his death?"

I was astounded by what they were implying—that the man I had loved was a cold-blooded killer who dumped a pregnant woman's body in the woods and buried her in a shallow grave. And then he committed death fraud and abandoned me intentionally.

No. Maybe I could accept that Dean had become involved with a client before he and I met—because they had just presented the evidence to prove it—but that didn't mean he was a killer and a con artist.

"I haven't received any notes or phone calls," I firmly replied. "I would have told you. And isn't it obvious that I believe myself to be a widow? I've moved on with my life."

Detective Russo nodded.

"Could we have that videotape?" Detective Johnson asked.

"I'll go get it." Feeling annoyed, I stood, went upstairs, dragged a chair across the floor to my closet, and climbed onto it. Weeks ago, I had placed the cedar box back on the top shelf, so I pulled it down again, set it on the bed, raised the lid, and found the videotape at the bottom, beneath the stack of love letters and photographs. It was not my only copy. My mother had one as well, so I didn't mind handing it over as evidence.

"I hope this helps in some way," I said when I returned to the kitchen. "And I'd appreciate it if you could keep me informed of any developments."

"We will. Thank you for this."

I walked them to the door and watched from the window as they got into their car and drove off. Then I turned to Joel, who was lying on the sofa, sucking his thumb as he watched the movie.

"Ready for lunch?" I asked.

Later, when I put him down for his nap, I sat in the living room and stared at the wall for almost an hour.

~

That night, when Gabriel came home from work, I was in the kitchen setting out plates for dinner.

"I ordered a pizza," I said as he kissed me on the cheek. "It should be here in a few minutes."

"Rough day?"

"Yes." Without hesitation, I told him everything—that the detectives had come by that morning with the results from the DNA sample.

Gabriel watched me with intense focus, his cheeks flushing with tension. "What did they say?"

"That the baby was Dean's," I told him.

A breath sailed out of his lungs. "My God." He moved a little closer. "Are you okay?"

"I'm fine," I said and backed up against the kitchen counter. For a moment, I stood there shaking my head. "I'm not sure what it all means.

I mean . . . obviously, he had relationships before he met me, but he never told me that he was involved with a client. That's illegal, you know."

"I know," Gabriel replied.

I sighed. "So if he kept that secret from me, what other secrets did he keep, and is that why Melanie Brown is dead? Because he didn't want anyone to find out? So he killed her and dumped her body in the woods? I don't want to believe any of that. I *can't*."

Gabriel pulled a chair out for me. "Why don't you sit down."

I moved forward, took a seat, and rested my chin on my hand. "In the end, it doesn't matter what I believe. Either way, it raises all sorts of questions and definitely implicates him in her murder, if that's what it was. They still don't know. Maybe her fall down a set of stairs was an accident. But there's also the question about Dean's disappearance." I looked up at Gabriel in utter disbelief. "You won't believe what they told me today. They said that Melanie Brown's doctoral thesis was about why planes disappear over the Bermuda Triangle. She was trying to use physics to explain it."

Gabriel drew back. "What?"

"I know. It's crazy. And now I'm imagining all sorts of things. Wormholes, time travel, magnetic fields that suck planes into outer space."

"What do the detectives think?"

"Johnson is skeptical about any of that kind of fringe science. Mostly, they think that Dean might have used the information to deflect the truth. To distract from it. They think he might have crashed his plane on purpose, out of guilt, or that he staged it all and is alive and well somewhere, living under a different name." I buried my head in my hands. "Oh God."

The doorbell rang, and I jumped. "That's the pizza. We'll have to talk about this later."

Gabriel stood up to answer the door, and we called the children to the table.

~

That night, after Gabriel turned off the light in our bedroom, we lay beside each other, staring up at the ceiling.

"I don't know what happened to Dean," I said, "and that's up to the detectives to figure out. We might not ever know. But I'm certain about one thing."

Gabriel rolled to his side and faced me in the glow of moonlight in the window.

"I used to think he sat on a pedestal," I confessed. "I admired him for how he overcame difficult circumstances and didn't want to repeat his father's mistakes. But he'd had an affair with a client, and he got her pregnant, and whether or not he was responsible for her death, he abandoned her to be with me. What does that say about his ethics? And if he did that and kept it from me, he obviously wasn't the man I thought he was. Our relationship wasn't as authentic as I believed it to be. Maybe he *did* just want me for my money."

"No," Gabriel softly said. "I'm sure that's not true."

I rolled to face him as well. "If there was ever any doubt in your mind about me still dreaming of Dean or wishing he would come back, you can let go of that. Even if he fell through the ceiling right now, I wouldn't want to be with him. You're the only man I'll ever want, Gabriel. I swear it. Whatever I was hanging on to . . . it's over now."

Gabriel pulled me close and held me in his embrace.

An hour later, while he slept soundly, I lay in anguish, rubbing a hand over my belly in small circles. I had told Gabriel that it was over, and I wanted it to be, but I couldn't get over the fact that Dean had been sleeping with a client when we first met.

I took a deep dive into my memories of our first few weeks together—the walk in Central Park, the cruise up the Hudson River with my family, the trip to Miami. Everything about Dean had felt so real; our connection was soulful. Yet my parents never liked him. My father did everything in his power to stop me from loving Dean. What had they been able to see that I couldn't?

If only Dean had opened up to me about what happened with Melanie Brown. He should have known I wouldn't judge him. I would have tried to understand. Why hadn't he told me? Did he think I was like my father? That I was unforgiving or that I demanded a spotless past? And what else had he hidden from me?

I stared at my closet door, and with every moment that passed, it grew harder to suppress my anger. How could Dean have lied to me about something so important? I wanted to pull that cedar box down from the shelf and take a blowtorch to it. Or watch it go up in flames in the fireplace downstairs. Gabriel would probably help me light the fire if I asked him to.

For a long while, I lay there fantasizing about that, but in the end, I didn't burn it. I rose from bed the next morning, fixed breakfast for Gabriel, and kissed him goodbye. Then I got dressed, took Rose to school, and dropped Joel off at my mother's place for a few hours.

When I returned home, I went upstairs, dragged the chair to the closet, and pulled the cedar box down one last time. I didn't open it because I couldn't bear to look at Dean's penmanship on the cards and letters or any photographs of him smiling with his arm around me. Nor could I bear to look at my perfect happiness in those pictures—because it wasn't real. I had been charmed and duped. And now I was embarrassed by my blindness.

I carried the box down to the damp storage room in the basement and stuck it in the farthest corner behind a cardboard box full of old books that I hadn't been able to part with years ago. They were musty now, and I never thought of them, so it seemed like a good place to store this evidence of my brief marriage to a man named Dean Robinson. I would keep it only because Rose was a part of this, too, and one day, she might want to know something about her real father.

That was the only reason I kept it. If not for Rose, I would have torched it.

2012
NEW YORK

CHAPTER 29
OLIVIA

It was a warm Sunday afternoon in mid-October, and I was on my knees in the backyard, planting tulip bulbs. Recently, the flower beds had burst into a spectacular rainbow of color for the autumn season, and my perennials were blooming gorgeously. Lavender-blue asters and pink and red sedums lined the southern edge of the yard. This was the spot I had chosen to plant a mix of tulips in anticipation of another color extravaganza next spring.

Sitting back on my heels, I wiped the perspiration from my brow with the back of my wrist and looked up at the clear blue sky. Church bells rang somewhere in the distance, and the faint sound of Gabriel's saxophone reached me from the basement, though the windows were closed. This morning he was playing "Autumn Leaves," which seemed appropriate. I sat for a moment in my faded denim jeans, looking around while I listened to the music.

A bumblebee roamed among the chrysanthemums, and the grass was pleasantly cool and slightly damp beneath my knees. The sensation lured me into the past, flooded my thoughts with memories of motherhood: lying on my belly in the grass with Joel and Ethan while we examined the vibrant blades up close and picked the best ones to blow like a horn between our thumbs; Ethan zooming down the little plastic slide that Gabriel had picked up at a yard sale down the street; Rose helping me water the plants in the garden, then setting up the sprinkler to frolic in with Ziggy and her younger brothers.

Today, Ethan—now fourteen—was at a friend's house, playing video games no doubt, and Joel was with his girlfriend, Angie. She was a pretty, dark-haired girl who played on the badminton team at school, while Joel was involved in soccer. They were together almost all the time and very much in love. Occasionally, Gabriel and I worried that they were getting too serious. They were only seventeen, in their final year of high school, and now they were applying to the same colleges in order to stay together after graduation.

Whenever Gabriel and I discussed it, the conclusion was the same. We liked Angie. She was a lovely girl, and she made Joel happy. Why not let them be? Because it certainly hadn't turned out well for my father when he tried to control my life. Sometimes I wondered what might have happened if he had expressed his concerns differently or given me the freedom to figure things out on my own. Maybe I wouldn't have dashed so quickly into Dean's arms and run off to Miami with him. But that was ancient history now, water under the bridge.

As for Rose, she turned twenty-one earlier this year, and she still struggled with what to do with her life. She had earned a degree in biology and was working in a commercial lab while sharing an apartment with some roommates from school. Each time we saw her, she expressed dissatisfaction with her job because she was a people person and wanted to do something that involved more human interaction. Some days, she wanted to quit her job and go back to school, but she kept changing her mind about what program she wanted to take.

"She'll work it out in time," Gabriel said, never seeming to worry about it much.

I hoped so. I just wanted her to be happy and fulfilled, but I knew it was rare to have everything figured out when you were twenty-one.

When I looked back at the person I was at that age, I could see I'd had no clue what I might want later in life. If someone had told me that I would lose interest in making films and choose a traditional, domestic lifestyle as a full-time mother, I might not have believed it.

And now here I was at fifty, spending a Sunday morning with my hands in the dirt in my backyard, in the same house that Gabriel and I had purchased together shortly before we were married. It was quieter now, without Rose and Ziggy, who we'd lost in 2001 after a brief illness due to a tumor in his belly. He was fifteen.

These days, I was working outside the home again after taking a part-time position in the Reserve Film and Video Collection at the New York Public Library. Mostly, I worked at the reference desk and enjoyed speaking to patrons about obscure films and documentaries they were searching for. I was still becoming familiar with the collection, and every day I discovered something new and interesting.

I sat back on my heels and realized Gabriel had stopped playing his saxophone. A light breeze blew across the treetops. Then someone knocked on the window glass in the kitchen, and I turned to see Rose waving at me from inside. I hadn't expected her to drop by, so it was a pleasant surprise.

Rising to my feet, I brushed the dirt from my hands and knees. The back door opened, and Rose stepped onto the stone patio.

"Hi!" she said with an odd cheerfulness that seemed strangely forced.

I made my way across the lawn. "Hi. I wasn't expecting you." When I reached the top of the patio steps, I pulled her into my arms. "I missed you."

"I missed you too," she replied, though it had only been a week since we last saw each other.

We stepped back, and I admired how lovely she looked with her hair in a braid. She was dressed casually in faded blue jeans, sneakers, and a white cotton sweater.

"How are things?" I asked.

She gave me a polite smile that unnerved me a little. "Okay. Sort of. Could we talk for a sec? Maybe we should sit down?"

She gestured toward the patio table, and I noticed Gabriel watching us from the back door. When he met my gaze, he poked his head out. "Want some iced tea?"

"That would be nice," Rose replied.

He went back inside to fetch it while we pulled chairs across the square flagstones and sat under the striped canvas overhang.

"What a gorgeous day," Rose said, and I knew instantly that if she was talking about the weather, something must be wrong.

"What's up?" I asked.

"Well," she replied hesitantly. "It's kind of big news, and I don't really know how to tell you."

The door opened, and Gabriel emerged with two glasses of iced tea. The ice cubes rattled in the tumblers as he set them down. "There you go." He hovered for a few seconds before saying, "I'll be in the basement." Then he turned and went back inside.

Rose picked up her glass and took a long sip.

"What is it, sweetheart?" I asked. "Whatever it is, you can tell me."

"I know. I just . . ." She took a deep breath. "I don't know what this means, Mom, and I'm afraid it's going to make you upset."

"I won't be upset. I promise." I tried to be patient while she twisted her school ring around on her finger.

"Okay, I'll just come out with it." Her eyes filled with tears. "I'm sorry, Mom. I should have told you about this before, but last spring, I signed up for FamilyHistoryToday.com. You know . . . that website that tests your DNA and checks your genealogy?"

"I know of it. Why did you do that?"

"Because . . ." She moistened her lips. "I was just curious about where I came from. Curious about my real dad."

"But I told you all about him," I replied, defensively.

Rose had known from the beginning that Gabriel was not her biological father. Even before she could read or write, I told her that her real father was a pilot, but he'd died before she was born. A few times over the years, she'd asked questions, and I never held anything back, except for the allegations about Melanie Brown's death. That wasn't something I'd ever wanted to bring up with her. I just didn't see the point because nothing was ever proved.

"If you had other questions, you could have come to me," I said. "I might have been able to answer them. I wouldn't have minded. It's why I kept that box full of pictures of him, so that you would know who he was."

She nodded. "I understand, and I'm grateful for that. And I don't know why I got sucked into that website. I guess I was just feeling a little lost. I don't know what I'm supposed to be doing with my life or who I'm supposed to be. I couldn't help but wonder if it had something to do with the fact that I never got to meet my real father, and I wish I could have."

I glanced back at the house. "Have you shared any of this with your dad?"

"Yes," she replied. "I told him just now, before I came out here. I wasn't even sure if I should tell you because I know it's painful for you, still. But he told me that it would be best if you knew."

I reached for her hand and squeezed it. "Of course. And he was right. I'm glad you told me."

She looked down at our clasped hands. "But there's more. Something else that I'm confused about, and it isn't going to make sense to you, Mom."

I inclined my head. "What is it?"

"I got a letter from that website on Friday," she explained, "and they told me that . . ." She paused. "They told me that I have a sister."

A sister?

My thoughts shot immediately to Melanie Brown's tragic end in the forest and the unborn child that died with her.

But no . . . it couldn't be that . . . could it? Had the FBI shared their DNA database with the genealogy website?

Then I wondered who else Dean might have been involved with before he met me or Melanie Brown. Could he have fathered other children back in Wisconsin? Or here in New York?

"Did they tell you anything else?" I asked. "Like where she lived?"

Rose nodded and seemed reluctant to reveal further details.

I sat forward again. "Please tell me. I need to know."

She began to cry and covered her face with her hands.

"No, sweetie," I gently said. "Don't be sad. Whatever it is, we'll work it out. If you want to meet this woman, that would be fine with us."

She wiped the tears from her eyes and fought to pull herself together. "It's not that, Mom. It's something else. And it's bad."

I felt like my blood was turning to ice water in my veins. I spoke firmly and perhaps a little harshly. "Tell me, Rose. You have to tell me now."

She slumped back in her chair. "Okay. They said this sister lives in Australia. But she's younger than me. She's only eighteen."

It took me a few seconds to get a handle on this. "She's younger?"

No. That couldn't be possible. That would mean that she had been born after Rose. *Conceived* after Rose was born. My stomach clenched sickeningly.

He's alive, I thought with an unexpected and shocking spark of excitement that came from somewhere deep within, from long, long ago. This was exactly what I had once dreamed of—my desperate, despairing wishes becoming a reality.

But then I was lurched back to the present. Denial came at me from all angles. It exploded in me like an atom bomb. "That can't be right," I said. "Maybe it was a clerical error. They sent a letter to the wrong person, or someone entered the DNA results incorrectly."

"Maybe," Rose replied. "That would be the simplest explanation. But I'd like to know one way or another. Wouldn't you?"

"For sure." I glanced at the back door again and noticed that Gabriel had not returned to his saxophone in the basement. Where was he?

"Let's go inside and talk to Dad," I suggested. "I'd like to know what he thinks."

Rose nodded, stood from the table, and followed me into the house.

Gabriel was at the sink washing a coffee mug. "Hey," he said, looking at me uncertainly. "Are you okay?"

I moved to the table and sat down. "Surprisingly, yes. Maybe because I don't see how this could be possible."

He set the clean mug on the drying rack and reached for a dish towel to wipe his hands. "It could be a mistake. Companies make mistakes all the time. There's always human error."

"How do we find out?" Rose asked.

"We'll call them tomorrow," he calmly replied. "Ask them to go over the records and double-check everything. We'll need to tell them that Dean was declared dead in 1990, so it's not possible for him to have fathered an eighteen-year-old child."

"Unless he's not dead," Rose said, being the only one forthcoming enough to voice what we were all thinking—that perhaps it was possible that he had survived the alleged plane crash where no wreckage had ever been found.

She turned to me. "But why would he pretend to be dead if he wasn't? You guys were happily married, weren't you?"

"I certainly thought so," I replied. "But it was complicated." I looked up at Gabriel, and he encouraged me with a nod as he moved closer and squeezed my shoulder.

"Maybe it's time," he said to me. "She's old enough. She should know."

"Know what?" Rose asked, and I labored to relax some of the tension in my body.

"About six or seven years after Dean disappeared," I slowly began to explain, "two detectives came to the door, and I learned about something that he had done. It changed the way I felt about him."

I paused, because this was difficult to put in plain words, but somehow, I managed. I told her everything about Dean's inappropriate relationship with Melanie Brown when he was her therapist. I also told Rose about Melanie's pregnancy and disappearance and her body being found in the woods.

"I can't believe that," Rose said, her cheeks turning red. "And why didn't you ever tell me? You must have known I would find out eventually on the internet."

"I always did plan to tell you," I tried to explain, "when the time seemed right, but it never did. Not until now."

She bent forward and buried her face in her hands. "My God, Mom. You made it seem like he was a good person. But you were lying to me."

"I wasn't lying," I insisted. "Especially not when you were little. Dean and I had a good marriage before he disappeared. Even then, I had a hard time letting go, because I loved him. I thought the world of him. It wasn't until much later that I learned about all this. It was devastating to me, and I wanted to spare you from that."

"You didn't want me to find out that I was the daughter of a murderer?"

"Hold on now," Gabriel said, interrupting. "We don't know that for sure. It was never resolved or proven that the woman's death was a murder or that Dean was responsible. It could have been someone else she was involved with."

"Because they were never able to question him," Rose said. "Because he conveniently disappeared over the Bermuda Triangle." She scoffed. "That seems pretty conclusive to me—that he faked his death to avoid getting caught."

Gabriel held up a hand. "Let's not make that assumption. The first thing we need to do is call the genealogy website and see if there's been a mistake. Then we'll decide where to go from there."

Rose sat back and thought about it. "Okay. I won't convict him just yet. Innocent until proven guilty, right?" We sat for a long time in silence, and then she checked her watch and spoke irritably. "I'm supposed to meet some friends for lunch. Maybe I should cancel that."

"Whatever you want to do is fine with me," I said. "This was a lot. You could stay awhile, and I'll cook you lunch. You could help me in the garden."

She considered that for a moment, then shook her head and stood up. "No. I'm going crazy right now. I need to see my friends."

"All right."

Gabriel and I stood up and followed her to the front hall, where she'd hung her jacket and purse. "I'll make the call tomorrow at work on my break," she told us. "And I'll let you know what happens."

We said goodbye, and she walked out.

After she was gone, Gabriel and I returned to the kitchen. "I don't know what to do with myself right now," I said.

He wrapped his arms around me, and I melted into the comfort of his embrace. When we finally stepped apart, I looked out the window at my flower beds. The bag of tulip bulbs was still waiting to be planted in the spaces I had cleared.

"I feel like I should call those two detectives who came here," I said, "but who knows if they're still around? I wonder who's looking after the case."

"They never charged anyone with murder, did they?" Gabriel asked.

"Not that I'm aware of. I'm pretty sure it's still an unsolved mystery." I faced him. "How does it work with DNA testing? Would the FBI have access to the data from public genealogy websites? Maybe they're already onto this and they're making an arrest in Australia at this very moment."

Gabriel reached into his back pocket for his phone. "Let me google that." He sat down at the kitchen table and began typing and swiping. "It says here that users' DNA results are private, and the company requires a warrant or subpoena before they would turn over data to law enforcement."

"So that means they're not aware," I said. "Unless someone tells them. Someone like me."

Gabriel set his phone down. "Looks that way." He stood up and approached me. "Whatever you want to do is fine by me."

I thought about that. "What I really want to do right now is try not to lose my mind as I let all of this sink in. Maybe I should go put those tulips in the ground."

"Want some help?"

"I'd love it. Thank you."

Somehow, Gabriel understood that I didn't want to talk about Dean anymore or how this might affect Rose. There was nothing I could do about that until we knew more about the letter from the genealogy website—which meant, for the time being, I was still bogged down in the unknowing.

Together, in silence, Gabriel and I went outside into the bright October sunshine. I got down on my knees again, picked up a trowel, and dug some fresh holes in the cool, damp earth.

CHAPTER 30
OLIVIA

I sat on the edge of the stone fountain outside the New York Public Library and unwrapped my sandwich. A week had passed since Rose came to the house and disclosed the facts surrounding her genealogy search, and ever since that day, I had not slept well. Most nights, I woke after only a few hours, tossed and turned with anxious thoughts, then finally gave up and watched television. It was only a problem when I had to rise early for work the next day. Today was one of those days, and I wished I could spend my entire lunch hour napping on a cot somewhere.

I was halfway through my sandwich when my cell phone rang. It was Rose, so I quickly answered.

"Hi, Mom," she said. "Do you have a second?"

My heart picked up speed because I could guess why she was calling. "Yes. I'm on my lunch hour. Did you hear back?"

"I did," she replied. "And they told me there was no mistake—that the girl in Australia is definitely my sister, but she has nothing to do with Melanie Brown. Her mother is alive and well and living in Brisbane."

A breath shot out of me, as if I'd been punched, because this sounded like proof that Dean hadn't died in the plane crash, like everyone had pushed me to believe. He had survived.

"Who's her father?" I asked, needing to know for sure.

Rose hesitated. "Well, here's the thing. The genealogy site has no record of who her father was. He wasn't even named on her birth certificate."

I looked up at the overcast sky and the stark, leafless branches on the trees and shivered. "So we still don't really know . . ."

"But wait, there is more," Rose said, clearly trying to bolster my spirits. "When I spoke to them, they told me that my sister was open to talking to me and maybe even meeting me in person if I was interested. That's why I waited to call you. I wanted to speak with her first and try and get some more information."

Something inside me froze. Was I sure I wanted to hear this? I had been living without answers for so long I was accustomed to it. It was a comfortable and familiar state of being. "Well? Did you talk to her?"

"Yes," Rose replied. "We just got off the phone a minute ago. Her name is Susie."

I forced myself to think of Rose and what this must mean to her. "My goodness. How was it?"

"Great," Rose replied. "Well . . . a little awkward for the first few minutes, but then we had an amazing conversation. You should hear her accent, Mom. It's so cool. I loved it."

I heard the excitement in my daughter's voice—my darling Rose, who had felt so lost and adrift lately—and had to smother the desire to ask more questions about the identity of Susie's father. I had decided, long ago, that it was better to focus on the living, not the dead, so I listened patiently, with fascination, while Rose continued to describe her phone call.

"She just started college, and guess what she's taking? Biology."

"No kidding. That's what you took."

"I know, right? Isn't that wild?"

"It is." I sat down on the edge of the fountain again.

"But she only took it because she didn't know what career she wanted. Sound familiar? But she's decided to switch to nursing next year. She wants to be an RN."

Rose told me more about Susie, and when she was finished, I checked my watch and realized I had only a few minutes left on my lunch break.

"Did you tell her why you signed up for the genealogy site?" I asked, circling back to the reason why she had found Susie in the first place. "Because you were curious about your father?"

"Yes, we talked about that. That's kind of the same reason she did it. She was interested in her biological heritage, which is what got us talking about her father. Here's what she told me . . ."

I had trouble catching my breath as I watched a group of elementary school students make their way up the wide library steps.

"It was a one-night stand for her mother," Rose explained. "She was thirty at the time, recently divorced, no children. She went snorkeling with some friends on the Great Barrier Reef and had a fling with a guy who operated the tour boat. His name was John, but she never knew his last name. She wasn't looking for anything serious with him, but she was feeling wild that weekend, after her divorce was finalized. Susie said her mother used it as a cautionary tale when she told her about it."

By this point, I was riveted, and I didn't care if I was late getting back to the reference desk.

"Did Susie ever meet him?" I asked.

"No. He knows about her, though. Her mother went back and told him that she was pregnant, but she also told him she preferred to raise the baby on her own and she didn't expect him to be involved at all. He agreed, so Susie never met him. She's never even seen a picture. Her mother got remarried when Susie was two, so she was raised by another father, just like me, and she had a good life. But she's been curious lately. Seriously, Mom, our lives are so weirdly similar."

I realized my hands were shaking. There was a fluttery sensation in the pit of my belly. Looking up at the concrete pillars at the entrance to the library, I said, "That is pretty remarkable." Then I checked my watch again. "Listen, it's past the end of my lunch break, but I still want to hear more. Did you tell her that your father, who might also be her father, was a suspect in a homicide case?"

"No, I didn't tell her. She was just so happy and excited to talk to me. I didn't want to spoil it."

"I understand." A small flock of pigeons hopped around, close to my feet, pecking at the ground, fluttering their wings. It made me feel disoriented, as if I were floating above them, strangely removed from the physical world. "So we still don't even know if that John person is Dean. Was she able to describe him at all?"

"Susie said her mother described him as handsome with blue eyes and blondish hair. That's all she knows."

Blue eyes. Blondish hair. That sounded like Dean, but there were plenty of handsome blue-eyed men in the world. I couldn't let myself make any assumptions.

But still . . . there was a DNA result. Real science that affirmed he was Susie's father.

"I find it so hard to believe," I said as I plodded up the library steps. "I mean, what are the odds that it could be a different person with the same DNA? A twin? I'm not a biologist, so I don't know how it works, but—"

"Mom. She also said he had an American accent."

"I see." I entered the building, where it was warmer, but I still felt cold. "Does he still work in the same place?"

"Susie doesn't know, but she said she would ask her mother to make some phone calls and try and track him down. She wants to meet him too."

I reached my desk and shrugged out of my jacket. "I'm glad you found her, Rose."

"Me too. And Mom . . ."

"Yes?" I waited nervously for her to continue.

"Susie and I want to meet each other in person. So I want to travel there for a visit. Would that be okay?"

I heard whispers, people milling about in the stacks. The world felt oddly secretive and remote. "Of course," I replied, hiding my fears and uncertainties from my daughter. "I want to meet her too." I sat down. "But I have to get back to work now. Maybe come over for dinner tonight? We can talk about what to do next."

"I have two weeks' vacation I can take anytime," Rose replied. "Are you serious, Mom? You'll come with me?"

"We'll talk about it tonight," I said.

But I knew I didn't have a choice. I couldn't go on living without answers to a question that had haunted me for more than twenty years.

Rose was quiet. "I'm sorry, Mom. I didn't mean to create all this drama. Maybe you would have been better off not knowing about this."

I unlocked my desk, opened the bottom drawer, and slipped my purse inside. "Don't be sorry, sweetheart. I'm glad you found out. Whatever happens, we'll get through it together."

Yet I felt as if my world were spinning out of control. I needed a moment to get my bearings.

~

I woke at dawn the next morning, just as a faint gray ribbon of light reached through the small opening between the drapes. The bed was empty beside me. Gabriel had already risen, which proved what I'd already suspected: He was troubled by our conversation at dinner the night before, when we'd made the decision as a family that Rose and I would travel to Australia to meet Susie. And to visit the place where

Dean might be living. Gabriel supported the idea, but now it was sinking in, for both of us.

I rose from bed, pulled on my bathrobe, and went downstairs to the kitchen. The house was quiet in the dim morning light. I noticed the door to the basement was ajar, so I padded softly down the wooden steps in my slippers and peered over the rail and into the rec room, where I found my husband. He was sitting on the sofa, polishing his saxophone with a soft white cloth.

"Hey there," I said as I made my way closer and sat down beside him. "You're up early."

"I couldn't sleep," he replied, glancing at me briefly.

"Neither could I."

He continued to polish the brass instrument until it gleamed in the lamplight. Then he set it inside the open case and said, "Coffee?"

"Definitely."

He closed the case, put it away, then followed me to the kitchen, where I set about brewing a fresh pot. Gabriel fetched two mugs and set them on the counter, and while the coffee maker gurgled and hissed, we stood, side by side, watching it fill the glass decanter.

"I wish I was going with you," he finally said. "Maybe I should."

"But next week is the music festival," I reminded him. "Your students need you."

"They do. But you need me too." He regarded me intently, his eyes searching mine. "Don't you?"

"Of course," I quickly assured him. "But Rose and I will be okay."

Gabriel faced me. His expression stilled and grew serious. "This morning when I woke up and imagined you on the other side of the world—in a place where you might see Dean again—I wanted to break something."

I heard the old jealousy in his voice and recognized the worry in his eyes because we'd been down this road before. He had never been completely confident that I loved him more than I had once loved Dean.

"You can come if you like," I replied. "Maybe you should."

He thought about that for a moment, then faced the coffee maker again. "No. You should go on your own. You and Rose."

I contemplated this firm, unequivocal decision. "I feel like maybe this is a test," I carefully suggested. "You want to find out for sure if I'll come back to you."

Gabriel folded his arms. "It could be that. What's that old saying? If you love something, set it free . . ."

"If it comes back, it's yours."

"If it doesn't, it never was."

I turned to him, touched his arm, and looked into his eyes. "I *am* yours, Gabriel. Surely you know that by now. I hope you can believe it."

The coffee finished dripping, and he filled both our cups. "I've always tried to believe it. Most of the time I do, but every once in a while, when the house is quiet, I feel you grow distant, like there's a sadness in you that has nothing to do with me, so I can't fix it. I just have to leave you alone with it."

I accepted the coffee mug he held out to me. It was warm on my cold hands. "You're right. Sometimes I do remember the pain I went through, and nothing can fix it or erase it. It's a part of me. But that doesn't mean I still want Dean. After everything we've learned about what he did, I feel only anger toward him. A sense of betrayal. There's a shadow over all the memories, like a dark thundercloud."

Gabriel leaned back against the counter. "I hear what you're saying to me. You want me to accept that you chose me—and that you will continue to choose me—but I can't help but worry that if he's there and you see him again, you'll feel a spark, despite everything that happened. You'll remember that passion you felt for him when you were young. I'm not sure you and I ever had that kind of passion. It was love and friendship when we got back together, not lust."

"But it was so much deeper and better than lust," I told him, needing desperately to make him understand. "What you and I had was a history of friendship and respect. But that doesn't mean it wasn't physical. There was definitely lust. There still is. But it was the icing on the cake, not the cake."

"But sometimes," he argued, "passion and lust can be more powerful than love. It can light you on fire and cloud your judgment, and just like that"—he snapped his fingers—"you're in someone else's arms. Or worse."

"No, Gabriel. My judgment will remain intact. I promise you that."

He faced me from a distance. "I know you would never want to be unfaithful, but if something does happen, I want you to think of me, here in our home. Remember how much I love you. How much I'll be missing you and waiting for you."

I closed the distance between us and laid my hand on his cheek. "Nothing will happen. And I will come home."

The morning sun beamed through the kitchen window and flooded the room with an auburn glow. Gabriel clasped my hand and kissed my open palm.

God, oh God . . . I didn't want to hurt him, and I knew he would have preferred that I not travel to Australia at all—that I simply report the DNA results to the authorities and let them take it from there. But I had to go, and Gabriel understood that. If Dean was alive, I needed to see him for myself and ask why he'd done what he'd done. Only then would I be ready to come home and finally put an end to the wondering.

CHAPTER 31
OLIVIA

Cairns, Australia, 2012

I stood at the railing on the balcony of our hotel and looked out at the Coral Sea. The day was hot and bright beneath a cloudless blue sky, and palm leaves fluttered gracefully in the breeze. The scent of suntan lotion reached me from the beach, and I looked down at Rose on the white sand, stretched out on her belly on a lounge chair, the side of her face turned toward the sun.

I wondered what she was thinking about. Her half sister, Susie, perhaps. They'd had time to get to know each other since our arrival in Brisbane, when Susie's mother, Patricia, welcomed us like family. We were jet-lagged and in need of a hot shower and a soft bed, and they picked us up at the airport and drove us to their home in a Riverside suburb outside the city, where we stayed for three days.

Initially, I refrained from asking questions about Patricia's brief relationship with Susie's father because it didn't seem polite. But on the second day of our visit, Susie took Rose on a tour of her university, and Patricia invited me out for lunch, just the two of us. We sat on an outdoor patio with elegant, white-clothed tables, and she ordered a bottle of chilled pinot grigio. As soon as it arrived, she sat forward and asked what I wanted to know about her one-night stand eighteen years ago.

"Everything," I replied, sitting forward as well and feeling a friendly connection.

With a nostalgic, faraway look in her eyes, she told me that Susie's real father was the handsomest man she'd ever seen in her life.

"He had thick, wavy, sun-bleached hair," she told me. "Blue bedroom eyes and broad shoulders, and he was captain of an old wooden sailboat. It was like something out of a dream. I couldn't take my eyes off him, and it was my friends who pushed me to flirt with him."

I listened to all of this with an unsettling mixture of understanding and jealous rage, because this was Dean she was talking about. *My Dean.* I tried to tell myself that, in actuality, the man she spoke of was a stranger to me, because the Dean I once loved was an imposter. My Dean didn't truly exist. It shouldn't matter that he had slept with the woman across the table from me. He had probably slept with many unsuspecting women over the past two decades.

"Go on," I said, regarding her steadily as I sipped my wine.

Patricia described a night of drinking and dancing, and that's when I stopped her. "Are you sure? The Dean I married never drank. Not a drop."

She sat back and shrugged. "Well, he certainly liked his whiskey that night."

A wave of skepticism washed over me. What if it wasn't the same man? "Keep going," I said.

There wasn't much to tell. Patricia revealed that she had dragged him back to her hotel room, where they'd made love, which she remembered fondly, but when she'd woken up the next morning, he was gone.

"That's it?" I asked. "He didn't say goodbye or leave a number?"

"He left a very sweet note on the hotel stationery," she replied. "He drew a little heart at the bottom. I wasn't offended. We both knew it was a one-night thing, and I was touched by the note. It was the first time

I had let myself flirt with anyone since my divorce. I just needed to let loose, and John was . . ." She paused. "He was lovely."

"Lovely?"

"Yes. He was a gentleman. When we were in my room, he kept stopping and asking if I was okay and if I was sure. For a few days afterward, I was completely infatuated with him, and I wanted to go back and see him again, but I resisted the urge."

"Why?"

"Because I knew he wasn't for me. I'm a city girl with a corporate career," she explained, "and he was a beach bum. You know the type. Flip-flops and shorts every day of the year. No television. No commitments." She sipped her wine. "I shouldn't stereotype him, though. There was something sad in his eyes. And it wasn't easy to get him to dance with me." She rolled her eyes at the memory. "I think he probably felt sorry for me. He didn't want to reject me and hurt my feelings."

I was gripped by every word of Patricia's story but dizzy from drinking the wine too quickly. By the end of it, I was convinced that her John and my Dean were in fact the same person. Whether he was a gentleman or not was up for debate, because my Dean had traveled across the world to hide a violent crime he had committed.

Now here I was, two decades later, standing on a hotel balcony overlooking the Great Barrier Reef, admiring the beautiful daughter we had created together. The child he had never met.

Was he really here? Alive?

Susie and Patricia had called dozens of snorkeling outfits in the area and had finally located a sailboat captain named John who fit the description. He had been running snorkeling tours for more than twenty years. I was grateful for their detective work and eager to walk to the marina where this man's sailboat was docked.

Rose had agreed that it would be best for me to go alone. I was the only person who could say for sure whether John, the beach bum, and Dean, the pilot, were one and the same.

She also understood that I had some personal ground to cover on my own.

~

Later that afternoon, I sat on a bench in the sunshine, watching from the boardwalk as a shiny new forty-five-foot cruiser motored into the marina with sails lowered. According to the tour company's website, the luxury yacht was named *Jade* and was available for private charters. There were no pictures of the owner on the website, and the contact information provided no physical location for the business, merely an email address and phone number.

As I sat waiting and watching, part of me wanted to believe that a total stranger might step off the boat in the next few minutes, not Dean, because Dean was dead. His plane had crashed off the coast of Puerto Rico in 1990, and I was chasing a ghost.

I promised myself that if Captain John was not my late husband, I would accept that as closure, once and for all, and fly home to New York.

The boat bumped up against the dock, and a young man in black shorts and a blue T-shirt hopped off to secure the lines. The boardwalk was crowded with tourists who obstructed my view, so I leaned this way and that to keep an eye on who was getting off the boat. I pulled my sunglasses down the bridge of my nose and squinted into the distance as passengers slowly disembarked. Two by two, they walked past me on the bench, and I tried to be discreet as I studied their faces and listened to their conversations.

Soon, they were all gone, and the young crew on the boat was tidying up. I continued to wait until they stepped off and said goodbye to the last man on board. I couldn't get a good look at him from where I sat on the bench, so I gathered up my bag and stood.

My stomach churned hotly with waves of apprehension, and my heart pounded hard and fast. Gabriel rushed into my mind at that moment. He was at home, taking care of the house and life we had built together, and the thought of him, like an anchor, gave me courage. I took a few slow, deep breaths before I put one foot in front of the other and started off down the length of the dock.

Seagulls called out to one another, and a bell clanged somewhere on the far side of the marina. The sun was hot on my bare shoulders, and I began to perspire as I walked. I was halfway down the length of the dock when a man finally stepped off the boat.

I stopped and stared. He was slim and fit with windblown golden hair. He wore faded gray shorts, a navy T-shirt, and aviator sunglasses. For some reason, he paused briefly, dropped his duffel bag, and bent forward to rummage around inside it. I stood motionless, studying the curve of his muscular back and the way his hands moved as he dug through the bag.

Then he straightened and rested his hands on his hips. His head turned, and he looked at me. The whole world seemed to disappear for a moment. All I felt was the mad rush of scorching blood through my body.

It was Dean. There could be no doubt.

I don't know how long we stood there, just staring at each other like that. Me in my ankle-length sundress, flip-flops, and sunglasses, completely immobile on the dock. Him with his hands on his hips, the sunlight glinting off his honey-colored hair.

There was a buzzing sensation in my ears.

Then his hands fell to his sides.

I slowly began to walk toward him, and he started walking too. He left his duffel bag behind him, splayed open on the dock.

We came together at last, a few feet apart, and stopped.

Years ago, in my many heart-wrenching daydreams, I had imagined that if by some miracle Dean and I were ever reunited, we would run toward each other and collide in a passionate, euphoric embrace. There would be tears and laughter and kisses. But I did not feel like laughing or hugging. I was built of cold stone in that moment with no desire to melt into his arms.

He was speechless for a time. Then he said simply, "Olivia."

My anger became a physical thing. I wanted to strike his chest with my fists or shove him backward. But I fought against those urges and nodded. "Yes."

"You found me," he said.

Words lodged in my throat. I felt empty and drained, as if my old self had been gouged out of me with a garden shovel.

"It appears so," I replied. "And I have no idea what to say. I can't believe it's you." My hands clenched into fists, and my mouth went dry.

"I can't believe it's you either," he replied.

His voice was . . . oh . . . so intimately familiar. I never thought I would ever hear it again.

Then I couldn't do it anymore. I couldn't stand there politely, as if we were old school chums. My gut was on fire, my rage irrepressible. I looked away, across the water.

"I'm so sorry," he finally said and dropped his gaze to the weathered boards on the dock.

I scoffed and removed my sunglasses to regard him in the full light. "Don't even do that. Don't say you're sorry, as if you forgot to take the car in for an oil change. You pretended to crash your plane into the ocean two decades ago, and you left me behind. You let me believe you were dead. You let me cry for you and grieve for you. But here you are." I waved a hand through the air. "Living the good life!"

He removed his sunglasses as well, and I saw, for the first time, the age lines around his eyes. "I'd hardly call it that."

"It looks pretty good to me." I turned toward the boardwalk, where tourists and families were strolling leisurely with helium balloons and ice cream cones. "I saw that hip young crew you get to work with every day. And look at your tan. You've been getting plenty of sun. And this boat! Well done. She's a beauty."

He shook his head and looked down at his feet. "How did you find me?"

I exhaled sharply. "Pure luck, really. My daughter, Rose, sent her DNA to a genealogy website, and she found out she has an eighteen-year-old half sister here. Her name is Susie." I paused when I noticed his gaze lifted abruptly. "Yes, you have two daughters. Both wonderful young women. But surely you knew that."

"I knew about one."

"Susie, but not Rose? Aren't you on Facebook? You haven't googled me over the years? Not even once?"

"I googled you a few times," he said. "But there wasn't much information available twenty years ago. I knew that you had remarried . . ." Dean stopped and looked toward the sea. "Mostly, I stay off the internet. No Facebook. I listen to the local news on the radio. That's about it."

"Best not to think about it, I suppose," I said harshly. "Just block it all out."

"That's exactly right," he replied.

Our eyes finally locked and held, and I tried to smother my anger so that I could think rationally.

"I know about Melanie Brown," I told him.

He slowly shook his head, as if he were looking at a mudslide and knew it could not be stopped. "What do you know?"

"That she was buried in the woods in New Jersey."

He tensed visibly.

"Two detectives came to my door," I continued to explain, "years ago. They did some DNA testing and connected you to her disappearance when they confirmed that you were the father of her child."

Dean's head drew back as if I had swung a two-by-four in his direction. "I beg your pardon?"

Suddenly, I realized that I might not know everything about the circumstances surrounding Melanie's disappearance, because Dean seemed surprised by this information.

"Surely you knew about that," I said. "That she was pregnant? At least five months."

Dean staggered backward a few steps, then crouched down and cupped his hands together as if in prayer. He pressed them to his forehead. "I didn't know that."

I stared down at him, my thoughts bouncing around in a cloudy haze of confusion and uncertainty.

"And she couldn't have known either," Dean said. "There's no way she would have kept that from me, and she was drinking all the time. But how could she not know?"

"It happens," I said. "If she was on the pill, she might have been having periods, and maybe she just thought she was gaining weight." I paused. "But just to be clear . . . you're telling me that you really were involved with her." There were so many details that I still needed confirmed and clarified.

"Yes." His fast response was like a punch in the gut.

I gave him a moment to take in the news I had just delivered, and then I wondered: What else did I not know? All I had done for the past twenty years was speculate about what happened to this man over the Bermuda Triangle and what he did or did not do to Melanie Brown. Now, at long last, he could tell me the truth.

"Did you kill her?" I asked.

He looked up at me with a pained expression. "No. At least . . . not on purpose."

Fearing I might be sick, I turned away from him and pressed the heel of my hand to my forehead. "Please tell me what happened."

He rose slowly to his feet and raked his fingers through his hair. "We can't do this here. We need to sit down."

Desperate for information and needing to sit, I followed him along the dock to his boat. He helped me step aboard, and the familiarity of his strong, warm hand clasped around mine stirred up a flood of memories. I still couldn't believe he was here in the flesh and that I was touching him, talking to him, looking at his face, his eyes, his hands. How many times, in the weeks, months, and years after his disappearance, had I dreamed of this?

As Dean strode across the cockpit of the boat and unlocked and opened the hatch, I wondered what he had thought when he'd seen me walking toward him just now, for the first time after more than twenty years. I had borne three children; I was no longer the svelte twenty-four-year-old I had been when we'd first met in his office and went walking in Central Park. I was a fifty-year-old woman now, and I had lived half a lifetime that he knew nothing about.

He led me down the companionway to the deluxe cabin below. The woodwork was smooth, polished teak, and the seat cushions were upholstered in gray leather. I took a quick glance at the master's quarters up front and set my bag on the floor.

"Please . . . ," he said in a somber voice, indicating the bench at the table. "Can I get you anything? A drink of water?"

"Do you have wine?" I asked, needing something to take the edge off. Something to wrap my hands around as I sat across from the husband I'd thought was dead.

"Red or white?" he asked.

"Doesn't matter."

He pulled a bottle of white out of the galley fridge, poured me a glass, and poured water for himself. We sat down at the table and faced each other.

"First," he said, "will you tell me about your life?" He paused and sat back. "Rose?" His voice shook as he spoke her name, and his eyes revealed a whole universe of sorrow.

I loathed the fact that I sensed loss and regret in him and felt sympathy in response. I didn't want to feel that way because this was a man who had kept secrets from me. I had never suspected a thing about his true character until two homicide detectives showed up at my door.

"Remember that last day when we went sailing," I said, "and I wanted to have a baby?"

He nodded, still with that same troubled, tortured expression.

"I had no idea that I was already pregnant." I picked up my wine, took a sip, and set the glass down again. "Would that have made a difference?" I asked. "Would you have stuck around if you knew?"

Without hesitation, he replied, "If I'd known you were already pregnant, I wouldn't have left you. I only left that night because I thought it best to make my exit before we took that next step. I didn't think I was cut out to be a father, and part of me worried that it was in my genes. I didn't want to pass that on."

"Make your exit . . ." I frowned. "As if our life together was some sort of theatrical performance?"

I couldn't help myself. I picked up my glass of wine and splashed it in his face.

Dean sucked in a breath of shock, then quietly dried his face with the back of his hand. We both sat motionless for a few seconds, without speaking.

"That drink was for you," I finally said. "Now I'll need a refill, please."

He didn't argue. He simply stood, fetched the bottle of wine, and poured me another glass.

"Let's back up a bit," I said as he sat down again. "Because I don't really want to tell you about my life, except to say that it's been wonderful. I married Gabriel Morrison, who you met once at that coffeehouse in SoHo. Do you remember him?"

"Yes."

I took another sip of my wine and stared at Dean coolly over the rim of the glass. In a way, I wanted to hurt him with that information, like a form of revenge for what he had put me through.

"Suddenly I'm wondering if I'm a bigamist," I said bitterly. "I suppose I am. But let's not get sidetracked. I want to know about your relationship with Melanie Brown and how she ended up in an unmarked grave." My tone was clearly combative.

"She was a client when I was a therapist," he told me. "I started seeing her for grief counseling before you and I met. I knew for a while that she was developing romantic feelings for me, which is not uncommon. It's called erotic transference, which is when—"

"I know what erotic transference is."

He stopped. "Then you know that sometimes it can go both ways."

My eyebrows drew together, quizzically. "Go on."

He hesitated and fixed his eyes on the center of the table between us. "I was going through a rough time after my aunt died. I was lonely and . . . there's no excuse for it. It was a terrible abuse of power, but I eventually gave in to Melanie's declarations of love and . . ." He paused. "I hate talking about this. But one day in my office, we kissed. I knew without question that it was wrong, but I was a mess and in need of . . . I don't know. Something." He cupped his forehead in his hand. "It was a mistake."

"How long were you involved with her?" I asked.

"About five months, but not by choice. I just couldn't seem to figure out how to end it because she could have destroyed my career if she told anyone about us, so I had to tread carefully."

I tried not to speculate about their relationship. Instead, I pressed him to continue. "What happened after that?"

He closed his eyes. "I knew that, in her mind, her love was real, but it wasn't real for either of us. I recognized that after the first forty-eight hours. But by that time, it was too late. I was involved, and I'd already violated the ethics of my profession, so I couldn't just walk away. Unfortunately, she'd ended her therapy, which was also a mistake. At the very least, I should have moved her to someone else, but I didn't. Obviously, I didn't want her talking about me. So I stayed, and I tried to help her, I guess. I was still her therapist in a way, and that was the crux of our relationship. It's what she wanted from me. I thought—I hoped—that maybe things would improve and that I could grow to love her. I did care about her. But then I met you, and it became an enormous sacrifice to stay with her only because she could report me if I didn't. It was a very unhealthy relationship."

"So you killed her," I said, leapfrogging over the ugly parts of the story, because, after all these years, I was impatient.

"No," he firmly countered. "I went to her apartment one night to try and end things with her, but she'd had a lot to drink, and she was emotional, and she shoved me out the door. I fell onto the landing, and she . . ."

He stopped talking and went very still. He stared off into space as if he had disappeared into the past. I was reminded of that day on my sister's sailboat when I spotted the dolphins.

"Dean?" I sat forward slightly.

He shook his head as if to clear it and began talking again. "She kept screaming at me to get out. Then she tried to push me down the stairs, but I grabbed hold of her to keep myself from falling, and we both fell."

His words echoed through my mind, and I felt a strange melting away of rage and suspicion. "It was an accident then."

"Yes."

"Why didn't you call the police or an ambulance?" I asked. "If it wasn't your fault . . ."

He squeezed his eyes shut. "But it was my fault. It was *all* my fault. I panicked. I was falling in love with you by that point, and I was so afraid of what would happen if anyone found out that I was involved with a client. You, especially. I didn't want you to see me that way when you thought so highly of me." He pressed the heels of his hands to his eyes. "I barely remember what happened after that. It was pouring rain, and I carried her to my car . . ." He began to quietly weep.

"Oh God." I felt sick. "I don't know if I want to hear the rest."

"I didn't want anyone to know," he continued to explain, regardless. "I just wanted it all to go away, like it never happened. I wanted to be with you. I wanted you to love me."

"I did love you," I said with a blaze of anger. "How could you have doubted that?"

He shook his head ashamedly. "It was still so early. I didn't know. It all seemed so precarious. I barely even remember everything I did. Just flashes of it." He paused. "Sometimes, when I start to think about it, I have to force myself to forget. I meditate. I do anything to steer my thoughts away from it. If I didn't, I'd probably just . . ."

"You'd just what?"

"I don't know. Get on my boat, sail to the middle of the ocean, and dive over the side."

I closed my eyes. "Please don't say that."

He grabbed big clumps of his hair in his hands.

"Why couldn't you have just told me?" I asked, more gently now. "After we were married, you sometimes had nightmares. They were about that, I assume?"

"Yes."

"You could have confided in me. I would have helped you, somehow. You didn't have to do what you did—fly off in your plane and never come home. That was a terrible thing you did to me. You caused me so much pain."

His eyes lifted, and they were red with tears. "If you only knew how many times I've had that conversation with you in my mind, where I tell you everything and you understand and absolve me and say that you'll love me no matter what. Back then, I wanted to tell you, but I couldn't bear the thought of your disappointment in me. You were so perfect and happy, and I wanted to protect you from the nightmares. I knew that my pain would become your pain, and I couldn't lay that on you. It was hell then, and it still is. I thought you would be better off without me."

I stood up and turned away from him because it was all so maddening. "But you cursed me with another kind of pain. The loss of you was horrible, especially without closure, without ever knowing what really happened to you. And later, finding out that you had kept secrets from me. I just wish, when it first happened, you had let me choose whether to stay with you or not. If you had called the police that night, maybe we could have worked through it. Survived it."

"Or maybe you would have never wanted to see me again."

"It ended up that way anyway," I reminded him. "You lost me. You destroyed what we had."

"At least I had you for a while."

I scoffed, and my anger resurfaced. "But you were in hell the entire time. So was it worth it? Those brief years we had together?"

"Selfishly, I want to say yes," he replied, "because you were my safe haven. But I hate what I did to you."

We sat in silence for a while. Dean sipped his water. "If I had called the police that night and you found out what I did, you would have cut me loose, and you would have gotten over me, I'm sure. We barely knew each other."

"Don't be so sure," I replied. "I thought what we had was special, even in those early days. Looking back on it, if you had told me everything, I probably would have stood by you. Are you forgetting that I let my father cut me off? I said goodbye to my entire family for you. That's how crazy in love with you I was."

He bowed his head. "Maybe I just didn't believe I was worthy of that kind of love. My father always told me I was worthless. My greatest fear was ending up like him. Alone. Disgraced. In jail."

"So *that* was your greatest fear?" I asked with disappointment. "Mine was losing you. Thank you for that—for letting me know where I stood in the hierarchy of what mattered to you."

His eyes lifted, and I had to fight a sudden wild impulse to let myself fall headfirst into the tortured depths of his soul and tell him that everything was going to be all right.

"Not a day goes by," he said, "that I don't think about you. But I had to let you go, especially after you remarried. I wanted you to move on and be happy. So I decided that my shame and loneliness would be my penance."

I faced him. "It wasn't your fault that she died, you know. If she pushed you . . ."

"It was my fault for becoming involved with her in the first place," he replied, "when I knew it was wrong. Sometimes I think about that, and it feels like it was someone else in my body. Not me." He gazed forlornly at me. "For a while, you were my escape from what I did. When we moved to Miami, it was easier to block it out, to pretend it never happened."

"Until I wanted to have a child," I said. "Is that why you chose to leave me that night?"

"No," he replied. "I had been thinking about it for quite some time. I was just waiting for the right set of circumstances."

"What circumstances?"

"I had to be alone in the plane. Usually there was a flight attendant. Often a copilot."

"How did you do it?" I asked. "How did you make your plane disappear? The detectives said that Melanie Brown was working on a project about how planes go missing over the Bermuda Triangle. Was there some technique you used out of that?"

He bowed his head. "No. It had nothing to do with whatever she was trying to prove. All I did was descend rapidly to a very low altitude until I was flying too low to be detected by radar."

I couldn't believe it. It was so simple. And yet it had created a monster in my mind, an obsession with mad theories and explanations.

"That's it?" I asked. "Then where did you go? You couldn't have flown all the way to Australia like that. Could you? You'd at least have to stop for fuel somewhere."

He seemed to have an easier time talking about this than about Melanie. "I flew to Colombia, ditched the plane there, got a fake passport from some people I'd met at one of Mike Mitchell's parties. Then I booked a flight to Sydney."

"What do you mean, you ditched the plane? Did you just abandon it?"

He shook his head, as if he didn't want to answer the question.

"Did you sell it? To who?" I was beginning to figure this out on my own. "Let me guess. Someone you met at one of Mike's parties."

He nodded solemnly. "They paid me cash. It was enough to get me here and buy a sailboat and start a business."

I turned away from him. "Oh God, Dean."

I stood at the counter in the galley, looking up at the sky through the small window over the cooktop. I found myself thinking of that day long ago in my father's study when he'd tried to convince me that Dean wasn't good enough for me. I had defended Dean and walked out on my father, who had insisted he was only trying to protect me.

I imagined my father looking down at me now and saying, *I told you so.*

I was a mother now. Maybe it was time for me to forgive my dad, because I finally understood his need to protect. And yet, if only he could have trusted me enough to figure it out on my own. Maybe I would have.

But Dean had been trying to protect me, too, in his own way.

A seabird soared over the boat. I watched it coast on the wind. When it disappeared from view, I let out a sigh.

I was so tired of people assuming I was too fragile or innocent to protect myself. What was it about me that made them think I couldn't handle hardship?

Except for Gabriel. He had let me come here on my own.

As I continued to stand on Dean's boat, the floor beneath my feet bobbed gently on the waves. Outside the tiny rectangular window, the sky was a spectacular shade of blue. I had never seen color like that before, and I wished Gabriel were there with me to admire it.

Then I looked back at Dean, who stared out the opposite window, his posture ravaged with emptiness and defeat. I thought of how angry

I'd been after I'd learned about Melanie Brown. I had banished the cedar box to the basement, as if it were something toxic.

But today, on this boat, my anger was dissipating. In its place, I felt the first blessed whispers of relief in knowing the truth, though it was marked by sadness for Melanie Brown and pity for Dean, for the mistakes he had made and had to live with. Mistakes he could never undo, unless he could find a way to turn back time, which was not possible.

If only he had been able to trust me enough to know that I would have stood by him if he had done the right thing. We would be past all that by now. Instead, he had chosen another path. He had withdrawn into his shell, to live with a nightmare that would never end.

I wondered if he felt any relief today, as I did. Confessing the truth to me, after all these years—perhaps it was like the pulling of an abscessed tooth. It had always been his worst fear for me to learn of his crime, but now the secret was out. At least between us. He no longer had to fear my censure. It was done. That part of it was over.

"What happens now?" he asked as I returned to the table and sat down across from him.

The thought of Detective Johnson and the card I still carried in my wallet coasted into my mind. For all these years, there had never been any breakthroughs regarding Melanie Brown's death or Dean's disappearance. But now there was this.

As far as I knew, there was no family or loved ones searching for Melanie. Perhaps that's why the file had been abandoned and left unsolved. There was no one to demand answers, no one to keep fighting for justice on Melanie's behalf. No one except for me.

"Can I ask you a question?"

Dean nodded.

"Whatever happened to the dissertation Melanie was working on?" I asked. "The detectives said it was never found. I'm curious what she discovered about all those missing planes."

Dean leaned back on the bench and gazed out the window. "She never really solved the Bermuda Triangle mystery, but she said she made some interesting discoveries about particle physics. In the end, I couldn't bring myself to read it, but I couldn't destroy it either. Not after what happened to her. So after the police questioned me, I ripped out the page where she mentioned my name, took the dissertation to the library, and stuck it on a shelf. I figured someone would stumble across it eventually and catalog it or return it to Columbia."

I frowned. "I don't think anyone ever did because I read everything I could get my hands on about the Bermuda Triangle. And surely the detectives would have found it when they were investigating. Which library?"

"New York Public. Main Branch."

"What section?"

"I can't remember. I was panicked."

It had been years since I had searched for information about the Bermuda Triangle. I'd wanted to put it behind me, but I decided I would look into it when I got home.

"Let's go outside," I said. "I need to feel the breeze."

Dean followed willingly but silently, and I realized he was not the same man I had fallen in love with. That man had become a prisoner, locked up with his fear and shame. It had left him broken.

When we emerged into the sunlight, I looked around at other sailboats that were tied to their moorings and at the people in shorts and tank tops on the boardwalk. I moved to the shiny steering wheel and ran my fingers lightly across the top of it. "She's a beautiful boat," I said.

Dean sat down on a bench and rested his elbows on his knees. "I only got her last year. She's bigger than my last boat. It made a difference with the bookings. We're busier."

I raised a hand to shade my eyes from the sun, which had moved lower in the sky.

"Listen," I finally said. "The reason I came all this way was because of Rose. If not for her, I probably would have spent the rest of my days never knowing what happened to you, but she found out about a sister she didn't know she had, and she wanted to meet her. So now, here we are, and I finally have the truth."

"Yes," he said.

He was staring down at his shoes, and I hated this. I hated it with every breath in my body.

"Dean . . ." I waited for him to look up at me, and then I spoke carefully. "You must realize that you have to turn yourself in."

He said nothing. He merely sat back and gazed out at the water.

"Dean?"

He wouldn't look at me. Then he stood up and walked to the rail, kept his back to me. Eventually, I approached and laid my hand on his shoulder.

"If only I had moved her to another therapist right away," he said. "If only I hadn't kissed her that day. She'd still be alive. And you and I could have spent the rest of our lives together."

Perhaps, I thought.

Or perhaps not.

The boat bobbed lightly on the gentle swells, and I wondered soberly if either of us would ever truly be at peace. Then Dean stepped forward and wrapped his arms around me. I was shocked and unsettled at first. I didn't want him to touch me in that intimate way. But then I understood that he was still living in a nightmare, and he needed comfort, release, or perhaps absolution. I tried to relax, and I rubbed my hand up and down his back, and we held each other for a moment, until the boat heaved on the sudden wake from another craft coming in from the reef.

When Dean stepped back, he inhaled deeply, as if he were drawing courage from the sea air. He faced the water again. "I'll do it," he said. "I'll go to the police and tell them what happened."

I was surprised by how easily he agreed to it. It made me realize how broken he was. There was no fight left in him, or perhaps he felt there was nothing worth fighting for. This supposed freedom on the Great Barrier Reef had never been real.

"Can I at least meet Rose before I do that?" he asked. "I'd like to tell her how sorry I am. For everything."

I considered it for a moment. Part of me wanted to say no, to shield Rose from the heartbreak and confusion of knowing that her biological father had committed a crime and had run from justice. But it wasn't my place to control her life in that way or steer her away from pain. I had to trust that she was strong enough to handle it.

I said yes because I knew that's what Rose would want as well.

"I'll text her and tell her to come right now." I dug into my bag for my cell phone and sent her a quick message. She replied immediately to let me know that she was on her way.

Dean and I stood a little longer, watching a flock of seabirds surround a fishing boat.

"I told her we'd meet her on the boardwalk," I said, after a time. "Maybe we should go now?"

Dean agreed, and together, we disembarked.

As we walked the length of the dock in solemn silence, my heart throbbed. I couldn't help but wonder what our lives might have been like if he had never become involved with Melanie Brown. I imagined it all for a shimmering moment, the vision flashing through my mind like a meteor shooting across the sky. Then I reined in my imagination because there was no point dreaming about what might have been. If things had been different, my life would not be the same today, and I could never want that. Not now, because I loved my life. I loved my husband and my children and the happy home that we shared.

Dean and I reached the boardwalk and took a seat on the bench to wait. Finally, I spotted Rose walking toward us. She was dressed in a long floral skirt and a slim-fitting turquoise T-shirt, and her hair was pulled up in a messy bun. "Here she comes," I said.

Dean stood and stared. "She's so grown up. I can't believe it. And she looks so much like you."

My eyes were on Rose the entire time. She walked with purpose, and I was proud of her for being brave and open to whatever might transpire.

As she drew near, she slowed her pace and removed her sunglasses. The three of us came together, and a gentle breeze off the water blew at my skirt.

"Rose," I said. "This is Dean. Your father."

She regarded him hesitantly, then stepped forward in a polite way and hugged him. He clung to her, and raw emotion welled up in me. I wanted to weep for all the lost happiness that could have been ours if not for the tragedy of Melanie Brown's death. I grieved not only for that young woman but for Dean and Rose.

When he stepped back and spoke, his voice shook. "It's nice to meet you. After all this time."

"You too. I think," she replied, truthfully.

He lowered his gaze. "I'm not sure where to begin. Could we sit down?" He gestured toward the bench.

Rose nodded and started off toward it, so I backed away and strolled to the railing to give them some space.

~

A half hour later, Rose and Dean stood up in the hot sun. They hugged again. Then Rose turned and walked toward me, and Dean returned to his boat.

"Where's he going?" I asked, with a touch of concern.

"To call his employees and deal with his business," she replied. "Mom . . . he says he's going to turn himself in."

"I know." Rose began to cry, so I took her into my arms. "It's the right thing, sweetheart."

"Is it?" she asked. "Are you sure?"

"Yes. What he did was wrong, and he knows it. He's always known it. He needs to face up to it."

"But it was so long ago," she argued. "Don't you think he's suffered enough? He's missed out on a life with you and me, and he knows that, and he's felt guilty about that woman for two decades. He still has nightmares about it. What's the point in him going to jail now? He's not a bad man. He just had a hard life when he was young. That's bound to damage you in some ways, which wasn't his fault. And he was lonely. That's why he got involved with her. You understand that, don't you? He tried to end it, and what happened to her was an accident."

I watched Rose and waited for her to wipe away her tears. "Yes, I understand that. But hiding her body in the woods and running away like he did wasn't right. He lied, Rose, and he broke the law. And now that we know he's here, alive, we can't lie on his behalf. I couldn't live with that."

She turned back toward Dean's sailboat. "We can't just let it go?"

The sun moved behind a cloud, and the air turned cool. "Would *you* be okay with that?" I asked. "Just letting it go?"

"I don't know." She hesitated. "I suppose not. I wouldn't want to lie."

A part of me understood Rose's reluctance. Perhaps Dean had been punished enough. But then I thought of Melanie Brown in a shallow grave and his fraudulent disappearance. The Coast Guard search, the theft of an airplane . . .

"I don't think Dean would want us to lie either. I think he's finished with hiding, now that he knows we know the truth."

Rose let out a heavy sigh and looked up at the clouds. "I don't want him to think we hate him. Because I don't. I feel sorry for him, Mom, because he can't undo what he did. It was an accident, and he regrets it, and I believe him about that."

"I believe him too." I pulled her into my arms and hugged her. "I'm proud of you, because you're right. We shouldn't hate him. I've spent too many years feeling angry. It's been like a poison in my veins. And Dean has spent most of his life living in fear, and he needs to be free of that, even if it means going to prison."

We both stepped back and looked toward his boat. I hoped he was doing what he said he would do. I hoped he was calling his employees and getting his affairs in order. But it wasn't easy to trust. I was conscious of Detective Johnson's business card in my wallet, just in case.

Rose took my hand, and we walked in silence back to the hotel. I was proud of her for her compassion and understanding, but I realized that I still had some work to do in that area. Everything I had learned that day had been a shock, a violent awakening to what had actually happened in the past and a truth I had never wanted to face—that I had once loved a man I never really knew.

The breeze off the water cooled me as I walked beside Rose. I did not let myself look back. I preferred, instead, to look ahead and immerse myself in thoughts of home. When I conjured it in my imagination—with all its comfort and warmth—it was Gabriel's face that I saw.

CHAPTER 32
DEAN

After sunset, it was a windless calm on the water, so I lowered the sails and lay on my back on the upper deck, letting *Jade* drift freely across the reef. Below me, in the dark, thousands of species of colorful fish populated the exquisite coral gardens that had become my escape over the past two decades. Lying alone, I contemplated the miracle of life on this planet. How tranquil it all seemed while my boat turned in slow, continuous circles. The fresh fragrance of the sea air filled my nostrils, and I marveled at the splendor of the night sky. The moon was full, and the Southern Cross hung above me in all its glory. The space station went by, like a traveling star. I watched it for about ninety seconds until it disappeared, as if by magic.

I thought of the first time I'd ever gone sailing after sunset. Olivia had taken me out on her sister's boat in Miami. We spent the night anchored in a little cove, far from the city lights. It was a calm, perfect night, just like this one.

But even then, I was screaming inside.

My mind was not screaming tonight, however, which made no sense considering that I had promised to turn myself in to the police and confess all my wrongs. It was my worst fear. Ending up like my father. Handcuffs. Prison. The shame of it all. It was what I had been running from for more than two decades.

All I could think of was Olivia on the dock, first looking at me with condemnation, then placing her hand in mine and stepping onto my boat. Olivia listening to everything I had done, telling me that she would have stood by me if I had called the police that night. If only.

Then I thought of Rose and Susie and all that I had missed. I'd never held either of them in my arms when they were infants. I never taught Rose how to ride a bicycle or swim. I did not witness the daily miracle of her development as a human being.

The sense of loss was bone deep. The dark shadow of my regret, inescapable. At the same time, I felt some relief and gratification to see the woman Rose had become. Smart, sensible, kind, and compassionate. Astonishingly forgiving toward me. Did my DNA have anything to do with that? Or was it all because of Olivia and Gabriel, who had given her a wonderful life?

And what about Susie? Would I ever meet her? Perhaps it was possible, one day.

I continued to lie there, spinning slowly in the moonlight, and felt a strange inner peace—something I had not felt in over twenty years. How quiet and serene it had become inside my head.

A memory of Olivia throwing the tennis ball for Ziggy drifted into my imagination. Olivia cooking breakfast in our condo. The smell of the bacon. Olivia sleeping beside me in our bed, her hand tucked up under her cheek, her eyelids fluttering as she dreamed. Her kiss. The softness of her skin. Her unfathomable, unexpected love for me. And today, a fresh, new memory of Rose on the bench beside me, telling me about her life and hearing my confessions. Rose, my daughter. Forgiving me.

Beautiful memories . . . all of them.

But there were other memories too. The first painful, devastating night I spent without my mother. The back of my father's hand and the hot sting of it on my cheek. The mad chaos of running away from a burning car I helped to steal, leaping over a fence to escape police sirens. Melanie pushing me onto the landing outside her apartment.

A light breeze blew across the deck, and *Jade* began to rock gently. I listened to the sound of my breathing, slow and steady, and looked up at the full moon and the mysterious galaxies that must exist in the great beyond. My life was so small in comparison, but not unimportant. All the atoms in my body had come from somewhere in this vast universe, and I had been shaped and molded by the world into which I had been born. I had played a part in bringing a beautiful person into this world. Rose.

Perhaps there was more shaping to do, more shifting and changing and spinning. More sunrises and sunsets to behold, for I had awakened from the nightmare. All I wanted now was peace and freedom. I knew where I would find it.

Another breeze gusted across the moonlit sea, so I stood up and raised the mainsail.

CHAPTER 33
OLIVIA

The sun was just coming up the next morning when I rose sleepily from bed, opened the sliding glass door in the hotel room, and stepped onto the balcony. The sea was aglow in the pink light of dawn. It was barely past six, but a young woman was on the beach doing handstands and cartwheels. I watched her for a few minutes and appreciated how carefree she looked.

Would I ever feel such lightheartedness again, after this trip to the other side of the world? I was still reeling from everything I had learned about Dean, and I had no idea how to move forward. Obviously, I longed to return home to Gabriel, but Rose wasn't ready to say goodbye to Australia yet. For one thing, she wanted to spend more time with Susie, but mostly she wanted to see Dean again and reassure herself that he wasn't going to take off like he did before and disappear without a trace.

We had talked about it over dinner the night before, and she admitted that she didn't feel able to trust him. "How can I," she asked, "after everything that happened in the past? I just don't want him to disappoint me, Mom. I really hope he doesn't."

"I hope so too," I replied.

Feeling a chill in the morning air, I went inside to take a shower. When I finished blow-drying my hair, I walked out of the bathroom and gently roused my daughter.

"Wake up, sleepyhead. The restaurant opens at seven, and I want waffles."

Rose groaned and rolled over. "I'm still not used to this time change," she said. "I wish we could sleep in."

"You can sleep in when we get home," I replied. "Today we're going back to Brisbane."

Rose sat up and rubbed her eye with her knuckle. "Okay, but I need to shower. Can I meet you in the restaurant?"

"Sure. Just don't fall back to sleep."

"I won't."

I waited until I heard the shower running before I gathered up my purse and headed downstairs. I was just crossing the lobby when a young man at the reception desk spoke to me.

"Good morning, Mrs. Morrison," he said. "There's a letter here for you." He retrieved it from under the counter and held it out.

"Who's it from?" I asked as I approached.

"I'm not sure," he replied. "It was dropped off late last night."

I accepted the envelope and read my name, which was scrawled with a black Sharpie. The penmanship was achingly familiar, like something out of a past life, and it caused my heart to beat at triple speed.

"Thank you," I said as I turned and made my way to one of the sofas in the lobby.

I sat down and felt a little dazed as I broke the seal and removed the handwritten letter. My body filled with dread.

Dear Olivia,

I am writing to say thank you. Thank you for finding me again. Thank you for crossing the world with Rose to get the closure you needed. And though it was painful for me to see you on the dock today, and to face up to everything I did, it needed to happen.

I also want to say that I'm sorry for all the pain and grief that I caused you. Yesterday, I told you that I had wanted to protect you from my nightmare, which was true, but that makes it seem like a selfless act—that there was some nobility in what I did—but the truth is, I was a coward. I've always known that. It was fear that drove me to flee. Perhaps also, subconsciously, I wanted to erase my life and the person I was and start over with a clean slate. But that meant I had to erase you, too, which was the greatest loss and worst mistake of my life. Worse than anything else.

But enough explaining. No more excuses. I am resolved to let go of my past and move forward. I thought, mistakenly, when I married you that I was moving forward, away from the life and misdeeds I wanted so desperately to leave behind, but I wasn't able to do that. Not while I was carrying a secret inside me. There was no escaping from that.

So, I will assure you now—because I want nothing but truth between us from this day forward—I will never run away again. I want Rose to know where I am if she ever wants to see me. Susie, too. You know the truth now, so there is no more fear. I'm no longer afraid of going to prison. I want my nightmare to end, and the only true way to be free of it is to confess everything and pay the price I should have paid all those years ago. You and Rose are more important than anything that's going to happen to me now. I want a chance to earn back your respect, and to give you some sense of resolution about the past.

For the first time ever, writing this letter to you, I feel at peace, more at peace than I ever was. You saved me once, years ago. You showed me what love was supposed to look like. And you have saved me again by encouraging me to face the truth.

I am now on my way to the police station. I don't know what will happen to me after that. I only know that I am grateful to have loved you, and that is something I will never regret. Please tell Rose that I am here for her if she ever wants to see me. I don't want to miss any more days of being her father, even if it's from behind bars for some of them. I'm not afraid anymore.

Sincerely,
Dean

As soon as I finished reading the letter, I let the tears fall. I stopped fighting the stubborn inclination to control my emotions or to bury them beneath my anger. Instead, I allowed myself to remember the love I once felt for Dean, and I cried openly and nakedly in the lobby of the hotel. I cried for the reopened wounds on my heart, but I also cried for Dean and what lay ahead of him. I cried for what could have been.

When I finally recovered from that fresh flood of grief, I slipped the letter into my purse and stood up to go to breakfast. I would sit down at a table and wait for Rose to arrive, and then I would show her the letter so that she would know she was loved. She would know that she could trust the father who had not been there for her, until now.

As for me, I had known for a long time that I was loved and that I could trust in that love. It was a forever love. A mature love. A love that had never let me down. I was a lucky woman, and all I wanted to do now was go home to my husband and tell him that he was everything to me.

EPILOGUE
OLIVIA

New York, 2017

The sultry sound of Gabriel's saxophone reached me from the basement window. I sat back on my heels in the yard, raised my face to the clear, blue October sky, and felt the warmth of the sun on my cheeks.

It had been five years since Rose had brought news of a half sister we hadn't known existed. It was remarkable how life could continuously unfold over time with surprises and changes, sometimes for the better. Sometimes not. But always, it was an adventure in its unfolding.

Rose was now a registered nurse. She worked daytime shifts in the OR at Mount Sinai. Susie was there as well, working in obstetrics—a result of her decision to join Rose in New York for the same nursing program. They had found an apartment together, close to the hospital, and were best friends as well as sisters.

As for Dean, he was serving time at a correctional facility in upstate New York, where he led group therapy sessions with fellow prisoners. Rose visited him now and again. She always brought news of him and told us that he was doing well. I wished only the best for him, and I believed with all my heart that with each new day, he was finding his way closer to some form of absolution and freedom from the past.

As for Melanie's physics paper, I located it as soon as I returned home from Australia. It turned out that it had been at the NYPL for years, shelved without a call number in the history section. A librarian finally discovered it and cataloged it in 2003, but that was long after the detectives had stopped working on the investigation. Naturally, I signed it out and read it, but it was mostly hard-core science that went over my head. Like Dean said, it didn't solve the mystery about what happened to all the missing ships and planes in the Bermuda Triangle, but maybe Melanie would have gotten there eventually, if she had lived. And who knows what else she might have accomplished?

I leaned forward again and fixed my attention on the rich soil in the garden bed where I was planting more tulip bulbs, this time on the opposite side of the yard. Gabriel had not been surprised to see me come home with a bag of bulbs that morning because I had been adding to the collection every year. I'm not sure why. Perhaps I enjoyed the annual reminder of something that had changed me—when Rose told me about Susie and the possibility that my first husband was alive and living in Australia. What happened after that had answered all my questions. I knew what was true, what was real, and what wasn't. Ever since that day, each spring, more tulips bloomed. Then summer came and brought roses, marigolds, geraniums, and begonias. All that color, constantly changing . . .

Joel and his girlfriend, Angie, had graduated from the University of Southern California and were still together and in love, living in LA and working in the film industry. They were young, so I was open to whatever heartbreak or joy might come their way. For now, all was well. As for our youngest, Ethan, he was working for the Coast Guard in Miami and considering a career in the military. If there was one word to describe the career choices of my children, it was *variety*.

I finished planting the bulbs and sat back to admire my fall garden. The asters and mums were in full bloom in sunset hues, and the goldenrod stood tall next to a cluster of snapdragons.

A rich red leaf from the maple tree floated down from the highest branches and landed on the soil in front of me. I picked it up, admired it, and rose to my feet. I collected a few more fall leaves to place in a vase on the windowsill in the living room.

The back door opened, and Gabriel stepped onto the raised patio with Dixie, our new puppy, a fluffy little black-and-white Havanese. She was soft as silk and enormously affectionate when she wasn't busy stealing Gabriel's socks. I watched her bounce clumsily down the steps and scamper toward me. Then I looked up at Gabriel's handsome face in the midday sun and exhaled a long sigh of contentment.

"It's official," he said, walking down the steps. "We've settled on this year's musical."

I strolled leisurely across the grass toward him. "What did you decide?"

"The kids want to do *Grease*, so I surrendered. Reluctantly. We start auditions next week."

We came together in the center of the yard, and I bent to rub Dixie's belly. "'Summer Nights,' here we come."

When I straightened, Gabriel reached for my hand, and our fingers wove together. "Did you finish planting the bulbs?" he asked. "I thought I might help."

"Too late. They're already in the ground. You could help me water them, though."

We went to fetch the watering can from the shed, and while Gabriel filled it with the hose, Dixie ran around in circles.

"Winter's coming, but spring will be here again before we know it," he said as he watered the new bulbs.

"Yes. Though I'm not sure how I feel about that. Time seems to be going so fast these days."

"Well, you know what they say. It only flies when it's fun."

I linked my arm through his and kissed him on the cheek.

Another bright-red maple leaf floated down from the treetops, so I picked it up and relished the notion that there were still more seasons ahead of us, more snowmen and sandcastles to build. Our children had flown from our nest, but Gabriel and I would remain here with Dixie. We would go for long walks in the summer and enjoy candlelit dinners on our patio in the moonlight. We would talk about our children and make plans for the future.

I watched Gabriel put the watering can back in the shed. Then I walked with him up the patio steps. He scooped Dixie under one arm, took hold of my hand, and kissed it as he led the way back into the house.

"Thanksgiving's just around the corner," he mentioned as we entered the kitchen. "How about blueberry crisp for dessert this year instead of apple? I don't know why, but I have a hankering for blueberries."

"Why wait?" I replied. "Let's make it tonight."

He turned and looked at me as if I'd invented fire. "Oh, my stars. I can't believe how much I love you."

I laughed and stepped forward into the warmth of his embrace, smiled up at him, and thanked him for loving me.

AUTHOR'S NOTE

Ever since I was a child, I've been fascinated by the mysteries of the Bermuda Triangle, which is what inspired me to plot a novel around the subject. Though *Beyond the Moonlit Sea* is a work of fiction, as are all its characters, I based a few plot elements on a combination of actual events and unexplained mysteries. One such event was Flight 19, which involved the loss of US Navy planes off the coast of Florida in 1945. There is plenty of information about that available online and in documentary films if you're interested. A simple search for *Bermuda Triangle* on YouTube will provide an abundance of material on the subject. As for Melanie Brown and her doctoral thesis, that is entirely fictional, but the particulars were inspired by a few important resources. Most especially, I'd like to acknowledge and recommend *Into the Bermuda Triangle: Pursuing the Truth Behind the World's Greatest Mystery* by Gian J. Quasar. It's a brilliant, comprehensive study of lost ships and planes, and it takes a deep dive into possible theories that might explain those unusual happenings. The book provided me with inspiration for Melanie Brown's research project, and I am indebted to the author. The book also led me to the work of Canadian scientist John Hutchison. In the novel, Melanie mentions her experiments to recreate "the Hutchison Effect." You can learn more about John Hutchison and his work at www.hutchisoneffect.com. Regarding this, it must be said that I'm an English major and I know very little about particle physics.

I did my best to learn what I could to support the drama in the novel, but any mistakes concerning the science are my own.

Lastly, special thanks are due to my early readers, Michelle Killen, Stephen MacLean, and Chris Taylor, for helpful comments about the story. Thanks also to friends Eve and Brent for assistance with research concerning the ethical principles of psychologists in 1986. I am grateful also for my outstanding agent, Paige Wheeler, and my exceptional editor, Alicia Clancy, and the entire team at Lake Union for doing incredible work and for being such a joy to work with.

QUESTIONS FOR DISCUSSION

1. When Olivia learns that her husband, Dean, has gone missing over the Bermuda Triangle, what was your expectation regarding the direction of the overall plot for the novel? Did you believe that Olivia would see Dean again one day? If so, under what circumstances?
2. When the character of Melanie Brown is introduced during her first therapy session, were you hopeful that her PhD project might provide the answer to Dean's disappearance?
3. In chapter 11, Dean is aware of the importance of discussing erotic transference with a colleague to ensure he maintains "a helpful and professional therapeutic relationship" with his client, Melanie. But something stops him from seeking help from a colleague. Discuss Dean's personal history and how you believe it played a part in his failure to ask for help and also in his failure to maintain a professional relationship with Melanie.
4. Consider the questions Olivia asks Dean during the interview for her film project on grief. Later, when they walk in the park, they talk about the afterlife. Discuss how the opinions they express to each other might have affected their actions and feelings in the future, in

particular Dean's decision to disappear without a trace, leaving Olivia behind to grieve for him, and also Olivia's inability to accept that he's truly gone. In chapter 6, she wonders if he's in heaven. Why would she change her mind about something she once believed when she was younger?

5. When Dean goes to Melanie's house for dinner in chapter 14 and we see how their romantic relationship is disintegrating, did you feel any understanding or sympathy for Dean at that point? Also consider Melanie's feelings and behavior in chapter 17 when she suspects that Dean is interested in Olivia. Discuss how first-person narration and point of view can influence how you, as a reader, might judge what is happening.
6. Do you believe Melanie and Dean could have been successful in their relationship if he had never met Olivia? Why or why not?
7. Describe how you felt about Dean's relationship with Olivia, from the moment he first meets her in his office to the moment when they decide to get married and move to Miami. Consider chapter 18, when they travel up the Hudson River together, and later when they cook spaghetti at Olivia's apartment. How would you describe their feelings for each other? Did you believe it was true love? Were you rooting for them as a couple? Why or why not?
8. The book opens with Olivia and Dean going sailing together, and there are many references to sailboats throughout the novel. What do you think the author was trying to convey? Consider how the sailboat represents themes or the state of mind of the characters at different times in the story.

9. In chapter 23, after Olivia moves back to New York, she expresses this thought about Gabriel: "But here we were, both single again, and I didn't know how to make him understand that I didn't want to start anything. I just wanted to be on my own." How did you feel about Olivia's resistance to loving Gabriel at that point? Did you feel she was taking too long to get over the loss of Dean? Discuss how grief can affect a person's ability to move on. Can you describe any examples from your own life where it was particularly difficult for you or someone you know to move on?
10. When Olivia travels to Australia and finally learns the truth from Dean, were you able to feel any sympathy for his plight? Do you believe Olivia ever truly forgives Dean? If you were Olivia, what would you have said or done when you recognized him on the dock?
11. After Rose meets Dean in Australia and Olivia wants him to turn himself in for his crimes, Rose says: "But it was so long ago. Don't you think he's suffered enough?" Did you agree or disagree with Rose? And in chapter 32, when Dean spends the evening on his sailboat reflecting upon his life, did you wonder if he might flee again? How would you have felt about the novel's conclusion if he had remained at large?
12. If Dean had called the police after he fell down the stairs with Melanie, and if he had confessed everything to Olivia right away, how might their lives have turned out? What do you think might have happened?

ABOUT THE AUTHOR

Photo © 2013 Jenine Panagiotakos, Blue Vine Photography

Julianne MacLean is a *USA Today* bestselling author of more than thirty novels, including the popular Color of Heaven series. Readers have described her books as "breathtaking," "soulful," and "uplifting." MacLean is a four-time Romance Writers of America RITA finalist and has won numerous awards, including the Booksellers' Best Award and a Reviewers' Choice Award from *Romantic Times*. Her novels have sold millions of copies worldwide and have been translated into more than a dozen languages.

MacLean has a degree in English literature from King's College in Halifax, Nova Scotia, and a business degree from Acadia University in Wolfville, Nova Scotia. She loves to travel and has lived in New Zealand, Canada, and England. She currently resides on the east coast of Canada in a lakeside home with her husband and daughter. Readers can visit her website at www.JulianneMacLean.com for more information about her books and writing life and to subscribe to her mailing list for all the latest news.